Story Quotes from THE FORESTER:

"In a shaky voice Susan yelled, 'I thought you were dead. Why didn't you call or write to me? You knew how I felt about you."

"The fury of wind, rain, lightning, and thunder was everywhere, and I feared I would be blown off the ledge or hit by a bolt of lightning."

"The trout turned and swam in my direction. I readied the net. Webbing spread out in front of him, and he sensed danger. Water exploded in front of me with escaping fish."

"Looking back, I saw a ball of fire consuming my helicopter. I got to my feet and ran."

"The both of you are so damn pig headed. You are impossible to deal with. I don't understand how two people, who say they love each other, can stop talking to each other for three months."

"I turned and saw a beautiful Native American woman sitting next to me."

"The corner stone of their success is an understanding that the whole resource is needed to protect any individual part."

"Shut up and let me talk. I want you to take my truck and go to Yosemite and take those pictures for your wife, and I don't want an argument from you."

"It's up to the timber companies to make it work with creditable management practices in the woods."

1

"The roar sent another wave of terror through me. Flames from the fire set the Bear's eyes ablaze and gave him a terrifying look. He blocked the only escape route."

"Sara's face flushed with anger. In a harsher tone she said, "You've done nothing to prevent these trees from being cut."

"In the stillness, I became aware of my heart beating and the invisible movement of the earth. With each passing second, the present retreated with the setting sun, and the future advanced with the rising moon. I was sitting on what seemed to be an edge of time."

"Holding me by my shirt with his left hand, he pounded my face with his right fist. I lost consciousness on the way to the floor."

"Sara had one year to live."

"A harsh voice growled into my ear. "This is George McCormick. I don't like you telling my son it's wrong to cut trees in northern Maine."

This Exciting Eco-Thriller Begins On PAGE 7!

THE
FORESTER

James Kraus

THE
FORESTER

Cover Photograph of White Pines
James Kraus

Cover Text & Design & Interior Text Layout
James Kraus

Published by Pen & Picture
Printed in the United States of America

ISBN 10-1478113111

Dedicated To

Gould Hoyt

Forester   Teacher   Friend

Acknowledgments

I would like to give a special thanks to Norman Bodek for his confidence in THE FORESTER and for his encouragement when I was not sure I would continue with the project. Also, a special thanks to Bill Christopher for his never ending persistence, encouragement, and counsel. Another special thanks to Barbara Rexilius for reading the entire manuscript twice and for her numerous suggestions, especially in the areas of medicine and Native Americans. Pam Michielen also read the entire manuscript and offered many suggestions. Ted Mack spent a lot of time reading the manuscript and making suggestions with grammar and text. His wife, Cathy, also helped in many ways. A very special thanks to my wife, Annie, for reading the manuscript twice, for her numerous suggestions, her encouragement, and her endless assistance with getting the words right.

I also appreciate the assistance and encouragement given by Kirk Peterson, Charles Alexander, Gary Chilson, Gould Hoyt, Mike Rechlin, Hans Michielen, Dr. John Gunn, Lori Knosalla, various helicopter pilots, and the Crow and Navajo people that I communicated with by telephone and email.

Story Timeline
References are made to story influences that occurred in the 1960s.
Most of the story takes place in the late 1980s.

CHAPTER 1

Sara had one year to live. The thought overwhelmed me as it had countless times. Trying to suppress my emotions, I glanced at Sara and managed a smile. She smiled back. I looked at the road and thought about how much I loved her smile and the warmth it always communicated.

It seemed I was spending more time staring at Sara's brown eyes, her facial expressions, and her curly hair flopping over her forehead. It was like I was falling in love with her again or maybe I was just realizing how much I really loved her. Maybe I...Sara interrupted my thoughts.

"I wish Annie didn't live so far away. She says she prefers the winters in New Jersey and doesn't miss the snow and cold in Maine."

"New Jersey has more jobs."

"There's also more traffic, pollution, and congestion," replied Sara. "But she feels they can make more money in a place like New Jersey than they could in Maine. That was your influence."

"There's nothing wrong with making money and enjoying the finer things in life."

"I believe the simple life is better," Sara said, pointedly. "I also think it's important to live close to nature. I know they live near a park where they can go for walks, but there's nothing close by that you could call woods."

"I think they made the right move. When they're making more money they can go wherever they want to."

Sara became quiet, apparently lost in thought, and then with her head resting on the back of her seat, she nodded off. She was still asleep when I exited the interstate for gas near Billings, Montana.

When I stopped at the end of the exit ramp, she woke up and unbuckled her seat belt. I turned left and drove under the interstate bridge.

Sara yawned and asked, "Where are we?"

I glanced at Sara to respond and a jolt of horror shot through me. A wall of steel was outside her window. A fraction of a second later chromed metal slammed into us. Sara screamed. Our truck slid and began to roll. Sara's body hit me...

Awareness returned. There was a noise I couldn't identify. Everything was veiled in gray. The noise echoed inside my head again. Shadows engulfed me and pulled me back to nothingness.

I couldn't move. A man was leaning over me. This time the noise became a siren.

A voice said, "We're on our way to the hospital."

I wanted to say, "Sara," but couldn't.

I drifted away again.

"My name is Doctor Smith, can you hear me?"

I was suddenly aware of the accident.

"Can you hear me?"

Someone was sticking something into my forearm.

I had to wake up and ask about Sara.

"Get an MRI of his neck and skull."

They were going to take me somewhere, and I didn't want to go anywhere until I saw Sara.

"No," I whispered.

"Can you hear me?" asked a nurse.

With all of my strength, I yelled, "Sara!"

A man's face came into focus. I became aware of my head hurting.

"Who is Sara?"

"My wife. Where is she?"

"What is your name?"

"Where's Sara?"

I tried to get up, but I couldn't move, and then I realized I was in a back and neck splint. Another doctor appeared from behind the curtain that partitioned the area.

"You're in the Billings Medical Center. A tractor trailer rammed into your truck. The driver must have been half asleep coming down the interstate ramp. They think he hit the accelerator when he thought he was hitting his brakes."

"My wife? Is she all right? Where is she?"

The doctor looked uncomfortable and wouldn't look at me directly.

"Where is Sara?" I yelled. "What happened to my wife?"

The doctor looked at me with a pained expression. "Your wife experienced the worst of the impact from the collision. The EMTs did their best, but, I'm very sorry. She died in the ambulance. They said she regained consciousness briefly. If you'd like to speak to the paramedic who was with your wife I believe he's still here."

"Yes."

The doctor left. Moments later a uniformed man appeared at my bedside. His lips thinned and there was a catch in his voice. "I'm very sorry. We did our best. Your wife's injuries were very severe. She came to for a few minutes and struggled to say something…it sounded like, 'Take my pictures, Kirk.' Does that make any sense to you?"

I stared at the man and mumbled, "Yes."

This wasn't possible. Minutes earlier, I was talking with Sara, and now she was gone. Tears started streaming down my face. The paramedic put his hand over mine, squeezed it, and then quietly left.

Sara was gone, snatched away from me. I wanted to tell her…so many things I wanted to tell her. I thought about our trip, her dream of taking photographs in Yosemite had been about to come true. Now it would never happen.

A terrible feeling of hurt and disbelief welled up inside me. I could see Sara's face. She was smiling. She always had a beautiful smile. I would never see her smile again. The accident was so sudden, so final. There was no warning. No time to prepare. No time to say good-by.

They rolled me down the hall and into the MRI room. After the scan, the doctor looked at the pictures and told me he didn't see

9

any problems. He called the attendant over to assist with the removal of the splint.

I asked if I could see Sara. The doctor replied that they could take me to her on the way to my hospital room but, he cautioned, I might prefer to remember her as she was. "I'm afraid the degree of trauma she experienced has made her hardly recognizable."

Again I remembered Sara's beautiful smile. That was what I needed to remember, not the mangled appearance the doctor's comment inferred. The attendant asked softly, "Do you still want to see your wife?"

I shook my head, "No," and turned away from him.

They slid me off the gurney and onto a bed. The nurse told me they were keeping me overnight for observation. The concerned look on her face and her gentle touch seemed to intensify my pain. My heart was breaking.

When everyone had left my room sobs came from deep within. I cried like I have never cried in my life. When I couldn't cry anymore, I gazed at the ceiling until they brought me supper. I couldn't eat.

The nurse returned with a paper cup with some pills in it and a cup of water. "These will help you get some sleep."

The nurse had a determined look on her face. I sighed, took the cup from her hand and emptied its contents into my mouth followed by a drink of water. My eyes began to feel heavy, and I fell asleep.

I woke up to sunshine highlighting the starkness of my hospital room. The ache in my heart was still there. They brought breakfast. I still couldn't eat. I drank some water to ease the dryness in my mouth.

A chaplain came in and tried to talk to me about Sara. His voice rambled on, but his words weren't connecting in my brain. I heard him say something about Sara being in heaven. He asked me if I wanted to pray with him. My answer was immediate and intense. "I don't believe in God."

The chaplain stood quietly. Eventually he said, "Do you want to talk about your wife's funeral arrangements?"

Taking a deep breath, I suppressed the urge to tell him to leave. I looked at him and realized he meant well. A conversation on our trip had actually been about this subject. Sara had said, "Please have me cremated and sprinkle my ashes in a beautiful place."

I glanced at the chaplain and said, "She wanted to be cremated."

"Do you want to have her sent back to Maine to have this done?"

I stared at him for a few seconds and said, "I need time to sort this out. You don't understand what our trip was about. Sara might prefer I continue on to California...I don't know what to do...I'm not sure what's best. I need to talk to my daughter."

"I understand."

The chaplain left, and I called Annie. She answered the phone and said, "Hello."

My voice shaking, I said, "Annie, its Dad."

"Is something wrong?"

A lump in my throat prevented me from responding.

"Dad? Are you all right?"

Fighting to get control of my emotions I said, "I have bad news. There was a terrible accident. A semi ran through a stop sign and broadsided us. I was driving. It hit the passenger side, where your mom was sitting. She didn't make it. She died in the ambulance on the way to the hospital."

Tears were running down my cheeks. Annie started to cry. I held the phone away from my head, and we both cried for what seemed like a long time. Still crying Annie quavered, "Mom is dead? I can't believe it."

"I know. I can't believe it, either."

We stopped talking. Again I tried to control my emotions. I think Annie was trying to do the same thing. After a time she asked, "Are you okay, Dad? Were you hurt?"

"I have a bump on my head, but basically I'm okay...at least physically."

"Did you have a chance to talk to Mom after the accident...before...before she...?"

"No. We went to the hospital in separate ambulances. She apparently came to in her ambulance. The paramedic said she mumbled something about me taking her pictures."

"You mean her pictures in Yosemite?"

11

"Yes."

"That was very important to her."

"I know. But right now I need to talk to you about your mom's funeral arrangements. She told me when we were driving out here that she wanted to be cremated. I was thinking of having that done here and flying home with her ashes."

"You can't go back to Maine without taking Mom's pictures. It was her dream. You have to go to California."

"I don't know anything about photography."

"It doesn't make any difference. Mom wanted you to go to Yosemite to take her pictures. It was her dying request. You have to do it."

I wiped tears from my face. "I don't understand what taking pictures will do for your mom. I feel I should go back to Maine and make funeral arrangements."

"Funerals were never important to Mom. She loved life too much. There's a reason for you to take these pictures."

"What's the reason?"

"I don't know. I just know you need to fulfill Mom's last request."

"I'll have to think about it."

"There's nothing to think about. I'll be very upset if you don't take these photographs for Mom."

"I'll get back to you and let you know what I decide to do. I have to go now."

I wanted Annie to support my decision to go back to Maine. Instead, she had sided with Sara. Annie had a habit of doing that, especially with Sara's positions on the environment.

I called Sara's sister in Seattle, who we had planned to visit on our way to Yosemite, and told her about Sara's death. She burst into tears, and I cried with her.

When we were able to talk, I explained that Sara wanted to be cremated, that I was making arrangements to have it done in Montana, and that I would plan a memorial service for her when I got home. She was hesitant about cremating Sara in Montana, but after thinking about it, she agreed it was the best thing to do. I also called Sara's friend, Cynthia, and told her the same thing. I didn't mention Sara's dying request to either of them.

12

The doctor came in and checked me over. He said I needed to take it easy for a couple of days. A nurse told me they were going to release me after lunch and asked me if I wanted her to call a taxi.

I nodded and said, "Yes, thank you."

A woman brought lunch. I didn't feel hungry, but I thought I should eat something. The chaplain came in as I was getting ready to leave. I told him I had decided to have Sara cremated in Billings and take her ashes with me. He said he would be happy to call a funeral home to arrange this.

After a brief conversation the chaplain hung up the phone and handed me the telephone number of the funeral home that would take care of Sara. He said I would be able to pick up her ashes in three days. He also gave me the phone number for the gas station that had my vehicle and travel trailer.

The cab driver drove me to a motel where I checked in for three nights. In my room, I forced myself to think about what I should do next and decided I needed to rent a car.

I called a car rental place and then took a shower. Resting on the bed, my mind turned to Sara and her last words. I thought about driving to California to take pictures for her.

I also thought about the Ansel Adams photographs of Yosemite that Sara had on the wall in front of her desk back home. They were extraordinary photographs taken by a master photographer. They were the photographs that had inspired Sara's dream.

I had no idea how to take these kinds of photographs. The more I thought about what I should do the more my thoughts jumbled into confusion.

A knock on the door interrupted my thoughts. It was a man with my car rental. I filled out the necessary papers and he left. I called the gas station that had my truck and travel trailer and was given instructions on how to get there.

The gas station attendant asked to see my driver's license and said he would have to keep my truck and trailer until the insurance companies inspected them. He said I could take my belongings as we walked to the two wrecks sitting by a chain link fence.

"They look totaled," I said.

"No question," he replied.

The trailer door was jammed shut, and the man got a wrecking bar to pry it open. I thanked him for his help, and he went back to work.

Inside the trailer my eyes went to the Ansel Adams photograph, Clearing Winter Storm that Sara had taped to the closet door. Emotion and loss grabbed me again as I gazed at the picture. I remembered talking to Sara in our trailer about the photograph a couple of days before she died.

"Clearing Winter Storm has always been my favorite photograph," Sara said. "Notice how the sun highlights Bridalveil Falls and how the dusting of snow etches the rocks. I love the way the rock formation called El Capitan is emerging out of the mist on the left and how the rising clouds look like they are opening up a gateway to heaven. I want to take a photograph as good as Clearing Winter Storm when I'm in Yosemite."

Sara looked very serious as she said these words. I didn't understand why taking a photograph could be so important to her. I said, "You'll take some great pictures, and you'll be there in a few days."

"I can't wait to look at Yosemite through the viewfinder of my camera. I want to see mist and clouds roll over the mountains, the evening sun turn Yosemite Valley into a warm glow, and waterfalls that look like they are falling from clouds. I want to be inspired with the same awesome beauty that inspired Ansel Adams and feel what he felt when he took his photographs."

"You will."

Sara looked at Clearing Winter Storm and then at me with an anxious expression. "I hope so." She paused and asked, "Do you like this photograph?"

I cleared my throat, stalling, and trying to think of an appropriate answer. "It's a nice picture, but I don't know much about photography. I'm not into photography the way you are."

Sara glanced at me with doubt on her face. "I hope you're not thinking I'm full of baloney. I know we don't agree on how we view nature and natural beauty. But it's important to me that you try to understand why we're driving all the way across the country so I can take photographs in Yosemite."

14

I took a deep breath and exhaled slowly. "I'm going to Yosemite because I love you. It's not necessary that I understand why you take photographs. I want you to be happy. If taking photographs makes you happy, then I want you to take photographs."

Sara's face brightened. "Thank you for saying that."

Thinking back on our conversation that day, I wished I had said something more positive about Sara's dream and her photography.

The words, "Take my pictures, Kirk" came into my mind and I felt the weight of them settling upon me. I stared at Clearing Winter Storm, studied the details of it, and realized it was no ordinary photograph. Was this the kind of photograph that Sara expected me to take?

The thought overwhelmed me. I knew nothing about photography, and I had no interest in learning anything about it. I felt an obligation to fulfill Sara's last request, but I had no idea how to do it. I removed the photograph from the closet door and put it on the front seat of my rental car.

Back in the trailer I picked up Sara's books from the floor. As I put them in a box I glanced at the titles. There was a copy of *A Sand County Almanac* by Aldo Leopold, a book of John Muir quotations, and two with photographs by Ansel Adams. There was also a book on how to do nature photography, which I placed on the front seat of my car.

Opening another closet door, my eyes fell on Sara's camera bag, her most prized possession. I opened the bag and saw its contents were none the worse from the accident. A pile of dirty clothes and pillows had helped to cushion the bag during the crash.

There was another photograph taped to the inside of the closet door, a photograph of the King's Pines. It was Sara's favorite photo of early morning sunlight streaming through the branches of three big white pines. For as long as I could remember Sara had been photographing those big trees. Several years ago she had a show in the public library entitled, *Pines in Winter*. As a result of that show, she received an invitation to publish a few of her pine photographs in the magazine, *Maine Outdoors*.

The King's Pines occupied twenty-seven acres of land, owned by North Country Woodlands, where I worked as a forester. These trees were considered to be the largest stand of big white pines in the northeast. Most of them were between three and five feet in diameter. A few were larger.

The previous CEO of North Country Woodlands, John Noland, named these trees the King's Pines as a historical reminder. During the colonial period, the king of England marked big pine trees in America with broad arrows to reserve them as masts for the ships of the Royal Navy. John Noland talked about making the King's Pines into a park, but it never happened.

When the new CEO, Mike Corey, decided to harvest the King's Pines, Sara was devastated. She blamed me for Mike's decision and began a courageous fight to save them. We stopped talking to each other, and she moved out of the house to live with her friend, Cynthia. The words we said to each other in the King's Pines on a snowy day in March came vividly to mind.

Snowshoeing a short distance I came to a big pine tree in a small clearing. There were pileated woodpecker holes in several places along its trunk. I estimated its crown to be fifty percent alive. I knew it was hollow on the inside, and it was just a matter of time before a strong wind blew it down. It was a good example of a tree dying on the stump.

I began to measure the tree with a diameter tape. Placing the tape's hook into a bark fissure, I pulled the tape around the tree. As I walked around the tree I looked up and saw Sara about thirty feet in front of me. She was standing behind her camera and tripod glaring at me.

We stared at each other, unable to speak. I wanted to say something neutral but couldn't think of the right words.

"You walked right past me," Sara said.

"I have a lot on my mind with a wife that's not talking or living with me."

Sara's face flushed with anger. In a harsher tone she said, "You've done nothing to prevent these trees from being cut, that's why we're not talking to each other."

"Mike makes the decisions at North Country Woodlands; it was not my decision ..."

Sara interrupted. "You never see the grey area of any situation. Everything must be black or white to you. Old trees die, so you cut them down."

Sara paused and glanced up at the big trees. Then she looked directly at me and said, "While we're here, take a look at these trees and see how beautiful they are. Listen to the wind caressing their needles. See how their branches twist and curve to form their majestic crowns. Try to feel the power and persistence of nature that these trees communicate and how they stand as a tribute to time and their own existence and success."

I didn't like the way Sara was talking to me. In a sharper voice I said, "I don't deny they have beauty, but I also see things you don't want to see. Look at that tree rotting on the ground over there."

I pointed to another tree and said, "There's one with its top knocked off by lightning. Its days are numbered. All of these trees are in decline. They're all past their peak of growth. It's foolish to let an investment like this rot on the stump when they can be used to build houses and to create jobs for people. It's beyond the time to harvest them."

Raising her voice Sara said, "These trees belong to our heritage. There are no other trees like them in Maine. School kids need to see them."

Sara paused and added, "From an ecological perspective they're not dying as foresters would lead people to believe. Only a healthy, stable forest can persist for centuries like this one has done. Old people can be healthy even though they are old and these trees are no different."

I fired back with, "Trees are not people. When they're decaying on the ground they're of no value to anyone."

"They may not be of value to people when they're decaying, but their nutrients will go into the growth of a new forest and that is valuable to nature."

"Most of the nutrients are in the branches and needles, and foresters leave them for recycling when they harvest trees."

"You have thousands of acres of trees to harvest on the land owned by North Country Woodlands," Sara said. "Cutting these big trees is not going to influence the financial survival of your company one way or another."

17

"The company has the right to harvest trees on their lands."

"These trees are rare and beautiful; there are no other trees like them. Your argument is based on money and greed, and it's a poor excuse to cut down an old growth forest."

"I've heard all of this before. I know how you feel. You never think about people and that they need resources to live. It costs money to preserve a forest. A company has to make a profit and..."

"And I've heard all of that before, only I haven't heard you speak so much about money. Money is all you think about."

"I like my promotion and big raise and not having to worry about money. I also like driving a new truck and my new TV and deer hunting rifle."

"When this country loses its wildlife, its wilderness, and its big trees it will be poorer, and all the money in the world is not going to buy them back. Talking to you is hopeless. Enjoy your money. It's all you're going to have."

I didn't want our conversation to end this way. I didn't want to talk about the trees. I wanted to talk about Sara and me, but it was too late. I had said all of the wrong things. I wanted to say I was sorry. But it wouldn't do any good. Sara was too upset. I was too upset.

Sara picked up her tripod and started to snowshoe toward the road. I followed her. I wanted to tell her I wanted her back and that I loved her. I wanted her to understand why we had to cut the pines. But she would never understand. I stopped moving and watched her vanish into the big trees.

I heard Sara start our old truck. The motor accelerated and then faded as she drove away. I went back to work feeling hurt, angry, and frustrated.

The photograph of the King's Pines on the trailer door came into focus. I wished we had not quarreled that day. I also wished the King's Pines had not become such a divisive issue in our lives.

Sara and I had different views on the environment all through our marriage. After a few years of heated arguments we began to realize our disagreements were hurting our relationship, and we promised not to discuss our opposing views with each other.

But when Sara learned the King's Pines were to be harvested it was too much for her to endure quietly. Memories of the evening that Sara appeared on the national news flooded my mind.

The door opened and a huge man filled the entrance to the Logger's Palace. Snow whirled around his bearded face as he entered the bar. Moose Harkens opened his red and black checkered coat and walked over floor boards that creaked with every step.

It was rumored that Moose stood six feet seven inches and weighed close to three hundred pounds. The third bar stool on my left groaned as he eased himself onto it. His words to the bartender kept his reputation intact for having a loud, foul mouth.

"I'll have the fuckin special and two beers."

I knew of no one who liked Moose except for a small following of equally obnoxious friends. Word was he knew how to make money in the logging business. He also had a reputation for tearing up the woods with his equipment.

North Country Woodlands hired him only once. When Nolan saw the damage he had done to standing trees with his skidder he personally told him to get off company land and never come back. I didn't like Moose. I think he knew it.

Moose downed his first beer and looked at the logger sitting next to him. "Are you working?"

The logger nodded. The bartender put a plate of spaghetti in front of Moose and refilled his empty glass. A commercial was ending on the TV behind the bar and the last news story was coming on. It began with a reporter standing in a forest.

"Not since the days of Paul Bunyan has there been so much talk in the woods about cutting trees. Only now the talk is between a man who wants to cut a forest of big white pines in northern Maine and his wife who wants these trees to be preserved."

A close up of Sara appeared on the screen. She looked beautiful standing in front of a big white pine. "We're talking about cutting the largest forest of old growth white pines in the northeast. When next summer ends these magnificent trees will be gone if North Country Woodlands goes ahead with their harvesting plans."

I appeared on the screen after Sara with footage the local TV station had taken earlier in the week. "Trees do not last forever.

Eventually they die of old age and fall to the ground. We can let them waste away or we can utilize their wood while it's still sound."

Moose glanced at me and snapped, "Your wife has a big mouth that hurts a lot of people who are trying to make an honest living."

A surge of anger went through me. I locked eyes with Moose and said, "I didn't ask for your opinion. I would suggest you mind your own business."

Moose stood up. "It's my business when your wife talks about letting trees rot on the stump, which puts people like me out of work."

"I've seen the kind of work you do in the woods."

Moose pointed to himself with his right thumb. "I'm the best logger in northern Maine. I'm the man to cut those big pines."

"You'll never touch those trees if I have anything to say about it."

Moose walked over to my bar stool and stood close enough for me to smell his rancid breath. "You're nothing but a fuckin tree hugger."

Before I could respond, Moose seized my neck and squeezed with his huge hands. My right hand fell into my plate of spaghetti as I gasped for air. I gripped the plate and swung it toward Moose's head with all of my strength. He tried to block the plate with his forearm but wasn't fast enough to stop it from slamming into his face. He released his choke hold on my throat and staggered backwards. I jumped to my feet.

"Fight!" someone yelled.

Moose wiped the spaghetti from his face and threw a fist in my direction. I dodged the blow and returned a strong shot to his face. Gritting my teeth, I delivered two more quick jabs to the same target. It wasn't enough to stop him.

He grabbed my shirt, lifted me off the floor and hurled me onto a table. I slid off the table and landed in a tangled mess on the floor. Moose was on me before I could recover and yanked me to my feet. Holding me by my shirt with his left hand, he pounded my face with his right fist. I lost consciousness on the way to the floor.

The next thing I was aware of was the bartender splashing water on my face. I tried to get up, and he helped me to a chair.

"Where is he?" I mumbled.

20

"He's gone, but he sure gave you a beating."

The bartender helped me to the bunk room where loggers slept when they were working away from home. In the bathroom I washed my face with a wet towel. Looking in the mirror I saw that the tissue surrounding my left eye had filled with blood. I also had several cuts and bruises on my face. I hurt everywhere.

Moose had insulted Sara leaving me no choice but to fight for her. While I didn't agree with Sara's position on the King's Pines, I felt good about defending her right to express the views she believed in.

Three days after Sara had appeared on the evening news Mike called me into his office and said, "The Nature Bank just called. They saw your wife on TV. They want to purchase the King's Pines and make them into a park."

I went to my office and called Sara. Cynthia answered the phone, and I asked her if Sara was there.

"She's not here. Is there something you want me to tell her?"

"Tell her the Nature Bank wants to purchase the King's Pines and make them into a park."

"Sara will be happy to hear that. I think you should tell her yourself. She'll be back after supper; she usually eats at McDonalds after work."

"I'll stop by then."

"There's something else."

Cynthia's voice suddenly sounded very serious. "I probably shouldn't tell you this, but we both love Sara and want what's best for her. We're planning a trip."

"You and Sara?"

"Yes. Sara always had a dream to take photographs in Yosemite National Park, photographs like Ansel Adams took."

"She never told me about her dream."

"I know. She didn't think you would understand. You always gave her the impression that you didn't think her photography was important. She wants to go to Yosemite while she still...still has time..."

Cynthia stopped talking, and I heard her sob.

"What do you mean while she still has time?"

"I'm sorry I have to be the one to tell you this, but you need to know before you talk to her. Sara's cancer is no longer in remission."

21

Cynthia sobbed again and added, "The doctors feel she only has a year to live."

Cynthia's words hit me like a sledge hammer. Neither one of us said anything for a while. Eventually I muttered, "Sara should have told me."

"She should have," replied Cynthia with anger in her voice. "But the two of you are so damn pig headed. You are both impossible to deal with. I don't understand how two people, who say they love each other, can stop talking for three months."

We didn't say anything for a few seconds.

In a calmer voice Cynthia added, "I'm sorry, I shouldn't have said that, but both of you have upset me a great deal."

"I didn't mean to upset you. Everything just got out of hand."

"Please promise me you'll be sensitive and understanding when you talk to Sara."

"I will. I want Sara back. I want to put this whole thing behind us."

"I'm glad. Sara also told me she would rather go to Yosemite with you, but feels that would be impossible because you have so much work to do."

I didn't know what to say. I felt terrible about Sara thinking I wouldn't take her to California. "Thank you for telling me this, Cynthia."

When I arrived at Cynthia's house she pointed upstairs. I found Sara in her room sitting on her bed. Our eyes locked for several seconds. Sara looked like she was going to smile. I wanted to see her beautiful smile that I had missed so much. Instead a guarded expression appeared on her face as she said, "Why are you here?"

I hesitated to answer for a moment trying to suppress the emotions I was feeling. "I have some good news that I wanted to tell you in person. The Nature Bank wants to buy the King's Pines and make them into a park. They called Mike this morning."

Sara's face lit up the way I had hoped it would. "That's wonderful. I'm so relieved."

A few more awkward seconds passed as I tried to muster my courage to bring up the subject of Sara's cancer. "Cynthia told me about your cancer, that it came back. Why didn't you tell me?"

22

"I didn't want you feeling sorry for me. We have not been very supportive of each other these past three months."

Tears rushed into Sara's eyes. She sobbed and said, "They had to remove my right breast. I'm not the same woman."

"Bullshit! You will always be Sara and that is all I care about. I love you just as much as the day we got married."

Sara looked at the floor and suppressed another sob. I could feel my eyes filling with tears. I waited to say something, but we both needed some time to control our emotions.

"Cynthia told me the two of you are planning a trip to Yosemite National Park so you can take your photos."

Sara nodded. "We are."

"Please, let me take you?"

"What about your job?"

"You are more important."

"Are you sure?"

"I'm sure. I want to go with you, if you'll let me. I also want us back in our own house; will you come home with me?"

"Well, I don't know."

I knew Sara was teasing me now because she was getting an impish grin on her face. "I do love you, in spite of your misguided opinions."

I laughed. "The least said about misguided opinions the better."

"Okay."

As Sara said that she jumped off her bed, threw her arms around me, and began to cry again. We held each other for a long time. She stopped crying and said, "I didn't mean to cry. I'm just so happy to have you back."

"I know. I feel the same way."

Sara called down to Cynthia, "Have you heard the news about the pines?"

"Yes, Kirk told me earlier."

"You no longer have a boarder. Kirk and I are going to California."

I pulled into our driveway, jumped out of the truck, and ran around the vehicle to help Sara. She got out by herself and politely said, "I'm not a cripple."

23

I picked her up on our porch and carried her into the house. She giggled. In the living room she hugged me and whispered, "It's good to be home with you."

We kept hugging and didn't say anything for a while. In the quiet I was aware of the clock ticking on the wall. All of a sudden I was more conscious of time and more afraid of it.

I lifted her chin with my hand and kissed her passionately. Before I knew what was happening we were in our room behaving like newlyweds.

Later, we lay in bed with moonlight filling our room. Sara's head rested on my shoulder. The window was open, and we could smell the early spring air. A coyote howled in the clear-cut behind the house.

I woke up to the smell of coffee and bacon. I heard Sara's footsteps, and then she appeared with a tray filled with breakfast. We sat with our backs against our pillows as we ate. After we finished our toast and coffee Sara asked, "Are you going to the office?"

"I have to tell Mike we're going to California. He's not going to be happy to hear I want time off with all the work we have to do. But I'm not worried about that. I better get going."

Later, when I told Mike that Sara only had a year to live and that I was taking her to California to fulfill a dream he said, "I need you here."

I stared at him for two or three seconds. "I have to take Sara to Yosemite."

Mike didn't say anything more. I went to my office to gather my belongings. Mike came to the door. "What are you doing?"

"I'm quitting."

"You can't quit. How long would you be gone?"

"Four or five weeks. Maybe more."

"Okay. I'll hold things together until you get back."

When we left for California Mike was waiting for a check from the Nature Bank to close the deal on the King's Pines. The Nature Bank had agreed to have the proposed park called, "Sara's Pines." I promised Sara I would place a sign on the site with this name on it when we got back from our trip.

I removed the photograph of the King's Pines from the closet door and placed it on top of the Ansel Adams photograph in my car. I then told the gas station owner to dispose of the two wrecks after the insurance company had seen them and gave him a check to cover his services.

Back at the motel I rested on the bed thinking about Sara. Random words entered my mind.

"Take my pictures, Kirk."

"I'll be very upset if you don't take these photographs for Mom."

"I want to take a photograph as good as Clearing Winter Storm when I'm in Yosemite."

Sara and Annie wanted me to go to California, but I had no idea how to take a photograph like Clearing Winter Storm. In less than three days I would have to make up my mind to go east or west, and I had no idea which way I would go.

Memories of Sara, our love, our disagreements, her dream, her cancer, and our last days together passed in front of me in a jumbled vision. All of it was haunting, all of it tugging on my emotions. A more powerful thought entered my mind and pushed the others away. Sara was gone.

CHAPTER 2

A rifle shot cracked the stillness of the snow-filled forest. I stopped moving, frozen to the ground by the closeness of the sound. Snow trickled down my neck as I brushed against a balsam fir. A second shot echoed through the woods.

For almost an hour I had been pushing a deer toward Mike, who I had positioned on a stand at first light. Mike had fired those two shots. I was hoping he had killed his first deer.

A buck exploded from the trees in front of me. Years of hunting produced a response of following the running deer with my rifle as he bolted for cover. Sights and deer aligned for a fraction of a second, and I squeezed the trigger. Powerful legs collapsed under the buck as he fell forward into the fresh snow. I watched the buck with my rifle ready for another shot, but he didn't move.

A quick examination of the buck showed that I had brought him down with a neck shot. There was no evidence of another bullet hitting him. Mike's two shots had missed completely.

"Did I get him?"

I whirled around as Mike stumbled into the small clearing. His eyes blazed with excitement, and he was breathing hard. Again he shouted, "Did I get him?"

"He came out of those trees and fell right there."

Mike grinned. "I can't believe I shot a buck on my first hunting trip."

I politely smiled back and said, "A six point buck is a nice trophy for a first hunt."

Looking a little embarrassed, Mike regained his composure and said, "Where did I hit him?"

"In the lower neck. I put a shot into him to make sure he wasn't suffering. But it was your shot that brought him down."

"You were right about that stand being a good place to see a deer," Mike said. "I like a man who knows what he's doing."

Glancing at his watch he added, "I have to get to a meeting."

"Okay. I'll stay here and field dress your deer."

"Thanks. I appreciate everything you've done."

While I was working my dad's voice echoed in my head. "Always conduct yourself as a sportsman. Being a good sportsman is the most important rule of deer hunting."

I gazed at the falling snow and felt a twinge of guilt about lying to Mike and violating my dad's sacred rule of deer hunting.

"Shit," I said out loud and continued in my head with, "Why would my dad or anyone else care about me shooting a deer for Mike. I had a good reason for doing what I did. No one would know the truth except for me, and I didn't plan on telling anyone."

Two days later Mike called me into his office and said he was promoting me to Chief Forester. I was elated. I was convinced that helping him bag his first deer had influenced his decision to give me the promotion I wanted.

Mike leaned back in his chair. "The only way I can save this company is to increase revenue. I want you to increase the number and size of our clear cuts."

I nodded approvingly. "I made that recommendation to Nolan several times, but he always ignored it."

"He also ran North Country Woodlands into the ground," replied Mike. "Include the harvesting of the King's Pines in your cutting plans."

My stomach tightened.

"I also want you to increase second home development where it's suitable on our lands."

I nodded. "I also recommended that to Nolan."

Back in my office I kept thinking about cutting the King's Pines. I agreed in principle with Mike's decision, but I knew Sara would be upset.

I also knew it was futile to try talking Mike out of cutting the big trees because he was a man who didn't like his decisions to be questioned. He had demonstrated many times in his career that he knew what he was doing, and he had made a fortune taking over businesses that were failing. I was confident he would save North Country Woodlands.

Before Mike purchased North Country Woodlands we had experienced one pay cut and there was talk of another. Everyone worried about the company's financial condition. Most of us believed John Noland when he said things would get better, but they never did.

Sara and I struggled every month to make ends meet. When we had trouble making our mortgage payments, Sara got a job at McDonalds to help out.

Jobs were not plentiful in Spruce Mills where paper manufacturing and timber related jobs were the economic staples. When young people grew up they had the same work options as their parents. Some found employment in Spruce Mills, but many left the area for other opportunities.

My college education and the harsh economic reality of northern Maine taught me that harvesting trees was in everyone's best interest. People needed wood for paper, building materials, and other products. I felt that clear cutting and other commercial forestry practices were the most cost effective way of doing this. I liked my job and felt that I made an important contribution to society. I also liked living in Maine.

Staying in Maine was also important to Sara. She loved the area and got upset when I talked about leaving if North Country Woodlands went under. She tried to accept the fact that harvesting trees allowed us to stay in Maine, but she was uncomfortable with it. She also hated the huge clear cuts that dominated the landscape surrounding Spruce Mills.

Many of these thoughts ran through my mind as I sat in my motel room thinking about my forestry career and my life with Sara. For the most part our life had been good except for our different views on the environment and having to struggle with money problems. Toward evening I decided I had to get something to eat. The owner of the motel suggested the restaurant across the road.

I found a seat at the bar next to two cowboys who were talking about ranching. I ordered a steak and a beer. One of the cowboys said, "I'm tired of environmentalists telling ranchers they are over-grazing their cattle and trying to put us out of business."

I finished my beer and ordered another. The alcohol quickly went to my head, and I began to loosen up. I decided to join the conversation.

"We have similar problems with environmentalists in Maine," I said. "Only in Maine they want us to stop cutting trees and building houses on lakes. They want to save the forests for themselves, but they also want their houses, furniture, and newspapers.

"Then they criticize the companies and the methods they use to produce the things that they create a demand for. They never make the connection that it is their consumption and their standard of living that create environmental problems."

"They never do because they live in never, never land," one of the cowboys said.

"They're a bunch of damn hypocrites," the other cowboy said. "My dad and his dad ranched all of their lives, and they never abused the land. If they didn't protect the environment we would have nothing today. Most environmentalists don't know the first thing about running a ranch."

The cowboys ordered another round of drinks, including a beer for me. I was getting drunk, and the alcohol was numbing my grief. I vaguely remember the two cowboys helping me back to my motel room and falling asleep on my bed with my clothes on.

The next morning I woke up with a terrible hangover and thinking about how much Sara hated to see me drunk. I felt better after a shower and ham, eggs, and coffee in the restaurant.

Back in the motel I picked up Sara's book on nature photography and turned to the section on shutter speeds and f-stops. Unable to concentrate, I put the book down and turned on the TV. My mind floated to Sara, and my thoughts were still with her when I took a walk, ate supper, and went to bed. Exhausted, I slept soundly, but woke up at three o'clock thinking about Sara.

My thoughts went back to our college days at the University of Maine where I studied forestry, and Sara studied photography. I was a loner and didn't have many friends. Sara was very popular and had what I considered a distinct beauty that set her apart from other girls. She said I had strong features, like a hero in a movie, but she always giggled when she told me this. I never took her description of me seriously.

I also thought about Vietnam and being drafted six months after we were married. I didn't like the war, but I liked flying helicopters. Sara wrote to me every day while I was there, and her letters were always filled with love and caring messages. I remembered how much I missed her, but somehow I knew I would see her again. Now I would never see her again. This horrible thought remained with me until daylight crept into my room.

After a shower and breakfast I drove to the funeral home. A man with an expressionless face handed me a bill and a metal urn filled with Sara's ashes. I paid him and placed the urn on the passenger seat of my car.

Three days ago Sara was sitting next to me. Now the seat contained an urn filled with her ashes, her camera equipment, two photographs, and a book. Struggling to control my emotions, I drove out of the funeral home parking lot and followed the signs to the interstate.

The decision I was dreading loomed up in my mind like a monster. Do I go east to Maine or west to California? A sign told me the interstate was two miles ahead. I kept debating with myself which way I would go. But confusion and uncertainty would not allow me to make a decision. Another sign read one mile to the interstate.

I needed more time to think. Maybe a few days taking pictures with Sara's camera would help me to have a better idea of the kind of photographs I could take. The more I thought about this idea the more I liked it. Reaching the interstate I turned west and headed for Livingston.

Sara continued to consume my thoughts. I wanted her back. I wanted to hear her talk about her photography and about Yosemite and her dream. I wanted more time to be close to her and more time to love her. I wanted to hear her laugh and watch her take her own pictures in Yosemite National Park. But she was gone, and I didn't know how I was going to live without her.

In Livingston I stopped at a grocery store to purchase food and film and then drove south on Route 89 toward Yellowstone National Park. The highway followed the Yellowstone River. To the east I could see a beautiful range of mountains. Stopping at a Forest Service picnic area that overlooked the river, I ate lunch and shot a couple of photographs of the mountains.

Sipping a coke, I thought about whether I should go to Yosemite or just drive home. Sara had not said I had to take her pictures this spring.

I thought about taking a photography course during the winter at a community college in Maine and flying to California next spring to take Sara's photographs. The more I considered this idea, the more I liked it.

A gray bird landed on the top of a nearby picnic table and began to eat crumbs of bread that someone had left there. I laughed to myself as I thought of Sara trying to photograph the bird. She always said photographs were everywhere.

A scream below caused me to look at the river where I saw a rubber raft and a drift boat floating next to each other. The man sitting at the oars in the drift boat was holding the two boats together.

Two men were standing in the raft and appeared to be arguing. Suddenly, the larger of the two men pushed the man with a white beard to the bottom of the raft. The older man tried to stand up, and while he was off balance, the other man shoved him over the side of the raft into the swirling river. I jumped to my feet.

The old man's life vest kept him on the surface, where he floated and bobbed in the powerful torrent. The other man jumped into the drift boat, pulled out a knife, and punched holes in the rubber raft. Air escaped from the raft as the drift boat headed downstream. The old man reached a rock and with great effort pulled himself onto it.

When I was certain the old man was safe on the rock, I ran to my car to look for a rope. While rummaging through my trunk, I began to doubt if I could throw a rope far enough to reach the rock.

My eyes fell on my fishing rod, and I realized I might do better with a cast. Quickly I assembled my spinning rod and tied the heaviest lure I could find in my tackle box to the end of the line. With the rope and rod in one hand I slid down the steep bank.

Arriving at the edge of the river, I yelled to the old man. He looked at me. I held the rope up so he could see it. He waved back. The rock looked beyond the range of a cast. I needed to get closer.

There was a pile of river debris close by where I found a sturdy stick to use as a wading staff. Cautiously I felt the bottom of the river ahead of me with my stick and inched into the churning

31

flow. The rushing water made it difficult to stand and to keep from being swept away. About fifteen feet from shore I stopped, not daring to go any further.

My first cast fell short of my target, but it gave me confidence that I could get my lure to the marooned man who sat motionless watching me. I tried another cast further upstream from him. This time the spoon came within inches of the rock. On the third cast the hooks grabbed the rock. The old man reached for the lure. I allowed line to peel from my reel as I stumbled back to shore on numb legs and feet.

I cut the spinning line with my pocketknife, tied it to one end of the rope, and signaled the old man to pull in the line. With stiff fingers he labored to haul the line and rope through the water. I fed rope into the river to keep pace with the line he was retrieving. The rope bowed in the current, and I worried the weight of it might break my fishing line. I was relieved when the man had the rope in his hands.

"Tie the rope around you," I shouted.

With difficulty the man tied the rope around his chest. He was suffering from hypothermia, and it took great effort to accomplish this simple task.

When he was satisfied the knot would hold he jumped into the icy water. I braced myself in the rocks beneath my feet and pulled on the rope. The man floated downstream in an arc toward the shore. His feet touched the rocky bottom. He tried to stand, but he didn't have the strength to fight the force of the river. I waded into the water to help him.

He was shivering uncontrollably and swearing in a shaky voice. I put his arm around my neck and dragged him to shore. Lowering him to the ground, I realized I would not be able to get him up the steep bank in his condition.

"I'm going to my car for towels and a sleeping bag. I'll be back in a few minutes."

The man nodded. I left him curled up on the ground, climbed the bank as quickly as I could and reached my car gasping for breath.

Returning to the river, I helped the old man out of his wet clothes, dried him off, and got him into my sleeping bag. I went back

32

to my car again for my camp stove, canned soup, candy bars, and dry clothes for both of us.

When the soup was hot I started spooning it into his mouth. He grabbed the spoon from me and mumbled, "I can manage."

He coughed and gave me a weak smile. "I'm Henry Johnson. Thanks for pulling me off that rock. I was beginning to think I was a goner."

"I'm Kirk Weber. Eat more soup. I have candy bars. I can also make hot chocolate."

"This is fine, but I'll have a candy bar."

I removed the wrapper from a candy bar and gave it to him. While he ate I studied his face and guessed he was in his late sixties or early seventies. He finished the candy bar and soup and, without saying a word, closed his eyes and went to sleep. He seemed to be breathing okay, so I let him rest.

I changed into dry clothes and sat on a rock waiting for him to wake up. His eyes opened about an hour later. When he saw me staring at him he grinned and said, "Are we going to lie around here all day? I've got to get back to my shop."

"Where's your shop?"

"A few miles upriver."

"Can you climb the bank?"

"Yes. Now help me out of this bag, and let's get going."

I helped Henry out of my sleeping bag and into dry clothes.

"Let me help you up the bank."

"I'm fine. I don't need help."

I bent over to pick up my things and glanced at Henry. He was struggling a few feet up the slope.

"Let me help you," I shouted.

"I'm okay," he hollered.

I gathered up the rest of my belongings and looked at Henry again. He was holding his chest. I ran to him as he fell to the ground.

CHAPTER 3

"Pills," whispered Henry. "In my shirt pocket."

I picked up his wet shirt from the ground and found a bottle in one of the pockets.

"One pill," Henry said holding up a finger.

I pushed one of the small pills into his mouth. A short time later he started to breathe in a more normal fashion.

"It's my heart," Henry said. "I guess my river adventure was a little too strenuous. I'll be okay after I rest for a while."

"What were those pills?"

"Nitroglycerine."

"Rest here and I'll get this stuff to my car."

When I returned Henry said, "I'm feeling better. Let me sit for a while longer, and I'll be fine."

"That's what you said last time. Maybe I should get some help."

"No, just give me a few minutes."

A half hour later Henry stood up and said, "I'm ready."

We took it very slow climbing the steep bank. I made Henry stop every few feet to give him time to catch his breath. He seemed to grow impatient with my stops, but I didn't want any more problems. I was relieved when he was finally sitting in the front seat of my car.

"Do you want me to drive you to a hospital?"

"No, I'm okay. Turn around and head up river."

We traveled about a mile and came to a distant hill on the left side of the road that was covered with expensive looking condominiums.

"WestSun Resorts is building that big resort up there," said Henry. "They call it Autumn Springs Resort after the springs that are the source of the Autumn River. The Autumn River, which flows past my fly fishing shop, is being diverted to build a reservoir in that large basin in front of that hill. It's a mockery of nature for someone to build a reservoir by destroying a rare and beautiful river like the Autumn."

I glanced at Henry and saw his face had reddened with anger. I wanted to ask him a question about the Autumn River, but I didn't want to say anything that would upset him even more. He stopped talking until we came to a gravel road.

"Turn here," he bellowed into my right ear.

Half way across a large bridge Henry pointed and said, "See that stream that comes into the Yellowstone River on the left, that's the Autumn River. It won't be there in a few more days."

Again I suppressed my urge to ask him a question.

On the other side of the bridge Henry told me to stop at a fishing access area on the side of the road. He got out of my car and climbed into an old truck with a camper in its bed. A flatbed trailer was attached to the rear of the truck, which he had probably used to transport his raft to the river.

Leaning out the window of his truck Henry yelled, "Follow me."

We drove a short distance and came to a log house with a sign over the door that read, Henry's Trout Flies & Tackle. Two fishermen were standing in front of his shop. Henry climbed out of his truck, fetched a key from under his door mat and unlocked his door. A bell jingled as he opened the door.

The shop was small and well stocked with trout fishing paraphernalia. Fly rods, nets, waders, vests, and other equipment sat on shelves or hung from hooks on the walls. Plastic boxes filled with trout flies sat on a counter in front of a work area for tying flies. A beautiful painting of an angler casting a fly to a large brown trout in a clear pool hung on the wall behind his counter.

The two fishermen wanted fishing permits, and Henry filled them out. He asked them to sign a petition opposing the Autumn River water divergent project, which they were happy to do. One of the fishermen said, "Is there anything else we can do to save the river?"

"At this point, I don't think anything can save it," Henry said shaking his head. "I'll mail this petition to the governor tomorrow, but he's already made up his mind."

"Damn shame, that's what it is, a damn shame," the fisherman said.

Henry took a couple of flies out of a box and said they matched the natural insects that were hatching on the river. The fishermen paid him for their permits and flies and left.

"Let's eat lunch," Henry said.

"Maybe you should lie down for a while."

"I'm fine, a little weak from being thrown into that cold water, but otherwise I'm fine."

I shrugged and followed Henry through a door to a small living room and then through another door to a deck with a spectacular view of the river and mountains in the distance.

Henry pointed and said, "That's the Autumn River. Runs clear year around. Only fluctuates a few inches between spring and fall. The finest trout in America are in those waters. Have a seat. Let me get out of your clothes and fix us something to eat."

I sat down and gazed at the river and mountains. Birds were coming to a bird feeder in a nearby tree. I picked up a pair of binoculars from a table, focused on the river, and watched trout dimpling the smooth surface of a pool.

Henry appeared with a tray of sandwiches, a couple of apples, and two mugs of coffee. He had changed his clothes, and an old cowboy hat sat on his head. Placing the tray on the table he said, "Help yourself."

"Thanks."

I took a bite from my sandwich and asked, "Why were those guys attacking you?"

"It's a long story."

"I've got time."

"I've lived in Montana for fifteen years. Retired early from an engineering job in L.A. Decided to come to Montana where there was still open country. I run this shop to supplement my retirement income.

"The Autumn is the best limestone creek in the country. Its nutrient rich water produces a ton of food that can grow trout up to five or six pounds. Mostly brown trout but there are also rainbows, which don't get as big. Outdoor writers are always up here writing articles about the great fishing. Thanks to them, I keep a steady supply of customers in my shop. The Autumn is catch and release water. I issue eight rod permits a day, which helps to lessen the impact on the fish from all of the publicity."

Henry took a swallow of coffee and continued. "Everything was fine for many years, until WestSun decided to build a huge condominium city for old farts that have plenty of money and want to get out of California because their state is all shot to hell with people and development.

"WestSun is planning to divert most of the river in four days. Trout Unlimited and other environmental groups have been fighting them in the courts. A couple of months ago a judge ruled with WestSun. I think someone got paid off."

"But why were those two guys roughing you up?"

"I think they work at Autumn Springs and were told to discourage me from doing an interview tomorrow with a Denver TV station about their water project. I think Susan Martin, who runs WestSun, is afraid the story will break into a national story and generate a lot of bad press for her project and company."

Henry took another gulp of coffee. "Those two jerks heard me talking in a bar last night about floating the Yellowstone River today and decided to wait for me in their drift boat. I think they wanted to scare me into backing out of my interview. But I don't scare off easily. I still plan on doing the interview."

Henry pushed his hat back on his forehead and said, "That's my story, now tell me about yourself."

I told Henry about Sara's death and the accident. I also told him about Sara's dying request for me to take photographs for her in Yosemite National Park.

A sad expression formed on Henry's face. He said, "I'm real sorry about your wife. I lost my wife five years ago. Lung cancer. She got it from the foul air in L. A. That's one of the reasons I took early retirement, to get her out of that filthy city. She loved Montana. Found a bunch of women in Livingston who loved quilting as much as she did. I miss Sally more than I can put into words. You never get over losing a wife if you really loved her."

Henry paused and looked at the mountains in the distance. "Are you on your way to California?"

I scratched the side of my head before I answered, "Not exactly. Sara loved the pictures Ansel Adams took in Yosemite. He was a master photographer. Sara was also an excellent photographer. I don't know anything about photography and how to take the kind of pictures Sara would want. I don't know what I can accomplish by going to California."

"It's the going that's important," replied Henry. "It was your wife's last request. How can you not go?"

"Photography was the most important thing in Sara's life. I feel it's important for me to take the kind of pictures she would have taken."

"It's obvious you've done a bit of thinking on this. I think you need to go, but it's none of my business. In any case, I wish you would stay a few days. I'm beholden to you. Stay and fish the Autumn before it's gone. I'll guide for you, no charge."

"Thanks Henry, but I have a pile of work waiting for me in Maine."

"Then at least stay overnight and get a fresh start in the morning."

Glancing at my watch I said, "Okay, Henry. I'll stay overnight. But I want to get an early start before those TV people get here. I know all about TV interviews, and I don't like them."

"I don't enjoy them myself, but sometimes they're necessary. I'll take a couple of steaks out of the freezer. I haven't had my portion of beef this week. Make yourself at home. I'll pull out the bed in the living room for you to sleep on. Feel free to use the shower. There are towels in the bathroom closet. I'm going to take a nap."

After an early supper Henry said, "I want to show you the Autumn River and their water project. We'll take my truck."

We headed up the road and Henry kept talking. "The Autumn River flows one and three-quarter miles from its source to the Yellowstone River. I own a quarter of mile of stream above and below my shop. The state owns three hundred feet from my property line to the Yellowstone River. WestSun owns everything above my land. Fishing was permitted on their property until they got uppity a few years ago and posted it. But I sneak up there to fish early in the morning when no one is around."

Henry cleared his throat and spit out his window. "WestSun owns all of the water rights because the source of the Autumn is on their land. That's why we had such a difficult time with them in court. Out here everything is water. Wars have been fought over water and cattle. But times are changing. Sooner or later they're going to think more about trout because trout generate a lot of money in Montana."

"What's the state of Montana doing about the problem of diverting water from The Autumn?"

Henry got a sarcastic expression on his face and said, "Montana Game & Fish? Nothing. They're shaking in their boots. We have a Republican governor. All he cares about is business and development.

"A few fish people spoke out against the water project, and their jobs were eliminated with the last budget cut. Game & Fish stated that WestSun has to maintain a minimal flow of water in the river, and that's all they've said about the project."

We came to a steep hill. Henry shifted into second gear and punched the accelerator to the floor with his cowboy boot. On the other side of the hill he stopped on a bridge and said, "Take a look at what's under this bridge."

We got out of the truck and looked at a large concrete ditch. Henry angrily said, "This is the Autumn River's new home. This ditch will carry seventy-five percent of the river to the reservoir."

"That leaves only twenty-five percent in the riverbed," I said.

"That's right. Barely enough to support a small population of small trout. The big trout are doomed."

"Why?"

"With most of the water diverted the size of the pools will shrink dramatically. The big trout will lose most of their food supply and the physical space they need to grow and prosper. Higher temperatures and lower oxygen in the water may also have a negative impact. Most of the big fish will die or migrate downstream to the Yellowstone if they are able to swim through the shallow riffles."

"Does WestSun know this?"

"They say there will be a good population of trout in the river. They've also hired their own biologists to issue positive statements to the press. The general public doesn't know who or what to believe. It becomes an argument dealing with numbers and size of trout, and everyone has an opinion. But if you press the biologists at Game & Fish they will tell you, off the record of course, that the big trout will not survive when the river is reduced by seventy-five percent."

Henry wrinkled his forehead. "People out here take water from rivers and streams for irrigation all the time, so there's a lot of sympathy for WestSun. They say if you own the water rights, than it's your water. I wish I had enough money when I first came to Montana to buy all the land that the Autumn flows through. But it cost too much. Come on, I want to show you the river."

Henry started to climb over the fence that ran parallel to the road. I looked at a no trespassing sign that was nailed to a fence post and hesitated to follow.

Henry glanced back and yelled, "Don't pay any attention to that sign. I walk on their land all the time. I want to show you where the Autumn River begins."

I reluctantly climbed over the fence and followed Henry through thick willow. Rushing water reached my ears, and then I saw a large pool with water bubbling up in the middle. There was no flow of water coming into the pool.

"This pool is called the Source," Henry said. "It's fed by a huge underground spring, which causes the water to shoot up like that. It's this spring that keeps the Autumn flowing at a steady rate all year long."

Henry had a sad expression on his face. I said nothing. He kicked a stone, turned around, and headed back to the road. I followed. We didn't talk on the way back to his shop.

Back on his deck Henry said, "People are moving here all the time from California. The locals are becoming slaves to developers. Development means jobs and money. But it also brings a lot of problems that no one wants to talk about. They won't be happy until this state looks like California."

Henry could really rant and rave. Sara would have loved him, and he would have loved talking to her. He was a very likable person, but I didn't agree with his ideas and opinions. If push came to shove, I would side with WestSun Resorts and the rights of private citizens and companies to manage their own land the way they wanted. But this was not my battle. There was nothing to be gained

40

by arguing with Henry.   Tomorrow morning I would be on my way to Maine.

Henry appeared to be talked out, and I couldn't think of anything appropriate to say. We sat in silence for a while.

Suddenly Henry waved his hands in the air and yelled, "Look at that river. It's not going to be here in a couple of days. They're going to kill a national treasure, and no one can stop them because the law is on their side. I don't understand how people can destroy a river like the Autumn. I just don't understand."

Henry rested his chin in his right hand and gazed at the river with an expression of defeat. In a way I felt sorry for him, but I knew there was also a case to be made for the developers. People had the right to develop the land they paid taxes on. Henry had his fly shop and his life style, but he didn't want others to have the same privileges he had, and that wasn't playing fair.

Henry stood up and walked over to the far side of his deck to look at the sun setting in the west.

"It's time," he said. "I want to show you one more thing."

He grabbed his binoculars from the table and said, "Come on."

Henry led the way down a trail to the river.   We came to a large rock and climbed up its slanted surface. From the top we looked down at a long, slick pool. Trout were rising everywhere to floating insects.

"This pool is called Looking Glass Pool," Henry said, "because at this time of the day the setting sun allows you to see into its depths."

Henry gave me his binoculars, and I raised them to my eyes. Long strands of aquatic vegetation waved in the current. Between the fluttering green tentacles were some of the biggest trout I have ever seen. I focused on a rainbow trout that looked about twenty inches long. Sunlight flashed on his pink stripe as he took a fly from the smooth surface.

"I just saw a big rainbow trout."

"The rainbows will get between sixteen and twenty-five inches," Henry said, "but the browns get up to five and six pounds. There is a big brown trout in this pool that I think is between seven and eight pounds. He rises late and does most of his feeding after dark. If we are going to see him it will be just before the sun drops below the ridge behind us."

Shadows grew longer. Slanting rays of sunlight gilded the landscape. Henry said, "We still have a few minutes of sunlight. I hope he shows."

The hush of late evening surrounded us. Henry pointed to a submerged rock in the middle of the pool and said, "The big brown rises like a submarine from a hollow beneath that rock."

I explored the water around the rock with the binoculars, but I didn't see a big fish. Lowering the binoculars, I glanced at Henry just as he yelled, "There he is!"

A huge tan shadow had materialized like a ghost above the rock. I said, "He's enormous. I've never seen anything that big in Maine except a salmon."

"I've had him on my line twice," said Henry, "but I couldn't hold him."

The big trout moved slowly downstream, and I lost sight of him behind a rock. As the sun sank behind us a gentle twilight stimulated a huge hatch of insects. The surface began to boil with rising trout.

"I want to save the big brown trout," Henry said.

"What do you mean, save him?"

"When they divert the river there will not be enough water in the ripples below Looking Glass Pool for him to swim to the Yellowstone River, which is just around that bend. He'll be trapped in this pool. The competition for food and space will be fierce. His size will be a liability, and he'll probably starve to death. I can't let him die like that."

"How can you save him?"

"I don't know. I've been trying to get Game & Fish to net him and move him to the Yellowstone River. But they won't come near this place. They're afraid of running into reporters and calling attention to themselves."

Back at his shop, Henry took two beers out of his refrigerator. We sat on his deck gazing at a sky filled with a tapestry of stars.

"I wish you could stay a few days and help me to think of a way to save the big brown," Henry said.

"I can't, Henry."

42

We made small talk for another half hour, and then Henry said he was going to bed. He looked tired. I think his river ordeal had drained him more than he realized. I threw my sleeping bag on the bed in his living room and went to sleep.

The next morning I was up early and had coffee made by the time Henry walked into the kitchen. We ate cereal and toast and Henry chattered about fishing in Alaska and New Zealand. By eight o'clock I was ready to leave. Henry shook my hand and thanked me again for pulling him off the rock in the Yellowstone River.

I thought about Henry as I drove to Livingston. He was ridiculous trying to save a fish that only had a couple more years to live. He was irrational, impractical, and idealistic, just like all of the other environmentalists in the world.

On the interstate I accelerated to seventy. My steering wheel began to shake. When I slowed to fifty the shaking stopped. I would have to deal with another delay, and I wasn't happy about it.

I got off the interstate at Big Timber and called the car rental place in Billings. The man on the phone told me not to drive the car and that he would bring another car to Big Timber. I suggested we meet in the cafe where I was calling from and gave him directions to get to the place.

I decided to buy a magazine while I waited. As I glanced over the magazines my eyes fell on a photograph on the cover of *Audubon Magazine*. It was Sara's favorite photo of morning sunlight streaming through the King's Pines. I picked the magazine up. Two words entered my mind, "Help Henry!"

CHAPTER 4

"Help Henry!" I repeated to myself.

The words startled me because it seemed like I had heard Sara's voice saying them. Of course I knew Sara was not talking to me. I laughed at the notion. But then, I thought, she might talk to me if she could, and "Help Henry!" would probably be what she would say.

I tried to rationalize that Sara's opinions would always be with me and that they might materialize in my mind in various ways. The more I thought about the words, the more convinced I became that seeing Sara's photograph on the cover of *Audubon Magazine* had triggered an association in my mind between Henry's desire to save the big brown trout and what Sara would want me to do.

I purchased the magazine, ordered a cup of coffee, and told myself I was not going to think about the words. The article contained three more of Sara's photographs and a text written by someone else. It mentioned that the King's Pines were the largest stand of white pines in the eastern United States and that they were to be cut this coming summer.

Apparently *Audubon* was not aware that the King's Pines were being preserved as a park by the Nature Bank. I made a mental note to call *Audubon* as soon as I got back to Maine and ask them to publish an update on their article.

Sara always sent photographs to national magazines, but she never expected to get them published. I wished she could have seen her photograph on the cover of *Audubon Magazine*.

Sara's words were still in my mind when my rental car arrived at noon. The man from the rental agency was apologetic and helped me to pack everything into the new car.

I placed the urn filled with Sara's ashes on the front passenger seat. Touching the urn made me think about helping Henry. With effort I shook the thought away, told myself I was going to Maine and headed to the interstate.

Waiting for the red light by the ramp to the interstate, I turned the radio on. "We need your help to save the Autumn River," were the first words I heard, followed by, "Call your state representative today before this national treasure is lost forever. Tell them you are opposed to the diverting of this magnificent river for creating a reservoir at the WestSun development. This announcement was paid for by Montana Trout Unlimited."

The light turned green, but I didn't move. The guy behind me began to blow his horn. I started to turn onto the ramp and came to a complete stop. Again, the guy blasted his horn. Rubber squealed as he pulled around me. He flipped me his middle finger as his car accelerated. Again the words, "Help Henry!" rose from the depths of my mind.

With caution I backed down the ramp and into the gas station on the corner, where I sat, not believing what was happening to me. After a while, I pulled out of the gas station and drove around Big Timber, unable to make a decision. It was crazy for me to go back to Henry's place. I had made up my mind to go to Maine. I was acting irrationally, but then I realized that Sara often acted irrationally, especially with environmental concerns.

"Okay," I said to myself. "I'll help Henry, and I'm not going to think any more about those damn words."

On the way to Henry's place, I kept glancing at the urn of ashes on the passenger seat and kept seeing Sara in my mind with a big smile on her face. I said to myself, "Sara, this is not fair. You're playing games with me, and you seem to have the advantage."

There was a Gone Fishing sign on Henry's door. I headed for Looking Glass Pool and passed several anglers fishing the river before I saw Henry in his favorite place. On the viewing rock I watched Henry without him being aware of my presence.

Curves of line gracefully moved through the air over Henry's head. With perfect timing he waited for the line to straighten behind him before he empowered the rod to bring it forward. The line flew in front of him, and he let it fall to the sheet of water. The fly made a soft landing on the slick water and floated on motions of current. A swirl erupted around the fly, sending expanding rings over the pool's placid skin.

Henry's rod bowed with the strength of the fish. His line sliced through the water. The trout jumped twice and bolted downstream with a burst of speed and energy. Henry followed the fish to the tail of the pool where he netted him. He admired his prize and released the fish. Looking up, he saw me on the rock and grinned.

I climbed off the rock and walked to the edge of the pool. Henry's hand was extended as he approached me, and we shook hands firmly. To my surprise, he didn't ask me the reason for my return, and I didn't offer one. The fact that I was there was enough for Henry. I guess it was also enough for me.

We walked back to his shop where he offered me a beer on his deck. Henry seemed to have more energy and to have recovered from his ordeal on the Yellowstone River. The bell in his shop signaled that someone had walked in.

Henry got up and said, "More fishermen. They're making special pilgrimages to fish the Autumn River for the last time. There are already twelve people on the river. I'm not issuing rod permits. No one will be turned away these last few days. I'm also giving everyone free flies as a token of my appreciation for their support over the years. Autumn River trout flies will be of little value after this week."

Returning to his chair, Henry took a gulp of beer and gazed at the river. Wrinkling his forehead, he said, "They never showed."

"Who never showed?"

"The TV people."

I had completely forgotten that Henry was to be interviewed by a Denver TV station.

"What happened?"

"I don't know. A guy from the Denver chapter of Trout Unlimited had arranged everything. He called this morning and said the TV crew wasn't coming. He was as surprised as I was. He thinks WestSun got to someone high up at the station, but he doesn't know for sure."

Henry stared at the river. I knew he was disappointed. After a long silence he said, "It's almost supper time. I never got a chance to

46

thank you properly for what you did yesterday. Let me buy you dinner and a couple of beers. Okay?"

"Sure, I could use a good meal."

We got into Henry's truck and headed south in the direction of Yellowstone National Park. Fifteen or twenty minutes later he turned onto a gravel road, traveled a short distance, and pulled into a parking lot filled with pick-up trucks. A sign on the building identified the place as The Yellowstone Saloon. We walked into a crowded room where most of the people were wearing cowboy hats and boots.

"This is where the locals hang out," Henry said. "Let's grab that table by the window."

Henry ordered a pitcher of beer and a chicken dinner for himself. I also ordered the chicken. I poured beer into our glasses, took a long swallow, and started to relax.

"Look at what just walked in," Henry announced.

Turning around in my seat, I saw two men standing by the door. One was unshaven, and the other man was just ugly.

Blood swelled in Henry's face. "They're the guys that jumped me on the Yellowstone River. I've got a few things to settle with them."

Before I could respond Henry was on his feet. I got a terrible feeling he was about to start a fight as I followed him.

The two men looked surprised when they saw Henry, but they stood their ground. They were not the type to back down from anyone. Sarcastically Henry said, "It's nice to see you boys again."

I had to give Henry credit for having more guts than brains. One of the men sneered and said, "How was the water in the Yellowstone River? A bit chilly for this time..."

The man's words were cut off by Henry's fist slamming into his mouth. Wobbling backwards, the man grabbed a chair to keep from falling. Henry advanced and tried to hit him again. The man dodged his wide swing and threw a punch at Henry.

I didn't see Henry go down because a powerful blow to my face had knocked me to the floor. Scrambling to my feet, I saw another punch coming and blocked it with my left forearm. At the same time I plunged my right fist into a soft belly, bringing the man to his knees.

Henry was on the floor with his opponent sitting on top of him. The man raised his fist to hit Henry. I dove through the air and hit the guy with a body block. Getting up quickly, I delivered a swift blow to his face before he could get to a standing position. Blood spurted from his nose as he fell.

Henry was gasping for breath and holding his chest. I reached into his pocket for his pills and pushed one into his mouth.

"You ought to get that bypass, Henry," someone yelled. "One of these days your ticker is going to quit on you."

Out of the corner of my eye, I saw the two men helping each other out the door.

"Take it easy, Henry," I said. "Those guys are gone."

A fat man with red suspenders said, "You really whipped their asses, and they had it coming for a long time."

I helped Henry to a chair. A few men congratulated us and gave us pats on the back. Then everyone went back to their drinking and left us alone. I made Henry sit for a while before I suggested we go back to his shop. He nodded, and I helped him to his truck.

"There's a shotgun in my camper, get it," Henry said.

"What for?"

"Don't argue. Just get it."

I got the shotgun and handed it to Henry.

"Why do you need a shotgun?"

"To shoot those bastards."

"Do you think they'll try something?"

"You can't trust them. It's best to be prepared. I think I'll keep my shotgun handy for a few days."

"It wasn't smart picking a fight with those two jerks when you knew you had a heart condition."

"A person my age can't afford to walk away from a fight."

I didn't say anything and started the truck. When we arrived at Henry's shop he went to bed. I fixed a sandwich from the turkey he had in his refrigerator. Sitting on his deck, I gazed at the warm glow on the mountains and said to myself, "What am I doing here?"

The next morning Henry looked fine. I couldn't believe how quickly he recovered from his spells. We ate breakfast sitting on his deck.

"I have an idea on how we might save the big brown trout," Henry said.

"How?"

"It's a long shot and it might not work, but it's the only thing I can think of."

"What is it?"

"If we can get the big brown to take a large fly, a fly with a hook that will hold him, I think we can push him downstream to the Yellowstone River, where he'll be able to survive."

"How far is it to the Yellowstone from Looking Glass Pool?"

"Two or three hundred yards. What do you think of my idea?"

"It might work. I can't think of anything better."

"Big brown trout do most of their feeding after dark," Henry said. "We'll have to fish at night."

"That's okay. I'll do whatever I can to help you."

"I'm glad you're here. We'll start fishing tonight when the setting sun moves the big brown out of his hiding place. We've got four nights to save the biggest trout in the Autumn River."

At dusk we watched the big brown leave his cave on schedule. Henry knew where the big trout did most of his feeding, and he positioned himself to reach the fish with a short cast. He fished over the huge fish for three hours. Several smaller fish were brought to his net, but none of his offerings brought a rise from the big trout.

Near midnight Henry took a break for coffee and a sandwich. He said, "I have no idea what he's feeding on. The hatches on these limestone creeks are very complex, with many different species of flies hatching at the same time. The fly you see fish taking on the surface, may not be the fly that interests a really big trout. That big brown might be feeding on nymphs on the bottom, and we would never know it."

Henry gave me a couple of nymphs to fish with a sinking line, and I fished for the next two hours with no success. Like Henry, I caught several fish, including a beautiful three pound rainbow trout. It was close to three o'clock when we quit fishing. On the way back to Henry's shop, I asked him if we might consider saving some of the fish we were catching by moving them down to the Yellowstone River.

49

"Not now."

"Why not?"

"It would take too much time away from our effort to catch the big brown trout."

"Why is the big brown so important?"

Henry took a deep breath and let it out slowly. "I would like to save all of the fish, but I can't. The big brown is special because he represents the very best that this ecosystem is capable of producing. He's at the top of the stream's food web. The whole river is present in this one fish. He has the best genes and the best ability to survive. He has proven himself by being what he is. He might also have an opportunity to mate in the Yellowstone River and keep the Autumn River alive in his young."

I looked at Henry but couldn't see the expression on his face in the darkness. I didn't place the same value on a fish that he did. His explanation reminded me of Sara's defense for the King's Pines.

"I have to save him because he's the king of the river," Henry continued. He paused and added, "And because I don't want to walk down to Looking Glass Pool and find him dead. Does that make sense to you?"

I didn't want to disagree with Henry so I said, "I guess."

The next evening Henry brought a net with a small mesh to catch insects floating in the current. After filtering the water with his net, he said, "There's not a fly coming down the river that we have not already presented to that big fish."

We started to fish and tried a variety of flies. Several nice trout came to net, but there was no action from the big brown. Again we fished to three in the morning.

At eight o'clock the next morning there was a knock on the door, and Henry let two men into his shop. One of the men said he was writing a magazine article on the Autumn River and wanted to get a photo of Henry fishing the river. Henry said he would meet him at Looking Glass Pool at eleven o'clock and went back to bed. I dozed off, but woke up with Henry making noise in the kitchen.

Over a breakfast of flapjacks we talked about the big brown trout. Henry said, "We've tried everything except big streamer flies. Maybe he's taking small rainbow or brown trout. A big trout will often feed on smaller fish. Let's try rainbow and brown trout

50

streamers tonight. We've got nothing to lose. We can't do any worse than we've been doing the last two nights."

"What time are they going to divert the river on Wednesday?" I asked.

"Nine o'clock."

"Maybe we should stay the entire night on the river."

"Good idea," Henry said. "We can sleep by the river. Bring a sleeping bag. We'll stay to sunup."

"I'll bring my camp stove to brew coffee," I said.

"Take whatever you want from the kitchen. Now I need to talk to you about something else. I know a guy who lives in Red Lodge who is a fantastic photographer. He got into fishing a couple of years ago, and I guided him on the Autumn and the Yellowstone. He still owes me for a couple of trips. I think he would be willing to teach you the basics of photography in lieu of my fee."

"I can't do that, Henry."

"Yes, you can. I won't take no for an answer. I know your wife was a very special person. Going to Yosemite is something you have to do for her. I also want you to take my camper."

"That's ridiculous, Henry."

"No it's not, because I'm going with you. After they divert the Autumn, there'll be nothing to keep me here. I think a change of scenery will do me good. Besides, I've never been to Yosemite. I know that sounds strange, since I lived in L.A., but I wasn't into seeing California when I lived there. I went to Alaska, New Zealand, and Montana to fish and hunt. Promise me that you'll think about it, okay?"

"I'll think about it, Henry."

There was no insect activity on the stream that night. The weather had turned cooler during the day with a feeling of rain in the air. An overcast sky made it difficult to see into the water and to determine if the big brown was in his usual feeding lane.

Henry started fishing with a large rainbow trout streamer. By midnight he had caught only two fish. He crawled into his sleeping bag, and I took over till he relieved me sometime after three. At six it started to rain as the black of night turned into a dismal grey morning. It was time to quit.

Henry left a message on his shop door explaining he had been fishing during the night and didn't want to be disturbed. We slept to four in the afternoon.

Over supper we talked about fishing strategies for our last night on the river. The weather had cleared, and the sun was warm. It looked like a good night for fishing. We decided to go back to big nymphs and to fish dry flies only if there was a hatch of big insects.

On the way to Looking Glass Pool we agreed to fish shorter shifts. As the sun began to set we saw the huge brown leave his den and cruise over tan and cream gravel. Henry said, "This will be the last time we see him with normal water levels in the river."

Henry began casting. On his second cast he caught a seventeen inch brown trout and gently returned it to the river.

Night descended upon us as thousands of white dots speckled the black sky. I made coffee and got ready for a long night.

At ten o'clock I began my shift. I caught a couple of nice trout, but failed to get a rise from the big brown. At midnight I began to get sleepy. I was glad when Henry took over, allowing me to crawl into my sleeping bag. Henry woke me at two. I didn't want to get up, but I knew if I didn't take my shift he would keep fishing. He was short of breath as he struggled to get into his sleeping bag. I was glad this was our last night of fishing.

A fog began to form on the water, making me shiver. I slipped on a red and black wool shirt and ate a sandwich before I waded into the river. I fished to four. When I went to Henry's sleeping bag to wake him, I found him sleeping peacefully. I didn't have the heart to disturb him.

I decided to rest for a while and then go back to fishing. My eyes grew heavier as I lay on top of my sleeping bag. Without realizing what was happening, I drifted into a sound sleep.

Screaming crows woke me. Low fog covered the land like a gray blanket. To the east, the red flush of dawn bounced off tiny droplets of moisture suspended in the air. The sight was beautiful and eerie.

I blinked my eyes and glanced at the river. Thousands of huge, black mayflies fluttered and danced above the water. Their performance seemed to have a mesmerizing effect on me. Breaking out of my trance, I woke Henry and pointed to the river.

Henry's mouth opened, and he couldn't speak right away. Finally he blurted out, "It's the phantom mayfly hatch. I didn't think it existed. I read about it in Gordon Smith's book on western hatches. He said it occurs once every three or four years on a few limestone creeks at dawn and that the hatch only lasts five or six days. I've lived on this river for fifteen years and have never seen it."

Feeding fish were everywhere. My eyes darted to the place where the big brown usually fed. As I watched, he rose to the surface and sucked one of the large insects into his mouth.

"There he is Henry, and he's feeding like he hasn't eaten in a month."

Henry searched through several fly boxes for a black dry fly. He looked at me with an expression of desperation and said, "I don't have anything black that will float. I'll have to tie a fly."

He set up a small fly tying vise. He then instructed me to hold the flashlight while he scrutinized little plastic bags of fly tying materials.

As Henry worked he mumbled to himself, "I'll use a number eight hook, black feathers for the tail and hackle, a dark gray quill will do for the wings, but there's nothing black for the fly's body. What am I going to use for the body?"

He looked at my wool shirt and said, "Your shirt. Cut me a piece of black wool from your shirt."

When all of the necessary materials were assembled, Henry began to tie the fly. First he attached the tail feathers to the hook with his tying thread. Then he took the wool from my shirt, secured one end of it to the hook near the tail and wrapped the rest around the hook's shank. Next, he cut two matching pieces from the duck quill for wings. When they were secured in an upright position, he wrapped hackle around the front of the hook and knotted his thread to keep everything from unraveling. Releasing the jaws of his vise, he held the fly up for me to inspect.

"It looks great Henry, but will it fool the big brown?"

"I hope so. Do you want to make the first cast?"

"No. I might screw it up. This is your fish, Henry."

Henry switched to his floating line, tied the black fly to his tippet, and dressed the fly with float preparation. He then waded into the river.

The power of the rod stretched the line behind him, and with a thrust of his wrist the line flew forward. At the precise moment, Henry released the surplus line in his hand, and it shot through the rod's guides. Losing energy, the line floated down to the river, allowing the fly to gently alight on the glassy water about fifteen feet above the rising trout.

Henry's body tensed for a strike as the distance between the fly and the big brown decreased. Five feet in front of the big fish, the fly abruptly went under. A rainbow trout leaped out of the water and came down on top of the big brown in a commotion of swirling water and spray. When the disturbance settled, the brown and the rainbow were gone.

"Shit," muttered Henry.

The old man kept staring at the place where the big brown had vanished. Phantom mayflies floated undisturbed over the area. Henry turned around and looked at me. He started to slowly wade back to shore. Disappointment was etched into his face.

The calm surface broke into a large dimple behind Henry. Rings grew and spread from a rise that could only have been made by the big brown. A lump rose in my throat and blocked my words for a second or two.

"Henry," I said as I pointed behind him. "Look!"

Henry turned around, hesitated, and returned to his casting position. I couldn't see the expression on his face, but I knew it had changed.

"Make it good, Henry."

The fly kissed the water. Its path was perfectly aligned with the big brown trout. Feathers clung to a bubble and then broke loose. The magnificent head broke the glass. Henry raised the tip of his rod, but again success was denied. The brown had chosen a natural insect instead of Henry's hastily tied imitation.

Once more the rhythms of line, rod, and wrist performed without a flaw. The fly drifted to its fate. I watched as if in a daze. Action seemed to move in slow motion: a huge head emerging from the water...the fly vanishing into massive jaws...ripples of a rise ring maturing in size...raising the rod to set the hook...line screaming from a reel.

54

In the confines of chest-deep water Henry labored to attain land. He extended the rod above his head as line poured and leaped from his reel. The knot that secured the thinner backing line to the heavier casting line bolted through the guides of the rod in pursuit of the trout fleeing upstream. Henry reached the shore and began to run after the huge fish.

Suddenly, the line lost tension. The trout had reversed his swimming direction and was heading downstream. Henry reeled frantically to retrieve slack line. This would be the trout's longest run and the most dangerous one for Henry.

As the fish neared Henry the line snapped tight and cut through the water. In seconds the trout was below him, and he struggled to follow it. His chest was heaving under the strain.

Run and reel was the name of the game. Don't let the fish take out all of the line. Keep him away from sharp rocks and snags that could wear the fragile leader to the breaking point. It all sounded so simple. Large trout could be lost with a flip of a tail. Henry and I knew how quickly it could happen.

The big brown had fought the hook before, and he knew how to use the current to his advantage. Out of Looking Glass Pool he swam and into the pool below, with a tired old angler stumbling and toiling to keep up.

I ran ahead of Henry and asked him if he was okay. Line was spilling from his reel like sand in an hour glass. He was losing the race. There was pain on his face. I knew his heart was in trouble.

"Let me take over, Henry."

He pushed me away.

"Do you have your medicine?"

"There's no more line," Henry screamed.

I looked at Henry's reel. In another instant the leader would snap and...

"Take the rod, you beautiful, stupid fish."

As Henry yelled these words, he threw his fly rod into the river. Then he collapsed. Frantically, I searched his pockets for his pills. I found the bottle that he kept his medicine in and quickly shoved one of the pills into his mouth. Henry clutched his hand to his chest. Between clenched teeth he muttered, "Its over...he'll die with the rest of the trout."

"Don't think about that, Henry. Try to relax."

"I can't relax," he yelled.

"You're not doing yourself any good. I'll go check on him if you promise to lie here quietly."

"Hurry up."

Cautiously, I waded into the pool. Near the middle of the river my boot felt a slight resistance. I reached into the water and grabbed the line that was stretched up and down the pool. Feeding the line through my hands, I waded upstream and found the rod lying on the bottom of the river. Lifting the rod from the water, I saw that the line was still attached to the reel. Turning, I walked with the current pushing at the back of my waders, reeling in the precious line as I got closer to the big fish, not daring to test the weight at the other end.

When most of the line was on the reel, I waded ashore and tried to see the big trout in the underwater confusion of highlight and shadow. My eyes found him resting behind a rock.

"We still got him, Henry. I don't know how, but he's still on the line."

I looked back at Henry and saw him holding himself up with one hand. With his other hand he motioned in a downstream direction. I knew he wanted me to move the big fish toward the Yellowstone River.

Applying tension to the rod, I carefully nudged the huge fish into the faster flow. He gave a swimming action with his tail and shot downstream with me running after him.

The sun rose higher in the cloudless sky. The big brown began to stay longer in one place, but I wouldn't allow him to do that. Each time he tried to rest, I forced him into the rush of the river, pushing fly rod and leader beyond their limits of strength.

Time passed with nothing eventful happening, except for the routine of gaining and losing line and the moving of the big fish closer to the junction of the two rivers.

We reached the Yellowstone. The trout swam into the swiftness of the big river. I felt a sense of relief. The trout was safe. The contest was over.

The brown darted around a rock in an attempt to find deeper water. I eased around the rock and put pressure on the rod to pull the fish toward me so I could remove the hook and release him.

My boots began to slip on smooth gravel. The fish turned and came in my direction. I readied the net. Webbing spread out in front of him, and he sensed danger. Water exploded in front of me as the fish tried to escape.

I tried desperately to dig my boots into the loose gravel, but it kept sliding under my feet. Water boiled around my back as I fought the powerful surge to remain in a standing position.

My feet slipped, and I fell into the cold water and rolled and tumbled with the river. The churning current pulled me under. My lungs were bursting. I popped above the surface, coughing, choking, and gasping.

Somehow, I had been pushed into shallow water, behind a protective rock. Directly in front of me the big brown floated on his side, gill plates pulsating from exhaustion. The hook had torn loose from his mouth. He was free.

I took him in my hands and gently moved him back and forth, forcing life-giving water through his gills. Gradually he revived, and I allowed him to slip from my fingers. He rested in the calm water for a while and then slowly disappeared into the depths of the Yellowstone River.

Hastily I returned to where Henry rested on the bank. He was still in great pain. I began to fear for his life and shoved another pill into his mouth.

"How do you feel, Henry?"

"Where's the big brown?"

"He's in the Yellowstone."

"Thank goodness. At least we have saved that much of the Autumn River."

"I have to get you to a hospital."

Henry shook his head to indicate he didn't want to be moved.

"Listen to me," he said. "I have something I want to tell you."

I eased my ear closer to Henry's mouth because he was barely speaking in a whisper.

"I've made out the title of my truck and camper to you. It's on my fly tying bench."

"What are you talking about?"

Henry pulled me closer and mumbled, "Shut up and let me talk. I want you to take my truck...and go to Yosemite...cough...and take those pictures for your wife...and... cough...and I don't want an argument from you."

Henry started to gasp for air, and then he stopped breathing. I felt for a pulse in his neck, but couldn't find one. I began to do CPR, and I kept at it for what seemed like a long time, but he did not respond. Henry had passed away.

CHAPTER 5

I covered Henry's face with my wool shirt and sat on a rock staring at his lifeless body. Shock and disbelief numbed my thoughts.

"Is that Henry?"

I jerked my head up. Two men were standing in front of me.

"Yes. He just died."

"How did it happen?"

I stood up, looked at Henry's body and said, "It was his heart. He had the big brown trout on his line and was running after him to keep his leader from breaking. We were trying to save the big fish by moving him down to the Yellowstone River while he was hooked. I guess it was too much for Henry. I tried to give him CPR, but he didn't respond."

Wrinkling his forehead, the man said, "Trying to save the Autumn was too much for him. I tried to get him to leave before they diverted the river, but he wouldn't go. He had to stay to the bitter end. It's a disgrace what they're doing to this river, and now it's cost Henry his life."

"Henry was a person who had to do what he had to do," the other man said. "We all loved him for the way he was. He had to do everything possible to save the Autumn River. What happened to the big brown trout?"

"He's in the Yellowstone River."

Three men and a woman arrived. I let the first two men explain the situation to them. Someone suggested we carry Henry to his shop. We lifted him into our arms and formed a sling to support his body. Arriving at Henry's shop, we laid him on his bed and covered him with a blanket. One of the men said he would call the sheriff's office to report Henry's death.

More people began to arrive. By nine o'clock there were at least twenty people in Henry's shop. A news team arrived. Shortly after, I was standing on Henry's deck when a reporter asked me for an interview.

I frowned and said, "I don't like doing interviews."

"You're the only person who knows what happened. I wish you would reconsider. A lot of people knew Henry and would want to know how he died."

The man sounded sincere. He also was right about me being the only person who could tell the story. While I didn't agree with Henry's position on the environment, I had gained a lot of respect for him during the last four nights.

"Under the circumstances," I said, "I guess I don't have a choice. But keep it short."

The reporter nodded and signaled the cameraman to come out on the deck. They asked me to stand by the railing with the river and mountains behind me. The red light on the video camera came on, and the reporter began the interview.

"I'm with Kirk Weber, the last person to be with Henry Johnson before he died. Can you tell us what Henry and you were doing on the river so early in the morning?"

I cleared my throat and said, "We were trying to catch a big brown trout to move him down to the Yellowstone River so he wouldn't die when the Autumn River is diverted. We fished all night.

"At dawn Henry hooked the big fish. The exertion of the battle was too much for him. He started to have chest pains. I gave him one of his nitroglycerine pills. I told him to rest, and that I would try to move the fish down to the Yellowstone River."

The reporter asked, "Was this the first time Henry had a problem with his heart?"

"No. He had two spells that I knew about, but he always recovered without much difficulty. After I released the big trout in the Yellowstone River, I ran back to Henry. When I got to him, he was still in pain. I gave him another pill. He said a few words, and then he stopped breathing. I tried CPR, but he didn't respond."

"Are you saying that you moved the big trout to the Yellowstone River while he was hooked?"

"Yes, that was our plan."

"Why did Henry want to save this particular trout?"

60

"Henry wanted to save all of the trout, as well as the Autumn River, but he couldn't do it. The big brown trout was special to him. He said that every part of the river's ecology was present in this one fish, and that he didn't want to find him dead after they diverted the river."

"That is an incredible story, Mr. Weber. Thank you for sharing it with us."

The reporter looked directly at the camera and said, "Henry Johnson and the river he loved will be missed by the hundreds of fishermen who came here to fish. But thanks to Henry and Kirk, a small part of this extraordinary river has been saved."

The cameraman turned off his camera, and the reporter thanked me again.

"The river has been diverted!" a man yelled.

Everyone ran to the deck and viewed the small amount of water trickling through the riverbed.

"Let's go see what's happening to the fish," someone shouted.

All of us ran down to the river, including the news team. Trout that had been hidden by deep water could now be seen.

A couple of men found a large rainbow trout trapped in a shallow ripple with its back out of the water. Jumping into the stream, they pushed the trout with their hands into deeper water while the camera man shot video of them.

We inspected several more pools and found all of them crowded with trout. I didn't see how they could survive in so little water.

On the way back to Henry's shop emotions were running high. One of the men began to shout obscenities at WestSun Resorts.

"They can't do this," someone yelled.

"They've killed the river," stated a man in an angry voice.

"They've killed Henry," said another.

"The trout will be next."

I could understand their feelings, but the law was on the side of WestSun Resorts. I did, however, sympathize with the fishermen who were saying they wished there was a way to save the trout.

Someone asked the reporter when the story would be aired. He said, "Tonight."

By noon the news team had left. People were standing around Henry's shop not knowing what to do. Some of them started to leave. Others felt obligated to stick around to keep an eye on the trout. I felt bad about the trout and worse about Henry. I also felt that I needed to get back to Maine.

In Henry's shop I found an envelope with my name on it and two sets of keys for his truck. I opened the envelope and pulled out Henry's truck title, which he had signed over to me. There was also a note which read:

Dear Kirk,

If something should happen to me, I would like for you to have my truck and camper. You will need good transportation to get to California to fulfill your obligations to your wife.

Also, would you please call my two daughters and let them know what has happened to me. Their phone numbers are on the back of this note.

I have only known you for a few days, but thanks for being a friend to me and the river.
Henry

Henry was so much like Sara. Both of them were strong-minded people when it came to saving the environment. Both of them also wanted me to take pictures in Yosemite.

"It's the going that's important," is what Henry had said.

Maybe taking photos for Sara was not the only reason I had to go to California. Maybe Henry was right? Maybe there was a reason related to the going?

I was already in Montana, and Montana was a lot closer to California than Maine. Maybe I should just get into Henry's truck and drive to Yosemite and not worry about taking the exceptional photographs that Sara would have taken. The more I thought about this idea, the more acceptable it seemed to be.

I took my belongings from my rental car and put them in Henry's camper. Again, I reserved the passenger's seat for Sara's ashes. I called the car rental agency and told them to pick up their car.

In the kitchen, I listened to a couple of men talking about Henry. One man said someone from a funeral home had picked up his body while we were down by the river. Another man said they needed to make arrangements for Henry's funeral and burial. A discussion followed about what Henry would want.

By evening, there were only eight men left in Henry's shop. They had campers and said they were staying overnight to watch the fish.

One of the men introduced himself as Jed Clarkson and explained that he was president of the local chapter of Trout Unlimited. He thanked me for everything I had done. He asked how long I was staying. I told him I was leaving for California in the morning.

At five o'clock Jed turned on Henry's small black and white TV set, and we watched the news. The local channel did a good job with their presentation, and everyone in the room seemed pleased with it. My interview was okay.

The national news came on next. We were surprised to see that the Autumn River was the closing story. It began with the shot of the two men pushing the large rainbow trout out of the shallow ripple into deeper water. My interview was next. The reporter closed the segment by saying WestSun Resorts had been approached for an interview and had declined.

"It's great coverage," Jed said. "But it's too late to save the river."

Several of the men began to gripe about WestSun Resorts. I was getting tired of their complaining. I had helped Henry because I thought it was something Sara would want me to do. But it was over, and I had to get on with my life. I told Jed I had to make a phone call and went to Henry's shop.

I dialed Mike's number. He picked up the phone on the third ring.

"Hello Mike, this is Kirk."

"I saw you on TV and was wondering if you were going to call. What is this nonsense about you saving a fish with an old man?"

"It's hard to explain, Mike. I got caught up in some strange events and..."

"They are very strange events, and I don't understand why you are involved with them. I thought you were on your way to California with your wife."

"I was. We were in an accident. Sara is dead."

Saying the words, "Sara is dead," triggered a release of emotions I didn't expect. Mike didn't say anything for several seconds. I was grateful for the time to pull myself together.

"I'm sorry about Sara. I know you loved her very much."

Neither one of us knew what to say next. I held the phone away from my mouth, took a deep breath, and let it out slowly.

Mike broke the awkward silence. "When are you planning to get back to Maine?"

With effort I said, "I don't know."

"I realize this is a difficult time for you, but I need you back here. I've had an unexpected problem come up. There was a fire in one of my hotels. I have to make an emergency trip to Florida. We have to renovate the building, and I'll be down there for at least a month."

I rubbed my forehead and without thinking I said, "I have to go to Yosemite and take pictures for Sara."

Mike didn't respond right away. I knew he wouldn't understand Sara's dying request. It was also too personal for me to tell him about it.

"Why?" asked Mike.

"Because it was very important to Sara. It's hard to explain. It's a personal thing."

There was another uncomfortable silence.

"This is all very confusing to me, Kirk. When are you planning to go to Yosemite?"

"I thought I might take a few weeks and drive down there now."

"Do you have to go this summer?"

"I'm here, and California is a lot closer to Montana than Maine."

"I know that," replied Mike with irritation in his voice. "Can't you go some other time?"

I didn't like Mike pressuring me to come back to Maine, but I wanted to keep my job. I hesitated to answer for a few seconds and then in a low voice I said, "I guess I can go next spring."

"That would be a lot better than going now. Getting back to work will keep your mind occupied and help you deal with your grief. Take a couple of days if you have to and then head back. I'll see you in a week or so."

I hung up the phone and stared at the painting on the wall of a fisherman casting a fly to a big trout. The fisherman seemed to look a little bit like Henry when he was younger.

I called Henry's two daughters and broke the sad news to them. Both of them had been worried about Henry for a long time and had tried to encourage him to get bypass surgery. I told them I would call them back and give them the names and phone numbers of some of his friends who wanted to help with his funeral.

Then I went back to Henry's living room and told Jed I was going to bed. He thanked me for everything I had done, and I went to Henry's camper. I climbed into the bunk over the truck cab and quickly fell asleep.

A knock on the door woke me. It was Jed. I told him to come in.

Stepping into the camper Jed said, "I'm sorry to wake you. I was afraid I might miss you in the morning. I didn't want you to leave without hearing the news.

"I was just talking to the president of the Helena Chapter of Trout Unlimited. He said a friend at Game & Fish just told him that the governor was very upset with the bad press that Montana received on the news tonight.

"He also said the governor has ordered all of the fisheries people in the southern half of the state to be here tomorrow to move the Autumn River trout to the Yellowstone River. WestSun Resorts has also agreed to restore the river's flow until the project is completed."

"That is good news," I said. "I'm glad they're doing it. Henry would be happy."

"It was Henry's death and your interview that made it happen. Without the publicity they would have let those fish die."

"Thanks for telling me. I have a lot of driving to do tomorrow. I have to get some sleep."

"I understand. Thanks again for everything you've done."

The next morning I looked at the river from Henry's deck and saw the flow had been restored. In Henry's kitchen a couple of men were making breakfast. I ate a bowl of cereal with toast and coffee and said good-by.

A Game & Fish truck passed me on Henry's road going in the opposite direction. Jed said I had helped to save the trout. Maybe I did. Although I think circumstances may have had more to do with it than I did. In any case, it was over, and I had to start thinking about my job in Maine.

I stopped at a gas station to fill Henry's tank and to buy groceries. Three Game & Fish trucks were also there. There would be a lot of people at Henry's place, including the press. I was glad I had left early. The last thing I wanted was another TV interview.

As I neared the Autumn Springs Resort I heard a helicopter. The thumping blades grew louder. Suddenly the chopper shot over my truck and came to a hovering position above a field next to the road. It made a short plummet toward the ground, checked its descent, and shot back up. It appeared the pilot was trying to land in the field but was having trouble doing it.

I stopped by the side of the road to watch. Again, the chopper made a jerky approach, and again the pilot pulled the aircraft back up. On his next attempt, the chopper hit the ground hard and stayed there.

A woman dressed in jeans jumped out of the helicopter and ran toward my truck. She was very attractive and seemed to have an air of poise and refinement about her.

"I need your help," she yelled.

"What's the problem?"

With an expression of concern she said, "My pilot is having dizzy spells. I have to get him to a hospital."

"Let me take a look at him."

I ran to the helicopter with the woman. We found the pilot slumped in his seat, holding his head in his hands.

"We had just taken off when Bill said everything was spinning and that he had to get us down," the woman said.

I said to the pilot, "How do you feel?"

"Dizzy. It let up for a few minutes and gave me a chance to land, but its back again."

I turned to the woman and said, "How far is it to the nearest hospital?"

66

"Bozeman is about sixty-five miles from here."

"I flew helicopters in Vietnam. I can fly us to a hospital a lot faster than we can drive."

The woman looked at Bill and then at me. "He needs to get to a hospital."

We buckled Bill into the rear seat, and I got into the pilot's seat. I took a quick look at the controls and instruments. The basics were there with a lot of sophistication that was not in the Huey Helicopters I had flown in Vietnam.

The woman looked worried as I started the engine. I tried to give her a reassuring smile as the blades began to whirl faster. The blades reached take off speed, and we lifted into the air.

With a burst of power we accelerated into a steep climb. We flew over the trees and then over a small mountain. The woman turned in her seat to check on the pilot and then gave me another nervous look.

The helicopter was a very recent model, and I knew it had cost a lot of money. I got the impression it belonged to the woman sitting next to me.

Looking down at the Yellowstone River, I set a course to Livingston. From there I followed the interstate to Bozeman.

A radio call to the airport control tower at Bozeman confirmed that the hospital had a heliport. The controller gave me instructions to the hospital and said he would notify the emergency room about my arrival.

A nurse met us with a wheelchair at the heliport. We helped the pilot into it, and the nurse took him to the emergency room. The woman and I went to a waiting room.

I purchased two cups of coffee from a vending machine while the woman was in the restroom. When she came back, she sat down and thanked me for the coffee.

I watched her take a sip of coffee and said, "I'm Kirk Weber."

"I'm Susan Martin. Thank you for helping us."

"Your pilot did an incredible job of landing the helicopter in his condition."

"Bill is an excellent pilot. I always felt safe when I was flying with him. I hope he'll be okay."

"Where were you going?"

"Denver. I have a company there."

"Is your company WestSun Resorts?"

Susan smiled with confidence and said, "I had a feeling you knew about WestSun. I saw you on TV last night."

"I guess the whole country saw me, including my boss, and he was not happy about it."

"Why?"

"He wants me back in Maine as soon as possible. We have a lot of work to do."

"Good help is hard to find. Was Henry a good friend?"

"I guess it looks like we were friends, but I'm not an environmentalist. I'm a forester. I've managed timber most of my life. I believe in using resources for people instead of locking them up. I also believe in property rights and that you have the right to divert your water to build a reservoir. But you made a few mistakes."

Susan's eyebrows went up. "What kind of mistakes?"

"You created a public relations disaster for your company by attempting to let those fish die, and by doing so you gave Henry the opportunity to tell the whole country that you and your clients don't care about those trout."

"Your interview told the country about the trout," Susan snapped.

"It did. I had no choice. A lot of people knew Henry, and they deserved to know how he died. I'm the only person who knew how it happened."

Susan gave me an annoyed look. "You're not making sense. You say you're for property rights and that I have a right to divert the water I own. Then you tell the world how Henry and you saved a stupid fish."

"Letting those fish die would have been a waste of a natural resource, and I'm opposed to doing that. I had no idea I would be on national TV, and I had no way of knowing my interview would motivate the Montana governor to move all the fish to the Yellowstone River."

With rising anger Susan said, "So what should I have done with those fish?"

"You could have moved them to the Yellowstone River before you diverted the Autumn River. That would have diffused a lot of the emotion Henry was able to generate. You might also have made a deal with the state of Montana to move those fish to the reservoir you are building. You could have used those wild trout as part of your advertising campaign to attract clients to your resort."

Susan gave me a calmer look. "Interesting strategy. But I still don't understand why you were helping Henry to catch a fish?"

"It's something my deceased wife would have wanted me to do. I don't think I can explain it very well."

Susan seemed to read the sudden emotion I was feeling. She said, "I'm sorry, I didn't mean to get into anything personal."

"It's okay. I still get emotional when I think of Sara. We loved each other very much. She has been gone only a short time."

"How did she die?"

"A truck plowed into our vehicle a few days ago. She died on the way to the hospital. We were on our way to California. Sara was dying from cancer. She wanted to photograph Yosemite Valley before she died."

"Why?"

"Sara was into photography. It was her dream to take the kinds of pictures that Ansel Adams had taken there. Sara had some unusual ideas, but I went along with her because I..."

"Because you loved her. I admire you for that. I'm sorry for asking so many personal questions. I get more curious than I have a right to be."

Our conversation was interrupted by a doctor walking into the waiting room. He looked at Susan and asked, "Are you Susan Martin?"

"Yes."

"I'm Doctor Jacobs, Bill Riley's doctor. He's doing better right now, but these spells can come back at any time. His symptoms could be an indication of a lot of things, some more serious than others. A brain tumor is one of the more serious problems. We want to send him to a hospital in Great Falls that has the staff and equipment to test for a wider range of neurological problems."

Susan thanked the doctor and he left. She then looked at me and said, "I have to get back to Denver. I like you Mr. Weber. You are honest and not afraid to speak your mind. In fact, I like you enough to offer you a job.   Will you fly me to Denver? I'll pay you a thousand dollars for your services."

Susan's offer took me by surprise.   I stared at her a few moments and said, "My boss was hesitant to let me take Sara to Yosemite, but changed his mind when I told him I would quit if he didn't let me go.   Now he has to go to Florida to take care of an emergency situation, and he needs me back there as soon as possible."

"I'll fly you back to Montana early tomorrow morning.   You'll only lose one day. Will one day make a difference?"

"I guess I can make up one day."

"Good. I'll call Autumn Springs and have some people meet us by your truck."

Two men were waiting by my truck when we landed in the field.   I packed a few things and asked Susan to have one of the men drive my truck to Henry's place and to leave the keys on top of the right rear tire.

Back in the air, I headed in a southeastern direction. We flew over the northeastern corner of Yellowstone National Park and landed in Casper, Wyoming for fuel. Back in the air we headed for Cheyenne and followed Interstate 25 into Colorado. Smog began to hide the mountains as we neared Denver. Below us rush hour traffic was building on I-25.

Susan instructed me to head for a cluster of high rise buildings and to land on a heliport by a swimming pool that was on the roof of one of the buildings.   A man greeted us at the heliport. Susan gave him a polite, "Hello Jeff."

I followed Susan down a flight of stairs to the pool, where three marble statues stood in prominent positions. They looked like Greek gods, but I wasn't sure. We came to a door, and Susan opened it with a combination lock. A carpeted hallway led to another door. Beyond this door we entered a beautiful, spacious room.

Paintings of cowboys, Indians, and wildlife hung on the walls, and bronze sculptures of the same subjects stood on pedestals in various places. One side of the huge room was a wall of glass with a view of the Rocky Mountains to the west.   The opposite wall contained a waterfall tumbling into an artificial pond with goldfish swimming under lily pads.

Susan said to have a seat. She disappeared into a bedroom and closed the door behind her. I sank into an overstuffed leather chair and gazed at a sculpture of a cowboy bulldogging a steer.

A woman dressed in a smart-looking suit came into the room and asked me if I would like something to drink. I told her I would have a beer. She returned with a frosted glass and a bottle of Coors.

"Is there anything else I can get for you?"

"This is fine, thank you."

The woman disappeared into a room, which I assumed was a kitchen.

I took a swallow of cold beer and glanced around Susan's living room, a room that was a pinnacle of wealth and success. She was obviously a woman who could do anything she wanted. I had no doubts she had been doing exactly that for a long time.

I began to imagine what it would be like to have money to invest in art, to have people wait on me, to have a private swimming pool, to own a personal helicopter, and to live in a palace on top of the world. Susan's lifestyle was impressive, and I felt envious.

I placed my empty glass on the table in front of me, which was covered with magazines. I picked up one of the magazines and saw that it contained short stories and poems about romantic love. In the table of contents I found a story entitled, "The Flower of Love." Susan was the author. I wondered why a woman like Susan would write short stories about love?

My thoughts were interrupted by the bedroom door opening. Susan strolled into the room wearing a mousey grey suit, a white wig, and wire rimmed glasses. Pointing to her white sneakers she said, "How do you like my disguise as the little old lady environmentalist wearing tennis shoes?"

"Why are you wearing a disguise?"

"It's a trick my dad taught me. He always felt it was a good idea not to be recognized when he went to a controversial meeting where there would be a lot of unfriendly people, like environmentalists.

"I like to see for myself what happens at big meetings. Second hand reports from my staff don't always give me the information and perspective I need."

I started to ask a question, but was interrupted by the woman in the smart suit coming into the room and asking Susan what she wanted for dinner?

"We only have a few minutes, so it has to be something fast."

"Is Mexican food okay?"

"That would be fine."

The woman left and Susan said, "You had a question?"

"What is this meeting about?"

Susan settled into the leather couch by the table and said, "The environmentalists have decided the only way to save Colorado from the curses of development is to legislate a state wide zoning plan, which will restrict building in what they call esthetically and ecologically sensitive areas. The property rights people have gone through the ceiling over this proposal.

"There's a meeting tonight to solicit public opinion on the zoning plan. There's bound to be an explosion from the property rights people, and I want to be there to see it. A member of my staff will be making a statement on behalf of the Colorado Real Estate Association, and I want to see how it's received. You should come."

"I think I will. Sooner or later, environmentalists back home will come up with the idea to zone Maine. I'm curious to see how people out here react."

"The meeting is in a local college gym," said Susan. "It's one of several being held around the state."

We ate a quick supper, and then Susan disappeared into another room, which looked like an office. I turned on the TV to watch the evening news. There was a story about the meeting and a brief overview of the proposed zoning plan. The door to Susan's office was open, and I could see her talking on the phone.

Susan came out of her office and told me we were ready to go. We took an elevator to the ground floor and got into the back seat of a waiting car. Two men sat in the front seats.

Susan made a gesture toward the men and said, "This is Matt, my executive manager. The driver is Dick, my personal body guard."

I shook hands with the men, and we sped away. Matt turned around and said, "Kirk, you and I will sit on the property rights side of the gym. Susan and Dick will sit on the other side with the environmentalists. Do not talk to or make any sign of recognition toward Susan or Dick at any time during the evening, or we'll blow Susan's cover."

I nodded and said, "I understand."

A block from the gym Dick pulled the car to the side of the road. Matt said, "This is where we get out, Kirk. Susan and Dick will drive the rest of the way to the gym. We'll walk, so we don't arrive together."

There were several signs hanging from cars and pickups in the parking lot. One sign suggested that the governor should be impeached for supporting the zoning plan. Another said, "Save Colorado While There Is Still Something To Save."

There were more signs held by people in front of the gym. Somebody handed me a pamphlet. It was an invitation to join the environmentalists for a rally at the University of Colorado in Boulder. I stuck the pamphlet into a pocket. Another person handed me a colorful brochure from the Sierra Club. I politely stuffed it into another pocket.

In the gym lobby, Matt filled out a registration card that placed him on the schedule to speak. The man at the registration table said the meeting would start with a slide presentation. After that a few politicians would give short speeches, and then people would be called to speak in the order they had signed their cards.

Matt and I found a couple of seats by a group of cowboys who were yelling at the environmentalists sitting on the other side of the gym. I tried to find Susan in the crowd, but I couldn't see her. I held my hand to Matt's ear and said, "Is Susan safe sitting over there?"

"People don't expect her to come to these meetings or to be dressed the way she is, and they certainly don't expect her to be sitting with the environmentalists. I used to worry about it, but she has been doing it for years. She's also the boss."

I nodded and said I thought she was taking a chance.

A man walked to the microphone to introduce the chairperson of the study commission that was responsible for writing the proposed zoning plan. The environmentalists cheered and the property rights people rose to their feet, jeering and booing. It was clear the property rights people were not going to quiet down and let the chairperson speak.

A large man dressed in western clothes came to the microphone from the property rights side of the gym. He removed his cowboy hat and waited for the noise to subside. I got the impression he was a leader with the property rights people.

Facing the property rights side of the gym he said, "If we want to be heard tonight, we'll have to sit through this slide presentation. I know it's not going to be easy, but please let the meeting continue."

The chairperson approached the microphone again to make introductory comments on the slide show. After asking for the lights to be turned off she started to narrate the slides as they flashed on a big screen. Photographs appeared of big houses on top of mountains and on the banks of rivers, urban sprawl around Denver, a stream running yellow from mining waste, low water in reservoirs, a coal fired power plant...

"Why are you opposed to progress and jobs?" someone yelled.

"Shut up and let her speak!" another voice hollered.

The chairperson paused for a few seconds and then continued unflustered. More photographs followed including houses burning from a forest fire, a dust storm over a town, smoke and haze hiding mountains, traffic jams on I-25, an aerial shot of a stream filled with rafts surrounding a fisherman, a map showing proposed pipelines to move water from western slope rivers to Denver, a No Trespassing sign in front of a house by a trout stream, a bulldozer pushing dirt to build a road in a mountain meadow filled with wild flowers, cars sitting in the parking lots of malls and ski areas, etc.

When the slide show ended the lights came on. A state legislator spoke next. He straddled the fence and received a good round of applause when he finished because nobody knew which side he was on. Another politician spoke and he received loud applause from my side of the gym. Three more politicians gave speeches, with two of them siding with the environmentalists.

The first speaker from the sign-up sheet was a person from the Sierra Club. He was shouted down several times by the property rights people, but each time he waited patiently for the verbal abuse to decline, and then continued in a calm voice. Another environmentalist spoke, and several ranchers and real estate people took their turns at the microphone.

Two hours went by with both sides supporting their speakers and shouting down their opponents. I figured it was getting close to the time when Matt would be called to speak.

I saw a man waving to us in front of the bleachers. I pointed to the man and said to Matt, "I think he wants to talk to us."

Matt stood up, and people opened a route for us to climb down the bleachers to the gym floor. When we reached the man, Matt snapped, "What is it?"

"I have to talk to you outside."

In the lobby the man said, "Are you with Susan Martin?"

"Yes, but how..."

"We don't have time for a lot of talk. I'm on your side. Susan is in a very difficult situation. I overheard a couple of environmentalists talking in the rest room. They know Susan is disguised as an old lady, and they know she's sitting with the environmentalists. They're planning to expose her when one of them speaks and start a riot."

"Damn," muttered Matt.

"We have to find her," I said, "and get her out of here!"

Matt and I rushed to the other side of the gym. Splitting up we began searching the crowd for a white wig. I heard the moderator introduce someone from the, "Save Colorado First Association."

I looked at the podium and saw a man with long hair and a beard standing there. I knew this was the guy who was planning to expose Susan. My heart raced as I strained my eyes to find Susan's white wig.

"We are dealing with the oldest enemy of the environment, money and greed," the man said. "Money is the reason Colorado looks the way it does. Money buys power and influence and..."

I continued to scan the faces in front of me. My eyes found Susan. I began to make my way toward her. The environmentalists rose to their feet, cheering and applauding, making it more difficult for me to get through the crowd.

When they sat down, I saw Susan glaring at me. It was obvious she was thinking that I was breaking her rules, and I was. But she had no way of knowing what was about to happen.

"...and the most powerful developer in the west, Susan Martin, should be asked to address the environmental concerns of her latest

75

project in the San Juan Mountains. People think she never attends these meetings, but she does, and she is here tonight, only she is wearing a disguise so she will not be recognized."

Two rows of bleachers separated me from Susan. Her expression of anger had changed to a look of fear.

"That's right ladies and gentlemen, Susan Martin is here tonight. Would everyone on the environmentalist's side of the gym look around for a woman wearing a white wig and a grey suit."

I reached Susan at the same time a man sitting behind her stood up and shouted, "Here she is!"

Dick stood up and pushed the man down. Another man tried to grab me. I shoved him away. The gym exploded with yells and shrieks. Several people from the property rights group ran over to the environmentalists' side of the gym and began fighting with them.

Another man stood up and took a swing at me. I ducked and Dick gave him a Karate shot to his shoulder. I grabbed Susan's hand and yelled, "We're getting out of here!"

I looked for Matt as we made our way down the bleachers. He was nowhere to be seen. People gave us hateful looks and shouted obscenities as we passed them. Nearing the floor, I saw Matt with two policemen standing in front of us.

Someone shoved me from behind. I whirled around to face him. He hit me in the face with his fist. The blow caught me off guard. I fell backwards between two people and my head hit the wooden floor of the gym.

CHAPTER 6

A light was shining in my eyes. I reached up to push it away.

"Thank goodness you're coming around," said a female voice.

My head hurt, and I found it difficult to move. With effort I focused on the nurse leaning over my bed. She had a flashlight in her hand and was smiling at me.

"We were getting ready to put a tube into your stomach to feed you," she said. "But now that might not be necessary."

I looked at the tube in my left arm and said, "How long have I been here?"

"This is your third day. You had us worried. Your vital signs and neurological checks were okay, so we didn't do anything too drastic. We took some pictures of your head. There were no fractures, but we didn't like you being unconscious. I'll tell the doctor you're awake."

I had to call Mike and tell him what had happened and that I needed a few more days to get back to Maine. I knew Mike's patience was growing thin, and I wasn't sure how he would react to another delay.

A man in a white coat came into my room and introduced himself as Doctor Taylor. He asked me my name and the names of the last three presidents. I answered his questions and he said, "Good, your memory seems fine."

We were interrupted by Susan coming into the room. She smiled and said, "I'm glad you're okay."

"He seems all right," replied Dr. Taylor. He looked at me and added, "We're keeping you over night and will see how you are in the morning. Can someone keep an eye on you when we discharge you?"

"He can stay at my place," said Susan. "I'll hire a nurse to take care of him, if that's okay with you, doctor?"

"A nurse might not be necessary but that would be fine if you want to do it."

"I want him to have the best of care."

"It sounds like you'll be in good hands," said Dr. Taylor. "I'll see you tomorrow."

After Dr. Taylor left, Susan said, "I was really worried about you."

"I guess that was quite a blow to my head."

"Do you remember that night in the gym?"

"I remember we were making our way down the bleachers and some guy hit me. I remember falling backwards, but that's all I remember."

"That was a mean crowd," Susan said.

"The environmentalists don't like you."

"They have always despised me, but the property rights people think I'm wonderful."

"What happened to you after I hit my head?"

"Matt and the police managed to get me out a side door and into a police car. They called an ambulance for you. I'm glad you're okay. We'll get you back on your feet as soon as possible."

"I can't afford to spend a lot of time recuperating. I told my boss I would be heading back to Maine four days ago. He's going to be upset when I'm not there. I have to call him and tell him what happened. I could lose my job."

"Forget your old job," replied Susan. "I'll hire you and pay you twice what you were making in Maine. I need a good helicopter pilot and someone who has a knowledge of natural resources who isn't afraid of development."

"What about Bill?"

"I received a phone call from the specialist who has taken Bill's case. He told me they found a brain tumor and that they are scheduling surgery."

"I'm sorry to hear he's so sick."

"He has an excellent doctor, and I hope he'll be back. There'll always be a job for Bill at WestSun. I've been thinking of buying another helicopter to help my executive staff get around faster and, if I do, I'll need two pilots."

I nodded.

"When you're not flying you can work in management. I also have a few tracts of timber in the northwest you can manage. I have plenty for you to do."

Susan paused and added, "I'll never forget how you tried to rescue me in the gym the other night. That kind of loyalty is rare nowadays, and I appreciate what you did. The best thing you can do is relax and get well. When you are better we can talk again about a job."

I smiled politely and said, "I don't know what to say. I need time to think about your offer."

"Take as much time as you need. I'm in no rush for an answer. I think you would be happy working here."

Susan left, and I kept thinking about her job offer and the recent events in my life. How could I refuse such a generous offer? There would never be this opportunity at North Country Woodlands, no matter how long I worked there.

When I was discharged from the hospital Susan provided me with a beautiful apartment and hired three nurses to monitor my progress around the clock. My apartment was on the floor beneath her penthouse, and she visited me every day for the rest of the week. She joined me for dinner a couple of times, and we talked about her business and her ongoing battles with environmentalists.

The following Monday the nurses left. When Susan came for her usual visit she handed me a paper and said, "Do you feel up to looking at a position paper we're presenting at a meeting?"

"I can do that."

"Good. Here's the story. We're being charged by an environmental group that we're pushing a herd of elk from their wintering grounds by building a golf course at our San Juan Resort. A wildlife expert from Colorado State University has prepared this paper for us on the ability of elk to move to new wintering grounds."

The next day I handed Susan the paper on elk and said, "I made a few minor suggestions on the last page, but otherwise the paper looks good."

Susan stopped coming to my apartment, and I started to receive dinner invitations to her penthouse. I was beginning to enjoy the attention she gave me.

I began to work with Matt on an environmental impact statement for a golf course in their San Juan Resort. Environmentalists were worried the runoff from the golf course would pollute a nearby stream. We took the position that we were taking adequate precautions to prevent this from happening.

Matt introduced me to Susan's staff, and I was beginning to talk with architects, engineers, accountants, lawyers, and hospitality people. A few of them lived, like I did, in apartments below Susan's penthouse, but most of them lived outside of her complex and worked in the offices below the living quarters.

All of them seemed to have a great deal of energy and enthusiasm for their work, and all of them expressed a strong loyalty to Susan and WestSun Resorts. Susan was a smart manager, and it was easy to see why she had a very successful company.

A young landscape architect put it this way, "Susan builds beautiful resorts and brings joy and happiness to the lives of many people. But there are people, like environmentalists, who think she destroys the environment. Nothing could be further from the truth. The resorts Susan creates are simply exquisite. I get a tremendous amount of satisfaction from working on them."

It was becoming obvious that I would be foolish to turn down Susan's job offer. I also could not put off any longer getting in touch with Mike.

I called Mike and did my best to explain what had happened to me. He was angry that I had waited so long to call, but when he heard I needed time to recover from a head injury he calmed down. He surprised me by wishing me luck with my new job. I was happy that we could part on good terms. I told Susan at supper I would be happy to accept her job offer.

Susan hired a private instructor to help me prepare for my helicopter tests. By the end of the month I was ready to take the written exam and to take my flight test. I passed both with flying colors and was fully qualified to fly Susan wherever she wanted to go.

After dinner one evening she asked me what I liked to do for recreation. I told her I loved deer hunting. Her eyes opened wide when I told her how to outfox a big buck.

With excitement in her voice, she said, "I've never been hunting. Maybe we can go this fall."

"I don't know much about hunting deer in the west," I said.

"That's okay, we'll hire a guide."

One afternoon, Matt came to the pool as I was finishing a swim to tell me Susan wanted to see me in her apartment. I quickly returned to my place, dressed, and took the elevator to Susan's penthouse.

Susan's apartment manager, Jean, greeted me at the door and brought me my usual bottle of Coors. She said Susan was taking a shower and would be with me shortly.

While waiting, I thumbed through a few of the magazines on the table and was surprised to see that Susan had written romantic poems and short stories in all of them. I wondered why she wrote about this subject so often.

Twenty minutes passed and I was starting to get fidgety. Susan entered the room, and when she saw me reading one of her magazines, she said, "Do you like poetry?"

"I don't read much of it, but I see you like to write poems and short stories."

"Writing is a hobby of mine. I wanted to study creative writing in college, but Dad said there would only be money for a business degree, so I studied business administration. But I also took a few courses in writing and poetry, which he didn't know about."

Pointing to the magazine in my hand Susan said, "That little magazine has published a lot of my work."

Susan's smile broke into a laugh and added, "I sometimes wonder if my publishing success is connected to my annual contribution, but I suppose its best I don't know for sure."

I chuckled. "You have an interesting hobby."

"I've always found it relaxing to write."

We walked to the leather chairs by the goldfish pond. Susan said, "Attitudes toward development are changing in Colorado. It used to be everyone was happy to see development because it meant jobs and money in the state's economy.

"But now environmental fanatics are getting people worked up over smog in Denver, houses on top of mountains, water shortages, traffic, stream pollution, and other ridiculous issues. They are really pushing this zoning plan, which could give us a lot of problems if it's approved by the voters in the fall."

81

"How did the zoning plan idea get started?" I asked.

"Apparently a private land zoning plan in the Adirondacks of New York State has received a lot of press in the environmental literature, and it has given environmentalists in Colorado some big ideas."

"I can't believe environmentalists are so pessimistic about progress," I said.

"Colorado has always been a boom or bust place. When the economy is good, the environmentalists talk about the environment, but when the economy is poor, they disappear, and all the talk is about jobs. A private land zoning plan in Colorado would block plans we have on the drawing board for future projects."

"I've been working with Matt on an environmental impact statement for the golf course in the San Juan development."

"I'm glad Matt has you working on that project. Texans love to come to the San Juan Mountains to escape from their hot summers. With the number of people retiring we could do very nicely with one or two new projects in southwestern Colorado. But if this zoning plan is passed our efforts will be severely limited.

"When you finish with the impact statement for the golf course, I want you to work on the campaign we're initiating against the zoning plan. Work with our public relations people, and help them to make our campaign more grass roots oriented.

"We want to get local merchants, small land owners, the hospitality industry, construction workers, real estate people, and everyday folks involved, and make sure the media covers everything that is favorable to our position. We have several contacts with the press that are sympathetic to development."

I nodded and said, "Okay."

"Emphasize jobs and the economy. Tell the working people they are the ones who will be hurt by a zoning plan. Get everyday folks concerned about their constitutional right to own property and their right to do what they want with it."

"I understand."

"Work with Matt on this. He has been with me for a long time, and he knows how to get a job done. He's my best attorney, and he understands the people in Colorado. People out here are very independent, and they don't want some bureaucrat in Denver telling them they can't build a house on their own land."

I told Susan I would see Matt the next day and that I would not let her down. She thanked me and told me to keep her informed with our progress.

The next morning I went to Matt's apartment. He invited me to have coffee on his balcony. For a while we sipped coffee and made small talk as we watched the morning sun on the distant mountains.

Matt told me about his great-grandfather homesteading in Colorado and that both his grandfather and his dad had run cattle on the western slope. In the course of our conversation I found out that Matt was very experienced with the strategies of environmental groups, since he had worked several years with the Wilderness Society before he came to work for Susan.

"Why did you leave the Wilderness Society?" I asked.

Matt glanced at the mountains and said, "I didn't like their position of locking up land in wilderness areas. I view land as a resource that should be used for the betterment of people. Susan also offered me more money."

Matt poured me another cup of coffee and said, "Susan likes to work with other groups so we're not leading the charge and getting the headlines. She funnels money into other businesses and organizations that are happy to use their influence with issues we have a common interest in."

Picking up the morning paper from a nearby table Matt said, "Have you seen this?"

The headline read, "Riot Breaks Out in Fort Collins Over State Zoning Plan."

I read further. "Crowd gets ugly at zoning meeting at Colorado State University, and three people were hurt. Governor Jackson plans to increase security at the remaining meetings."

"This is becoming a very emotional issue," I said.

Matt stood up and said, "People have a right to be upset over restrictions on their land. It's our job to make it even more emotional, so they use their emotions to vote against the zoning plan. We have a lot of work to do before Election Day."

Looking at his watch Matt said, "You'll be working with Ted Rollins, who has a lot of experience with local people. Don't hesitate to ask me for help if you need it. Remember, we're all pulling in the same direction. I've called a meeting at nine o'clock, so we better get going."

There was a group of people waiting for us in the conference room. Matt walked to the head of the table and said, "Today is the start of our campaign to defeat the zoning plan. We have a lot of work to do, so let's get started. Susan wants us to work on five areas in this campaign. The assignments have been made. I want you to meet for an hour with your partners to discuss specific strategies and ideas."

I left the conference room with Ted, and we went to his office. Ted was very enthusiastic and had a lot of ideas to discuss with me. At the end of the hour we had a good list of ideas to take back to the conference room.

Matt asked for a brief report from each group. Ted suggested that I present a few of our ideas.

I stood up and said, "Our assignment is to motivate everyday folks to take a position against the zoning plan. We want to organize a demonstration in front of the state capital building and a caravan of vehicles with banners and signs on I-25. We want to sponsor a TV commercial with an appeal to the average person. We also plan to call the leaders of various clubs and organizations and ask them to organize their own protest activities according to their own interests."

I sat down and other people presented their reports. There were questions and discussion on various topics. Matt said he liked all of the ideas. The meeting broke up at noon.

After supper I began calling leaders of clubs and organizations and found the people I talked to very receptive to our ideas and suggestions. Many people told me they were fed up with the environmentalists, and that there was no reason to own private property in Colorado if it couldn't be developed. Everyone seemed pleased that WestSun Resorts was taking a leadership role in opposing the zoning plan.

Two days later, Jean delivered a written dinner invitation to my apartment. This was the first time Susan had sent me a formal invitation.

I smiled politely and said, "This sounds like a special dinner."

"It is. I would suggest you wear a coat and tie."

I did as Jean suggested, even though I hated wearing a tie. When Susan opened her door wearing a beautiful evening gown, I was glad I had dressed appropriately.

"You look stunning," I said.

In a charming voice Susan said, "Thank you, it's nice of you to notice. Come in and thank you for dressing. Dinner tonight will be very special."

We walked over to the goldfish pond, and Jean took our orders for drinks. It seemed I always sat with Susan by her goldfish pond, and I got the impression this was her favorite place in her luxurious apartment.

Susan took a sip of her drink and said, "I've decided I wanted to have a special dinner to celebrate a few things. I'm happy you have completely recovered from your head injury, and I'm pleased you have become a valuable employee. I also want to thank you in a special way for rescuing me from that terrible meeting and for being concerned for my safety."

"There's no need to thank me for what I did that night. You were in a difficult situation. I didn't want to see you get hurt. I also like my job and salary. I'm the one who should be thanking you."

Susan laughed and said, "Okay, we'll celebrate a mutual thank you. I hope you like lobster because I've had several pounds flown in from Maine. I thought it might be a special treat for you."

"I like lobster. I don't imagine there's a lot of fresh lobster in Colorado."

"There isn't. The cowboys ran them out of town a long time ago, too much competition for beef."

We both laughed. Jean came in and announced that dinner was ready, and we went into the dining room. I saw Susan to her seat and then sat at the other end of an elegantly prepared table.

I glanced at the crystal glasses, the hand painted china, the exquisite silverware, and the platters of sumptuous food in the flickering light of two candles. Across the table from me sat one of the richest and most beautiful women in the west, who was being gracious and grateful to me, and I was having a private dinner with her. Was I really experiencing this or was it just a dream?

85

"I wasn't sure that lobster would be enough," said Susan, "so I ordered shrimp and a few other seafood items so we would have a variety of things to eat."

"It looks great."

"Please help yourself and be generous with your portions."

"I promise I'll eat as much as I can."

"Good. I'll watch to make sure you don't miss anything."

We filled our plates and ate quietly, savoring the delicious food. Jean came in with a bottle of champagne and showed the label to Susan. She nodded her approval. Jean opened the bottle, poured a small amount into a glass, and Susan took a sip. Smiling she said, "It's perfect."

Jean filled two glasses, left the bottle in a bucket of ice, and returned to the kitchen.

Susan watched me take a sip of champagne. I smiled and said, "The champagne is great, and the food is delicious. You have an excellent chef. I've eaten a lot of lobster, but never with a sauce like this."

"My chef is an expert in French cuisine. The variety of his sauces is unlimited."

"He has a real talent," I said.

"I hope you don't mind if I talk a little business," Susan said. "Matt tells me you have a knack for influencing people, and you have a wonderful ability to grasp the significance of a situation. I think you might do well in a position with more responsibility."

Susan took a sip of champagne and continued, "In four or five months one of my resort managers will be leaving. I have been considering you for the job. The salary is one hundred and sixty thousand dollars. The resort is near Vail, so you will not be very far away. You could keep the helicopter there and fly to Denver when I need you to fly me somewhere."

"I'm enjoying what I'm doing now, and I think we'll defeat the environmentalists in November."

"You'll have plenty of time to finish the campaign before this position becomes available. I like having you here, but Vail is not very far by helicopter. You can fly in for dinner, and you can keep your apartment here. You have plenty of time to make up your mind.

If you decide to stay in your present position that is also fine with me."

"I'll think about your offer and see how my present job goes for the next few months."

"That sounds reasonable."

Susan changed the conversation by saying,   "I hope you haven't forgotten that you promised to take me deer hunting this fall. Maybe you could scout around for a place. We have good hunting near many of our resorts, but I would like to go to a new place. You know, check out the competition, meet new people, find a place where I don't know anybody."

I laughed and said, "A place where they don't know you, is that possible? I'll do my best, but it's a tough assignment."

Susan laughed as she scooped out a piece of lobster from a claw and dipped it into a dish of special sauce.   She looked at the succulent piece of lobster and said, "Matt tells me you're driving a rental car that has been giving you trouble."

I watched Susan put the piece of lobster into her mouth and said, "It wouldn't start the other day. The car company sent over another car, and I haven't had any trouble with it."

Susan swallowed and said, "I think you deserve something better. I'm giving you an early bonus."

As Susan spoke, she reached across the table and handed me a set of car keys. "I hope you like driving sports cars.   It's in the basement garage."

I stared at Susan with my mouth open and a sudden loss of my ability to talk. Realizing she had flustered and embarrassed me, Susan looked down at her plate to give me time to regain my composure.

"I don't know what to say?"

"I hope you enjoy driving it," replied Susan.

"I'm sure I will. Thank you."

Susan tactfully changed the subject, and I put the keys in my pocket. We talked about our high school and college days and as the evening progressed, I caught a glimpse of a fun-loving Susan she kept hidden most of the time.

After dinner, we sat in the chairs by the swimming pool and watched the sun set behind the Rocky Mountains. It was a hot summer evening in Denver. The roof top provided a nice breeze.

A police siren cut through the air from the streets below. Susan seemed to ignore it. I listened to it and thought about the world beyond the roof top, a world much different than the world Susan and I were in.

"Have you been to Europe?" Susan asked.

I shook my head and said, "No, I haven't."

In a charming voice she said, "Perhaps we can go sometime."

It was close to midnight when I said good night and left Susan standing by the pool. I was tired, but I had too much to think about to sleep.

My relationship with Susan was changing dramatically. She had always been friendly and sociable, but now she was getting more serious with a special dinner, talk about a trip to Europe, and an outright gift of a sports car. Why was she doing these things?

She was obviously trying to impress me, and she was doing it, but she was also scaring me. I wasn't sure what she would expect from me in return.

Susan was very beautiful and very rich, and she no doubt had her pick from a lot of men. Any guy in his right mind would be attracted to her. As I lay in bed listening to the hum of the air conditioner, I began to realize my emotions were in chaos.

Sara had died just three months ago, and I still felt intense grief over her loss. I had not disposed of her ashes, which were still in Henry's truck, and I had not taken her photographs in Yosemite.

The last two and a half months had provided a distraction from my grief. I liked my job and the money I was making. But now it seemed I had another woman in my life, and I wasn't ready for a serious relationship.

Maybe I was reading too much into our evening together, and maybe I was jumping to too many conclusions. But there had been too many signals for me to ignore. I needed time to get over Sara, and I needed to slow things down with Susan.

The next morning, I got up early and went to the garage to see my new car, a red Porsche convertible. It was gorgeous. It was also overwhelming.

88

I looked at the car and said to myself, "You own a Porsche and a beautiful, rich woman likes you. So, take the car for a drive and enjoy the good life."

I opened the car door and sat in the driver's seat. The smell of new leather filled the interior. I looked at the instruments on the dash board and shifted the stick. With a turn of the key the engine roared to life. I goosed the accelerator a couple of times and cautiously maneuvered the car out of the garage.

Still being cautious and somewhat self-conscious, I drove the car through the streets of Denver with the top down. I headed for I-25 with the wind blowing in my hair. A good-looking woman standing on the sidewalk waved to me. I grinned back. Turning onto the ramp to I-25, I chuckled to myself and thought how wonderful life could be when you're driving a flashy sports car.

I headed for I-70. With ease the car climbed the steep incline into the mountains. I exited at Idaho Springs and headed toward Estes Park. For the next hour I spun around twisty curves, up and down hills, and was completely enthralled with the car.

I pulled into a small mountain town and parked in front of a cafe. Two women in a corvette checked me out as I got out of my new car. I liked their admiring glances, but I was not interested in meeting them. But I did enjoy their reaction to the red Porsche convertible.

I ordered breakfast and listened to the waitress talking to a man about the state zoning plan. The waitress was in favor of preserving the open landscape of Colorado. The man supported more development. It was a heated discussion, and I stayed out of it. I quietly ate my breakfast and then drove back to Denver.

The next couple of weeks kept me busy. I spoke to ranchers, real estate people, construction workers, retirement organizations, and many everyday folks who had a dream of someday owning a piece of Colorado. We were building support for our position, but Matt kept saying we couldn't let up on the pressure until the zoning plan was defeated in November.

One day Matt knocked on my apartment door early in the morning and said, "Susan wants you to fly me to Summit Resort and help me take care of a squatter problem. We've had several complaints from our clientele about unsightly Mexican shacks on the road to the resort in Horse Canyon. WestSun owns the land the

89

Mexicans are squatting on. We've asked them to leave, but they refuse to go, so we need to convince them to move."

I looked at my watch and said, "I'll meet you at the heliport at nine."

At Summit Resort we borrowed a car from the manager and drove down Horse Canyon. A stream tumbled over red rocks next to the road. The canyon was very scenic until we came to the shacks.

The structures had been assembled from an assortment of materials and were crude and ugly. Grass grew around an old car without tires that sat next to one of the buildings. Pieces of junk and debris littered the area around the dwellings.

I followed Matt to one of the shacks. His fist shook the thin wooden door. The knocking produced a skinny Mexican at the entrance. I caught a whiff of stale beans and body odor from the building's interior. Behind the scrawny man, I saw three kids playing on the floor and a heavy woman sitting by a cheap Formica table.

Matt spoke in Spanish. I didn't understand what he said to the Mexican, but I saw anger flame in the man's face. He responded by yelling something in Spanish and slamming the door in Matt's face.

In the car Matt said, "They'll need more than words before they understand we mean what we say."

We drove further down the canyon, turned onto a main highway, and arrived in a town an hour later. Matt said we needed to get a motel room and meet later with a man that could persuade the Mexicans to leave.

After eating supper in a cafe, we drove to a dingy bar outside of town. The bartender took our order for two beers and talked about football. People began to fill the bar as we drank our beer. A large Mexican walked in and sat at a table in a corner. Matt said, "That's our man."

I followed Matt to the man's table. He recognized Matt, but there was no warmth in their greeting. We sat down, and I studied the man's unshaven face and the scar on his cheek.

"I have work for you," Matt said.

The man nodded.

"Do you know where those Mexican shacks are in Horse Canyon?"

The man nodded, again. He lit a cigarette and blew smoke toward the ceiling.

In a business like tone Matt said, "We would like those Mexicans persuaded to move on."

"I can take care of that."

"Good," replied Matt.

"When will I be paid?"

"When the job is done," said Matt. "We'll include a bonus if the Mexicans are gone by the end of the week."

"They'll be gone in three days."

Matt stood up, and I rose with him. Matt said, "Good."

We left and drove to another bar that was cleaner and more respectable. Matt ordered a shot of whiskey and a beer. I ordered a beer. Matt threw the whiskey into his mouth and took a big swallow of beer. He told the bartender to pour him another whiskey. He swallowed the whiskey in a gulp and chased it with the rest of his beer.

Matt began to talk. I nursed my beer and listened, knowing I would have to drive him back to the motel.

"You're not the first guy that Susan has taken a liking to. She is incredibly beautiful, charming, and rich. There is hardly a man alive who wouldn't fall for her. But be careful. You're the one who'll get hurt. Susan's romances don't last very long."

"It sounds like you're talking from experience?"

Matt took a deep breath, exhaled, and said, "You could say that. I'm the only guy she ever married. Susan gives easily with material things, like trips, cars, money, clothes, and such. She wants desperately to be loved, and she wants to love a man in return, but she has problems with the giving side of a relationship."

"I don't understand."

The bartender refilled Matt's beer glass. He pointed to his whiskey glass, and the bartender poured another shot into it.

Matt cleared his throat and said, "You're a nice guy, and I don't want to see you get hurt."

"What do you mean?"

Matt poured the whiskey into his mouth and swallowed. His eyes seemed to bulge from his head as the whiskey hit his stomach. He sucked air into his lungs and let it flow out in a deep sigh.

"I was married to Susan for about a year," he muttered. "As I said, she wants to be loved more than anything in the world, but she can't get past a mysterious obstacle that is like a wall in her life."

"What's the obstacle?"

"I wish I knew."

Matt took a swallow of beer and added, "I suggested we go to a marriage counselor, but it was too late to save our marriage. She had already filed for a divorce. Our marriage was over in eleven months. Susan is the boss. She is the one who makes all of the decisions, whether it's in her business life or her personal life."

I took a sip of beer and said, "Do you still love her, Matt?"

Matt looked at me, hesitated, and said, "We all love her, Kirk."

"Why did you stay after your marriage broke up?"

"Susan asked me to stay."

"I don't understand why you didn't move on."

"I like my job most of the time, except for days like today, when I have to hire a heavy to burn out some Mexicans."

"I didn't hear him say he would burn those shacks down."

"He didn't have to. That's the way men like him operate."

"Does Susan condone that kind of work?"

"She knows that sometimes we have to play hardball in our line of work. I don't tell her when we have to be tough with people. But I do have the liberty to help those people financially after they have moved, which I will do through a local charity."

We left the bar, and I drove to our motel. Matt staggered into our room and flopped down on one of the beds. I took his shoes off and covered him with a blanket. The next day we flew back to Denver.

Susan was on a business trip and would be gone for a week. I was thankful we would not have to meet socially for a while.

Two days later, I met with Matt. He said, "The Mexican problem has been taken care of."

"What did that man do?"

"He applied pressure. I will get a check to those Mexicans in a couple of weeks."

"Why didn't we take them to court if they were trespassing?"

"Because a court case gets into the newspapers and generates bad press. We tried to buy them out, but they wouldn't accept our offer. This method works with no publicity for us, and they get more than the value of their shacks out of the deal."

"Maybe, but it's not right."

"There are a lot of things in this world that are not right. Those Mexicans were trespassing and that isn't right. They'll get enough money to buy something better than what they were living in. So stop worrying about it."

Susan returned from her trip late at night. The next morning there was a dinner invitation under my door.

We began the evening sitting by Susan's goldfish pond. Our conversation turned to my relationship with Sara and how we managed to be married for such a long time.

I told Susan how Sara and I met in college, about our excursions into the Maine woods, and how we fell in love on a camping trip. I explained how we viewed nature in different ways and that we didn't pay much attention to our differences until we had been married a couple of years.

Over dinner, I explained, "It took several disagreements for me to accept the fact that Sara was a true-blue environmentalist. After a while, we agreed our quarrels were hurting our marriage and that we needed to give each other the freedom to go our separate ways.

"Sara pursued her photography and her environmental concerns. I went fishing and hunting and managed timber. I guess we just learned to give each other the space that was needed for our relationship to survive."

"Your differences never caused a problem?"

Raising my eyebrows I said, "We managed to avoid sensitive subjects for a long time, but a few months ago events in northern Maine changed all that."

"What happened?"

"We had our biggest fight over a stand of big pine trees, and for a long time we didn't speak to each other. Sara was so upset that she moved out of the house. She wanted the big trees preserved and North Country Woodlands, where I worked, wanted to harvest them to help with their bottom line."

"How did you solve the problem?"

"The Nature Bank saw Sara on TV talking about the trees and decided to buy the land and make it into a park."

Susan took a sip of coffee. I looked down and in a low voice said, "Then I found out her cancer had spread to the rest of her body. I felt like a jerk that we had spent so much time not talking to each other."

I paused, looked at Susan, and added, "The doctors said she only had a year to live. Her dream had always been to take photographs in Yosemite National Park. So we headed for California."

Susan stared at me with tears in her eyes and said, "I'm sorry."

Emotions prevented me from saying anything for a while. Susan broke the silence. "Do you have a picture of Sara?"

I took out my wallet and handed Susan a small black and white photo. "This was taken about five years ago."

"She was very pretty."

I nodded.

Susan stared at Sara's picture and said, "I admire the love you had for each other."

I didn't say anything. Susan handed the photograph back to me and said, "You had a very close relationship. That's very important in life."

I looked at Susan and saw a terrible sadness in her face. I asked, "Was there a special man in your life?"

"One or two."

Susan looked at her plate and bit her lower lip. I wished I had not asked the question.

Suddenly Susan jumped to her feet, took a couple of steps toward her bedroom, stopped, turned around, and with a wave of her hand said, "You know, all of this can get in one's way..."

"What do you mean?"

Sounding totally frustrated Susan said, "I guess it's hard for most people to understand, but all of the men in my life fell in love with my wealth, instead of me. One particular man, I thought I was in love with, put on a great act, until I found him fooling around with other women in the office. He played me for a real sucker. I had given him everything. And then there was Matt, who I really hurt..."

When Susan mentioned Matt, she burst into tears. I was beginning to feel uncomfortable. I didn't like the conversation we were having. But I couldn't ignore the fact that Susan needed someone to share her feelings with and that she trusted me to confide in. I felt sorry for her.

Susan wiped her tears away with a handkerchief and said, "I don't know why I'm telling you all of this. You've been so honest with me. But you asked about my relationships with men. I don't like talking about them, because they were all failures.

"I'm sorry. I shouldn't ask so many personal questions. But you had a successful marriage, in spite of conflict. It's encouraging for me to think that a marriage can survive, even when there are strong opposing views."

"I'm no expert on marriage. I only know what Sara and I did."

"I think you did a lot of things right. Will you excuse me for a few minutes?"

Susan went into her bedroom. Returning, she sat down and with an innocent expression on her face, she asked, "Do you think I'm attractive?"

"You're a beautiful woman."

I could tell Susan was happy with my answer. She said, "I know you're trying to get over a terrible personal loss and that you loved your wife very much. But would it be asking too much for us to be more than business acquaintances. I would like for us to be friends. Is that okay with you?"

I hesitated to answer and then I said, "I don't see why we can't be friends."

"I know we're both very busy and that you need space," replied Susan. "But maybe we could do a few things together. Like go to dinner and a movie, or go for a drive in the mountains, or whatever."

I was beginning to feel pressured. I wasn't ready for a relationship with another woman, but I also didn't want to send the wrong message. My emotions were saying, "No." But a more practical part of me was saying, "Yes." There was a tremendous future ahead of me working for Susan, and I didn't want to put it in jeopardy.

The next month was filled with work, and there wasn't much time for Susan and me to see each other socially. Maybe Susan was beginning to lose her romantic interest in me. As long as she liked my work, I was willing to let our relationship become less personal.

By early fall, Matt was feeling confident the zoning plan would be defeated in November. We had contacted all of the state legislators, and most of them were saying this was not the time for the state to adopt such a restrictive plan.

Fresh snow came to the high mountains in early September. A week later, Susan and I went for a drive in the foothills. We stopped for a drink at a restaurant and sat on a deck enjoying a view of the peaks. The golden leaves of a nearby aspen tree fluttered in a breeze.

Susan stared at her drink for a while. Then she looked at me and said, "I think I'm falling in love with you."

I looked at the distant range of mountains and felt my stomach tighten. I said, "This is happening too fast. I'm not over the loss of Sara. I haven't fulfilled my obligations to her. I need time."

I thought for a few seconds and added, "I think it would be good for me to get away for a while. I'm planning to go to Yosemite in a couple of weeks to take Sara's pictures. I want to keep my job, but I can't make the kind of commitment you want, at least not now. You've been good to me. I hope you understand what I'm trying to say."

Susan's eyes misted. "I understand. I admire you for your love and devotion to Sara. Please take all the time you need to fulfill your wife's last request. And please come back when you're done with what you have to do."

CHAPTER 7

I was glad to be in the air. Early morning sunlight stretched across the plains, illuminating Colorado's Front Range. Below, traffic was building in the south lane of I-25 going into Denver. I was heading north to meet Susan in Montana.

Susan had flown into Billings from a conference on the west coast, and she had called me from the airport to tell me to pick her up at Autumn Springs Resort. I was planning to make a quick stop at Henry's place to pick up Sara's ashes, her camera, and a few personal belongings.

When I returned to Denver, I would take a leave of absence to go to California to take Sara's photographs. Susan had told me she would honor our working relationship even if things didn't work out on a personal level. In many ways a business relationship with Susan would be more desirable and less complicated.

There was a lot for me to think about. I was thankful to have time away from my job to take Sara's photographs and to decide what kind of a relationship I wanted with Susan.

I had chosen a course that would take me over the northeastern corner of Yellowstone National Park because it was shorter. Clouds began to thicken. I hoped I wasn't flying into snow.

Further north I began to fly over a secluded section of the park and a range of mountains. Near the summit it started to snow. As I descended on the other side it began to snow harder.

I saw a meadow. A helicopter appeared in the air space below me. It was a Huey Helicopter, the chopper I had flown in Vietnam.

At first I thought someone might be in trouble because the pilot was flying close to the ground. Then I saw two men in the meadow, and just beyond them I saw a huge grizzly bear moving in their direction. I had stumbled onto a poaching operation.

I quickly surmised that the other helicopter was circling to herd the grizzly toward the poachers on the ground. Both the other pilot and the poachers were looking away from me, and for a few more seconds they would not be aware of my presence. I decided to use my element of surprise to help the bear.

Skimming above the meadow, I flew closer to the poachers. The bear stopped about fifty yards in front of the two men and fearlessly rose up on his rear legs. A burst of red suddenly appeared on the grizzly's shoulder. One of the poachers had shot the bear.

The other man was raising his rifle as I came into a hovering position above them, and my sudden presence prevented him from firing a shot. The man lowered his rifle and shook his fist at me. Anger rushed through me. I brought my helicopter further down on them in retaliation. With terror on their faces they dropped to the ground. Pulling my chopper up, I saw the grizzly limping toward nearby timber.

I gained altitude quickly, knowing my next concern would be the other chopper. Looking to my right, I saw the poacher's helicopter coming after me. The chopper's side door opened, and a man appeared with an assault rifle in his hands. Pointing his rifle at my chopper, he opened fire. Several rounds ripped through my helicopter.

Smoke poured into the cockpit as I looked for a place to land. More bullets tore into my chopper. I brought my helicopter down and made a rough landing. I pushed the door open and jumped to the ground. Blades whirled overhead and flames burst from my helicopter as I dashed in the direction of nearby trees. There was more gunfire. I kept running as fast as I could in the slippery snow.

A loud explosion filled the air behind me. I hit the ground and covered my head. Burning debris flew over me. Looking back, I saw a ball of fire consuming my helicopter. I got to my feet and ran.

Above the roar of the flames, I heard the other helicopter pursuing me. I strained every muscle in my body to reach the timber. Bullets sprayed around me.

I came to a large fallen tree and dove under it. The helicopter came to a hovering position above me. I could see the man pointing his assault rifle at me. Bullets splintered wood and slashed the snowy earth on both sides of the tree. The gun fire stopped.

I peeked out from my hiding place and saw the man in the chopper's doorway banging his rifle with his hand. His weapon had jammed. In a flash I was on my feet running for the trees. The helicopter followed me.

Twenty yards to the trees…fifteen…ten….five….then a spurt of bullets as pine trees closed around me. The confines of the forest slowed me down, but I kept moving as fast as I could. I swerved to the right as bullets riddled the trees to my left. My feet slipped in the snow, and I fell to the ground.

I lay in the snow fighting to catch my breath. The helicopter sounded like it was landing in the meadow, probably to pick up the two men on the ground. I got to my feet and listened for the chopper to take off.

My clothes were soaking wet from falling and brushing against snow covered trees. Shivering, I heard the pilot shut his engine down. Panic seized my body as I realized they were coming after me. With a new surge of adrenalin, I got up and ran further into the snowy forest.

There was no escaping my tracks. My only hope was to stay ahead of the poachers until they got tired of chasing me. I crawled over and under blow downs and tried to avoid dense clumps of trees. Slick snow made it difficult to run, and I kept stumbling and falling. Out of breath, I stopped to rest, straining my ears to listen for the poachers behind me.

A brief span of quiet was broken by voices. They grew louder. One of them yelled, "Let's get out of here, the weather will take care of him."

Another said, "If he's as cold and wet as I am he won't last very long."

The voices grew fainter. They had turned back. I felt a sense of relief, but my problems were far from over.

I put my hands into the pockets of my jacket and found a candy bar. I pulled it out, ripped off its wrapper, and shoved it into my mouth. I searched other pockets for matches but found none. In a zippered pocket I found a wad of traveler's checks I had picked up for my trip to California. Nice to have money I thought, but it wouldn't help me survive in the middle of a wilderness in a snow storm.

My situation was desperate. I had no warm clothes, no matches, no compass, and no food. Roads and shelter were miles away, and I had no idea which direction to walk to get to them.

The sound of the poacher's helicopter taking off reached my ears and then faded in the distance. I was completely alone. Shivers ran up my spine from the cold and the stark reality of my predicament.

I decided to go back to the meadow. I didn't expect to find anything, except charred pieces of metal. But I might find smoldering debris that would enable me to keep a fire going with wood from blow downs. It was my only hope. I had to get back to the meadow.

I tried to hurry, but my muscles didn't want to move. My boots slipped in the snow, and I fell again.

Holding onto a pine branch, I pulled myself to a standing position. A curtain of big flakes surrounded me, making it difficult to see. Dents in a smooth white surface were quickly taking the place of my tracks in the snow. Soon there would be no dents, and I would lose my lifeline to the meadow.

I came to a place where I had slid down a steep hill when the poachers were chasing me. Now I had to climb up the slope.

Greasy snow made it difficult to reach a small tree a third of the way up the inclined surface. Holding onto the tree, I tried to push myself further up the hill to another tree. I let go of the tree, took a step, fell on my stomach, and coasted feet first down the hill. Three more times I tried to get up the hill with no success.

I decided I might do better if I cut across the hill. Half way up the gradient, I stepped on a loose rock under the snow. My ankle twisted as the rock moved, and I felt a sharp stab of pain. Losing my balance, I tumbled down the incline again.

My eyes shut as I grimaced in pain. Gradually the pain eased up. I opened my eyes to see the snow falling harder. My body was shivering vigorously and rapidly losing heat. The dents in the snow were almost gone.

I told myself I would live through this ordeal. I didn't know how, but I would survive. I would go to California, take Sara's photographs, and return to my job in Denver.

Denver? A few hours ago I was shaving in my apartment, surrounded by luxury and wealth. My future was bright. I was getting my life together. I wanted to be back in Denver. I was making a lot of money in Denver. My Porsche was in Denver. Susan was in Denver. I had to get back to the meadow, and back to Denver.

I reached up and grabbed a branch of a nearby pine tree. Snow fell on me. My bare hands were numb from being cold and wet. With great effort, I pulled myself to a standing position on my good ankle.

"Shit," I yelled.

I lowered my sprained ankle to the ground and slowly shifted my weight to it. There was pain. I clenched my teeth and tried to bear it. I let go of the pine branch, took a step, and fell again. It took several minutes for the pain to subside this time.

I started to think about the poachers and the grizzly bear. Why had I stuck my nose into something that was none of my business? Maybe I liked grizzly bears. Maybe I did it because of Sara. Was Sara trying to influence me again?

Sara was always trying to save something. I remembered all of the nights she sat at her desk writing letters to save rivers, forests, wildlife, wetlands, wilderness, or whatever. I didn't agree with trying to save everything. People had a right to use natural resources. They needed houses, furniture, and paper.

Trees were renewable. Water, wildlife, and grass were renewable. Resources needed good management. That's what resources needed. Good management. Every class I ever took in forestry was about good management. Foresters knew about good management. We could do the job, if environmentalists would just leave us alone.

Why did I help Henry? Why did I try to save the grizzly? It was Sara. Sara had influenced me, whether I wanted to admit it or not. It was Sara and her pictures of the King's Pines in the *Audubon Magazine* that had persuaded me to help Henry. Leave me alone, Sara.

I wanted to go back to Denver to enjoy my new life. I had everything in Denver. Why did I want to go to California? Maybe I should just let a relationship develop with Susan and put Sara behind me.

But I loved Sara. She was idealistic and naive, but I had loved her anyway, and she had loved me. But why did she love nature so intensely? Why did she always feel a need to change things in the world, and to change me? I didn't know. I didn't know anything. Sara had never experienced the realities of a wilderness that could destroy a human being. Neither had I, until now.

101

I had to get back to the meadow. But how would I get up the hill when I couldn't stand? I looked around for a fallen branch to use as a crutch, but I couldn't find one.

I decided to crawl up the hill. It was the only way. When I got to the top, I would try to walk. I was never this cold. It was almost impossible to move my arms and legs.

I positioned my hands and knees in a crawling position. My knees hurt on the ground beneath the snow. Progress was slow. Struggling, I reached the middle of the slope. There was a big rock in my way. I couldn't get around it. There was nothing to grab onto. I began to slip, slide, and roll sideways. I slid head first to the bottom of the steep hill on my back.

I didn't want to move. I felt scared and helpless and very cold. I wasn't going to make it to the meadow. My thoughts were becoming scattered and unrelated. They didn't make sense. Nothing seemed to make sense.

I thought about deer hunting in Maine. I loved deer hunting and being in the woods after a fresh snow. At least I thought I did.

I thought about the deer I had shot for Mike. I had deceived him into thinking he had shot the deer himself. I had done it to advance my career, and it had worked.

Why was I thinking about Mike at a time like this? Was it because I felt guilty about deceiving him? What was happening to me? What I did to Mike was nothing compared to what other people did every day to advance their careers.

Sara came into my mind again. She was so innocent. She would never think about deceiving anyone. Maybe that was why I loved her.

Sara was a very loving person. She always went to church and gave money to the poor, even when we were barely making ends meet. Sara always said we had to help poor people, and to take care of nature. How could you not love a person like that? Everyone loved Sara.

"But Sara wasn't in touch with the real world," I mumbled. The sound of my babbling seemed out of place in a forest filling with snow.

I thought about the Mexicans living in the shacks in Horse Canyon. I felt guilty about what Matt and I did to them. I didn't like

102

being a part of that situation. We should have helped those people to find another place to stay. Why hadn't I thought of that and suggested it to Matt or Susan? Susan was a smart woman. I couldn't believe she would endorse such tactics. Sara would have helped those people.

Susan and Sara were opposites. Lots of people were opposites. So what? The world needed opposites. John Muir and Gifford Pinchot were opposites, so were loggers and environmentalists, and Jimmy Carter and Ronald Reagan. Why was I thinking about Carter and Reagan? Where were all these thoughts coming from?

Bits of stray information kept entering my mind that didn't make sense. It was difficult to think. I wanted to stop thinking. Stop worrying. I wanted to rest and go to sleep. My teeth were chattering.

I had to find my tracks. What tracks? Why did I want to find tracks?

"I'm going to die out here," I muttered. "Somebody help me. It's okay to shoot a deer. It's okay to cut a tree down. Sara was okay. Susan was okay. I shouldn't have lied to Mike. I should have helped those Mexicans. I'm cold, so very cold."

I wanted to stand up, but I couldn't move. Thoughts were slowing down. I didn't want to think. I couldn't think.

"I'm not greedy," I murmured. "I've worked hard all my life...other people did better...had more money were happier...Sara... I love you Sara..."

CHAPTER 8

Warm. I was warm and alive. Beneath my body I felt a warm, hard surface. I opened my eyes and focused on an orange glow flickering on a stone ceiling above me. I turned and saw a beautiful Native American woman sitting next to me with the gentle eyes of a deer. She said, "You've been asleep for twelve hours. How do you feel?"

"Weak. I feel weak."

"We were worried you might not make it. If my husband had not brought you here when he did, you would have died in the storm."

"Where am I?"

The woman smiled. "You are in a safe and warm place. Drink this."

The woman helped me to drink broth from a cup. It tasted good. I looked past the woman and saw a huge Native American man sitting by a fire. Beyond the man, snow was falling on pine trees. I looked down and saw I was in a sleeping bag.

"Where am I?" I asked again.

"You're in a cave."

"Why is it so warm in here?" I asked.

"The earth beneath you is warm."

"I don't understand."

"It's the natural heat of Yellowstone. The cave is always warm because of the fire that burns in the earth. The rock beneath you conducts the heat from below. It's the same heat that makes the geysers and hot springs."

I stared at the two Native Americans feeling confused and bewildered. Several times I blinked my eyes, not believing what I was seeing and hearing.

Maybe I was really dying from exposure, I thought, and all of this was some kind of fantasy playing in my mind. I closed my eyes wondering if the fantasy would disappear, but the cave and the two Native Americans were still there when I opened them.

The woman smiled and said, "Don't look so anxious. We are real. We're not going to disappear."

"Who are you?"

"Drink more broth and sleep. I'll answer all your questions when you feel stronger. You need more rest. You've been through a terrible ordeal. You're lucky to be alive."

"Yes, I remember. Poachers were trying to kill a grizzly bear. They wounded the bear in his shoulder."

"My husband told me you stopped them from killing the bear."

"I didn't want the bear to die. They shot down my helicopter. I ran into the timber to get away from them. They left me to die in the storm."

The woman fed me a piece of meat and said, "You are safe here."

When I was finished eating, she went back to the fire and sat by the man. I had food in my stomach. I was warm, and I felt safe. I closed my eyes and was soon asleep.

When I opened my eyes the woman and the man were asleep, and the fire had gone out. A couple of candles provided a slight amount of light.

I got out of my sleeping bag and hobbled to the edge of the cave to relieve myself. I wore a large wool shirt that I assumed belonged to the big man. It was painful standing on my ankle, but I was glad it was not broken.

It had stopped snowing and diamonds glistened on the snow-covered trees in the moon light. It was cold beyond the cave. I crawled back into my sleeping bag and marveled at the warmth that came from the rock floor.

"Are you all right?" asked the woman.

"Yes, I'm feeling better. But I want to sleep more."

"Go back to sleep. We'll talk in the morning."

When I opened my eyes sunlight was streaming through the cave entrance. The smell of cooking food reached my nostrils. Glancing at the man and woman, I realized that both of them were wearing buckskin.

When the man saw I was awake, he brought my clothes to me. They were dry. I put them on and hobbled to the campfire.

The woman was cooking on a one burner camp stove, which seemed out of place in the cave. I was about to ask her why she had no fire in the fireplace when the man spoke.

"You're limping."

"I sprained my ankle trying to get back to the meadow."

"I'll make a crutch for you."

"I don't need a crutch."

Grinning the man said, "It'll give me great pleasure to make a crutch for a white man because they need all the help they can get."

I had heard that Native Americans have an unusual sense of humor, but I wasn't sure how to respond, so I said nothing. The man looked disappointed that I didn't say something.

I turned to the woman and said, "Why are you cooking on a camp stove when you have a fireplace?"

"We only build fires at night or when there is a storm or low clouds to hide the smoke from a passing airplane. There's a natural updraft for the smoke through the hole above your head. The Great Spirit was very creative when He built our cave."

I looked up and saw an opening in the rocky ceiling of the cave. Except for the camp stove, it seemed like I had traveled back to the eighteen hundreds. Who would believe this even if I had the courage to tell someone?

The woman handed me a cup of broth, a plate of meat, and a piece of bread. I ate slowly and tried to make sense of the cave and the man and woman who treated me with kindness.

I was drawn to their faces. They both had strong features and a warm brown complexion with a coppery undertone that was striking. The woman's black hair was parted in the middle and had been worked into two braids, which fell in front of her. There was something about her that reminded me of Sara. The man was very muscular and gave the appearance of possessing enormous strength and endurance.

The woman refilled my cup with broth and gave me dried fruit to eat. I had many questions to ask, and I didn't know where to begin. They seemed to be waiting for me to speak first.

"My name is Kirk Weber. Thank you for rescuing me and for giving me food and a warm place to sleep. You saved my life. I am grateful. But who are you and why are you living in a cave?"

"My Native American name is Song Sparrow," the woman said. "My husband is Strong Bear. He saw you save the great bear and was impressed with your courage. He didn't want you to die so he brought you here. He has allowed you to learn a great secret, a secret that is known by no other white man. You must never tell anyone about our cave."

Without hesitation I said, "You have my word that I will never tell anyone your secret."

"That is all we ask," replied Song Sparrow.

"It's a small request compared to what you've done for me."

Song Sparrow glanced at Strong Bear, and he nodded.

"Is the grizzly still alive?" I asked.

"He's alive, but he's very weak," replied Strong Bear. "I'm afraid he might die during his long winter sleep. We are feeding him buffalo meat to build up his strength."

I held up a piece of meat and said, "Is this buffalo?"

"Yes," said Song Sparrow.

I knew it was illegal to hunt in a national park. If they had killed a buffalo, than they were no better than the poachers.

"Buffalo," I said in a harsh voice. "You killed a buffalo in Yellowstone National Park?"

Anger flared on Strong Bear's face. Song Sparrow looked indignant. Without thinking I had insulted them. My voice had been filled with arrogance and self-righteousness. I couldn't believe I had said such a stupid thing. Strong Bear got to his feet, grabbed a pack, and left.

Song Sparrow paused before answering my question. "We understand the laws of the National Park Service, and they are noble laws. But they are white man's laws, and they do not cover every situation.

"The buffalo my husband killed was seriously injured during the rut. He was in great pain, and my husband felt he wouldn't survive the winter. It was an act of compassion to put him out of his misery, and it was a way to help the grizzly."

I looked at the floor of the cave.

"My husband killed the buffalo to provide food for the great bear because he's having difficulty moving around to feed on his usual diet of pine nuts, berries, roots, and other plants. Grizzlies also eat elk and buffalo. The buffalo meat may help him to survive.

"There are many buffalo in Yellowstone, but only a few grizzly bears. We took only a small amount of meat for ourselves. We carry all our food to the cave. We never hunt the animals in Yellowstone for our sustenance.

"We killed one buffalo that would have died an agonizing death. Your ancestors killed millions of buffalo in the late eighteen hundreds and destroyed the food supply for my people. What your people did was a great atrocity against humanity and nature. Where were your laws back then?"

I glanced at Song Sparrow and mumbled, "I don't know."

An uncomfortable silence fell between us. I needed to say something.

"I am sorry I misjudged you and your husband."

Song Sparrow stared at me without emotion on her face. "I will accept your apology, but Strong Bear has also been offended by your words."

"I'll apologize to Strong Bear when he returns."

I wanted to say something more conciliatory, but I couldn't think of the right words. Song Sparrow went to the back of the cave and stayed there for a while.

When she came back I said, "I don't always say the right thing. I didn't know all the facts."

Song Sparrow nodded in an accepting way.

"Please tell me about your cave. I find it difficult to believe that a place like this can really exist."

"Our cave is natural like all of the volcanic activity in Yellowstone. You do not question the fire that makes the geysers and mud pots. Our cave is a gift of nature."

"But why are you living here?"

"We are Crow and live on the reservation, but we come to the cave to live the old ways when we can no longer tolerate your world. It's our refuge and a terrible reminder of how good life was for my people at one time."

"How did you find this cave?"

"My great, great grandfather found this cave many years ago before Yellowstone became a national park. His enemies wounded him after a long chase and left him for dead a short distance from here.

"It began to snow a great blizzard. My grandfather was dying when the Creator led him to this cave. During the blizzard a deer wandered into the cave seeking warmth. My grandfather killed the deer for food.

"My grandfather's wounds eventually healed, and the cave became a special place for him. He came here many times with his family, and its secret was handed down from generation to generation.

"My father brought my brother and me to the cave before he died, because he did not want its secret to die with him. I was eighteen years old, and I swore to him that only my husband and my children would know of the cave's existence."

I looked at snow sifting down from a sky that had turned gray and asked, "What do you do when you're not here?"

"We try to help our people. Both of us have been educated at your universities. My husband is a teacher. I'm a lawyer."

"Why did you become a lawyer?"

"To change the injustices your people have imposed upon my people. Working with your laws is the only way things can improve for Native Americans."

I didn't know what to say. I didn't know very much about Native American injustices.

We suddenly heard a helicopter. I looked at Song Sparrow and said, "Are the poachers coming back?"

"They're searching for you. We heard them when you were asleep. When they didn't find your remains in the charred helicopter they probably figured you had escaped from it and wandered into the wilderness. They will probably give up searching when they conclude you died in the storm and that your tracks and body are covered with snow."

"I would rather stay here than let them find me. It would be difficult to explain how I survived. I also don't want them to find your cave."

"You can stay here as long as you need to. We can take you to the road when it's time for you to go."

"It will take a while for my ankle to heal. Tell me about Strong Bear and what he does when he's not here."

"He tries to teach our history and culture to our young people, but it's difficult to compete with TV and other distractions from your world.

"He is also an herbalist and a medicine man. His mother taught him the remedies of the forests and meadows, and his father taught him to be a highly skilled medicine man. He has helped many of our people."

Our conversation was interrupted by Strong Bear entering the cave. Song Sparrow greeted him and said, "How is the grizzly?"

Strong Bear frowned. "He's eating the buffalo meat I brought to him, but he's still very weak. I'm worried his wound is infected and that he will die during the winter."

"What can we do to heal his wound?" asked Song Sparrow.

"I followed the bear to a place where he scraped away the snow and dug in the earth for roots. He rolled over the roots in an attempt to rub them into his wound."

"That was strange," I said.

"It was not strange for the bear," replied Strong Bear. "He's trying to use the roots to heal his infection, but he's having trouble working the medicine into his wound."

Light snow was falling as darkness crept into the cave. Strong Bear started a fire, and when the flames began to lick the wood he sat down across from me. He cut a piece of buffalo meat into strips and waited for the fire to burn down to coals. He then placed the meat on a grill that he positioned over the glowing embers.

I took a deep breath and let it our slowly. "I owe you an apology, Strong Bear. Song Sparrow has explained to me why you killed the buffalo. It was the right thing to do."

Strong Bear looked at me expressionlessly. He nodded and said, "I accept your apology."

Strong Bear turned the meat over on the grill. Looking at me, he said, "Native Americans have always respected nature. We also respect the policies of the National Park Service that try to protect nature. But your people have a long history of not respecting mother

110

earth, and you continue with this poor relationship with most of the things you do."

"I'm a forester, and I think we do a good job of managing our forests."

"It brings tears to my eyes when I see mountains that foresters have stripped of their trees. Is that what you call good forestry? I don't understand your profession."

"There are some bad clear-cuts, but there are also a lot of good harvest cuts. You and Song Sparrow remind me of my wife, Sara. When she was alive she talked about nature the same way."

"Do you miss your wife?" asked Song Sparrow.

"Yes."

Song Sparrow looked sympathetic and glanced over at Strong Bear, then asked, "What was Sara like?"

"She loved nature and was always writing letters to save rivers, trees, and wild places. She loved being in the woods and loved photographing nature. She read a lot of books on nature and kept telling me I should read, *A Sand County Almanac* by Aldo Leopold."

"You should have listened to her," said Song Sparrow.

"I should have done a lot of things. But I also had to make a living and that's not easy in northern Maine."

"Like you, Leopold was a forester," said Song Sparrow. "He's one of the few whites who has given me hope for your people and for your forestry profession. If foresters would follow what he writes, they could help your people to live in harmony with the natural world."

My face grew warm as I tried to think of a way to defend white people and foresters. Most of my arguments were based on material progress, profit, and economics. I knew these arguments would not impress Song Sparrow and Strong Bear.

"How did your wife die?" asked Song Sparrow.

"In an automobile accident."

A puff of wind blew snowflakes into the cave.

"Did Sara want you to make a journey?" asked Song Sparrow.

With surprise I asked, "How do you know about my trip to Yosemite?"

111

"You mumbled words in your sleep. We heard you say, 'Have to take pictures for Sara,' and another time you said, 'Have to go to Yosemite."

"It was Sara's dream to take photographs in Yosemite National Park. Just before she died she asked me to take her pictures for her."

"Your wife wanted you to go to Yosemite because it will be a journey of learning."

"I don't see what taking a few photographs will accomplish, but I will do it because it was Sara's last request."

"Your wife was a wise woman," said Song Sparrow. "She knew your journey might help you to change how you view nature. But you must go with an open heart and mind."

I stared at Song Sparrow and said nothing. She handed me a plate of food, and we began to eat.

A low fog was outside when I got up the following morning. Strong Bear had left the cave early. When he returned he carried a bundle of roots he had dug up. He built a fire and positioned a large pot of water in the flames.

"What are you doing?" asked Song Sparrow.

"These are the roots the bear was trying to roll on. I'm hoping that boiling them will allow me to extract a substance that I might use to heal his injury."

"How will you apply the herb to his wound?" I asked.

Strong Bear smiled and said, "I'm not sure. But I'll think of a way."

"It sounds dangerous applying medicine to an injured grizzly bear," said Song Sparrow.

"I'll do nothing foolish. Let's see what happens to these roots when they simmer for a while."

The water came to a boil. Strong Bear broke some of the roots into small pieces and put them into the pot. Every few minutes he took one of the roots out of the water and squeezed it.

Eventually one of the roots emitted a yellow paste, and he beamed with delight. He took the roots out of the pot and squeezed the yellow paste into a leather pouch.

Strong Bear looked at Song Sparrow and said, "Perhaps the bear will recognize the paste as the roots he rolled on if I place it near his food. He might apply the medicine to his injury himself."

Sunshine broke through clouds during breakfast the next day and brightened the entrance to the cave. Strong Bear left when he had finished eating and returned late in the afternoon with another supply of roots. He boiled roots into the night, and by the time we were ready to go to bed his leather sack was filled with the herbal medicine. We were hopeful his plan would work.

Three days passed with Strong Bear spreading the paste on a piece of leather near the place where the bear came to eat the buffalo meat. When he returned in the evening of each day he looked disappointed and said, "The bear is not rolling in the paste."

When he returned on the fourth day he looked more worried and said, "The bear was not at his usual feeding place today. This is the first time he has not come to the rock where I leave the buffalo meat."

"Perhaps he's getting ready to hibernate, "said Song Sparrow.

"Other bears are showing no sign of hibernating," replied Strong Bear. "But his weakened condition might cause him to hibernate early. We'll see what tomorrow brings."

"I want to go with you tomorrow," I said. "My ankle is feeling better, and I think some exercise will do it good."

Strong Bear looked at me, smiled, and said, "Okay."

Morning came with sun and cold. After breakfast Song Sparrow went to the back of the cave and returned with a down parka, a wool hat, gloves, and a pair of snow boots. The clothes were dusty and looked like they had been in the cave for a long time.

"These belonged to my brother," said Song Sparrow. "He died in the cave."

"I'm sorry. How did he die?"

"He was dying from cancer when Strong Bear brought him here on the sled. He wanted to die close to nature and not in a hospital. He died in the spring, several years ago. We buried him at the edge of the meadow where he watched the animals."

"Are you sure you want me to wear his clothes?"

"He was the same size as you. You'll need warm clothes when you leave the cave."

I tried the boots on and said, "They're a good fit. Thank you."

Song Sparrow also gave me a small pack that contained food and some basic outdoor essentials. I thanked her again.

After lunch, we left the cave with Strong Bear leading the way to a place where butchered buffalo meat hung from two trees. He untied a rope from a tree and lowered a leg to the ground.

He removed the tarp that covered the leg, cut off a piece of meat, secured the tarp around the leg, and pulled it back into the tree. He then wrapped the piece of meat with a smaller tarp and secured it to his pack frame.

We walked a short distance through the forest and entered a small canyon with steep walls and a roaring stream. Strong Bear led the way to a group of rocks in the stream that could be used as stepping stones to the other side.

"The cave and this small canyon are not near any major trails," said Strong Bear. "This area appears to be a place the National Park Service leaves undisturbed for grizzlies. Their policy also helps to keep our cave a secret."

We followed a narrow ledge up the side of the canyon, walked through more trees, and stopped to rest at the edge of a meadow. Buffalo grazed in the distance.

"This is where the poachers come to kill grizzlies," said Strong Bear. "They have killed two grizzlies that I am aware of."

He pointed to the other side of the meadow and added, "The remains of your helicopter are over there.

"They have stopped looking for you so it is okay for us to take a shorter route to the bear's feeding place. I have been using a longer route that is more hidden in the forest to lessen the chance of the searchers finding my tracks.

"We always travel in the trees at the edge of the meadow when there is snow to avoid making tracks in the open that might be seen from the air. Follow me. I will break trail."

"How did you get me to the cave?" I asked.

"I carried you."

I was amazed how easily Strong Bear traveled with the heavy load on his back. He was a powerful man and moved liked a creature of the forest.

My ankle ached from the cold and the exercise, but I was determined not to complain. I was glad to be outside after being in the cave for several days.

We hiked about an hour. When we stopped by a flat rock it was snowing.

Strong Bear uncovered a piece of leather that was buried in the snow and shook snow and frozen paste from it. He then added fresh paste to the piece of leather and spread it out so it covered an area about two feet in diameter. The bear had a good dose of paste if he was going to roll in it.

We went to some rocks a safe distance from the feeding place and waited for the bear. The light began to fade and it was getting colder. I glanced at my watch, and when I looked back at the feeding rock the grizzly was there. Strong Bear looked relieved that the bear was still coming to the feeding rock.

The bear ate some of the meat. When he finished eating he sniffed the yellow paste for a few seconds. Strong Bear whispered something in his native tongue.

We watched the bear glance in our direction, and then he slowly limped away from the rock and the paste. I was disappointed, and I knew Strong Bear felt the same way. He said, "He's going to his sleeping place."

The bear headed up a steep hill and vanished in the shadows. I shivered and said, "Where does he sleep?"

"There's a crevice further up that hill he crawls into. He has a good vantage point up there to survey the surrounding country."

My ankle had stiffened from the cold, and it hurt on the way back to the cave. It was difficult crossing the stream in the canyon with only a flashlight to light the way. I was hobbling when we arrived at the cave.

Song Sparrow motioned for us to sit by the fire and placed food and mugs of hot tea in front of us. When we finished eating Strong Bear said, "I'm worried that the bear's infection is getting more severe. He seems to be in greater pain and walks slower, and his limp is getting worse. I'm afraid he'll die in his winter sleep if we don't get the paste on his wound."

"I hope you'll do nothing foolish," said Song Sparrow.

Strong Bear looked thoughtful and then gave a slight nod.

115

Song Sparrow looked worried.

We went to bed early. I did not fall asleep right away but started to think about Sara. Song Sparrow had said she was a wise woman. I never thought of Sara as being wise, but now I was beginning to see her in a different way.

Our views were often polarized, especially with forestry and the environment. I had always thought Sara was naive and idealistic with her thinking and values. Song Sparrow had caught me off guard with her statement, but there was truth in it. I needed to think more about Sara and what Song Sparrow had said about her.

I thought about Susan living in her penthouse with every luxury known to modern civilization. I tried to imagine her living in a cave with two Native Americans. The thought made me chuckle.

I thought about my Porsche, my beautiful apartment, and the hundred and twenty thousand dollars Susan was paying me. I also thought about Susan telling me that she loved me and the kind of life I could have with her. I would have money and a very comfortable life by going back to Susan.

Many conflicting thoughts filled my mind, and I needed time to sort them out. Exhaustion finally pulled me into a deep sleep. I began to dream.

Sara and I were walking through a forest. Sunlight dappled wild flowers, ferns, and moss that grew around the base of fir, hemlock, and cedar. The day was warm and bright and we stopped to pick blueberries and raspberries. We also ate a substance that grew on rocks that had a consistency like bread. Everything was delicious, and we were very satisfied with our meal.

We strolled along a stream and glanced at cascades of emerald water bubbling into transparent pools filled with feeding trout. Birds were everywhere, singing from branches and flying from tree to tree. Rabbits, squirrels, raccoons, and other animals went quietly about their normal activities, and our presence did not seem to disturb them.

We came to a gorgeous pool below a waterfall and sat there, enjoying the beauty and tranquility of the surrounding landscape. A doe came to drink at the pool on the opposite bank and looked at us with serenity in her eyes. She walked a short distance and was joined by a buck, and together they disappeared into the forest.

116

Sara dove into the pool and swam to the waterfall. She climbed onto a rock where tiny drops of spray caught the sunlight and formed a rainbow around her naked body. She waved to me, and I waved back to her. Slipping into the pool, she swam to the other side of the stream, where she climbed onto another rock to let herself dry in the warm sun. She looked beautiful, and I felt an intense love for her.

I dove into the pool and swam to the rock she was sitting on. She giggled, stood up, and ran into the dense vegetation. I pulled myself out of the water and ran after her, but I couldn't find her. I anxiously searched the area, calling her name several times. There was no answer. Sara was gone.

I woke up shouting, "Sara."

Strong Bear was looking at me from his bed. "You were having a dream, it's okay now."

I looked at him and said, "It'll never be okay because Sara is never coming back."

"You'll see her on the other side."

I tried to go back to sleep but kept thinking about my dream. I was awake when sunlight entered the cave. Strong Bear was already up and watched me limp to the fireplace.

"You should stay in the cave and give your ankle a rest," he said.

I felt tired and agreed with him. After lunch, Strong Bear went to feed the bear, and I took a nap.

When I awoke, Strong Bear had not returned to the cave. It was dark outside, and Song Sparrow was worried. By midnight we were still waiting for Strong Bear. I told Song Sparrow I was going to bed, but I couldn't sleep. When I got up to relieve myself, Song Sparrow was in bed, but I knew she wasn't sleeping. We both wanted Strong Bear to appear at the cave entrance, but he did not come.

Returning to bed, I fell into a fitful slumber, and then Song Sparrow was shaking me awake. When I opened my eyes she said, "Strong Bear is not back. I need to go look for him. Can you walk on your ankle?"

"I think so."

I got out of my sleeping bag and walked around the cave. My ankle was a little stiff, but it seemed okay.

We ate a quick breakfast and hurried through the timber in the predawn light. It was cold and dark in the canyon, and we used flashlights to find our way.

The sun broke over a distant ridge as we circled the meadow. A mountain to the right of us caught a gleam of dawn.

Song Sparrow was fast on her feet. I fell behind with pain stabbing my ankle as we followed the tracks in the snow to the bear's feeding place. Song Sparrow glanced at the feeding rock and gave me an anxious look. I pointed to a slope and said, "The bear sleeps up there."

We started to run up the craggy incline but quickly slowed with the steepness of the grade. At the top of the hill we stopped to catch our breath. Song Sparrow pointed to a mix of tracks in the snow made by Strong Bear and the grizzly, tracks that headed toward a cliff. An expression of horror came to her face as she stared at the trampled snow.

In desperation she called out to Strong Bear in her native tongue. To our surprise and relief Strong Bear answered her. We ran to the edge of the cliff and looked down. About fifteen feet below us Strong Bear stood on a small ledge.

Strong Bear grinned and shouted, "The bear chased me last night. This was the only place I could go where he couldn't follow me. Lucky for me his injury slowed him down, or I would not have escaped his anger."

"Why was the bear angry with you?" asked Song Sparrow.

"He didn't like me applying the healing paste to his wound while he was asleep. I thought I might wake him, so I tied a rope to a tree to help me get to this ledge. I didn't think an injured grizzly could climb down a rope, and I was right."

"You promised me you would do nothing foolish," replied Song Sparrow.

"It wasn't foolish. I had a plan to escape from the bear, and it worked. But I didn't anticipate the bear grabbing my arm with one of his claws, which has prevented me from climbing up the rope. I've been studying the surface of the cliff in the increasing light, and I have found crevices for my feet. I can make the climb with the two of you pulling me with the rope."

"How bad is your wound?" asked Song Sparrow.

"It's not serious, but it's painful when I try to climb the rope. So, I decided to wait for daylight to study the cliff."

"Can you hold onto the rope with one hand?" asked Song Sparrow.

"I can manage. Don't worry. Pull when I tell you to. Everything will be fine. Give me a minute to tie the rope around my chest. Find a place to brace yourself when you pull on the rope."

"We'll leave the rope tied to the tree to act as a brake in case you slip," I said.

I knew the two of us couldn't pull Strong Bear up the cliff, but if we could help him to keep his balance with the rope, there was a good chance he could make the climb using only one hand.

Song Sparrow and I found rocks to push against with our feet. When we were ready, she called to Strong Bear to begin climbing.

The rope tightened in our hands. We pulled with all of our strength. The rope came slowly toward us. My ankle hurt as I applied pressure to it, and I groaned in silence. Strong Bear called for slack, and we gave it to him. Then, he called for us to pull hard.

We gave a mighty tug. Strong Bear's head appeared by the edge of the cliff. Grabbing a nearby tree with his good hand, he hauled himself onto the snow in front of us. He grinned as Song Sparrow ran to him and threw her arms around his large body.

"I'm thankful you're all right," she said, "but I'm angry with you for doing a foolish thing."

"It was the only way to help the bear. I thought his injury would slow him down more than it did."

"It was a dangerous thing to do. The bear could have killed you," replied Song Sparrow.

This time Strong Bear didn't answer. It was prudent for him to remain silent because Song Sparrow was upset and determined to have the last word. When she saw that Strong Bear was not going to argue anymore she said, "Let me see your injury."

Strong Bear pushed his blood stained sleeve back, exposing an ugly gash in his forearm. Song Sparrow got her first aid kit from her pack, applied an ointment, and bandaged Strong Bear's arm.

Chuckling Strong Bear said, "We could use some of the paste I used on the bear."

"The ointment will do just fine," replied Song Sparrow. "You promised me you would do nothing foolish."

Strong Bear looked at me and said, "Song Sparrow told you that you should have listened to your wife. Perhaps I should have done the same with my wife. I'm sorry for the worry I've caused, but it's painful for me to see the bear suffer."

On the way back to the cave, Strong Bear and Song Sparrow walked ahead of me, talking in their native language. By the time we got to the cave they had patched things up between them. We stayed in the cave for the remainder of the day, resting, and celebrating Strong Bear's success and foolishness.

I slept soundly that night. When I woke up Song Sparrow and Strong Bear were fixing breakfast. Strong Bear asked me if my ankle was strong enough to hike to the feeding rock. I told him I needed to stay off of it for a while. Song Sparrow announced that she was going with him. Strong Bear nodded with a smile. It was clear he would make no more attempts to put the healing paste on the bear.

"How will you apply the paste this time?" I asked.

"I'll try spreading some of the roots in the paste. Maybe the bear will recognize the roots as the medicine he tried to apply himself, and maybe they will encourage him to roll in the paste."

When they returned to the cave in the evening both of them looked anxious and disappointed. Strong Bear took his pack frame off and said, "The bear did not show by the rock. We'll try again tomorrow."

My ankle was feeling better the next day, and I decided to go with them. Strong Bear wanted the bear to receive two or three more doses of the paste, and he was worried the bear might hibernate before this could happen.

We left the buffalo meat on the rock and the paste and roots on the piece of leather. We then went to the rocks to watch. Daylight began to fade, and the temperature started to fall. We waited.

Shadows invaded the light, and from the growing darkness the bear materialized like a ghost by the feeding rock. He smelled the meat, and then he lowered his nose to the paste and roots. He placed one of his paws on the roots and moved them through the paste. It looked like he was playing with them.

Strong Bear spoke softly in his native tongue. Song Sparrow whispered some kind of a prayer. I muttered, "Roll in the paste."

Time seemed to stop. The three of us continued to plead in our own way. The bear looked at us and then at the piece of leather. A message of some kind seemed to reach him because he lowered himself to the ground and rolled his injured shoulder in the paste.

I looked at Song Sparrow. There were tears on her cheeks. Strong Bear looked grateful. A lump came to my throat. None of us talked. We stared at the bear and then at each other.

Song Sparrow reached out for one of our hands. Standing there in the wilderness holding hands, I had the strangest sensation we were also holding onto the bear.

The bear rolled for a minute or two. Then he got to his feet and headed for his sleeping place with his shoulder covered with yellow paste.

On the way back to the cave Strong Bear said, "The bear has stopped eating, which means he'll hibernate in a few days."

Trickles of white floated down from a leaden sky the next day. We had seen the last of the sun, but we had two more days with the bear applying the paste to his wound. On the third day the bear did not show. We headed back in a snow flurry that quickly turned into a raging blizzard.

"The bear will probably hibernate during the storm," said Strong Bear. "I hope he'll be well when he wakes up in the spring."

Song Sparrow glanced at me and said, "When the storm is over it'll be time for you to begin your journey."

I looked at her and felt sad. I would miss my two friends and my stay in their cave, but I knew it was time for me to go.

My ankle had healed slowly because I had walked on it too soon, but exercise had also helped to make it strong. I would have no trouble hiking to the road.

It was dark when we arrived at the cave. Strong Bear made a large fire, and Song Sparrow prepared supper. After eating we sat by the fire. Occasionally a gust of wind blew snowflakes into the cave that melted before they could land on us.

Strong Bear seemed to be brooding about something. When Song Sparrow asked what was bothering him he said, "I hope the bear has applied enough of the paste to heal his wound. We may never know if he lives."

"I think he'll survive," replied Song Sparrow.

"Perhaps, but he'll always walk with a limp," said Strong Bear.

Strong Bear added more wood to the fire, and we went to bed. I fell asleep quickly and slept soundly for three or four hours, until I woke with a jolt of fear running through me.

I had heard a roar that I first thought was in a dream, but as I blinked my eyes and focused on the pale orange ceiling, I realized the roar had been real. Pushing myself to a sitting position, I looked at the entrance of the cave and saw the grizzly standing erect on his hind feet behind the fire. As I gaped wide-eyed at the bear, he roared again.

The roar sent another wave of terror through me. Flames from the fire set the bear's eyes ablaze, and snowflakes swirling around his head gave him a terrifying look. He blocked the only escape route from the cave. Again his roar echoed with paralyzing power.

Strong Bear got out of his sleeping bag and stood with the fire between the grizzly and himself. He stared for a few seconds at the bear's wound. The bear stood perfectly still.

When Strong Bear was satisfied with his examination he said something in his native tongue. The bear continued to stand there. Strong Bear repeated his words. The bear brought his front paws to the ground. They looked at each other for a few moments, and then the bear turned and disappeared into the storm.

I looked at Song Sparrow sitting up in her bed and said, "What did he say?"

"Your wound is healing...now go."

Strong Bear watched the falling snow for a while. Then, he went to his bed and lay down next to his wife. Peaceful sounds of sleep reached my ears minutes later.

I did not sleep for the rest of the night. I lay on top of my sleeping bag staring at the rocky ceiling, trying to understand what I had witnessed. The fire died down. The cave grew darker.

I was not a religious man, and I didn't believe in God. I also had no knowledge of mystical or spiritual experiences. There was no reference point in my life I could fall back on for an explanation.

Near daybreak, I began to rationalize the bear had come to the cave to hibernate, or to look for food, or more healing paste. It looked like the fire had stopped the bear from entering the cave, and Strong Bear's presence had encouraged him to leave.

It was still snowing hard when I got up and went to the campfire to sit. A few coals contained heat, and I added wood to them. Strong Bear and Song Sparrow got up later and prepared breakfast.

When we finished eating, Strong Bear went to the back of the cave and returned with three pairs of snowshoes. He inspected them carefully and leaned them against a wall. He then sat down and began to talk to me.

"You seem to have difficulty with what happened last night?"

I nodded.

"What happened last night is as much a mystery to me as it is to you. Only you are not in a position to accept it in the way I can accept it, because you and your people live in a culture that is disconnected from the natural world.

"Most Native Americans believe that all life is connected by a life force that comes from the Creator. It took thousands of years for our people to find ways to accommodate our human needs to the needs of the land, and to this spiritual power. When you took our land, we lost the essence of this power that nourished our bodies and spirits.

"The Navajo believe that, 'When we lived in harmony with the land, we walked in beauty with the Creator.'

"Your journey may help to remove a few of your barriers with nature, but it is impossible for you, or your society, to understand what has taken many years for Native Americans to learn and to cultivate."

Strong Bear stopped talking and stood up. He picked up one of the snowshoes and began to repair it with a piece of rawhide.

It kept snowing the rest of the day and into the night. We rested with none of us feeling a need for conversation.

123

I kept weighing Strong Bear's explanation for the bear's behavior against my own conclusions. I knew bears were unpredictable animals, and it was reasonable to think the bear had come to the cave to hibernate, or to look for food, or more paste.

While I had trouble accepting Strong Bear's explanation for the bear's behavior, I also could not completely reject it. I kept seeing the way the bear stood while Strong Bear examined his wound. The way he looked when Strong Bear talked to him. The experience haunted me, and I would never forget it.

At supper Song Sparrow said, "We'll pack for our hike to the road when we finish eating. The storm is subsiding, and the weather will be clearing. We'll leave before sunrise."

I was in a deep sleep when Strong Bear woke me. I felt drowsy, but was eager to get going. After breakfast Song Sparrow gave me a small pack filled with food to take with me.

We put on our snowshoes and stepped into the fluffy snow. Strong Bear broke trail. We hiked through the pines, crossed the stream, and made our way around the meadow.

Moonlight gleamed from fallen snowflakes and shrouded the world in a whitish, grey brilliance. Shapes of buffalo and elk appeared like pale shadows in the surreal light. A hush dominated the frozen landscape. The only sound came from our breathing and the squish of snow compacting under our webs.

An hour or two later, sunlight started to paint crimson into the clouds over the eastern horizon. We stopped to eat and to watch the color fade into the sky of a new day.

We kept hiking for the rest of the morning and stopped at noon on top of a hill. The sound of a car passing below reached our ears.

"You'll be able to catch a ride on the road," said Strong Bear.

"It's difficult for me to say good-by," I said.

"Go with our friendship," Song Sparrow said. "But please do not speak to anyone about our cave or your experience with us. That is all we ask."

"You have my word that I will tell no one your secret. Thank you for trusting me and for sharing your cave and food with me."

Strong Bear held out his hand, and I shook it. Song Sparrow gave me a hug. I started down the hill.

Suddenly, I felt an overwhelming urge not to return to my world. I turned around and caught a glimpse of Song Sparrow disappearing into the forest. I tried to swallow the lump in my throat, but it wouldn't go away.

There was no going back. The cave belonged to Song Sparrow and Strong Bear. I had been a visitor. With sadness, I turned and walked down the hill to the road.

I would keep their secret. I would also never forget what I had learned in the cave.

CHAPTER 9

I stopped in the middle of the bridge to look at the Yellowstone River and wondered if the big brown trout had found a suitable place in the huge volume of water. The Autumn River entered the Yellowstone on the left with only a trickle of water in its riverbed.

Trees along the river had lost their leaves, and their branches appeared stark against the deep blue sky. The snow that had fallen in Yellowstone National Park had not reached the lower elevations, but there were crowns of white on the distant mountains. I took a deep breath and let it out slowly. The air smelled fresh and clean.

I walked up the road to Henry's shop. His truck was in the driveway where someone from Autumn Springs Resort had dropped it off. I found the keys on top of the right rear tire and opened the passenger door. Sara's ashes were sitting on the front seat where I had left them.

I picked up the urn and held it to my chest. It gave me a strange feeling of being both close to and distant from Sara. I placed the container back on the seat and let myself into Henry's shop with the key I found under his door mat.

The place smelled musty. I opened a few windows and went to Henry's back porch. A faint sound of moving water came from the river.

Collapsing in a chair, I opened the pack Song Sparrow had given me and found bread, dried fruit, and buffalo meat. I had not eaten since early morning, and I was hungry.

I felt very alone sitting on Henry's porch. Solitude was not always a welcome companion, but I knew it would be a requirement on my journey.

Toward evening I left Henry's porch and headed down the trail to Looking Glass Pool. Only a dribble of water flowed in the riverbed.

Most of the rock that had concealed the big brown trout's crevice in Looking Glass Pool was exposed above the motionless water. Two small trout occupied the cavity that had belonged to the large fish.

On the way back to the shop, I found a memorial to Henry by a large cottonwood tree on a rise overlooking the river. A simple plaque stated his name, the dates of his life, and the words, "He loved and understood the Autumn River, but he could not enlighten enough of us to save it."

I stayed for a while at Henry's memorial and thought about him and our struggle to move the big brown trout to the Yellowstone River. Sara was the reason I went back to help Henry, but at the time, I had not been very enthused about Henry's ridiculous idea to rescue the big fish.

A slight breeze moved up from the river and caressed my face. Looking at the plaque again, I realized I now had a better feeling about helping Henry to save the big trout.

Back at Henry's shop I retrieved Sara's book on nature photography from Henry's camper and took it to the kitchen. On a shelf I found a can of coffee and scooped a generous portion into Henry's old coffee pot. The sound and smell of percolating coffee filled the kitchen. When it was ready, I poured a cup and went to Henry's deck.

A yellow radiance gleamed on the mountains. It was a scene I was sure Henry had viewed many times. I missed him and the conversations we had on his deck.

When it was too cold to stay outside, I went in and poured myself another cup of coffee. Sitting at the kitchen table, I opened Sara's book on photography and read about the ability of light to transform everyday landscapes into extraordinary photographs.

I went to Henry's shop and walked around glancing at his merchandise. At his fly tying bench I looked at his trout flies. They were works of art and perfection. Everything reminded me of Henry. It was not the same place without him.

I found a small library of fishing books and looked at the titles. One book had the word "Journal" on its side. I pulled it from the shelf, opened it to the first page, and read, *The Journal of Henry Johnson* on the *Autumn River*. I flipped through a hundred and twenty-seven pages, all hand written and numbered.

Back in the kitchen I made another pot of coffee and began to read Henry's Journal. The hand writing was clear and easy to read. The words formed in my mind as if Henry was speaking them.

"The Autumn River is a magnificent fusion of water and life. Water pours out of the ground so fresh and pure that it is a paradise for all the creatures that live within its bounds. I have never seen such an abundance of aquatic insects, such healthy trout, and so much beauty. The Autumn River is an ecological miracle."

"I am friends with the Autumn River because I walk its banks, fish its pools, and observe its natural phenomena. Being friends with a river is not like being friends with a person, but it can be done. Most of the effort comes from me."

"When I am quiet and patient, the river responds by revealing its ecology and beauty, and on rare occasions, its most guarded secrets. I try not to disturb events and processes that have taken years to develop."

"We have shared many experiences, this river and I, and our relationship has become personal and spiritual. The Autumn has taught me to love nature, and the Maker of it all."

"A river can teach a great deal about life. Everything that comes into a pool must enter through its surface or from upstream. One pool's waste does not destroy life in the next pool. The inhabitants have worked this out. There are rules. Waste is recycled in a river. That's the way it is with nature. If trout and insects can manage this, why can't humans?"

"The Autumn's flow of water is always steady and dependable. It follows the commands of the land, obeying every drop in elevation, every rock and curve in its path; slow and deep in one place, fast and turbulent in another. The water of the Autumn knows the architecture of pools and ripples. Water makes a river."

"The river provides an incredible web of sustenance for all of its creatures. Aquatic insects eat algae, plant fragments, and other insects. Trout eat mayflies, caddis flies, and minute crustaceans. There are millions of insects in the Autumn River. The trout number much less. It takes many insects to make a trout."

"A mayfly is a perfect design of nature. As nymphs they have streamlined bodies, which allow them to cling to rocks in strong currents. As adults they float like tiny sailboats on a pool's surface. Adult mayflies fly away when they leave the stream, but only for a short distance and a short period of time. The following evening the females return to deposit their eggs in the river and to die. A year later, every pool and riffle will have a great abundance of mayflies."

"Dimples on the water's surface identify the coming together of trout and floating insects. A dimple is a series of circles, each within the other, spreading tiny waves across the top of a pool. Water and dimples travel downstream. Trout and insects are more permanent residents."

"The swiftness of falling water and the quickness of trout were made for each other. Sleek and slim, trout cut through the water with ease and grace. A blend of colors and markings help to conceal them in the gravel and rocks of a stream and to protect them from predators that come from land and sky."

"When I hold a trout in my hands, for only a second or two, I know this is a creature made by an Artist, and that trout are worthy to live in some of the most beautiful places on earth."

"A thin membrane separates my surroundings from the trout's environment. I exist above this boundary, the trout below it. At times, I have sat quietly on the bank within a few feet of a trout. While physically close, our worlds are miles apart."

"In Looking Glass Pool, evening light reveals the presence of every stone and pebble and flashes on the speckled sides of trout as they dart and rise for drifting insects. Watching trout in the Autumn River is like watching fish swim in the clarity of mountain air."

"Water coming into Looking Glass Pool bubbles and froths, slows and deepens, and takes on a glassy quality. At the tail of the pool, the glass crinkles and cracks as it travels over rocks and boulders.

"In the deepest part of this magical pool there is a cavity under a big rock that has concealed a very large brown trout for a very long time. During the day, he stays hidden and it's impossible to detect his presence. But when the sun hangs above the ridge in the west, he leaves his den and glides over cream and tan gravel to a feeding lane of current, where he dimples his silver ceiling for floating insects. This big trout is a sly old fox, and he has my deepest respect and love."

"There is only one Autumn River. I know this. The Autumn is too special for nature to make more than one. It has taken me many years to discover this truth. I try to tell people about its significance, but words do not convey its ecological essence, its beauty, or my feelings for this incredible river."

It was close to midnight when I finished reading Henry's Journal. I decided to take his Journal with me to read it again and to think more about it.

Henry's truck needed a little persuasion to start the next morning. He had said it needed a tune up, and I decided to get it done in Livingston.

I drove slowly down Henry's road and stopped on the bridge to look at the Yellowstone River. Again I wondered about the big brown trout. I hoped he was alive and well.

In Livingston I pulled into a gas station and told the mechanic to prepare my truck for a long trip. Over lunch in a cafe I studied road maps and saw several national parks in Utah.

"Utah," I said to myself. "It will be warmer there than it is here. I'll head for Utah."

After lunch I went shopping. In an army surplus store I purchased a jungle hammock. I had used a jungle hammock in Vietnam and had liked the flexibility it offered for sleeping outside. It had a roof to provide shelter from rain and mosquito netting to keep bugs out. The hammock was a practical piece of equipment that would allow me to camp wherever I could find two trees.

130

I picked up my truck at three-thirty and went grocery shopping. Later I found a pay phone and called Annie. When I heard her voice I said, "Hello, this is Dad."

"I've been worried about you. I haven't heard from you for a long time."

"I'm sorry. My life has been rather hectic since I talked to you. I want to tell you that I'm going to Yosemite to take your mom's pictures."

"I'm glad. I was afraid you weren't going to do it."

"I know."

"What made you change your mind?"

"I've had some experiences that helped me realize I need to do this."

"What kind of experiences?"

"Personal experiences that are hard to explain. What's important is that these experiences have motivated me to learn everything I can about photography and to practice taking pictures between now and when I get to Yosemite. By then I hope I will be able to take the kinds of photographs your mom would like."

"I'm glad. You'll be gone a long time."

"I will. I'll send you post cards to let you know where I am and what I'm doing."

"Okay."

"I have to go, but I wanted to let you know that I'm fine and that I'll be taking your mom's pictures."

"I'm happy you called. I love you and good luck with your photography."

"Thanks. I love you, too."

I hung up, got in my truck, and drove out of town. That night I slept in a Forest Service campground. I woke up to falling snow and was happy I was heading south. I had seen enough snow in Yellowstone. I ate cold cereal and finished my coffee on the road.

In the weeks ahead I took many pictures and each one taught me something about photography. At first I photographed everything, but the more I read and studied the pictures in Sara's books, the more selective I became with subject, light, and composition.

I began to pay more attention to how the time of day, the weather, and the seasons influenced the land's ability to produce photographs. I studied the shape of rock formations and the types of light that made them radiate color and detail. I searched for trees that had unique crowns and positions in the landscape. I watched for graceful curves in streams and for water and rock combinations that complemented each other. I discovered subjects in the miniature world of frost, plants, and stones. I found photographs in every place I visited, and I tried to be ready for them whenever and wherever they materialized.

I was looking for a good photograph as evening sunlight warmed the colors and formations of Bryce Canyon National Park. Interplay of shadows and highlights appeared and vanished as clouds scudded across the sky.

My eyes fell on a lone juniper at the base of a massive wall of eroded rock. I switched to my zoom lens and framed a good composition. Darkness panned across the landscape with a passing cloud, followed by a short duration of intense light. I released my shutter and hoped that moment of dramatic beauty was preserved on the film in my camera.

The predawn light was bright enough to see trees outside my jungle hammock. Ropes creaked as I eased to the ground, shivering in the early morning cold. I dressed quickly and attached my camera and 400mm lens to my tripod. I slowly approached a meadow where I had seen mule deer the night before.

Sun brightened the mist in the east. Wet grass soaked my boots. I stopped and waited. Shadows emerged from the fog. One of the shadows had magnificent antlers.

I saw a route through aspen trees that would bring me closer to the feeding deer. I jumped across a small stream and stopped behind a clump of small pine trees where I watched three does browsing fifty or sixty feet in front of me. I set up my camera and tripod and shot several photographs in the vaporous light. There was no sign of the buck I had seen earlier. The does walked further away.

I was about to leave when the buck appeared and started to strut in my direction. When he was close enough for a photo he lowered his head to browse. A shaft of sunlight fell on a tree behind the buck. He raised his head into the light and his eye caught a sparkle. An incredible photograph was in front of me.

My thumb moved to the film advance lever. There was resistance. My last picture had been shot earlier when I was photographing the does. Pushing the film release button, I turned the small handle to rewind the film. Cold fingers opened the camera back and, with difficulty, I removed the exposed film. Looking up I saw the buck running away.

Not knowing whether to laugh or cry I decided I still had a lot to learn. Today's lesson was to always check the film frame counter after taking several photographs to see if there was enough film for another shot.

Tentacles of ice had grown across the backwater of a brook during the night, entrapping floating cottonwood leaves. Yellow leaves, air bubbles, and frozen ice daggers had arranged several photo possibilities.

The thin ice would not support me, but I managed to find logs and rocks to position myself near the compositions I wanted to capture. I took great care to avoid destroying the fragile mosaics as I moved to various places. By midmorning the works of art were starting to melt. I hoped I had frozen their beauty on film.

Fresh snow resembled white hats on the tops of rocks in the stream. Spruce and fir branches, heavy with snow, drooped downward. Pink tinted the sky, blushed on the snow, and reflected in the pool of slow moving water.

I snapped a picture, waited a minute, and released the shutter again as the light grew more intense. Twilight fought darkness and provided enough time for an early moon to rise large and bright above the trees and stream. I expected the pink to vanish, but it persisted, allowing me to shoot several photographs of the stream, the tree silhouettes, and the moon surrounded by pink clouds.

I found a tiny lake on a ranch in Arizona that had several species of wintering ducks. After talking to the rancher he gave me permission to photograph the ducks and let me borrow his waders and wading donut.

I constructed a floating blind on the donut with lumber, sticks, and brush. I also made a wooden frame to hold my camera and telephoto lens. With my camera in this position, I hoped to get photos of ducks that looked like they were taken by other ducks.

Early one morning I ventured out and began shooting pictures. Everything was going fine until I heard a loud splash behind me and the sound of something large swimming in my direction. The ducks took off squawking.

I turned the donut around and saw a huge black shape closing in, the rancher's male Labrador retriever. Apparently the big dog had made up his mind I was in need of retrieving. I tried to get away, but the dog was faster. I grabbed my camera as he lunged for the sticks supporting my blind.

"Damn dog," I yelled as he headed for shore with pieces of my blind in his mouth.

The rancher roared with laughter when I told him what had happened. He also assured me that he would keep his dog tied during future excursions on his pond. In the days ahead, I got some terrific photographs while the "duck blind retriever" watched from his dog house.

I was exploring back roads in northern Arizona looking for landscapes to photograph. The ponderosa pine forest in this country had good potential for pictures. Pulling a short distance off a gravel road, I found a nice place to camp.

The sun had already set, but what remained of the evening was absolutely beautiful. I walked around the big trees and took several photos of them. The evening gave no hint of the weather that was moving in from the north.

I woke up the next morning to heavy wet flakes that reminded me of the big storm in Yellowstone. Getting out of my camper I found a foot of snow on the ground.

Foolishly, I had pulled down a grade to hide my presence from people passing on the road. I tried several times to drive my truck up the small hill, but the snow was too deep and slick. I walked

134

to the road, but it had not been plowed, so it did not matter if I could get up the hill.

I decided to spend the morning photographing pine trees covered with snow. When I returned to my truck for lunch it had stopped snowing, and the sun was searching for an opening in the clouds. After lunch I climbed into my sleeping bag and turned down my heater to conserve fuel.

I started to read, *A Sand County Almanac*. It was an enjoyable book, and I liked Aldo Leopold's style of writing. I read for several hours, took a break for supper, and kept reading until I fell asleep. There was no snowplow the next morning so I kept reading until I finished the book.

At first Leopold's book read like a nice collection of essays about nature, but in the last few chapters he had a lot to say about a land ethic and ecological relationships. Sara had helped by highlighting his most important quotes with a yellow marker. Her attention to details made me chuckle.

Like most professions, forestry was still evolving and building on its knowledge base. Foresters didn't have all the answers, but Leopold believed many answers could be found in a land ethic.

He wrote, "*Examine each question in terms of what is ethically and esthetically right, as well as what is economically expedient. A thing is right when it tends to preserve the integrity, stability, and beauty of the biotic community. It is wrong when it tends otherwise.*"

Another quote that impressed me was, "*A land ethic of course cannot prevent the alteration, management, and use of these resources, but it does affirm their right to continued existence, and at least in spots, their continued existence in a natural state. In short, a land ethic changes the role of Homo Sapiens from conqueror of the land-community to plain member and citizen of it.*"

It was obvious Leopold loved wilderness, but with this quote he legitimized the use and management of natural resources by people. Leopold said it was okay to cut timber, to hunt wildlife, and to graze cattle, as long as the ecological health of the land was protected in the process. I was beginning to realize that it was this premise that the profession of forestry needed to consider in all of its activities.

135

But I also knew that protecting the health of the land was not easy to put into practice. To do so meant identifying and understanding ecological relationships and formulating management strategies to protect them.

Under the pressures of economics and politics, foresters were often coerced to take too much of profit generating resources and to ignore or play down the damage done to the ecological health of a forest.

Leopold put it this way, "*If the land mechanism as a whole is good, then every part is good, whether we understand it or not. If the biota, in the course of eons, has built something we like but do not understand, then who but a fool would discard seemingly useless parts? To keep every cog and wheel is the first precaution of intelligent tinkering.*"

He also wrote, "*A system of conservation based solely on economic self-interest is hopelessly lopsided. It tends to ignore, and thus eventually to eliminate, many elements in the land community that lack commercial value but that are essential to its healthy functioning. It assumes, falsely, I think, that the economic parts of the biotic clock will function without the uneconomic parts.*"

Leopold impressed me, and I kept thinking about what he wrote. In college, none of my professors mentioned Leopold, and for most of my career I would have dismissed his views as nonsense. But now I was beginning to see things differently, and I started to wonder how his ideas might be put into practice.

By noon the snow was melting. While eating lunch I heard a snowplow on the road. I quickly waded through the snow and asked the driver to help me get my truck to the road.

By the end of March I had photographed several national parks, including the Grand Canyon. My money was holding up, but I didn't know if I would have enough to make it through spring. I started thinking about getting a job to make sure I would not run short of cash when I was in Yosemite.

One day a man in a cafe suggested I drive up a nearby canyon to photograph waterfalls on a small stream. Half way up the canyon I came to a small Forest Service campground and selected a site to camp for the night. There was very little traffic on the road, and I was the only person in the campground. I considered myself lucky to find such a peaceful spot.

During the night, I was awakened by a knock on my camper. Half asleep, I opened the door. Someone grabbed my arm and pushed me to the ground. I tried to get up, but a blow to the back of my head knocked me out. When I came to, I was being dragged by two men to a tree where they tied me up. They went into my camper and began to loot it.

"You bastards," I yelled.

One of the men came out of my camper and punched me in my stomach a couple of times. He persuaded me to keep my mouth shut.

In the darkness I couldn't see what they were stealing, but I knew they would take Sara's photography equipment. They made a couple of trips to their truck, and before they left one of them walked over to me and pulled my watch from my wrist. After they were gone, I wiggled and squirmed and was able to get free.

Inside my camper I found they had taken all of Sara's photography equipment, my fishing equipment, several pieces of clothing, and two hundred dollars from my wallet. Sara's wooden jewelry box, which contained a valuable locket she had inherited from her grandmother, was also gone. My traveler's checks were still hidden behind a panel in the wall of my camper, so I still had most of my money. I also had my jungle hammock, sleeping bag, and all of Sara's books.

My biggest problem was that Sara's photography equipment was gone, and it would cost a lot of money to replace. I drove to the nearest town in the morning to report the robbery to the authorities. They said they would get on the case, but I was convinced I would never see Sara's photography equipment again.

In a cafe, I bought a photography magazine and began to check out camera prices over a cup of coffee. If I bought used equipment, I could replace all of Sara's gear, except her 400mm lens, for a little less than two thousand dollars. That was more than I had in traveler's checks, and I still needed money for my living expenses.

I decided to drive to Flagstaff to look for work. I found a job stocking shelves in a grocery store making seven dollars an hour. With that salary, it would take a couple of months before I had enough money for photography equipment. I found another job pumping gas in the evenings and on weekends, and by the middle of June I had saved enough money to purchase what I needed.

A big mail order store in New York City shipped me the equipment. When it arrived, I shot a couple of rolls of film to test it out. The slides came back from the lab sharp and perfectly exposed. I was pleased with the gear and knew it was capable of producing excellent photographs.

I gave the people at the grocery store notice that I would be leaving in a week. On my last day of work a few of my co-workers took me to a restaurant to buy me a beer and wish me luck. When they left, I moved to the bar, ordered a hamburger and fries, and began to watch the evening news.

The anchor man started the broadcast by saying, "Last night we covered a story about Native Americans traveling down the Missouri River, the Ohio, and the upper Mississippi to meet at Cahokia Mounds State Historic Site in Illinois. Tonight, we have a terrible follow-up to that story.

"At two o'clock this afternoon a helicopter swooped out of the Missouri sky, and while it hovered above the waters of the Missouri River, a man opened fire with an assault rifle on a flotilla of twelve canoes. The chopper then disappeared, leaving behind five dead and seven wounded. We go now to Ralph Jacobs at the St. Louis Memorial Hospital who has more information on the people who were injured."

Jacobs appeared on the screen and said, "The Native Americans were not prepared for the attack that was made on them this afternoon. An attack that many are saying was made by an American hate group.

"Three of the hospitalized Native Americans are in critical condition. The other four have suffered wounds not considered to be life threatening. I have with me two women who have just come out of the hospital and have agreed to talk to us."

The camera zoomed back, and to my horror I saw Song Sparrow standing with another woman. The reporter said, "Can you tell us about the condition of the people you visited?"

In a shaky voice Song Sparrow said, "Both our husbands are in intensive care. My husband was shot in his chest and stomach. He is unconscious, and I could not speak with him. His prognosis is not good. We are outraged over this attack. This journey was a peaceful effort to show the American people a part of their history that took place hundreds of years ago and..."

Tears choked off the rest of Song Sparrow's sentence, and she turned away from the camera. The reporter said, "I'm sorry. This has been a terrible day for you and for all of America. Our hearts go out to all of you."

I did not stay to hear the rest of the report. Strong Bear was seriously wounded, and he was in the St. Louis Memorial Hospital. That was all I needed to know. I ran out of the restaurant and through the parking lot to my truck.

Inside my truck, I pulled a road map out of the glove compartment and studied it. The map showed that the quickest route to St. Louis was to go to Denver and then pick up I-70 going east. I drove out of the parking lot, stopped for gas, and headed north with evening shadows growing longer and darker.

CHAPTER 10

I couldn't believe Strong Bear had been shot. I owed him my life. I would do anything I could to help him. Anger began to mix with my feeling of shock. I wanted the people who were responsible for this atrocity brought to justice.

Darkness fell, and I kept driving with Strong Bear filling my mind and heart. I thought about him carrying me to the cave, about him applying the healing paste to the grizzly, and about what he had said to me about Native Americans and nature the last night I was in the cave.

Strong Bear couldn't die. Not like this. Not shot down by jerks on a mission of terror and hate.

It was close to four o'clock when I pulled into a rest area somewhere in Colorado and crawled into the back of my camper. I slept soundly until I was awakened by the blast of a trucker's horn. I got up, made coffee, and quickly ate a bowl of cold cereal. Then I was back on the road, stopping only for gas and coffee. By late afternoon I was in Denver and on I-70. My road map said it was 860 miles to St. Louis.

Again I drove into the early morning hours until I was completely exhausted. I pulled off the interstate and found a place to park where I would not be disturbed. Falling into a deep sleep, I slept for six hours and woke up when the camper got too hot for sleeping. I made a quick breakfast and ate standing in the shade of a cottonwood tree.

Back on the interstate I pushed Henry's truck to its limit as I began to fear I would arrive too late. Driving through the night, I arrived in St. Louis the next morning. It took time to find the hospital and more time to get through the line at the parking lot. With every delay, I grew more impatient and anxious.

In the hospital I asked a nurse where the intensive care unit was located. She said, "Go down this hall and take the elevator across from radiology to the third floor."

I hurried down the hallway and pushed the elevator up button. The elevator door opened. A bunch of people got off. I held the door open for a man pushing a wheelchair onto the elevator with an elderly woman sitting in a slumped position. The man asked me to press the second floor button for him. I punched the three button for myself. We stopped at the second floor, and the man guided the wheelchair into the hallway. The elevator door closed. I impatiently hit the three button again.

On the third floor I asked a nurse at intensive care if Strong Bear was there. She looked confused and said, "I don't think we have anyone here by that name."

"I was told Strong Bear was in intensive care."

"Let me check on him."

My frustration continued to build with every delay. I glanced down the hall and saw a Native American come out of a room and start to walk in the opposite direction. I dashed after him and got to him just before he entered the elevator.

"Excuse me. Maybe you can help me. I'm looking for Strong Bear."

The man's eyes narrowed with suspicion. "Who are you?"

No sooner had I said, "I'm a friend," when I realized I looked and sounded like a person who couldn't be trusted.

The man turned to get in the elevator without answering me. I followed him and said, "I don't blame you for being suspicious of white strangers after what happened. I'm a friend of Strong Bear and his wife, Song Sparrow. I was in Flagstaff when I saw Song Sparrow on TV. She said Strong Bear had been shot and that he was in this hospital. I drove night and day to get here."

The elevator door opened. I followed the man down the hall and said, "I have to know if Strong Bear is alive. Do you know anything about his condition? I owe him...he saved my life...just tell me if he's alive."

The man stopped and stared at me with piercing eyes. "Strong Bear died early this morning."

141

"Strong Bear is dead. He can't be dead. He was a powerful man."

"He was. But not powerful enough. Your people have a long history of killing Native Americans, and you're still doing it. I don't want to talk to you."

"I don't blame you for not trusting me. Before you go, can you tell me where I can find Song Sparrow? I have to see her. I have to tell her how sorry I am for what happened."

The man's eyes narrowed again. He turned to leave without answering me. I ran outside and tried to stop him on the sidewalk.

"Please tell me where I can find Song Sparrow. I'm not one of those jerks who fired on your people. I have to tell Song Sparrow how sorry I am. I have to help her in any way I can. Please believe me."

The man stopped again and said, "I'll talk to Song Sparrow and see if she knows you and is willing to talk to you. Do you have a car?"

"I have a truck."

"My truck is in the parking lot across the street. My name is John. You can follow me to where we are camped."

"Thank you. My name is Kirk Weber."

John got into an old pickup with a large green canoe tied to it. I got into my truck and followed him through the streets of St. Louis to an expressway. After a short drive, we came to the entrance to Babler State Park where two national guardsmen stood next to a Hummer. I could hear a helicopter circling overhead.

John showed one of the military men a piece of paper, and he motioned for us to drive in. I followed John past several campsites where Native Americans and military people were camped. He pulled into a campsite, and I parked next to him.

I got out of my truck and said, "What is the military doing here?"

"The president ordered them here for our protection after the attack. They're going to be with us until we finish our journey to Cahokia. Wait here while I talk to Song Sparrow."

John left me sitting in my truck and returned about a half hour later with a woman.

"Song Sparrow will talk with you. Come with us," he said.

We walked to the far end of the campground and entered the woods on a trail, which led to a small clearing. Song Sparrow was sitting on a bench under a large white oak. John motioned for me to approach her. Song Sparrow looked at me. She had been crying, and her eyes showed deep sorrow.

Kneeling in front of her I whispered, "I'm sorry."

Tears rushed into her eyes.

"I started to drive here as soon as I heard about the attack. I was in Flagstaff. I only wish I could have gotten here sooner. Did Strong Bear regain consciousness?"

Song Sparrow wiped her eyes and between powerful sobs said, "Only for a few minutes. He told me that he wanted me to continue our journey to Cahokia and to speak for him. I told him I would honor his wishes."

Song Sparrow turned away from me unable to say anything more. Her shoulders trembled with sobs. I reached out to touch her and cried with her. When there were no more tears left we sat on the bench and stared at each other. Words were not necessary to express what we felt.

The woman came to the bench. Song Sparrow stood up, and we walked back to the campground in silence. When we arrived at their campsite I asked Song Sparrow if I could participate in their journey to Cahokia.

"I'll talk to John and see if it is okay with him."

John and I went to our campsite. I climbed into my camper and went to sleep.

A knock on my door woke me up a few hours later. It was John. I asked him if he wanted something to eat, and he nodded. I opened two cans of soup and made a couple of sandwiches.

We sat at my small table and ate in silence. When we were finished eating I asked, "Were you in one of the canoes when your people were attacked?"

With bitterness in his voice John said, "Yes."

"Can you tell me what happened?"

John glanced down at the table and said, "We were about twenty miles west of here. Our spirits were high because our journey was almost finished. We had been on the river for three and a half weeks. We were used to people waving at us from shore and coming

143

alongside our canoes in their boats. A lot of people seemed happy that Native Americans were showing the country their heritage.

"The press flew over us several times in helicopters to take pictures of us. We didn't think about danger when the attack helicopter came alongside of us because we thought it was the press taking pictures again. The side door of their chopper opened, and we saw two men with assault weapons. They started shooting at us.

"People jumped into the water to escape the bullets. Some of the wounded and dead fell out of their canoes. Others fell into their boats from their seats. Bullets sank three canoes. We pulled our dead and wounded into the remaining canoes. Everyone was covered with blood. It was a massacre."

John stopped talking. I could tell he was seeing the slaughter in his mind. He grimaced and in barely a whisper said, "I will never forget the screams, the pain, and the hysteria."

At this point, John seemed overwhelmed with grief and anguish. I didn't want to press him for more information. But he wanted to finish his story.

"The gunmen stopped shooting at us, and the helicopter flew away. Several ambulances came for our wounded. The police questioned us into the night. The next day they had us looking at photos of helicopters. We identified the chopper as a Huey Helicopter."

"I'm sorry, John." I paused and added, "I want those bastards brought to justice as much as you do."

"We all want justice, but for Native Americans there has always been a shortage of it."

"I know, John. I know."

After John left, I crawled back into my sleeping bag. Thoughts of the massacre ran through my mind. I thought about Strong Bear and what I had seen him do in Yellowstone. He had saved my life, and now I would never be able to repay him.

I was awake when John knocked on my door the next morning. I invited him in and asked him if he wanted some breakfast.

"I don't have time. We're getting ready to go to the river to finish our journey. There's going to be a brief ceremony for the dead before they take the bodies to the reservations. I thought you might want to come."

144

"I would."

"Song Sparrow spoke to me, and we would be happy to have you travel with us in our canoe."

"Thank you."

The whole camp, including the military personnel, was ready to leave in an hour. John told me I could travel with him in his truck. A rainy mist sprayed from a steel grey sky as we left the campground.

On the way John explained, "There'll be a ceremony for the dead in a small park. When it's over we'll get in our canoes and finish our journey. Tomorrow there'll be a Powwow at Cahokia. The publicity from the shooting has brought many people into the area. The police are worried about a large crowd."

"Do you think there could be another incident?"

"There will be guardsmen and police everywhere. It would be stupid for someone to try something, but you never know. This is not what we wanted. We wanted a peaceful celebration of Native American history and culture, not a circus."

"How did the idea of a journey to Cahokia get started?"

"It was the idea of Chief Flowing Water of the Mesquaki Tribe in Iowa. He wanted Native Americans to do more to show our history to the people of the country.

"At first his idea was not well received, but he was persistent, and eventually he was able to persuade a small number of tribes to participate. Three committees were formed, one for the eastern people to float down the Ohio, one for the northern people to come down the upper Mississippi, and one for the western people to travel the Missouri."

"Why was Cahokia selected as a destination?"

"Cahokia was the largest Native American city on the Mississippi River and a major trade center between the eighth and thirteenth century. Many of the mounds that were a part of the ancient city are preserved in a state park, so it is a physical place that still exists. Chief Flowing Water wanted more tribes to participate, but Native Americans don't like spectacles. Many of our people are not represented."

"Why did you come?"

"Strong Bear talked me into it. I'm Blackfoot. We were once the enemies of the Crow, but Strong Bear said native people must forget the quarrels of the past. He said all Native Americans must come together in solidarity if we are to survive in the world of white people."

"Did you help with the organizing?"

"I did. But Strong Bear and Song Sparrow did most of the work for the western delegation."

Nearing the river we saw military personnel blocking off the road in front of the park. Helicopters circled in a sky that was beginning to clear. Several men were carrying caskets into the park from nearby hearses. There were several hundred Native Americans in the area, many of them in traditional dress. Members of the press were also present, but the police were keeping them at a distance.

People stood in silence by the coffins. The men looked angry. Most of the women were crying. Song Sparrow stood behind Strong Bear's casket with tears rolling down her face. I stood a distance behind her. I felt terrible. A man walked to the edge of the river, made a gesture toward the caskets and began to speak.

"These men and women came in peace, as we all did, to follow trade routes that were established on these rivers over a thousand years ago by our ancestors. We came to show the people of this country who we are and that we are part of a history that belongs to all Americans. Let us never forget the people who lie before us, and let us wish them a safe journey to the Spirit World."

It was a short ceremony. John had explained to me that the ceremony was to be generic, out of respect for the traditions of each tribe and clan. When the dead arrived at their reservations there would be a more elaborate ceremony. After the man finished speaking the coffins were loaded into the hearses, and a convoy of vehicles drove away.

Sunlight broke through the clouds as we began to unload the canoes and carry them to the river. There were nine canoes, all of them between twenty and twenty-four feet in length. In Maine, we would have called them big water canoes.

John sat in the stern of our canoe, and I sat in the bow. Song Sparrow sat behind me. In front of John sat Song Sparrow's friend, Cloud Watcher.

We pushed out from shore. The muddy current of the Missouri caught our canoe and pulled it downstream. We began to

146

paddle.   A military boat and two police boats were on the river waiting for us. Two helicopters hovered overhead.

Some of the Native American men wore loin cloths and some form of a feathered head dress. A few wore buckskin, even though the weather was hot. The rest, including Song Sparrow, John, and Cloud Watcher wore jeans and a T-shirt with Native American art work and the name of their tribe printed on the back of it.

We settled into a comfortable paddling stride as the weather got hotter and more humid. There was little conversation in our canoe. The tragedy of the shooting hung heavily upon us.

I glanced back at Song Sparrow and saw a far off look in her eyes. Strong Bear's death had devastated her. I shared the heartache I knew she was feeling.

We paddled all morning in silence, with houses or a farm breaking the cottonwood, willow, sycamore, and brush along the shore.   At noon we ate a few sandwiches, and then we went ashore to use the bathrooms in the campers that were following us on land.

It was after two o'clock when we entered the Mississippi River and found the northern flotilla of eleven canoes waiting for us with their escort of military and police boats. We greeted them as warmly as we could under the circumstances and continued our journey down the big river.

There was more shipping on the Mississippi, and we watched tugboats pushing large barges up and down the river. The wake from the barges rolled under our canoes, and we had to scramble to keep our boats from turning over in the large swells.

The muddy water of the Missouri hugged the western side of the Mississippi for a distance.   Gradually the two rivers mingled together, each giving up some of its color and identity to the other. Industrial buildings and other forms of development increased along the shoreline as we got closer to St. Louis. The sun began to set, and then we saw Gateway Arch silhouetted against the last light of the day.

We crossed the river and found the ten canoes that had floated down the Ohio River waiting for us. They had traveled upstream by truck and van from the confluence of the two rivers and had put their canoes into the water to give us an official welcome. The journey on the three rivers was over, except for the Powwow at Cahokia.

A large group of people was waiting for us in a park on the eastern shore. Many of them were Native Americans, but there were also white people, military personnel, police, and reporters with video cameras.

People started to cheer as we got closer. A group of Native Americans dressed in traditional dress began to dance to the beat of a drum. Several people helped us carry our canoes up the bank. John asked me to stay with our canoe while he went to look for his truck.

The western sky burned orange, and the river caught its fire. I glanced at Song Sparrow. She had a sad expression on her face, and I knew she was thinking of Strong Bear.

The ancient city of Cahokia was a few miles east of us, and the modern city of St. Louis was west of us. The closeness of these two cities gave me a strange feeling of contrast.

As I watched the sun setting behind Gateway Arch I realized that the Arch and the City of St. Louis represented the westward expansion of white people into land that had originally been occupied by Native Americans. Cahokia was a city long before St. Louis came into existence. I wondered how many Native Americans were thinking about the different roles these two cities had played in the lives of their ancestors?

John returned with two men, and with their help we carried our canoe to his truck and secured it to the boat racks. He said Song Sparrow and Cloud Watcher would travel in a van to the campground, and that I could go with him in his truck.

That night I slept soundly until John woke me early the next morning. He said we needed to leave soon. I ate a hurried breakfast and was ready to go when he knocked on my camper door a second time. Again, we traveled in his truck.

John said we would park his truck at Horseshoe Lake State Park and ride in a van that was transporting people to Cahokia State Park. On the way he explained that the delegation from the Ohio River was camped at Horseshoe Lake and that the people from the upper Mississippi were camped at Pere Marquette State Park. He also said most of the local campgrounds were filled with people who had traveled to Cahokia to attend the Powwow.

Our van driver dropped us off in front of the visitor center. John and I followed a group of people around the building to a large open area that had been the central plaza of the ancient city. At one end of the plaza there was a huge mound of earth with two terraces. A man in a uniform was giving an interpretive talk, and we joined the people listening to him.

"...and in the eleventh century the Mississippian people built a wooden wall 12 to 15 feet high around 300 acres of the central city.

"Behind me is Monks Mound, which is the largest mound in the park. Its base area covers fourteen acres and it is one hundred feet high. It was constructed with twenty-two million cubic feet of soil that was carried in baskets from nearby pits.

"On top of the mound there was a building, which may have been used for ceremonial purposes. It may also have been the residence of the leader at Cahokia. The Mississippians may have built as many as one hundred and twenty earthen mounds in this area, but only sixty-five of these mounds are preserved in the park."

When the interpreter finished his talk, he told us the main program would begin at ten o'clock at the speaker's platform behind him. He also informed us that after the speeches there would be Native American dancing, displays of art work, socializing, and tours of Cahokia Mounds Historic Site.

People were already gathering in front of the speaker's platform to hear the program. Hummers and police cars were parked near the podium. Helicopters circled the park.

We walked back to the front of the visitor center and found Song Sparrow and Cloud Watcher. Song Sparrow was studying her notes and making sure she was prepared to present Strong Bear's speech. She gave me a warm greeting. I was pleased to see a brighter look in her eyes.

By nine-thirty people were still arriving. I estimated there were three to four thousand spectators in the area. There seemed to be more white people than Native Americans, probably as a result of the national publicity the massacre had received. John and I moved to a place where we could see the speakers and watch the crowd.

At ten o'clock a man in a park uniform climbed the steps of the speaker's platform and tapped the microphone to make sure it was working. He welcomed everyone and expressed his condolences to the Native Americans for the terrible tragedy they had endured. When he finished with the appropriate formalities he introduced the governor of Illinois. A heavy bald-headed man came to the microphone and received a weak round of applause.

"It's a great honor for me to welcome all of you and to extend a special welcome to the Native Americans who participated in the journey to Cahokia Mounds State Historic Site. I also wish to express my sympathies to the families whose loved ones were killed a few days ago, and to assure them that the authorities are doing everything possible to bring these killers to justice.

"This park represents one of the most outstanding examples of Native American culture on this continent. You belong here. This is your day. I will now turn the program over to your moderator, Chief Flowing Water."

Loud clapping and cheering erupted from the Native Americans as Chief Flowing Water walked to the microphone dressed in beautiful traditional clothes. He said something in his native tongue and then started to speak in English.

"This is a very sad day for all Native Americans, and we must never forget the violent deaths of our people. We also must not forget why we wanted to be here.

"We have followed the ancient water routes of our ancestors who carried pottery and copper from the Great Lakes, obsidian from the Yellowstone country, mica and crystal from the Appalachians, gold and silver from Canada, and conch shells from the Gulf of Mexico. But unlike our ancestors, we do not carry trade goods. Instead, we carry a desire to unite our people and to show the world our history.

"The culture of the Mississippians lasted for more than five hundred years. During that period of time, great urban centers came into existence, among them: Ocmulgee, Etowah, and Spiro. But none of them was as great as Cahokia.

"Between fifteen and twenty thousand people lived in this city, and thousands more lived in outlying settlements and farms along the Mississippi and its tributaries. It was the great rivers that united our ancestors and enabled them to build great civilizations in America. Today we honor all Native Americans by being here."

Chief Flowing Water ended his talk and the Native American audience responded with a tremendous round of applause. The reaction from the white audience was more subdued. When the

150

clapping subsided he said, "Our first speaker was to be Strong Bear, but he was seriously wounded in the massacre and died a few days later. His wife Song Sparrow will speak in his place."

Resounding applause came from the Native American audience as Song Sparrow walked to the microphone. She looked a little nervous, but I knew she would do fine.

She cleared her throat and in a steady voice said, "Cahokia was here several hundred years before Columbus set foot on American soil. This ancient city and this park speak loudly of the fact that Columbus arrived on a continent that was already discovered and settled with numerous human beings.

"Historical writings tell us that Columbus, and the Spanish that followed him, brought disease that decimated much of the Native American population in America. Many of those that survived suffered from starvation, torture, war, and in many cases outright murder.

"*Five Hundred Nations* by Alvin Josephy states that Columbus came back on a second trip with seventeen ships and that he enslaved countless Native Americans to mine for gold. When they revolted he used his cavalry and dogs to attack and kill many of them. Others had their hands, ears, or noses cut off, were burned alive, or hanged."

Song Sparrow paused and a hush came over the crowd. Several video cameras continued to record her presentation for the evening news.

"Native Americans know we cannot change the atrocities that happened to our people years ago, but we can demand that American museums, history books, and holidays be truthful and factual.

"Today I am petitioning the federal government that the glory, honor, and celebration with parades and festivities not be given to Columbus, because he violated the ethics of social justice with so many horrors."

A huge round of applause erupted from the Native Americans. Many white people were not clapping, and others gave weak applause. Song Sparrow looked pleased, but the police and military people in front of the speaker's platform appeared uneasy. I quickly glanced through the crowd and saw happy expressions on the faces of Native Americans, but many whites looked confused and anxious.

My eyes fell on two men whose faces were filled with anger and hate. One man had long, stringy, blond hair, an unshaven face, and a conspicuous hook nose. The other man was heavier with balding brown hair and a kinky beard. They were men I would not easily forget. Song Sparrow continued with her speech, and I watched the two men.

"If America is to achieve true greatness and fairness it needs to put to rest the injustices of its past. Today we are proposing to the President and to the Congress of the United States that we stop celebrating Columbus Day. In its place we propose that Americans celebrate Discovery Day, a holiday that would give formal recognition to all the people who discovered America."

An enormous uproar of cheering and clapping exploded from the Native American audience and continued as Song Sparrow left the podium. Many white people were again not clapping. Others responded with polite applause.

The two men I had been watching began to walk toward the speaker's platform. John and I headed in the same direction.

Chief Flowing Water introduced the next speaker as we reached Song Sparrow, who was standing next to two state policemen. Song Sparrow said, "The police want me to leave. They don't want any more trouble."

I nodded in agreement.

"They want to give us an escort out of the park," said Song Sparrow, "and I want to get to Montana as soon as possible for Strong Bear's burial ritual."

I glanced at the crowd while John was talking to the troopers and saw the two men I had seen earlier. Both of them were glaring at us. I knew in my gut they wanted to make trouble for Song Sparrow.

I looked at Song Sparrow and said, "I'm going with you to Montana to make sure you get there safely."

I looked back at the place where the two men had been standing. They were gone, and their sudden disappearance made me more nervous.

"The police have two cars waiting for us," said John.

Song Sparrow and I got into the back seat of one police car, and John and Cloud Watcher got into the other one. We drove out of the park, stopped to pick up John's truck at Horseshoe Lake State

Park, and headed for our campground. On the way, I kept glancing through the rear window to see if a car was following us, but I didn't see any vehicles that looked suspicious.

It didn't take long for us to pack and to get on I-70 heading west. The state police left us at Columbia, and we continued to Kansas City without them. Song Sparrow rode with me in my truck, and Cloud Watcher traveled with John. We didn't say much until I asked, "Was it Strong Bear's idea to change Columbus Day to Discovery Day?"

"Yes. He did a lot of research on Columbus and felt the true story of Columbus needed to be told to Americans. He campaigned in Montana on this issue and got a fair amount of press coverage, as well as some hate mail. He thought it was a good subject to talk about at the Cahokia Powwow."

"Americans deserve the truth," I said. "Do you think the President and the Congress would change Columbus Day to Discovery Day?"

"It will take more than one speech to change entrenched customs and traditions."

At Kansas City we picked up I-29 and headed north. In Council Bluffs, Iowa we got two motel rooms and were on the road early the next day. Over supper we decided to travel through the night because Song Sparrow didn't want to miss Strong Bear's burial ritual.

The sun broke over the eastern horizon as we crossed the Montana border. Song Sparrow was sleeping, and the early morning light that fell on her face made her look even more beautiful. I could easily understand why Strong Bear had loved her so much.

We stopped for breakfast at a café, and Song Sparrow called the reservation. Returning to our table she said, "They were worried I might not arrive in time for Strong Bear's smudging ceremony. I told them to schedule the ceremony at two o'clock this afternoon and that we would drive directly to the cemetery."

We hurried through breakfast and lost no time getting back on the road. By noon we were on the reservation. As we neared the cemetery Song Sparrow became very quiet. I glanced at her and saw a tear on her cheek.

153

When Song Sparrow saw the crowd at the cemetery she burst into tears. Several people ran to her as she got out of my truck. Many of the women were crying. The air was hot and still.

Cloud Watcher explained to me that many of the traditional burial practices were no longer observed by the Crow, but most families still requested a medicine man to conduct a smudging ceremony. She also explained the purpose of the ceremony so I would understand its significance.

The hearse arrived. Strong Bear was removed from his coffin and placed on a platform. He was dressed in buckskin, and his appearance reminded me of the way he looked when I first saw him in the cave.

A smudge fire of bear root smoldered at the base of the platform. The ceremony began with a medicine man moving the smoke with an eagle feather over the body of Strong Bear. As the medicine man waved the eagle feather he prayed softly for Strong Bear's spirit to make his journey in a good way. Wisps of smoke passed over Strong Bear's body and drifted upward.

A sharp call of a bird pieced the hushed air. We all looked up at the cloudless sky. A golden eagle hung motionless in the air. The eagle gracefully moved his wings a couple of times and glided toward the crest of a distant hill.

When the eagle had disappeared over the horizon, Cloud Watcher whispered, "Strong Bear's spirit has passed to the other side. He is with his ancestors."

After the smudging ceremony, Strong Bear was returned to his coffin, its top was closed, and it was lowered into the ground.

People stayed a while longer, and then Song Sparrow left with her family. Cloud Watcher took John and me to a guest trailer. John planned to leave the next morning to travel to his reservation, and I planned to leave to go to Yosemite. I was hoping to see Song Sparrow before I left. She surprised me by calling after supper.

"Thank you for your help."

"I wish I could have done more. I owe Strong Bear everything. I wanted to talk to him again."

"He liked you, and he didn't like many white people."

"I know."

"I need time by myself. I'm going to the mountains tomorrow. I called to say good-by."

"Will you write and let me know how the investigation of Strong Bear's killers is going."

"I will. Good luck with your journey."

"Thank you. Will you continue with Strong Bear's work to change Columbus Day to Discovery Day?"

"I have to, for Strong Bear, and because it's the right thing to do."

"I hope it happens."

CHAPTER 11

I arrived in California in the middle of July and camped in a private campground near Yosemite National Park. The manager of the campground told me they had been getting a lot of rain and that the falls had plenty of water in them. I was happy to hear this, but I was not happy to hear that visitors had to see the valley on a bus.

I must have looked annoyed because the campground manager shrugged his shoulders and said, "Too many people. Too many cars. The Park Service has been talking for years about bussing people into the valley.

"So they decided to do it for one year to see how visitors would react to it. I don't think they will continue doing it after this year; a lot of people are opposed to it. Riding on a bus is better than fighting the traffic, but it's not as convenient as having your own car. You can't go where you want, when you want. But you can still see the valley, and it's worth seeing no matter how you travel through it."

The next day I parked my truck in a large parking lot and waited with a few hundred people to board the buses. When my bus was full, we headed into the valley.

We stopped at several overlooks, and I got off the bus with everyone and took some mediocre photographs. Eventually we stopped at the place where Ansel Adams had taken his photograph, Clearing Winter Storm.

My eyes went from El Capitan to Half Dome and then to Bridalveil Falls. According to my park brochure, El Capitan was a massive piece of granite that rose 3,604 feet above the valley floor. Half Dome was a huge, hulking shape of rock that looked like a monk's hooded head at the far end of the valley. Bridalveil Falls fell out of a crevice in a cliff on the right side of the valley. I wished Sara was with me to see it.

In Clearing Winter Storm, a ray of sun had spotlighted Bridalveil Falls, mist and clouds had shrouded part of El Capitan and other formations, and dramatic light had intensified the composition. In front of me the sky was hazy and the rock formations lacked detail and definition, but I wanted to take a photograph anyway.

People walked around me as I set up my tripod. A few of them spoke softly and tried to express their feelings about the beauty of the landscape in front of them.

Suddenly the tranquility was broken by a loud voice barking an order, "Move, you're in the way of my shot."

I turned around and saw an overweight man holding a video camera and swinging his arm for me to get out of his way. I stepped aside. He snapped instructions to his plump wife to stand where I had been and to smile and wave to the folks back home.

When I finally got a chance to take a picture, the bus driver was telling us to board the bus. I quickly framed a shot, tripped the shutter, and got on the bus.

There seemed to be more buses and people on the overlooks as the morning progressed. There was also more competition for the choice photo locations, so I decided to forget about photography and just enjoy the scenery.

The bus driver commiserated with me when I told him how disappointed I was with all the people. He said I would find less people in the back country and suggested I get a trail guide and a camping permit at the visitor center.

Back in the campground I ate supper and looked at a book of Ansel Adams's photographs. I turned in early and lay in my bunk wondering if Sara would have been disappointed with all the people.

The next day I followed the bus driver's advice and purchased a trail guide book at the visitor center. I also obtained two camping permits for back country sites. I didn't like all the regulations the Park Service required, but I knew management was necessary to protect the ecology and beauty of the park.

The ranger at the visitor center explained that all of the popular parks were experiencing crowding. I wondered if John Muir or Ansel Adams had any idea of the impact their writings and photographs would create years later.

On the trail to my first backcountry campsite, I stopped to sit on a rock by the edge of an alpine meadow. A couple of hikers said, "Hello," but most were content to enjoy the quiet of the outdoors without talking. All of us seemed to be searching for the solitude that our presence was destroying.

In the next few weeks I hiked into several beautiful places and shot photographs of rock formations, meadows, wild flowers, streams, and wildlife. I also made a few more bus trips into the valley, hoping to see dramatic light create an exceptional photograph, but it didn't happen. By the end of August I still had not taken the outstanding photographs I knew Sara would have wanted.

Feeling discouraged one night, I drove to a nearby town for a couple of beers. A Porsche pulled into a parking place on the other side of the street as I got out of my truck. Staring at the car, I realized I had forgotten about my Porsche, Susan, and my job in Denver. The thought entered my head that I was foolishly chasing fantasies of light when I could be making a lot of money in Denver.

I wondered what Susan would say if I called her? Would she be surprised that I was still alive? Would she offer me my old job? Would she say she still loved me? But how would I explain not coming back after the helicopter crash?

Maybe that wouldn't be a problem. Maybe I could just tell her some people rescued me who wanted to remain anonymous and that I needed time to get over Sara, to take her photographs, and to think about our relationship. But was I ready to make a commitment to Susan?

I thought of Sara, Henry, Song Sparrow, and Strong Bear. They were the people who wanted me to come to Yosemite. But for what purpose? It was still not clear to me what I would accomplish by taking photographs for Sara, or what I was supposed to achieve on my journey?

I saw a phone in front of a gift shop and headed for it. I found Susan's private number on her business card in my wallet and dialed it. While the phone was ringing, I turned around and saw a large print of Clearing Winter Storm in the gift shop window. The photograph brought a mental image of Sara's smiling face into my mind. Susan answered the phone and said, "Hello."

Holding the phone away from my ear, I began to feel uncertain about what I was doing.

"Hello," repeated Susan.

I was not ready to talk to Susan. Hanging the phone up, I stood there thinking about how close I had come to making a big mistake.

"Damn redskin!"

The words echoed out of a walkway that connected the sidewalk with a parking lot in back of the stores. Running into the alley, I saw two men holding a Native American while another man delivered blows to his face.

Without thinking, I ran toward the man who was swinging his fists and hit him with a body block, knocking him to the ground. We got up together, and I threw a solid punch to his face before he knew what was happening.

One of the other men hit me from behind, and the impact threw me into the wall of the nearby building. Instinctively my hands went up to cushion myself. I whirled around, saw a fist coming at me and ducked. The man yelled as his knuckles smashed into the wall. Before he could recover, I pounded him with a couple of strong hits to his protruding gut. He fell to the ground holding his stomach.

Looking around, I saw the Native American standing over the third man who was holding his bleeding nose. We grinned at each other and watched the three men stagger to their feet.

One of the men hollered, "Let's get out of here!"

They ran to the parking lot, and moments later we heard a squeal of rubber. Glancing at the Native American I said, "You have a couple of nasty cuts on your face, and you're going to have a black eye. I've got a first aid kit in my camper."

"Thanks for your help, but don't worry about me. I heal quickly."

"Some first aid can't hurt," I replied. "I'd also like to know why those jerks were beating you up."

On the way to my camper the man explained, "I applied for a job to drive a bus in the park on the same day one of those guys applied for the job. I got the job and he didn't, and he has been pissed off at me all summer because an Indian got the job he wanted."

I grinned and said, "We gave him and his buddies something else to be pissed off about. I'm Kirk Weber."

"My name's Dennis."

Inside my camper I handed Dennis my first aid kit, and he went into my bathroom. When he came out he had a band-aid on his forehead. I said, "Have a seat, I'm making coffee."

I poured coffee into two cups and said, "How do you like driving a bus in Yosemite?"

"I like it most of the time when people are friendly and nice, but sometimes you run into people who are loud and rude."

"I think I've met one of them with a video camera."

Dennis laughed and said, "Photographers can be a pain, but they just want a few pictures to show the relatives back home."

"I've been trying to take special photographs for my wife."

"Everyone wants to take photographs like Ansel Adams took. But good photographs don't happen very often. At times the valley can look spectacular, but you have to be in the right place at the right time."

"I'm learning that. But my time and money are running out."

"Ansel Adams was very patient."

"I'm trying to be patient."

"Why is it so important for you to get good photographs?"

"My wife always dreamed of coming to Yosemite to take special photographs. She liked Ansel Adams and loved his Clearing Winter Storm photograph. She died on the way to the hospital after an automobile accident. Before she died, she asked me to take photographs for her in Yosemite. I'm trying to do that, but nature isn't cooperating."

"I'm sorry about your wife and your photographs. They're forecasting thunder storms tomorrow afternoon. After a storm the light can be awesome. I know of an old Indian trail my grandfather told me about that's supposed to have a great view of the valley. I've never been up it, it's a little too steep for me, but I can show you where it is."

"Can you show me tomorrow?"

"Meet me in the parking lot at eight. The trail is along a narrow stretch of road, so you'll have to get out of the bus quickly. Plan to travel light because the trail is steep and difficult."

Early the next morning I put the essentials I would need into my backpack, which included: jungle hammock, sleeping bag, windbreaker, camera, two lenses, light tripod, film, rope, water, trail

160

food, and a plastic bag filled with Sara's ashes. I planned to stay one night and to return the next day.

At eight I boarded Dennis' bus and sat to the right of him. About thirty minutes later he stopped the bus and motioned for me to get off. I must have looked perplexed when he pointed to a rock wall because he said, "Over there. You'll find the trail. Good luck."

I jumped off the bus and watched Dennis drive away. Standing on the side of the road, I studied the rock wall and saw nothing that resembled a trail. Feeling confused and frustrated, I began to think my new friend had pulled a joke on me.

I looked harder and noticed a narrow ledge slanting up and across the vertical surface. Above this ledge, I saw a crevice that a climber could use to steady himself with his hands. The ledge angled up about fifty yards and disappeared around a hump in the rock. I had no idea what was beyond that bulge. I wished Dennis had given me more information, but he probably thought I would figure it out.

At first the climbing was easy because the granite wall arched away from my body, enabling me to lean on it. I made it around the protrusion I was worried about and found that the fissure I was holding onto abruptly disappeared. Glancing down I saw a wider sill for my feet, which would allow me to proceed without the aid of a handhold.

Progress was good until I came to a place where the foot trail was missing for six or seven feet. Looking up, I saw a rim of rock above me that I could hang from with my hands. The road was two or three hundred feet below me.

I took a deep breath, exhaled, and mumbled, "What am I doing here?"

I took my pack off and tied one end of my rope to it. The other end I tied to my belt. Without the pack on my back it would be easier to make the crossing.

Standing on a nearby rock, I gripped the upper lip and carefully inched my way across the scary obstacle, which only took a few seconds to navigate. When my feet touched the flat place on the other side, I stopped to catch my breath. I then pulled my pack with the rope to the side I was standing on. I thought about Sara and wondered what she would say if she saw what I was doing to get her photographs.

161

Progressing further, I eased around another swell in the wall and to my surprise the lower shelf broadened again. It was easy going for several hundred feet until I came to another section without a place for my feet.

There was nothing to hang onto above me, but eight or nine feet below me was a very wide ledge. There were crevices and protrusions in an inclined slope that I could use as a ladder to make a descent to the horizontal area.

The angle of the slope helped me to keep my balance and the climb was easier than I thought it would be. Reaching the lower shelf, I took a break for a drink of water, and continued on.

The next challenging section had a slant of slick granite angling down fifty or sixty feet from a wide ledge to a drop off below. My feet had a good place, but there were no handholds.

Then I noticed the curve in the wall would help me to keep my balance, but it was still a frightening place to cross. On the other side I came to a wide place that had a spectacular view of the valley. It also looked like a good spot to camp.

My knees felt wobbly as I leaned against the side of the mountain. I had found a perfect place to take photographs. All I needed was a little help from Mother Nature.

"Well," I muttered to myself. "This is where I spend the night."

I was glad I had brought my hammock because the ledge was covered with rocks and stones. Spending a night on the ground would have been a miserable ordeal. I pulled the hammock out of my pack and tied one end to a pine tree and the other end around a knob on the rock wall. Climbing into the hammock, a gentle breeze rocked me to sleep.

After a nap, I ate some trail food and decided to explore beyond my camp. Another slick of granite had to be traversed to get off my camping shelf. On the other side the trail widened, but the view disappeared. I came to a plateau and hiked for a distance until thunder cracked overhead.

Turning around, I headed back as fast as I could. As I neared my camp thunderheads choked off the sun and darkened the terrain. I was amazed how fast the storm had materialized. A bolt of lightning zigzagged across the menacing sky, followed by a loud clap of thunder.

162

More lightning and thunder erupted as I crossed the slick granite to get to my camp. I quickly climbed into my hammock as a wall of torrential rain moved across the valley and slammed into my precarious perch. To the left and right of my camp, rain water ran down smooth faces of rock making it hazardous to risk a crossing.

Lightning slashed blackness. A deafening boom of thunder stunned me. Wind hurled my hammock against the side of the mountain and blew the downpour through my mosquito netting. In seconds, I was soaked.

There was no place to go! No place to hide! The fury of rain, wind, lightning, and thunder was everywhere! I feared I would be blown off the ledge or hit by a bolt of lightning!

There was nothing I could do except ride the storm out in my hammock. I was at the total mercy of the elements.

I reached down, opened a zipper on my pack, and took out the plastic bag that contained Sara's ashes. Holding the bag close to my chest, I thought about Sara. I was here because of her. I knew she would appreciate what I was doing. I wondered if she was watching me from...from...wherever she was.

Thinking of Sara seemed to lessen my fear. I began to watch the storm in a more detached way. Streaks of white continued to flash over El Captain, Half Dome, and Bridalveil Falls, but I no longer felt threatened by them. Nature's power dominated the landscape, and it began to have a captivating effect on me.

I don't know how long I lay in my hammock watching the storm, but at some point I realized it was losing its intensity. Rain and wind began to taper off, bolts of lightning came less frequently, and the thunder sounded more subdued.

I eased out of my hammock, opened my pack, and was thankful to find its contents dry. I replaced my wet shirt with my windbreaker. I took my camera out of the pack and fumbled with the screw to attach it to my tripod.

A shaft of sunlight streamed through an opening in the clouds and gleamed on Bridalveil Falls. Mist rising up from the valley floor caught the sun's color and flamed orange. The upper sky remained black, contrasting dramatically with the luminous earth below.

Clouds hurried across the landscape, concealing ridges and formations and revealing others previously hidden. Water vapor filtered the sun's rays into spotlights of dramatic hues and intensities.

Portions of blackness would unexpectedly burst into light, only to be retrieved again by darkness. A rainbow rose up from the valley floor to the right of El Capitan and vanished into the ominous clouds above.

Half Dome remained hidden in the ebony that shrouded the far end of the valley. Black clouds scudded across the sun and darkened the entire landscape. I stopped shooting photographs and waited.

A lance of dazzling light penetrated the darkness and fell on Half Dome. The flush grew stronger and brighter. I quickly changed to my short telephoto lens and shot several photos before the cloak of blackness fell for the last time.

For fifteen or twenty minutes photographs had appeared and disappeared everywhere as sky and landscape exploded into a kaleidoscope of continuous beauty. I kept focusing, composing, and releasing the shutter of my camera in an attempt to capture as much as I could on film.

When I realized that nature's show had ended, I stood in a daze, not quite believing what I had seen. The landscape had been like a painting by one of the great nature artists that no one ever thought could be real. Only this painting kept changing every few seconds as light and darkness battled each other for earthly dominance.

I reached into my hammock for the plastic bag that contained Sara's ashes. Holding the bag over the edge of the cliff, I shook its contents into the air. The ashes drifted away from my hand. For a second or two they hung together directly in front of me, and I felt Sara's presence in a powerful way. Then a gust of wind scattered the ashes, and I did not feel Sara's presence any more.

"Good-by my love," I whispered.

Shivering, I started to prepare for the night. I pulled my sleeping bag out of my pack and put it inside my hammock. There was no change of clothes because I had traveled light. I took off my wet pants and underwear and climbed into my sleeping bag to get warm. Between handfuls of trail food and gulps of water I continued

164

to think about the spectacular event I had just witnessed. I knew I would never see nature's curtain rise on a performance like this again.

A full moon rose up from a cluster of clouds and filled the valley with silver light. I thought about light and why it was so important to John Muir. Beyond the fact that Muir had lost his eyesight temporarily from an accident, he had always maintained that light was nature's most compelling manifestation.

The valley was always there, but on rare occasions, nature brought light, darkness, clouds, color, and landscape together in awesome arrangements of beauty that made the valley only a stage for the main event.

Lying in my hammock, I realized that all of the events and circumstances of the last year had occurred in a mysterious timetable to bring me to this ledge on this special evening. I wondered if my journey was over.

I slept soundly and woke up at dawn feeling refreshed and energized. The valley looked different in morning light, and I took several more photographs. The climb to the road seemed less difficult than the day before, and I took time to linger where the trail was wide and safe.

That night in my camper, I climbed into my sleeping bag and picked up one of Sara's books that contained John Muir's writings on Yosemite.

I read, "After ten years of wandering and wondering in the heart of it, rejoicing in its glorious floods of light, the white beams of the morning streaming through the passes, the noonday radiance on the crystal rocks, the flush of the alpenglow, and the irised spray of countless waterfalls, it still seems above all others the Range of Light."

I turned the light off over my head and lay there in the darkness thinking about photography and nature. Looking through the viewfinder of my camera was helping me to see nature in a different way. Was it possible that I was learning to see nature the way Sara saw it?

Before I fell asleep, I decided it was time to head back to Maine.

CHAPTER 12

Wipers swept raindrops from my windshield as I looked at the familiar sights of Spruce Mills. It was the second week in September, and the maples were showing autumn color. Fall was a beautiful season in Maine, and I was looking forward to photographing its splendor. I was also looking forward to photographing the King's Pines.

I wanted to photograph the big trees because Sara had loved them and because I had reached a point in my life where I could appreciate their beauty. I also hoped to share something with Sara when I looked through the viewfinder of my camera, something I could not put into words.

Outside of town, I turned onto the gravel road that would take me to the King's Pines. Strands of grey mist hung on a hill to my right where the red color of maples contrasted with the dark green of conifers. I passed a marshy lake, a dilapidated barn, and then a blue house with people living in it. After the buildings the forest closed in on both sides of the road.

I glanced to my right, knowing the big pine trees would soon come into view. Just a few more feet, and I would see their huge trunks and enormous crowns. My front tires hit a rut. I looked at the road and then to the right again. My eyes focused on a clearing. A clearing filled with large stumps!

"Shit!" I yelled.

I hit the brake, jumped out of the truck, and slammed the door shut. I walked into the clearing in a daze, glaring in all directions, not wanting to believe what I was seeing. But my eyes were telling me the truth. It was my mind that could not accept the fact that all of the King's Pines had been cut!

Feelings of sadness, disappointment, frustration, and shock all ran together into a more powerful emotion that I cannot describe.

Falling to a slump on the ground, I felt thankful that Sara was not able to see the destruction of her cherished pine trees.

When Sara and I had left Maine all of the arrangements had been made for the Nature Bank to preserve the big trees. They had agreed to buy the land and to establish a park. I had every reason to believe the trees would be protected. What had happened to change the fate of the King's Pines? Who was responsible for their demise?

Thinking back, I sadly remembered my true feelings with the big pines. I had gone along with the Nature Bank idea to please Sara.

But at the time I had thought that old trees beyond their prime should be cut. I had firmly believed that the cutting of old growth forests was good forestry. In a way, I was also responsible for the cutting of the big trees, and this awareness made me feel terrible.

But why had I thought that it was okay to cut them? The answer had to be found in my education and the attitudes, philosophies, and economics that had governed the forestry profession in Maine for a long time.

In the sixties all my professors had said that the timber harvest was the most important objective in forestry. Most of my forestry education had dealt with managing timber for the sawmill and not much more.

I had learned that other forest values like recreation, water, and wildlife were acceptable, providing that timber came first, and it always did because timber paid the bills. That's what most foresters said. That's what most foresters practiced. That's what most bottom lines demanded.

In a daze, I walked back to my truck and drove to my house. It began to rain as I pulled into my driveway. I grabbed a small knapsack and went inside.

I went to Sara's desk, dug out several prints of the King's Pines, and spread them out on the floor. They were beautiful. As I looked at them I realized that Sara was an excellent photographer. I wished I had realized this when she was alive.

I made a cup of coffee and called Annie. She answered the phone.

"I'm back in Maine. I wanted to call to tell you that I'm fine."

"I haven't heard from you for a long time. I've been worried about you."

"Sorry, I got busy taking photographs in Yosemite."

"Did you get some good pictures?"

"I don't have them back from the lab, so I don't know for sure how good they are. I was able to photograph the valley after a big thunderstorm, and it was incredible. I'll send you some prints."

"I would love to see them. How does it feel to be back in the house?"

"It's strange being here without your mom."

"It'll take time to adjust."

"I suppose so."

"I have to go, dad. I'll call you in a couple of days."

"Okay."

After a simple supper of canned soup and a tuna fish sandwich, I looked through Sara's files of slides and prints. She had hundreds of excellent pictures, which I had never seen.

In addition to photographs of the King's Pines there were photographs of wild flowers, wildlife, autumn colors, lakes, streams, mountains, and other landscapes. I marveled at all of her photographs and loved and missed her more than ever.

I went to bed with an overwhelming feeling of Sara's presence in the house. In every room memories rose up filled with the life we had spent together.

Lying in bed, I found myself waiting for her to finish brushing her teeth in the bathroom. When moonlight paled the darkness of our bedroom, the sound of a distant coyote reminded me of the countless nights we had listened to their wild calls. Tossing and turning took the place of sleep. By dawn I knew I could not spend another night within those haunting walls.

I fell asleep sometime after first light. When I woke up bright sunlight was streaming through the bedroom window. I wanted to smell coffee and bacon and to hear Sara making breakfast in the kitchen. My heart ached with the memories that I sadly realized could never happen again. I got up, dressed, and fixed a meal of cold cereal, toast, and coffee.

After breakfast I called Mike's office. A secretary answered the phone and said, "North Country Woodlands, may I help you?"

"Is Mike there?"

"I'm sorry, Mike is no longer here."

"When did he go?"

"I'm sorry, I don't know. I'm new here. Would you like to speak to Bill Graham?"

"Who's he?"

"The forest manager."

"I'll talk to him."

A confident voice said, "May I help you?"

"Who authorized the cutting of the King's Pines?" I said with anger in my voice.

Graham replied with irritation in his voice. "Who is this?"

I forced myself to calm down before I answered, "My name is Kirk Weber. I used to work at North Country Woodlands. I'm sorry for coming on so strong, but I 'm upset over the cutting of the King's Pines. When I left a year ago the Nature Bank had agreed to buy the land and to preserve those big trees in a park."

In a condescending tone Graham said, "Mr. Weber, a lot has happened since you left. When was the last time you were in touch with Mike?"

"A little over a year ago, but..."

"Mike left six months ago when WestSun Resorts purchased North Country Woodlands."

I was stunned. Susan had purchased North Country Woodlands.

"Who authorized the cutting of those big pine trees?"

"I did."

"Why?"

"North Country Woodlands was operating in the red when I arrived. I was told to make a profit and to turn the company around. The King's Pines were a source of revenue for us."

"I don't understand. The Nature Bank was in the process of buying that property."

"They never came up with the money for the purchase."

I paused and said, "It's obvious a lot has happened since I left. When were the King's Pines cut?"

"In August."

I had been in Yosemite in August. I paused again. There was nothing more for me to say.

"Thank you for the information."

"I've seen your name on several reports in the office. You and Mike had some great ideas for getting North Country Woodlands back on its feet. We're building a resort on North Pond like you suggested, only much larger than what you had planned. If you have some time, I would like to talk to you about some of your suggestions. There might be a job for you here."

I had decided on my way back to Maine that I didn't want to see Susan again and that decision included not working for her. Apparently Graham didn't know about my job in Denver, and I wasn't going to tell him about it.

"Thank you Mr. Graham, but right now I have some other things I have to do."

"If you change your mind, get back to me."

"Thanks. Good-by."

Susan had purchased North Country Woodlands. It didn't surprise me. I had talked to her several times about the company. Buying North Country Woodlands was just another business deal for her and another opportunity to make money.

After I had taken Sara's photographs in Yosemite, I had felt a strong urge to return to Maine. But now that I was here, I wished I was somewhere else. The King's Pines were gone, and I was miserable in my house where all I thought about was Sara.

I decided to go to the woods to take photographs, which was a good excuse to get out of the house.

I packed a few things and tied my canoe to the top of Henry's camper. I still had several rolls of film, a camper to live in, and a few dollars for expenses. The woods would provide a refuge and give me time to think about what I would do next.

I had no idea where I would go when I pulled out of my driveway, but it didn't matter. I headed north and turned onto the first gravel road that went into the woods. When it started to get dark, I pulled to the side of the road, made supper, and went to sleep. Over breakfast the next morning, I decided to head to Baxter State Park where I knew I would find wild land.

Early one morning, I entered a bog covered with dew. The sphagnum moss trembled as I stepped into a wet quagmire of lacy growth.

Spider webs glistened with tiny pearls of moisture. Drops of water clung to blades of grass and needles of spruce and tamarack. In one spot, I found a dragonfly grounded by the weight of minute drops of water on its delicate wings. I discovered beauty in tiny drops of water.

Another morning I paddled my canoe through a chain of islands engulfed in mist. Loons hidden in the vapor called to each other. I had heard loons many times, but this was the first time I actually listened to the mystery of their echoing music. The rising sun shot pink into veils of rising clouds, and then an orb of orange burst above a shoreline of spruce, fir and pine.

Hillsides blazed red, orange, and yellow. Autumn light and color painted reflections on the glassy surfaces of lakes and ponds. Frost coated leaves sparkled with tiny daggers of ice in the early sunshine.

Along a stream I observed brook trout spawning. In the woods I found bucks preparing for the rutting season. On top of a mountain I saw the sky mirrored in a lake below. Nature surprised me over and over again with its beauty, a beauty that I had looked at all my life, but had never really seen.

I took photographs of everything. When I ran out of film I continued to explore and enjoy the wonders of nature. Most of the autumn leaves were on the ground when I headed home.

On the way back to Spruce Mills, I stopped to look at land that Two Brooks Timber had recently opened to no-fee hunting. I spent an afternoon scouting for deer and saw a nice four point buck. North Country Woodlands was charging a fee to hunt on their land, and I decided to hunt on Two Brooks Timber land instead.

Returning to my house, I felt better about being there even though everything in it reminded me of Sara. It helped to focus on the positive memories we had shared within its walls.

The slides I had taken in Yosemite had arrived from the lab, and they were beautiful. I had a couple made into large prints and framed. They looked great hanging on the wall in front of Sara's desk. I sent Annie a good assortment of smaller prints.

Winter was coming, and I needed to buy firewood and get my snow blower repaired. I was running out of money, and I began looking for work.

A friend asked me to give him a hand with his firewood business a couple of days a week. I also applied for a part time job at the local building supply store, and they hired me. The two jobs paid enough to cover my bills, and for the time being that was all I needed.

Deer season was quickly approaching, and I spent most of my free time scouting for deer on Two Brooks Timber lands. A week before opening day, I came upon a set of deer tracks going into a swamp that were the largest I had ever seen. I decided to focus my efforts on getting a shot at this huge buck.

I had to work at the building supply store on the opening day of deer season, but the next day I was in the woods at dawn. It had snowed a couple of inches during the night, making it easy to see where the deer had been traveling. Positioning myself in a clump of fir and spruce near the swamp, I waited for the big deer where I had seen his tracks.

A couple of hours went by with no sign of a deer. I decided to walk around the swamp with the hope of finding the big buck's tracks. Moving slowly, I stopped every few hundred feet to scan the terrain in front of me for the shape of a deer. Continuing with this move and stop method I circled the swamp. Daylight began to fade, and I went back to the place I had waited earlier. No deer appeared, and I returned to my camper as darkness descended.

Pale yellow was in the eastern sky when I entered the woods the next morning. Cold temperatures during the night gave a crunch to the snow, which could warn a deer of an approaching hunter.

This time I found the big buck's tracks leaving the swamp and heading up an adjacent mountain. At first the tracks followed an established deer trail, but then they veered into thick brush. I cut to the west and picked up the buck's tracks ascending the slope on another deer trail.

Nearing the summit, shots broke out above me. I stopped moving. Someone yelled, "I missed him!"

I froze with the thought of gunfire coming in my direction and began hurrying down the mountain to give the hunters shooting room. Suddenly, a huge buck erupted from the woods in front of me. Startled by my presence, he abruptly changed course and vanished into nearby trees. In two or three heartbeats the buck had appeared and disappeared. I had seen enough to know he was enormous.

During the next few weeks I returned to the big buck's territory several times, but I never saw him again. Several deer were carried out of the woods, and weekly kills decreased as the season progressed.

The last day of the season began with four or five inches of fresh snow on the ground. Heavy wet flakes spilled out of a slate colored sky as I entered the woods. I was sure the big buck had bedded down in the swamp during the storm. This was the one place I had not hunted. It was time to penetrate the buck's secret domain.

Walking was slow and difficult in the swamp's dense vegetation. Clumps of snow fell on me or hit the ground with a soft thump as I brushed against nearby trees. My body snapped a brittle branch on a dead spruce. The sound was horribly loud. A blue jay shrieked an alarm.

I stopped and studied the snow-covered trees ahead of me for the buck's presence. Slowly, I took a step, and then another, and another, until I reached a patch of compressed snow. There were fresh tracks without snow in them leaving the bed. A breaking branch had provided the warning the buck needed to escape.

I began to move faster, hoping I might catch a glimpse of him that would allow a shot. Traveling a short distance, a branch beneath the snow caught my boot and sent me tumbling. Picking myself up, I brushed snow from my clothes and pursued at a slower pace. The buck would be on his guard, but I hoped I might get close enough for a shot. Tomorrow the season would be closed.

The buck's tracks went through tangles of black spruce and balsam fir and into thickets of white cedar. I crawled under and over blow downs and pushed through thick growth. I came to a place where he had stopped to rest. Examining his tracks, I saw he had nervously shifted his weight from leg to leg as he waited to see if I was following him.

Snow had stopped falling by the time I pushed the buck out of the swamp and up the mountain. At mid-slope his tracks left the deer trail and went into the woods. I followed them in a circle to a clump of trees next to the trail I was just on. I had walked past him without

173

knowing he was hidden there, watching me. I laughed to myself and accepted the fact that he had fooled me.

For his next trick, he found several sets of deer tracks and added his own to the already trampled snow. I pursued, searching for the place where he would abandon the confusion of tracks and head in another direction.

"He knows how to bamboozle hunters," I said out loud to myself.

At three in the afternoon, the sun was breaking through the clouds. I stopped to munch a sandwich and to drink coffee from my thermos.

This was a deer that had outsmarted many hunters, and he was having no trouble misleading me. I wondered what my dad would have done in this situation. Then I remembered him saying, "Think like a deer, anticipate his next move, and beat him to it."

It seemed reasonable to think the buck would return to the swamp in the evening, and I had a good idea which trail he would use. I stuffed the remains of my lunch into my pack and hastened to the other side of the mountain.

The sun was crawling to the west and pulling pink clouds with it when I walked out on a rock overlooking a small ravine. Making myself comfortable, I watched the trail for a half hour or so with no activity. I began to think I had outfoxed myself, but I wasn't going to quit. If the buck showed I would have an easy shot at forty yards.

Shadow covered the trail below me. Sunlight dwindled. The air was getting colder. It looked like the big buck had given me the slip again, but I was determined to stay until the fading light gave way to darkness.

It reminded me of the grizzly bear in Yellowstone the way the buck became visible. In one second I saw nothing, and in my next breath he was standing in the open with his head held erect. His antlers had twelve points. He was the biggest whitetail deer I had ever seen.

I slid the safety off on my rifle. Instinctively, I drew a line from my eye through the cross hairs of my scope to a place just above his heart. I let air pass slowly out of my lungs to help steady my hands. My finger felt the slight resistance of the trigger, but it

174

wouldn't squeeze it. I lowered my rifle and tried to swallow the lump in my throat.

What was wrong with me? The biggest buck I had ever seen in my life was standing in front of me, and I couldn't shoot him.

I raised my rifle again and brought the cross hairs into a perfect alignment for a killing shot. Sweat beaded up on my forehead as my brain told my finger to pull the trigger. But it wouldn't do it.

Confused and bewildered by my inability to shoot the huge buck, I watched him strut down the trail with dignity and grace. A lump was still in my throat when I swallowed.

"Damn," I said out loud. "Why didn't I pull the trigger?"

All of a sudden I heard Song Sparrow's voice in my head, "Your wife was a wise woman. She knew your journey might help you to change how you view nature."

I knew my life had changed, but I had no idea it had changed so profoundly. I had hunted all my life and never had any problem killing a deer. I had always wished for a shot at a trophy buck. Today I had an opportunity to fulfill my dream, and I had passed it up.

Not being able to shoot the buck was a choice based on values that were beginning to solidify. It appeared I was destined to save something in nature, something rare and beautiful. Sara, Henry, and Strong Bear tried to save trees, a fish, and a bear from being destroyed by others. I had saved a trophy buck.

CHAPTER 13

Three weeks before Christmas I got a job working in a sports shop at a local mall. My hours were long, and I was tired when I finished at nine in the evening. I worked a couple of weeks after Christmas, and then they let me go. On my last day of employment they gave me a discount on a cross country ski outfit, and I went skiing and photographed the winter landscape.

In the evenings I began to catch up on my correspondence and reading. I wrote to Song Sparrow and asked her how the investigation of Strong Bear's murder was going. Early in the fall the Missouri River massacre was mentioned in a TV news story about mass killings in America but that was the only time I heard anything about it.

I started to read the *Journal of Forestry* and other professional magazines that had piled up over the years. I read articles on high-yield production forestry, which was the principal management method used to grow trees in northern Maine. A few articles were about sustainable forestry, a new management concept designed to protect and sustain the integrity of a forest ecosystem while managing and harvesting timber.

With sustainable forestry, cutting is limited to small segments of a forest or single slow-growing trees. This technique provides space, nutrients, and light for the remaining trees to grow faster, and leaves a variety of tree species, sizes and ages in a forest. Large trees are often left for reproduction, ecological, and aesthetic purposes. This practice maintains a diversity of ground plants to provide food and cover for wildlife. The outcome is an ongoing supply of timber, wildlife, water, recreation, aesthetic, and other forest values from a healthy forest ecosystem.

Harvesting in large clear cuts, artificially planting one or two tree species in uniform spaced patterns, creating an even-aged forest, spraying with herbicides to control unwanted tree and ground cover species, and other high-yield production practices were not acceptable in sustainable forestry. The high-yield method produced a large amount of wood from a monoculture crop of trees that generated large profits. Other forest values were not usually a major priority with this type of management.

Production forestry was about controlling nature. Sustainable forestry was about working with nature.

One cold night I was sitting at Sara's desk reading a forestry magazine when I paused for a moment to look at her pine photographs on the wall. Suddenly, I remembered my promise to place a sign in front of the King's Pines with the words, "Sara's Pines" on it. I had completely forgotten about my promise to Sara, but now there were no big pines and no reason to put up a sign.

The more I thought about my promise, the more frustrated and depressed I felt. I closed the magazine and stared at the cover photograph of a forester planting a pine tree. Again I glanced at the photos on the wall. An idea came to mind.

Smiling I said to myself, "I'll plant a new generation of white pines on that site, and I'll use Sara's pine photographs to make a memorial to her. Then I'll have something to put a sign in front of. The big pine trees will live in her photographs, and in three or four hundred years some of the planted seedlings might grow into a new forest of big white pines."

I was thrilled with my idea. Jumping up I yelled, "I'll do it!"

I went to the refrigerator to get a beer to celebrate. Returning to Sara's desk, I started to go through folders in a file cabinet that contained photo prints. As I went through a folder that was labeled "The King's Pines," I found a piece of paper with two Bible quotes typed on it.

"For by the greatness of the beauty, and of the creature, the Creator of them may be seen, so as to be known thereby." (Wisdom 13:5)

"For what can be known about God is evident to them, because God made it evident to them. Ever since the creation of the world, his invisible attributes of eternal power and divinity have been able to be understood and perceived in what he has made. As a result, they have no excuse; for although they knew God they did not accord him glory as God or give him thanks. Instead, they became vain in their reasoning, and their senseless minds were darkened." (Romans 1: 19-21)

Beneath the typed quotes were two sentences Sara had written in her own handwriting. *"Nature is a pathway to God. If we destroy nature we destroy the pathway."*

I read the Bible quotes and Sara's handwritten sentences a couple of times and thought about them. I did not believe in God and found it difficult to make a connection between God and nature. I put the piece of paper back in the folder and continued to look for more photographs.

When I had assembled a selection of what I considered to be Sara's best pine photos, I put them into a large envelope to keep for the project I was planning. Next, I made a list of the things I would need to build the memorial.

The following morning I called Bill Graham. He was pressed for time, so I came directly to the point. "How much do you want for the land that the King's Pines grew on?"

"I don't know. All land sales have to go through the Denver office."

"Even for twenty-seven acres?"

"Even for twenty-seven acres."

"There's nothing on that land of any value," I said. "The trees are gone, and it's in a poor location for development."

"I'm sorry. I'll have to get back to you."

"When will you have an answer?"

"I'll call you when I have a price."

I hung up and hit Sara's desk with my fist. Graham was making a big deal out of selling a few acres of worthless land. I also realized it was just a matter of time before Susan found out I was alive.

I called the bank next and spoke to a woman about a loan to cover the purchase of the land. She explained I would have to come in to fill out the necessary papers and that all loans had to be approved by the bank president.

My next call was to Professor Holt, a retired teacher who had taught my forest management class when I was in college. I knew he had worked on getting seeds from the King's Pines to grow seedlings. He explained that the seedling stock he had developed was still being used by the state of Maine but that it was in short supply. I told him I

178

would need enough seedlings to plant twenty-seven acres for a memorial I was building to my wife.

"Your wife had a lot of spunk," he replied. "She deserves to have a memorial. It was a crime to cut those trees. Let me make a few phone calls, and I'll get back to you. I still have a few connections with the state."

I thanked Professor Holt and hung up.

Next, I called the largest sawmill in northern Maine, knowing it was the only mill that had the equipment to handle the big trees.

"Hello Ross, this is Kirk Weber calling."

"I heard you had left the area."

"It's a long story, Ross. Someday I'll bore you with the details. But right now I'm interested in some big saw logs. Did you get the logs from the King's Pines?"

"I did. Most of the wood is gone, but there are several logs, including some of the biggest ones, lying in the yard. I saved them for a guy from Boston who wanted to put them in a lodge he was building on one of the big lakes. He went bankrupt, and I got stuck with the logs. I was getting ready to cut them up."

"Don't cut them. I'll be up there tomorrow and take a look at them. I might buy them just the way they are."

"What are you going to build, a mansion?"

"No, a memorial to my wife. See you tomorrow."

After lunch, I started to draw up preliminary plans for a pavilion that would use several big logs as vertical uprights to support a roof. I planned to have a display area for photographs and interpretive messages and a small deck that would provide a view of the seedlings.

The following morning, I drove to Ross's sawmill and picked out several big logs for the uprights and a few smaller ones for cross beams. I told him I would get him a list for additional materials as I worked out more details on the building plan. He said he would cut the smaller lumber from the big pine logs I didn't want, and he promised to deliver all of the wood by early spring.

Graham called at the end of the week and said, "The price for the land is twenty-one thousand."

"That's an outrageous price for that property, and you know it."

"I'm sorry, but that's our price."

"Okay, I'll pay it."

Graham was following orders. There was nothing to be gained by arguing with him.

I called the bank. A woman told me it would be better to take out another mortgage on my house, which I agreed to do. I also told her I would need a total of fifty thousand dollars to cover all of my expenses.

A week later, Dr. Holt called to tell me he had found enough seedlings to do the planting. He also said he would have the seedlings delivered at the end of April. Everything was coming together, and I was happy I had found a way to keep my promise to Sara. I decided to celebrate and went out to dinner at the Lake View Inn. Arriving home, I went to bed feeling good about the progress I was making.

A shelf had been blasted out of the side of the mountain for the road. On my side of the road there was a sudden drop off and a guard rail that gave a false sense of security. On the other side there was a wall of rock. I was in the downhill lane and was driving in second gear to keep my brakes from overheating.

Rounding a bend, I saw a small compact car in front of me. It was going slower than my car, and I had to use my brakes to keep a safe distance behind it. The driver turned to look at me. It was Song Sparrow! Why was Song Sparrow on this road? Where was she going? It seemed odd we should meet like this?

We came to a steep section of road. A large pickup truck pulled alongside my car and passed me. The driver in the truck was the man with a hooked nose that I had seen in the audience at Cahokia when Song Sparrow was speaking. A chill went through me.

The truck accelerated and pulled alongside of Song Sparrow. Tires squealed as Hooked Nose turned his truck into Song Sparrow's car. The two vehicles collided and rebounded. Song Sparrow struggled to keep her car from smashing into the guard rail.

The truck slammed into Song Sparrow's car again. This time she lost control and swerved into the guard rail. I speeded up, hoping to maneuver between the two vehicles and confront Hook Nose, but there was no room for my car.

180

We came to a section of road without a guard rail. Again, the truck crashed into Song Sparrow's car, and this time it pushed her car off the road. Song Sparrow screamed as her car plunged into space.

I woke with a jolt and sat up in bed. Cold sweat covered me. My heart was racing. It had been a dream, a terrible nightmare. Climbing out of bed, I went to the bathroom and threw water on my face. I kept telling myself it was just a dream. But it had seemed so real, so terrifying.

I had to call Song Sparrow. I had to hear her voice and know she was okay. I looked at my watch. It was five o'clock in the morning. I would have to wait to call her. There was no sense going back to bed. I wouldn't sleep. I went down stairs and made a pot of coffee.

At eight o'clock, I called information and asked for the phone number for the Crow Reservation. Dialing the number, I waited for someone to answer, but no one did. Then I realized there was a two hour time difference between Maine and Montana. I would have to wait until ten o'clock to call her.

I went upstairs, showered, and came back to the kitchen to eat a bowl of cereal. Time passed slowly. At ten o'clock I called the reservation, and a man gave me Song Sparrow's phone number. I quickly dialed the number and felt a sense of relief when I heard her voice.

"This is Kirk, are you all right?"

"Yes, why wouldn't I be all right?"

"I had a terrible dream about you last night."

"I'm fine."

"I'm glad to hear that."

"Tell me about your dream."

Song Sparrow caught me off guard. I didn't expect her to ask about my dream. But it was logical for her to do so. I didn't want to tell her about my dream because I was afraid it would upset her.

"It was a weird dream that's hard to explain, but it made me anxious about you trying to change Columbus Day. You're calling a lot of attention to yourself. Those killers are still out there, and I'm sure they are opposed to changing Columbus Day. Do you understand what I'm trying to say?"

181

"I do, and I appreciate your concern, but I have to keep working on Discovery Day because if I don't, it will never happen."

"I wish you would wait until they catch Strong Bear's killers."

"I can't do that. It could take months. It also may never happen. If I stop working on this I would lose the momentum we have gained."

Song Sparrow was a stubborn woman, just like Sara, and like Sara, it was impossible to change her view on something once she had made up her mind. There was nothing else I could say, so I changed the subject.

"Have you heard anything from the FBI?"

"No, they've been very closed mouth on whatever they're doing."

"I'm sorry to hear that. They should have come up with something by now."

"They should have. The only time I hear from them is when a new agent is assigned to the case."

"That's not good."

We talked a few minutes longer and then hung up. The expression on Hook Nose's face at Cahokia appeared in my mind. It was a look of hate, and it frightened me. I also knew in my gut that he was a man who would not hesitate to hurt Song Sparrow.

A week went by. I was still thinking about my dream and worrying about Song Sparrow. I was also busy looking for work, and midwinter in northern Maine was not a good time to find a job.

A friend called and suggested a job with a maple syrup operation in the southern part of the state. I called the owner of the sugar bush and learned he was recovering from a heart attack and needed someone to help him. The pay was not great, but he offered room and board. I needed the money so I took the job.

I started laying out plastic tubing for sap collection the last week in February. The sap began to flow the second week in March, and my work schedule went from eight hours to twelve hours a day until the season ended. The owner asked me to help with clean up and the bottling of syrup, so I stayed to the end of April.

I arrived home the last week in April and found a letter from Song Sparrow in my backlog of mail. I quickly opened the letter and read it.

Dear Kirk,

Thank you for calling and for being concerned about my safety. I hope you will understand that I have to continue with Strong Bear's work.

I received a letter from the FBI. The agent who wrote the letter stated that they have been investigating white supremacy groups in Missouri and nearby states, but so far they don't have any leads. I don't have much confidence in their investigation. They never seem to come up with much when a case involves Native Americans.

If anything develops, I will contact you.

Song Sparrow

I wrote back saying that I wished she would cut back on Strong Bear's work until his killers were brought to justice. I expressed my disappointment with the FBI investigation, and I also told her about my plans for Sara's pavilion.

Ross called two days later and said he would deliver my building materials the next day. I met him at the clearing and instructed him to drop the wood near the pavilion site. A couple of days later the seedlings arrived, and I stored them in a friend's barn. I was eager to begin work on Sara's memorial.

The weather turned cold and rainy, the kind of weather that would help to keep the seedlings in a dormant condition during planting. A drizzle was falling when I arrived with a load of trees in my truck. I placed a bunch of seedlings in a planting sack and went to work.

Normally, foresters plant trees in straight rows, eight feet apart. I decided to break up the spacing and straightness of the rows so the trees would look more natural when they developed into an old growth forest.

The planting procedure was simple. I opened a slot in the ground with a planting bar and positioned a seedling in the hole. Then, I shoved the bar into the ground in front of the tree and pushed soil with the flat blade around the seedling.

Late in the afternoon, a reporter from the local paper came to take a picture and to ask me a couple of questions. It was a short interview, and he said the article would be brief. I was not interested in publicity, but I gave him the information he wanted and thanked him for coming.

The next day was just as wet and miserable as the previous day. I was on the planting site at seven. I worked for about four hours in a light drizzle and then took a break for lunch.

I glanced at my truck and saw a woman walking across the clearing. It was Susan.

Under my breath I said, "Damn."

Susan stopped a few feet in front of me, and we stared at each other with neither one of us saying anything. I was too surprised to speak.

In a shaky voice Susan yelled, "I thought you were dead. Why didn't you come back to Denver? Why didn't you call me or write? You knew how I felt about you..."

Her words were cut off by a sob.

"I'm sorry," was the only thing I could think of to say.

Through tears she screamed, "I'm pissed off at you. It took me a long time to get over you. Then one of my staff tells me that you wanted to buy a piece of land."

Susan's words were cut off by more tears. I waited for her to stop crying. Eventually she got control of herself and said, "I don't understand why you didn't get in touch with me? I thought we had something special between us."

"It's hard to explain. I'm...well...I'm a different person. I just reached a point in my life where I had to put a lot of things behind me."

"You could have let me know you were alive," Susan bawled. "You could have written a letter or called."

"I'm sorry if I caused you pain and grief. The helicopter crash gave me an opportunity to start a new life without any ties to the past. I didn't think you would ever know I was alive."

Shaking with anger Susan yelled, "Bullshit! How did you survive in that blizzard? They looked several days for you. You were given up as dead and buried somewhere in the snow."

Trying to remain calm I said, "How I survived is not important. What is important is that I had experiences after the accident that changed my life."

"What are you talking about? What changed you? You had a terrific job. You were making great money. Most men would have killed for what you had. I don't understand. You're talking crazy."

"I guess by the world's standards I sound crazy. That's understandable. But I don't care what people think. Other things are more important to me now."

"What things are you talking about?"

"I'm more concerned about the environment."

Susan's eyes and mouth opened with shock and disbelief. "Don't bullshit me," she growled.

"I came very close to dying in that storm after the crash. Some people saved my life and helped me to recover. I've had a lot of time to think. For the first time in my life I see beauty in nature."

In a sarcastic voice Susan said, "Beauty in nature. Now I've heard everything. Are you sure you didn't hit your head in that crash?"

"After the crash going to Yosemite to take Sara's photographs became the most important thing in my life."

"You were planning to go to California when you got back from Montana," Susan snapped. "Your trip was settled. I told you to take as much time as you wanted. You're not making sense."

"It's not easy to put into words. But I'll try. I visited a lot of beautiful places, took a lot of pictures. Photography helped me to realize the natural world was a place with meaning and purpose and beauty. It helped me to appreciate nature."

Susan's face remained angry while I talked. "I read books written by Aldo Leopold, John Muir, and other famous naturalists. I began to see nature through their eyes and to understand what Sara was trying to tell me all the years we were married."

Susan's expression turned to confusion as I continued. "Much of what I experienced had more to do with feelings and emotions than with facts or logic. I know this sounds weird. But these experiences had an enormous impact on me."

I paused and added, "If I called you or came to Denver to tell you this, I knew you would react the way you're reacting now, so I thought it best not to get in touch with you."

I knew Susan had no idea what I was talking about from the way she looked at me. She said, "I think you're so full of shit that it's coming out of your ears."

"I know it sounds like bullshit. But that's what happened, and...and that's why I'm planting these trees."

"I don't understand."

"Do you remember me telling you in Denver that Sara and I stopped talking to each other because we had a big fight over the cutting of some large pine trees?"

In a calmer voice Susan said, "I remember you saying something about that."

"Well, I now agree with Sara's position on not cutting the big trees...the trees that were growing here. But as you can see they were cut."

Susan looked at the large stumps surrounding us. Then she looked at me with more confusion and uncertainty on her face.

"I want to bring those big trees back...for...for Sara. But it'll take three or four hundred years for these seedlings to reach the size of the trees that were here."

"Why were they cut?"

"Because the company that owns this property was only interested in their bottom line."

"What company?"

I hesitated and then said, "Your company."

"I don't know what you're talking about."

"You gave Graham orders to get North Country Woodlands out of the red. He did the rest and sent all those years of growth to the sawmill. Those trees were just another number in the profit column on a piece of paper. It happens all the time."

"You told me those big trees were going to be preserved by the Nature Bank. What happened?"

"The deal fell through."

"That's not my fault. I had no way of knowing those trees were not protected or that Graham had made a decision to cut them."

"Would you have saved them if you did know?"

Susan stared at me without answering my question. She glanced at the stumps and then at the freshly planted seedlings. Then she looked at me with indecision on her face.

I didn't want to fight with Susan. She and Graham had done what business people do. That was the problem. The human world didn't run on ecology. It ran on economics.

I left Susan glaring at me, walked to my truck, and poured myself a cup of coffee from my thermos. Susan walked to her rental car. In my rear view mirror, I saw her look in my direction for a second or two. Then she got into her car and drove away.

It was getting dark when I headed back to my truck to call it a day. Approaching the road I saw Susan's rental car pull up behind my truck. She got out of her car and stood by the road waiting for me. I stopped a short distance in front of her. There was determination on her face. She spoke first.

"I didn't fly all the way from Colorado to talk about trees."

"I have nothing more to say."

"I came to see you."

"It's over."

"Did you care for me when you were in Colorado?"

"I don't know."

We stared at each other unable to speak for several moments. Susan looked at the freshly planted seedlings. Then she looked at me and whispered, "I'm sorry about the trees."

"It's a little late."

"I know. But I didn't know they were going to be cut. I didn't know how important they were to you. I didn't know you were alive. When you run a business the size of my operation, there are a lot of details you have to put in the hands of your staff."

Susan was starting to sound emotional again, and I didn't want a repeat performance of our earlier conversation. I had told her in Denver the big pines were on North Country Woodlands land, but she may have forgotten. It didn't matter now. The trees were gone. Talking about them wouldn't bring them back.

Trying to be considerate I said, "Look, for what it's worth. I'm not mad at you. What happened, happened. I don't want to get into another big discussion. I'm sorry. You're sorry. Let's let it go at that. You go back to Colorado and live your life. I'll plant my trees and live my life, okay?"

I tried to sound firm, and I was hoping Susan would do exactly what I was suggesting. But she had a funny look on her face that made me realize it was not going to be that simple.

"That's not good enough," she said. "I want to help you plant your trees."

"No."

"You're not being reasonable. If I'm responsible for cutting those trees, than you have to let me do something to correct my mistake."

"I don't need help."

"It's only fair you let me undo some of the damage you say I caused."

Susan's argument made sense. I didn't have a good reason for not letting her help. With reluctance I said, "Okay. I start at seven. Dress for the weather. They're forecasting another rainy day."

Susan smiled. "I'll be here at seven."

The next day Susan was waiting for me dressed in a rain suit. The weather was raw and wet. I rationalized that if this was what she wanted, I was not going to discourage her or say any more about it.

I showed her the planting technique, told her I would work the planting bar and that she could place the seedlings into the holes I dug. I gave her a sack of trees to carry, and we worked in silence for most of the morning.

At lunch Susan asked me what I was building with the big logs stacked in the clearing. I told her about my plans to build a memorial to Sara and her pine trees.

"What will that accomplish?" she asked.

"When we thought the big trees would be preserved in a park I promised Sara I would put a sign out here with the words "Sara's Pines" on it. Now there are only stumps, and a sign would be a joke. But after I plant these seedlings and build a pavilion to house her photographs, there'll be something to put a sign in front of. It's the best I can do."

"Why were those big trees so important to your wife?"

"I've asked myself that question many times. I still wonder about the answer. She thought they had an ecological value and that they were beautiful. She also liked photographing them. But I think it really came down to the simple fact that she loved them."

188

"Did you feel that way about those trees?"

I stared at Susan for a moment or two and said, "I do now. Yosemite changed a lot of things."

Susan looked thoughtful, like she was searching for an appropriate response. Unable to find a suitable comment she said, "We should get back to work."

Planting trees is tedious work. Susan was getting tired, but she didn't complain. We were getting more accomplished with two of us working than I could do by myself. Time passed.

"I've never done anything like this," Susan said.

I laughed. "You mean manual labor?"

Susan smiled politely and said, "You don't have to be sarcastic. I mean doing something for the environment. I wished I had seen those big trees before they were cut. Would it be possible for me to see some of your wife's photographs?"

Susan's request caught me by surprise, but she sounded sincere. "I can show them to you. Follow me home when we're finished working."

We arrived at my house muddy, wet, and cold. I suggested to Susan that she take a shower and gave her some of Sara's clothes to wear. While she showered, I spread some of Sara's best pine photographs out on the kitchen table.

Waiting for Susan, I thought about her plush penthouse and wondered what she thought of my simple house. Then I thought that it didn't matter what she thought. Status and money were still influencing me. I told myself I had to stop putting so much value on what wealthy people thought.

Susan's voice interrupted my thoughts as she entered the kitchen. "Your shower was great, and your wife's clothes are a good fit."

Susan sat next to me and looked at Sara's photographs. She studied each picture carefully and looked at all of them before she said, "They're beautiful. Your wife had an extraordinary talent. They belong in a book."

"I wish I had seen her talent when she was alive. I looked at the pine photos she had on the wall many times, but I never saw what I see now."

"Why didn't you talk to Sara about her photography?"

"Because I thought photography was a waste of time and that anyone could point a camera at something and take a picture.   I learned on the way to California that taking good photographs was not as simple as I thought.   When I came home and looked at Sara's pictures, I realized what an exceptional photographer she was. Now all I have are her photographs."

"I'm sorry."

I swallowed and said, "You surprised me, Susan. Why did you come back to help me plant trees?"

Susan shrugged and said, "I don't know. You made me think. Maybe I don't have an answer."

Susan left a few minutes later. I showered, made supper, and went to bed early.

A cold drizzle was falling when I got out of my truck at the clearing the next day. I glanced at the newly planted seedlings and felt good about getting them into the ground.

Susan arrived while I was filling two planting bags with seedlings. She looked tired, but managed a cheerful, "Good morning."

I returned her greeting and added teasingly, "I thought you would be arriving much later."

"You said seven o'clock.   I expect my employees to be on time, and I practice what I preach."

Susan picked up a sack of seedlings and said, "I'm ready."

I was impressed with Susan's show of enthusiasm and thought for a second or two if I was being too hard on her. Then I told myself she wanted to help, and that I needed to respect her wishes.

We worked for a couple of hours without saying much except for occasional small talk.   At ten o'clock I poured two cups of coffee from my thermos, and we sat in my truck chilled to the bone with the heater blasting hot air into our faces.

Susan looked miserable. I tried to think of a way I might suggest that she could leave after lunch.   But I knew she would protest if I suggested anything that sounded like I was being easy on her. After our break we started planting by the road and worked to the far end of the clearing.

A loud, obnoxious laugh shattered the murmur of light rain. My head jerked around, and my eyes fell on Moose, the last person I wanted to see.

"They told me in town you were planting pine seedlings, but I didn't believe them," he bellowed.

Moose spit out a stream of tobacco juice and yelled, "Did they tell you how much fun I had cutting your big pine trees? You said I would never cut them. You were wrong about that."

I glanced at the expression of disbelief on Susan's face. Then I looked at Moose and said, "I'm sure you got a great deal of satisfaction from cutting them. There's no sense talking about trees that are gone. The best thing you can do is to leave."

Nothing would be accomplished by quarrelling with Moose. I knew he had cut the big trees, but it was of no consequence now. If Moose had not cut the trees someone else would have done the job. Loggers were not hard to find in northern Maine. I turned away from Moose and dug a hole with the planting bar.

Moose kept talking, and we kept working. He followed us yelling and screaming about the stupidity of our tree planting effort and that we would be dead before the seedlings grew into large trees. We said nothing. I could tell he didn't like being ignored.

In a fit of frustration and anger he screamed, "Don't you care that I cut those trees?"

I turned around, locked eyes with Moose and said, "You'll never understand why the King's Pines should not have been cut. It's a waste of time for me to explain anything to you."

Moose held his fist in front of my face and yelled, "I cut those trees, and I'm glad I did it."

"I don't have time to listen to you."

Moose screamed something at us that I couldn't understand and began stomping on our freshly planted seedlings like a little kid throwing a tantrum. We ignored him and went back to planting trees.

When I glanced at Moose again he was half way to the road. He trampled a few more seedlings just before he reached his truck. Tires spun in the gravel as his truck roared down the road.

Susan turned to me with a look of disgust and said, "What's his problem?"

"I don't know what makes him tick. He has been like that for as long as I've known him. The best thing we can do is forget him and get back to work."

At the end of the day I told Susan she was welcome to come back to my place for a shower and supper, and she accepted my invitation.

I made hamburgers while Susan showered. When she came downstairs, I asked her if she wanted a beer.

"A beer would be great."

After supper we sat in the living room, too tired to talk. I went upstairs to take a shower. When I came downstairs I found Susan asleep on my couch. Waking her I said, "I have a spare bedroom, maybe you should sleep here."

Susan yawned and said, "That might be a good idea. I don't think I can make it to my motel."

The next morning, I was up before Susan and started to make bacon and eggs. A short while later Susan came into the kitchen, smiled and said, "It's hard to sleep when you smell coffee and bacon."

I handed her a cup of coffee and said, "How do you like your eggs?"

"Over easy."

Susan sat at the kitchen table and picked up an old copy of the local newspaper that was on one of the chairs. I cracked four eggs on the side of the frying pan and watched them bubble in the hot grease. I thought about how strange it was for me to be fixing bacon and eggs for another woman, who had just spent the night in my house.

Susan interrupted my thoughts. "I see environmentalists are petitioning the governor to implement a zoning plan on Deer Head Lake. The idea of zoning land seems to be growing. By the way, we defeated the zoning plan in Colorado. But those damn environmentalists will be back in a couple of years, and we'll have to fight the same battle again."

"I'm sure they'll be back, only now I would support them," I said. "Zoning is needed in parts of Maine. Colorado also needs to regulate development."

With disbelief on her face and in a raised voice Susan said, "How can you say that after you worked so hard to defeat that issue?"

"That was back then. I told you, I've changed. There's nothing wrong with development, but it has to be controlled in scenic places and fragile ecosystems."

Susan jumped to her feet and threw the newspaper on the table. In a sharp voice she said, "And I suppose you think I should restore the water to the Autumn River."

"I do."

With eyes blazing she demanded, "Why?"

In a calm voice I said, "Because it destroyed a river that had a rare and unique ecology. The Autumn River was one of a kind. There are no other rivers like it, anywhere."

"What has happened to you? There are plenty of rivers in Montana, and they all have trout and water. How can you say there are no rivers like this one?"

"Because I know this river. I've spent time with it. I've listened to Henry, and I read his Journal about the river."

Susan raised her eyebrows and said, "Henry wrote a Journal about the Autumn River?"

"Yes, a beautiful Journal. You should read it."

"I'm not going to read Henry's bullshit."

"It's not bullshit. Henry spent years studying the Autumn River. He loved its ecology and beauty, and he knew many of its secrets."

Susan laughed. "I bet he did. He was a crazy old coot, and you've become just like him."

"I learned a lot from him."

"I can't believe what I'm hearing. You've become an environmental wacko."

I laughed. "I never thought I would be called an environmental wacko. Sara would have loved to hear that. But it didn't happen overnight. Learning about nature takes time and patience."

"I don't have time to sit by a river. I have a company to run."

"You might do a better job building your resorts if you had more respect for nature."

"You've never been to Autumn Springs Resort. You've never seen the beautiful lake we built for swimming, fishing, and boating."

"I don't want to fight with you. You built an artificial lake filled with hatchery trout. Nature created the Autumn River with an incredible ecology that supported wild trout. No reservoir can replace the Autumn River."

"Water is water and fish are fish."

"If you spent time with the Autumn River you would know that is not true."

"I don't have time for this and stop lecturing me."

"I'm sorry."

"Don't be sorry. I'm not going to tear down my resorts because you think they are unnatural or because fish came from a hatchery.

"A lot of people find happiness in my resorts. They provide jobs for local people and keep the economy going in many places. And I'm sick of listening to whining, mealy-mouthed environmentalists who do nothing in this country but block progress."

Susan stomped out of my kitchen. I followed her into my living room where she stopped and said, "You can have that land you are planting those pine trees on, but that's the only concession I'm going to make. You have changed, but I'm still the same person."

Susan left me staring at her and went upstairs. Glancing at my coffee table, I saw Henry's Journal sitting there. Susan's day pack was on the couch where she had left it the previous evening. Without thinking, I picked up Henry's Journal and slipped it into her pack.

Susan came downstairs carrying a small bag, picked up her pack, and stormed out of my house. I followed her.

Standing by her car she said, "I wasted my time coming back to see you."

Without looking at me again she got into her car and drove away.

CHAPTER 14

I was glad Susan was gone. But I wished I had not given her Henry's Journal. I had acted on impulse, hoping that she might read it and understand why the Autumn River was so special. After thinking about it, I concluded that the chances of this happening were slim. It was more likely she would laugh when she found his Journal and throw it away.

The thought of losing Henry's Journal depressed me because it was an incredible insight into the ecology and beauty of the Autumn River. Henry was alive on those pages, and I wanted to read his words again. But his Journal was gone, and I didn't want to ask Susan to send it back to me.

A week after Susan left, all of my seedlings were in the ground. I went out to inspect them on a warm, sunny day. They looked healthy, and I was confident some of them would grow into an old growth forest.

Arriving home, I found a letter in my mail box from Two Brooks Timber. It was a job offer to do timber inventory work. Being strapped for money, I took the job, knowing I would only have weekends to work on Sara's memorial.

The following Saturday a friend with a large log loader set three of the biggest logs in upright positions in the ground to construct the front of the pavilion. He did the same with three more big logs in the rear of the structure.

I took Monday off and watched cement being poured for a pad around the upright logs and for the deck in front of the building. With the help of a few friends we worked the cement into a level floor.

Two men helped me the following Sunday to trim the massive uprights so they could accommodate horizontal cross logs. We secured the cross logs to the uprights with steel plates, which were held in place with large lag bolts. This construction method stabilized the structure by connecting all of the uprights together with horizontal cross logs.

The roof trusses were delivered already assembled, and they went up quickly. We put a green aluminum roof on the building, and added a wooden floor to the building interior and deck.

My pavilion design called for two outside walls and one interior wall to hang photographs and interpretive signs on. The three wall plan made the building easily accessible to the public.

I added two benches to the deck to encourage people to sit and view the seedlings for a few minutes. My hope was that people might spend a little time thinking about the beauty of the King's Pines, and why they were cut.

My summer was taken up with continuous work, but I liked my timber inventory job, and I felt good about what I was doing for Sara. I finished the pavilion by staining it with a warm, earthy, brown color.

I decided to take a break the second week in September by spending a couple of days on a secluded pond near Baxter State Park.

The evening had the feel of fall in the air when I carried my canoe and camping equipment to the pond. There was no one at the pond, and I was happy to have some time by myself. I selected a campsite on a point of land covered with a mix of white and red pines. A gentle breeze mingled a reflection of crimson from maples and greens from spruce and balsam.

After supper, I sat in front of my tent sipping coffee. In front of me the setting sun glazed orange on the water as it sank into trees on the opposite shoreline. Behind me, the moon climbed above a jagged horizon of spruce and fir and threw a silver glitter onto the pond's surface. A loon called from the water in front of my camp. A barred owl hooted from the woods behind me.

In the stillness, I became aware of my heart beating and the invisible movement of the earth. With each passing second, the present retreated with the falling sun, and the future advanced with the rising moon. I was sitting on what seemed to be an edge of time.

I have no idea how long I sat there captivated by the events surrounding me. Eventually, I went to my tent and climbed into my sleeping bag. The voices of the loon and the owl continued to break

196

the hush and lulled me into a deep sleep. It was still dark when I woke up hours later and listened to coyotes howling in the distance.

Looking through the back window of my tent, I saw millions of stars through pine branches. Needles stirred in a slight breeze. A shooting star streaked across the sky. Somewhere a bird sang a few notes and then stopped.

I took my sleeping bag to my canoe and paddled to the center of the pond. Crawling into my bag, I lay in the bottom of my boat and gazed into the universe. Grey tentacles of mist ascended and swirled around me, creating an illusion of my canoe floating through space.

Light crept into darkness. Color came to sky and earth. Streaks of sunlight fell on my canoe. Vapor dissolved in warming air. Honking geese shattered silence. I took a deep breath and let it out slowly.

For a fraction of a second an invisible veil seemed to lift, and I thought I caught a glimpse of a greater beyond. In those few ticks of time, I realized the mystery of natural beauty was revealed in moments like this and that these experiences help to bond humans to the earth. A powerful sense of peace came over me, and, at the same time, I also felt exhilaration from being alive.

I paddled to my campsite and ate breakfast. The Navajo words that Strong Bear said to me came to mind. "When we lived in harmony with the land, we walked in beauty with the Creator."

My experience on the pond was a brief visit into nature's harmony and beauty. Strong Bear had talked about an entire way of life that had been compatible with nature. A way of life that he had admitted he did not fully understand. I wondered if this kind of human relationship with nature could ever exist again?

My thoughts turned to sustainable forestry. The more I thought about it, the more I realized that this type of management was more in harmony with the land than what I had practiced for most of my career. I began to wish that I could manage a forest with sustainable forestry methods, but this type of thinking was not popular in the culture of production forestry, which dominated northern Maine.

Evening drew near; I broke camp and carried my canoe and camping equipment to my truck. I did not want to leave, but I had to work the next day.

With the pavilion finished, my attention turned to selecting photographs to hang in the exhibit area and to writing the text for the interpretive signs. I went through Sara's photographs several times and, after much deliberation, I picked what I considered to be her best shots of the big pine trees.

I sent the negatives to a photo lab to have them made into large prints. I would then send them to another company to have them encased in fiber glass to protect them from the elements.

The writing of the interpretive messages was the job I was dreading the most because I was not a good writer. The interpretive messages had to be special because they were for Sara.

Two Brooks Timber laid me off at the end of September, and I began to spend most of my time working on the interpretive messages. I called Dr. Holt, and he recommended several articles and books on white pine. I made a trip to the University of Maine to use their forestry library and to talk to a few professors.

Back home, I spread my research materials out on Sara's desk. The information looked good, but now it had to be transformed into messages that would convey the love Sara had for the ecology and beauty of the King's Pines. I knew what I wanted, but I wasn't confident I could put it into words.

On a piece of paper I wrote down a list of topics that included: white pine ecology, forest beauty, starting a new forest, time and growth, age and size, forest health, timber management, and the value of old growth forests. Starting with the topic of white pine ecology, I tried to compose an opening sentence. It was terrible. I crumpled the paper and threw it on the floor. My next attempt also landed on the floor.

I went to the kitchen, ate lunch, and read over my notes on white pine ecology. Back at Sara's desk more pieces of paper hit the floor. I gave up on ecology and tried writing about time and growth. More failures hit the floor.

I pounded the desk with my fist and decided to go for a walk. Returning at supper time, I grabbed a beer from the refrigerator and turned on the TV to watch the news. I ate a frozen dinner, downed two more beers, and stopped worrying about writing interpretive messages.

The next morning was cold and sunny. I could not face another day struggling with a blank piece of paper. After breakfast I decided to visit Sara's memorial. As I neared the clearing I got a nervous feeling in my stomach.

The pine seedlings came into view. My eyes fell on a large rubber-tired skidder with its cable attached to the side cross log of Sara's pavilion. Moose sat in the big machine, and when he saw my truck he gunned the throttle. Chained tires spun in the soil, grabbed the earth, and the skidder lurched forward with a blast of acceleration. Wood cracked as the side cross log broke away from the uprights and the roof trusses that were attached to it.

I jumped out of my truck as Moose climbed out of his machine. He stood next to his skidder with a grin on his face, waiting for me to do something.

Foolishly, I charged head first into his big belly. Two enormous hands picked me up and threw me to the ground. I jumped up and dove at him again. Smashing blows to my face knocked me down with everything spinning.

When my vision came back into focus, I saw Moose winding the cable into his skidder. From the ground, I watched him drive over my seedlings. He headed to the far side of the clearing and cut across a steep bank that led to a woods road.

Suddenly, his front right tire struck a pine stump, and the right side of his skidder shot into the air. For a fraction of a second the machine hung balanced on its two left tires. Then it rolled onto its left side. A spine chilling scream cut the frosty air.

I got up still feeling dazed and ran toward the toppled machine. Without stopping, I climbed up on the side of the skidder and looked into the cab.

Blood flowed around a pine branch protruding from Moose's chest. His eyes were glazed in pain. He tried to say something. I pressed my ear to his mouth and heard him whisper, "Mil...Mildred....."

"Don't talk. I'll get help."

Dark blood trickled out of Moose's mouth and choked him as he made a last gasp for air. There was a spasm in one of his hands and that was his final movement.

The skidder had rolled onto a fallen white pine, a tree that Moose had not taken to the mill because it was filled with heart rot. Several dead branches on the lower tree had broken down to sharp spikes of various sizes. It was one of these spear-like branches that had pierced Moose's chest.

Moose had died a horrible death. Ironically, one of the King's Pines had killed him. I closed the lids of his eyes and put my coat over his face. A feeling of wooziness came over me. I eased myself to the ground and waited in a kneeling position for my head to clear.

When I felt better, I got to my feet, staggered to my truck, and drove to a house down the road. A grey haired woman answered my knock on the door.

"There's been an accident at the King's Pines. Moose Harkens is dead. May I use your phone to call the police?"

"Come in," the woman mumbled. "The phone is over there on the table. The number for the police is on that paper taped to the wall."

The phone rang twice and a female voice answered, "Spruce Mills Police."

"This is Kirk Weber. I want to report an accident."

The dispatcher listened to me explain the details of Moose's death. When I finished talking she told me to go back to the clearing and wait for a police car.

Back at the clearing, I looked at the damage to Sara's pavilion. It could be rebuilt, but it would take a lot of work.

Minutes later a police car with flashing lights appeared on the road. I greeted the officer and explained what had happened. We walked to the skidder.

Pointing to the pine tree on the ground I said, "His skidder rolled onto that tree. One of the branches punctured his chest and killed him. There was nothing I could do to help him."

The officer nodded and said, "It's obvious what happened. I'll take care of things here. I think its best you go home. If we need you we'll call."

The phone was ringing when I got home. It was a reporter from the local TV station. He said, "Would it be possible to meet you at your pavilion for an interview?"

"I would rather not be interviewed. You can get all the information you need from the police."

"You can give us more details than the police."

"I'm sure the police can provide you with the information you need."

Moose's accident was the lead story on the local news. I was glad I had turned down the request for an interview.

After the news Sara's friend Cynthia called and said, "I can't believe Moose would do such a terrible thing."

"I wish it had not happened. He died a horrible death."

"Why did he want to pull down your pavilion?"

"I don't know."

"He was a strange man," Cynthia said. "Can you rebuild the pavilion?"

"It can be repaired."

"Don't be discouraged. Sara would be happy with what you're doing out there."

"I hope so. I have to go."

The next day the police called and asked me why Moose would want to tear down my pavilion. I said, "I have no idea. He didn't like environmentalists, and he didn't like me or my wife. That's all I can tell you. Moose was a mystery to a lot of people."

"That's what I'm hearing from the people I've been talking to."

After lunch, I drove out to the clearing to make a list of the materials I would need to rebuild the pavilion. When I arrived I saw several vehicles parked along the road.

A log loader was lifting the side cross log into its original position over the two uprights. Several men stood in the clearing, and I recognized them as loggers who had harvested timber for North Country Woodlands at one time or another.

I asked one of the men, who I knew as Frank, why they were rebuilding my pavilion.

"Moose violated your rights to do what you want with your own property, and we didn't like that."

A man in a red coat added, "Moose gave loggers a bad name, and what he did to your pavilion has not helped our reputation."

"We decided we wanted to help you to compensate for what Moose did," said Frank. "We think we can finish the job before winter sets in."

"What do you want me to do?" I said.

"Nothing. We'll take of everything."

I stayed for a while and then drove home. For the rest of the day I worked on interpretive messages with no success.

The evening news carried the story of the loggers rebuilding Sara's pavilion. Frank was interviewed, and I was glad to see loggers getting positive publicity. After the news I received a few phone calls from people who were very supportive of the loggers and wanted to make sure I had seen them on TV.

Cynthia called the following night and said, "I wanted to call you last night, but I had to go to a meeting. I was surprised to see loggers repairing Sara's pavilion. It's not like them to work on something that's pro-environment. Why are they doing it?"

"They say Moose violated my property rights by pulling down Sara's pavilion. They also felt he generated bad publicity for loggers, and they wanted to do something positive to help their reputation."

"This whole thing has caused a lot of confusion among my students, and they have been asking a lot of questions I can't answer," said Cynthia.

"What kind of questions?"

"Many of them don't understand why you planted pine trees and built the pavilion. They also don't understand why Moose was trying to pull down your pavilion. They're even more confused that loggers are rebuilding it."

"I guess it's confusing to a lot of people."

"Would it be possible for you to talk to my students about all of this?"

"I'm not comfortable speaking to groups."

"I don't feel I have enough knowledge about forestry and environmental issues to give my students the answers they need to know," replied Cynthia.

"I don't like giving speeches."

"You don't have to give a speech. Just talk to them and answer their questions. Please think about doing this. I'll call you back in a couple of days."

I hung up and said, "Shit!"

The next couple of days I spent looking for a job and trying to think of an excuse to get out of Cynthia's request. When Saturday came and Cynthia had not called, I began to hope she had forgotten about her invitation.

Saturday was my grocery shopping day. I drove to the store in a drizzle, purchased the usual staples and pushed a shopping cart to my truck in a downpour. After loading my groceries into my camper, I sat for a few moments in my truck eating cookies and watching raindrops hit my windshield.

There was a knock on my side window. I turned and saw a small, frail woman glaring at me through the rain streaked glass. I rolled down the window and said, "May I help you?"

"My name is Mildred Harkens. If you have a few minutes, I would like to talk to you."

I stared at her not knowing what to say. Her face was etched from worry and stress, and her eyes were puffy and red from crying. She looked miserable, and I instantly felt sorry for her. I could not deny her a few minutes.

"All right, but please sit in my truck where it's dry."

Mildred walked around my truck, opened the passenger door and sat down. She looked like she was going to cry. I felt uncomfortable. She bit her lower lip for a second or two and then blurted out with, "I want to tell you that I'm very sorry for what my husband did to your wife's pavilion."

Mildred looked down and silence filled the air with tension.

"I'm sorry about Moose. He died a few minutes after I got to him. I wanted to get help, but there was no time."

"Moses brought this upon himself."

"I wish it had not happened," I said.

"So do I, but Moses couldn't leave you or those trees alone."

Searching for something neutral to say, I said, "You called him Moses. I thought his name was Moose."

"Everyone called him Moose because he was so big, but his real name was Moses."

Mildred coughed a couple of times and continued. "My husband felt the world closing in on him. He saw land taken out of timber production all across the country. He saw loggers going out of business. He thought he would be next. He blamed environmentalists and people like you and your wife."

Mildred frowned deeply. "He also blamed the timber companies for not paying a decent price for his wood. He owed the banks a lot of money on his logging equipment, and he worried about making the payments. It was always a struggle for him to make ends meet."

"Logging is not an easy way to make a living," I said.

Mildred controlled a sob and said, "I'm not excusing him for what he did. Moses always showed the world a tough guy outer shell, but it was just a shell that he used to protect his vulnerability. He worked in the woods all his life. He didn't know anything but logging. He felt threatened by you and your wife.

"Cutting those big pines was like a victory to him, but he was wrong about that. I tried to tell him, but he wouldn't listen. Those trees were beautiful. I'm sorry he caused so many problems."

"He was a difficult man to deal with," I said. "He also gave me a lot of lumps and bruises."

Mildred started to talk, but a sob choked her words. She took a tissue out of a pocket and wiped her tears away.

"I'm sorry for the way he treated you. I don't blame you for not liking him."

"He didn't have many friends," I said.

"He didn't. But he had another side. A side he only showed to me and the kids. In spite of what you may think, he was a good husband and a good father. He wanted our kids to go to college. He didn't want them working in the woods."

Mildred blew her nose in another tissue and continued to talk in a shaky voice. "Moses had a terrible temper. It was his downfall. He yelled, and he beat people up. But he was never mean to me or the kids. We knew him as a gentle man."

I paused and said, "I never saw that side of him."

"I know," said Mildred. "I'm not excusing the things he did. But he did have another side, a side the kids and I loved very much.

He was a complex and frustrated man, but I always found him to be loveable. I'll miss him."

"I'm sorry Mrs. Harkens." I paused and added, "I think your husband would want you to know that he said your name just before he died."

Mildred's eyes filled with tears again. In a soft voice she said, "Thank you Mr. Weber for telling me that."

I nodded. I saw understanding and sadness in Mildred's eyes. Moose could not have been an easy man to live with. Somehow she had remained a loving and caring person through it all, and I admired her for that.

Mildred got out of my truck and disappeared into the pouring rain. Moose had been lucky to have her as a wife. I hoped he had realized how special she was. I started my truck and drove home. For the rest of the day I worked on interpretive messages and thought about Mildred and Moose.

I ate supper watching the news. A commercial came on. I brought my supper dishes into the kitchen and poured myself another cup of coffee. Returning to the living room I was surprised to see Song Sparrow responding to a question in the closing segment of the program.

"Modern Americans need to realize there were millions of people living here when Columbus arrived. We need to celebrate a holiday that recognizes all of the contributions made by all of the human beings that were involved with the discovery and settlement of this continent. Discovery Day will allow us to do that."

My stomach tightened as I watched Song Sparrow talk. An image of the man with a hooked nose came into my mind with the same expression of hate on his face that he had at Cahokia. Images from my nightmare also came back. I feared for Song Sparrow's safety and worried about the danger she was putting herself in by being on the national news.

I picked up the phone and dialed Song Sparrow's number. There was a busy signal. I hung up, waited, called again, and got another busy signal. After several more busy signals, I gave up and decided to call her in the morning.

I tossed and turned for most of the night, thinking about the man with a hooked nose harming Song Sparrow. I was awake when daylight crept into my room. There was no sense trying to sleep anymore. I got up, made breakfast, and waited until ten o'clock to call Song Sparrow.

She answered the phone, and I was relieved to hear her say, "Hello."

"This is Kirk. I tried to call last night, but couldn't get through."

"A lot of people called last night."

"I saw you on TV, and I'm worried about you bringing so much attention to yourself. I wish you would stop talking about Discovery Day until they capture Strong Bear's killers."

"I have to continue with Strong Bear's work."

"Strong Bear wouldn't want you getting yourself killed."

"I have to do this for Strong Bear. I can't worry about what might or might not happen. It was suggested to me last night that I have one of our reservation police officers go with me when I give a talk, and I plan to do that. But I can't stop working on this when we're getting national exposure."

"I know you feel strongly about this, but would you please think about what I'm saying, and not make so many appearances until they catch Strong Bear's killers."

"I appreciate your concern, but I can't stop now."

I was getting nowhere with Song Sparrow. She changed the subject by asking me about Sara's pavilion. I told her about Moose pulling it down and that we were rebuilding it.

"I have to go," said Song Sparrow. "There's someone at the door. Thank you for calling. I appreciate your concern."

I hung up and went upstairs to take a shower. I kept thinking about Song Sparrow and the man with a hooked nose for the rest of the day.

Cynthia called in the evening and asked me if I was ready to talk to her class. I said, "I was hoping you had forgotten about me."

She chuckled and said, "I haven't."

"I guess I can do it, but let's keep it simple. I'll show a few of Sara's slides of the King's Pines, and then I'll explain why I planted the pine seedlings and built the pavilion. We can then open it up to questions, okay?"

"That sounds great. Can you come Friday at ten o'clock?"

206

"Yes, that's a good time."

All eyes were focused on me when I walked into Cynthia's classroom. Cynthia gave me an introduction, and I told the class I would start by showing a few slides. When Cynthia turned the lights back on I began my talk.

"I would like to tell you why I planted pine seedlings and built a pavilion where the King's Pines once grew. When it appeared that the big trees would be preserved in a park by the Nature Bank, I had promised my wife I would place a sign on the site with the words, "Sara's Pines," on it...because...because those big trees were very special to her. But after the trees were cut there was nothing to place a sign in front of.

"So I planted seedlings that have the potential to grow into a new generation of big pines. I also built a pavilion to have a place to hang some of my wife's photographs of the big trees. My idea was to have the King's Pines live in my wife's photographs and that all of this would provide a park-like area where I could put a sign. In this way I would be able to keep my promise to Sara."

As I talked, I noticed some of the students looked interested, but others had expressions of indifference and boredom on their faces. A few glared at me with anger and distrust. One student in a front seat looked at his watch and yawned.

"My wife saw beauty in those big trees. Moose Harkens saw only logs for the sawmill. For most of my forestry career, I thought the same way as Moose. Only recently have events in my life brought me to a realization that the ecology and beauty of big trees are also important. I now feel it was a terrible mistake to cut those trees. I think this is a good place for me to stop and give you a chance to ask questions."

A girl with red hair raised her hand and asked, "Why are loggers rebuilding your pavilion?"

"They feel Moose violated my rights to do what I want with my own property. They also didn't want the reputation of loggers to suffer because of what he did."

A male student with long shaggy hair in the back of the room spoke without raising his hand. "My dad said North Country Woodlands paid those loggers to rebuild your pavilion. He also said they are a bunch of wimps for selling out to environmentalists."

207

"I don't know anything about them being paid. I appreciate what they are doing."

The student snarled and said, "I don't think it's a good thing."

The female student sitting next to the student with shaggy hair said, "Environmentalists closed down a logging job and put my dad out of work. My dad says you can't eat scenery and that's what we'll be doing if environmentalists get their way."

When the girl finished speaking everyone was staring at her. There was a terrible quiet in the room.

"I'm sorry about your dad being out of work," I said.

Another student raised his hand and said, "I feel you have the right to build a pavilion on your own land and that North Country Woodlands also had the right to cut those trees because they owned the property when they did it."

The male student in the back of the room said, "What's so special about a bunch of big trees that are dying?"

"That's a difficult question to answer," I said. "As some of you may know, the timber dollar value of a forest is measured in the number of board feet of useable wood that is present in merchantable trees. The King's Pines had this dollar value. They also had beauty, which is difficult to express in dollars. Beauty does not have a simple unit of measurement like board feet, but it does have a value that comes from the human heart."

"Here comes the bullshit," replied the girl in the back of the room.

Her comment brought snickers from other students. I could feel my face redden. I had ventured onto thin ice, and I knew it.

"Those big trees represented the best white pine," I said, "that soil, water, and sunlight can produce in terms of genetics, size, vigor, and beauty. They stood the test of time by being what they were and for these reasons they should not have been cut."

The male student in the back of the room snapped back with, "When it's time to eat, you go look at some big trees, and I'll have a big mac with fries."

The class laughed.

"I have no problem with you eating a hamburger because there are plenty of cows in the United States. But if you wanted to eat the last grizzly bear in North America I would try to stop you from doing it. In a way, those big pines are like the last grizzly bear because there are no other trees like them."

"The last grizzly would die just like those old trees were dying," said the girl in the back of the room. "So what difference does it make if they died a little sooner and people get to use the wood instead of letting it rot on the ground?"

I had said the same thing to Sara a few years ago. Now, I was on the other side of the fence. I gave her Sara's answer. "When this country loses its wilderness, its wildlife, and its big trees, it will be poorer, and all the money in the world is not going to bring them back. People, like all of you, have to decide if you want a future without these things."

The two students in the back of the room were turning my talk into a circus, and there was nothing I could say to change their views.

I glanced at Cynthia. She stood up and was about to say something when a girl in the middle of the room spoke for the first time.

"I liked your wife's photos, Mr. Weber. If those big trees were still alive, I would paint a picture of them."

The male student in the back of the room started to mimic the girl's statement. Cynthia cut in and said, "Jed, I expect you to respect everyone's right to make a comment."

I looked at the girl and said, "I'll get you a color print of the big pines that you can use for a painting."

She smiled and said, "Thank you Mr. Weber."

In a high-pitched voice Jed said, "Thank you Mr. Weber."

"Jed!" yelled Cynthia. "Go to Mr. Clark's office and tell him you don't know how to behave in class."

Jed got up from his seat and stormed out of the classroom, letting the door slam behind him. Cynthia thanked me, and I received a weak round of applause. I walked into the hall with Cynthia and said, "That was a disaster. Why didn't you tell me about those two in the back of the room?"

"Jed and Lisa usually don't say much in class. I didn't think they would challenge you the way they did. I'm sorry."

"The economics of northern Maine is a powerful influence," I said. "Timber and pulp pay the bills for many families in this part of the country. I understand that. I should have expected to be challenged."

Cynthia nodded and said, "Both of their dads are loggers. Lisa has had a tough time of it with her dad being out of work. I think you did a terrific job. Thanks for coming."

After supper I sat in front of the TV and thought about Jed and Lisa. I couldn't blame them for being upset with me. I had thought like they did for most of my life. The ringing of the phone interrupted my thoughts.

A harsh voice growled into my ear. "This is George McCormick. I don't like you telling my son it's wrong to cut trees in northern Maine."

"I didn't say we shouldn't cut trees. I told them we should not have cut the King's Pines."

"Why not? There was a lot of good wood in those trees. Moose Harkens is being made out to be the bad guy. He shouldn't have pulled down your pavilion, but he did what any logger would have done with those trees."

"I'm sorry, I don't agree with you. There were no other trees in the northeast like those pines. They should not have been cut."

"The northeast is full of white pine, and I don't have a problem with cutting them. I know a few people on the school board, and I intend to speak to them about what is being taught in our high school."

"Fine. You have a right to..."

My sentence was cut off by McCormick hanging up on me. I called Cynthia and told her about my phone conversation.

"I'm not surprised some parents would react negatively," she said. "Spruce Mills is a small town, and there are not many opportunities for employment. I think what you said to my class was very educational."

"I hope this doesn't create problems for you with the school board."

"Education is hearing both sides of an issue. If I have to defend education to the school board, I'll do it. Don't worry about me; you said nothing that wasn't educational and proper."

"Northern Maine can be a hostile place when you're on the wrong side of the fence," I said. "I don't think you've heard the end of this."

"I can handle it. I think you did a great job. I also think you should do more public speaking."

I laughed. "I don't think so."

Cynthia hung up, and I went back to watching TV. There was a knock on my door. It was Susan.

CHAPTER 15

I stared at Susan, speechless. She looked at me, her eyes soft, and whispered, "May I come in?"

Recovering from my surprise I mumbled, "Yes…please come in. I never expected to see you again."

Susan stepped into my hallway, and we both stood there feeling awkward. She seemed unsure of herself. I was baffled by her sudden appearance. I made a clumsy motion toward my living room, and we went in and sat down.

Without saying a word Susan opened a brief case and handed me Henry's Journal. I took the Journal from her and set it on the coffee table. I was about to say something when Susan said, "Please, I'm the one who needs to talk."

She glanced at Henry's Journal and took a deep breath. Our eyes met in an uncomfortable way. "As you know, I have an interest in writing. I know good writing when I see it. Henry's Journal is a beautiful piece of literature. I want to have it published."

"I don't understand."

"I read Henry's Journal while sitting next to my goldfish pond. The more I read, the more I became unhappy with the artificial world that surrounds me.

"I sit by a goldfish pond made of plastic and phony rock. Even the lily pads are made of plastic. I see the mountains from a helicopter or from my penthouse. I swim in a pool on top of a high rise building. I have never been in a forest. I don't know or understand the natural world, and the more I read Henry's Journal, the more I wanted to experience nature the way he wrote about it."

Susan got more emotional as she talked, and I thought she was going to burst into tears. I wanted to say something, but I couldn't think of anything to say. She continued as a tear rolled down her cheek.

"I'm responsible for the cutting of the big pines your wife loved and for the destruction of the Autumn River that Henry loved, and that makes me feel terrible. I now realize that those trees and that river were beautiful."

I never expected Susan to make such a statement. I looked at her dumbfounded. She maintained eye contact with me, but appeared to be thinking about what she wanted to say next.

"My dad was a ruthless wheeler-dealer businessman. He taught me all the rules for making money. I was a good student. By the world's standards, I've been very successful, but it hasn't brought me happiness."

She took a handkerchief out of a pocket and wiped the tears on her face. With effort she said, "My father taught me to always be in control, and I've tried to control everything in my life, even the men. With business it worked, with men it was a disaster. I've had countless romances, all of them failures. I want to love a man and to have him love me for the person I am, and not for my money."

Realizing Susan was having difficulty putting into words what she wanted to say, I gave her my full attention, quietly waiting for her to continue.

"When true love didn't work, I started to buy the affections of men. I was doing it with you. But I didn't realize I was also buying my own distrust for the men that got close to me.

"At first I thought you were like all the rest, but you had a special love for your wife. I respected that love. I was also envious of it. You and your wife had the kind of love I have wanted all my life. When I found out you were still alive, and that you walked away without saying anything to me, I couldn't handle it."

"You don't have to tell me this. It's none of my business," I said.

"Please, I've done a lot of thinking about what I want to say to you. I'm sorry about the way I bungled our relationship. I'm also sorry about those big trees and the Autumn River."

Susan swallowed and continued. "One day, I was feeding my goldfish. They were making swirls in the pond, and I tried to imagine a big trout taking a fly from the surface of Looking Glass Pool. But thanks to me there is no Looking Glass Pool and no big trout in the Autumn River. I thought an artificial lake was more important to my guests than a natural river. I can't bring those trees back, but I can bring back the Autumn River. Looking Glass Pool is now full of water, and my staff is really pissed off at me."

With surprise I said, "The water is back in the riverbed?"

"The river is back, and I've given orders to have the divergent dam destroyed. I've also purchased Henry's land from his two daughters, and I'm donating all of the Autumn River land to the state of Montana to be made into a park. I want Henry's fly shop to be made into a visitor center. I also want to build a memorial to him with interpretive signs, like you're doing for your wife."

"What about the reservoir at Autumn Springs Resort?"

"I told my staff to build a golf course where the reservoir existed and to tell our guests to fish the Autumn River."

"I can't believe you've done this."

"It's done, and I feel good about it. Someday I hope to see a big trout in Looking Glass Pool, like Henry described in his Journal. I might even take up fly fishing, if I can find someone to teach me."

I laughed. "You mean me. I'm not much of a fly fisherman. Henry was the fly fisherman. But I'll give it a try. This calls for a celebration. Would you like a beer?"

Susan inhaled and let the air out slowly. "A beer would be great."

We drank beer, and Susan talked about her plans to change Henry's shop into a visitor center. When she paused to take a swallow of beer I said, "I have a question I want to ask you. Why did you pay loggers to rebuild Sara's pavilion?"

"After I read Henry's Journal, I felt bad about leaving Spruce Mills in a huff. I told Bill Graham to keep me informed on any new developments with your project. He called me when he heard Moose had pulled your pavilion down. I told him to hire some people to help you rebuild it and to keep it a secret."

"The loggers told me they were helping me because they were concerned about property rights and their reputation."

"They are. They also told Graham they didn't want money for what they were doing."

"That's hard to believe. A lot of those men need work to put food on the table."

"I don't understand why they wouldn't accept compensation for their work," replied Susan. "I told Graham to get publicity out on what they were doing and to have a special dinner for them. I also told him to give them hiring preference for future logging jobs at North Country Woodlands."

Susan looked thoughtful and asked, "What needs to be done to finish Sara's memorial?"

"The photographs are ready to be hung, but the interpretive messages are giving me problems."

"What kind of problems?"

"I'm having trouble writing them."

"Let me write them. It's the least I can do since I sneaked away from your tree planting job."

We both laughed.

"If you compile a fact sheet for your topics," said Susan, "I'll write the messages using your information."

We spent another half hour talking and then Susan left. I spent the next few days assembling fact sheets and mailed them to Susan.

Cynthia called Saturday morning and told me she had talked to the principal, and he would be supportive if the school board tried to give her a hard time.

Later that day a woman stopped me in the grocery store and told me her daughter liked my talk. I was happy to hear that one student had gotten something out of my visit.

On Sunday the men finished repairing my pavilion. I brought sandwiches and beer for them to show my appreciation. A long Indian summer had given them plenty of time to complete their work.

A week later Graham had his special dinner for the loggers, and I was invited. I thanked everyone again and told them I hoped to see them working at North Country Woodlands in the future.

Deer season was only a few weeks away, and I had to make up my mind if I would go hunting. As the season approached, I decided I needed meat for the winter and that I would hunt for a small buck for this purpose. My experience with the big buck had convinced me that I was no longer a trophy hunter, but hunting for winter meat was something that would help my budget and help to keep deer herds healthy in forests that had too many deer.

I also decided that I might try to photograph the big buck. In many ways this would be more challenging than hunting him with a rifle. A big advantage with using a camera is that I could photograph the big buck when deer hunting season was closed.

Bill Graham called a week after I bagged my deer and wanted to know if I was interested in a job at North Country Woodlands. It was obvious Susan had made a suggestion to him. I needed a job, and my feelings toward working for Susan had changed after her visit. I accepted the position.

Two weeks after Thanksgiving, Susan called and asked me if we could meet over dinner. Several heads turned when Susan and I walked into the Lake View Inn. I laughed to myself when I thought about the gossip my dinner engagement would generate in Spruce Mills.

After dinner, Susan opened her brief case and handed me the interpretive messages she had written. I read them while she waited patiently for me to finish.

"They're great," I said. "I'll use them just the way they are."

Susan smiled and looked pleased. "I'm glad you like them. I noticed you didn't have a message about Sara."

"I thought about it, but that's as far as I got."

"It seemed to me," said Susan, "that people will see your sign and wonder who Sara was. So, I wrote a message about Sara. You don't have to use it, if you don't like it."

Susan handed me another piece of paper, and I slowly read the message.

"Sara Weber loved the big white pines that grew here. She valued their ability to persist through the years, and she felt their destiny belonged to nature. She preserved their beauty in numerous photographs. She fought countless battles to keep them in existence. But people do not always agree about the fate of big trees. When these seedlings become an old growth forest they will offer a future generation the opportunity to make a better decision."

My eyes misted. I looked at Susan. She smiled.

"Sara would have liked this," I said.

"I'm glad you like it."

Susan handed me a brown envelope, and I put the messages into it. She took a sip of coffee and cleared her throat before saying,

216

"There's something else I want to discuss with you. Bill Graham wants to move on. I would like to offer you his position."

"That's quite an offer," I said after a pause. "I hope you don't mind if I take some time to think about it."

"Take all the time you need. It's a good job, pays well, and you know North Country Woodlands better than anyone."

"That's not the reason I'm hesitating to take the job. Three years ago I would have taken the position without a second thought. But as you know, I've changed my views on the environment."

Susan nodded.

"Forestry is changing. There's a new school of thought called sustainable forestry that places more emphasis on protecting the ecological health of a forest when we harvest timber. I would only consider the job if you were willing to make a commitment to sustainable forestry."

"That's okay."

"It's not that simple. Sustainable forestry is in its infancy. Many of its management techniques are still in their development stages, and they need to prove themselves over a period of time."

"I see. Will sustainable forestry impact profits?"

"It will not generate the big profits that huge clear cuts produce because this method leaves a larger percentage of a natural forest intact to protect its ecology. In time, profits get better as a sustainable forest gets more productive."

Susan stared at me. It was obvious she was not happy with my comments.

"I also want to take some time to think about this," said Susan.

"I'll let you know in a week if I want the position, and you can let me know if you still want to hire me. Fair enough?"

"Fair enough."

"Regardless of whether I take the job or not," I said, "I'm grateful that you wrote my interpretive messages."

Susan face broke into a grin. "I was happy to write them."

The next morning I called Dr. Holt. His wife answered the phone and said her husband would call back when he returned from his walk on the beach. An hour later the phone rang, and it was Dr. Holt.

"Hi Kirk. Sorry, I missed your call. Most mornings I walk by the ocean at Popham Beach. Today was cold and windy, the kind of weather I love. What can I do for you?"

"What do you know about sustainable forestry?"

"I read everything I can find on the subject. Why are you interested in sustainable forestry?"

"I may have a chance to manage North Country Woodlands, and sustainable forestry is the management method I want to practice on their lands."

"We need to talk. Can you come down here for a few days?"

"I can be there by early evening."

"Good. Plan on staying at my place."

I said good-by to Dr. Holt and packed a few things. Before leaving Spruce Mills, I stopped at the local library to make copies of my interpretive messages. I then mailed them to a company to have them made into fiberglass signs.

It was late when I arrived at Dr. Holt's house. We chatted for a while and then went to bed. The smell of coffee woke me early the next morning. Dr. Holt came upstairs to make sure I was awake and to tell me breakfast was ready. We ate and talked softly so we would not wake his wife.

The sun was beaming rays of light over the horizon when we began our walk on the beach. Waves crashed and gulls shrieked.

"I love the smell of salt air," said Dr. Holt. "I should have been a sea captain instead of a forester. The tide is coming in. High tide is the best time to be on the beach. I come here whenever I can to see the dawn of a new day.

"My wife thinks I'm crazier than hell. She came here only once to see the sunrise when we first moved to Bath. She always says she had two trips that morning. Her first trip and her last trip."

Dr. Holt chuckled at his wife's joke, and I laughed with him. Then his face grew serious. "Why do you want to manage a timber company with sustainable forestry?"

"To see if it is possible to preserve the ecological health of a forest while producing a reasonable harvest and profit."

"That sounds like a sensible goal. Sustainable forestry gives foresters another option for timber management. It's the middle ground between preservationists who want to lock everything up in

218

wilderness areas and companies that want to produce timber by planting one or two tree species and then cutting them all down in a big clear-cut."

"Will sustainable forestry work in northern Maine?"

"Environmentalists want retailers to sell green wood, and the timber companies are feeling economic pressure to be greener. There is talk of third party inspections in the field and certification to maintain ecological standards in a sustainable forest. This will help consumers feel confident they are buying green wood.

"Sustainable forestry is just a concept right now. If the big timber companies can make money with it they'll promote it and say they are putting these methods into practice. How loyal they will actually be to these practices in the field remains to be seen."

"You don't sound very encouraging."

"It's up to the timber companies to make it work with creditable management practices in the woods. If they use it as just a public relations and marketing program, and throw a bunch of colorful brochures and confusing terms at the public and continue with business as usual, they will get some mileage out of it and fool people, at least for a while, but the truth will emerge sooner or later. I have my doubts, but I would love to see sustainable forestry become a successful forestry option in northern Maine."

We watched a couple of gulls squabble over a dead fish, and then I said, "I was hoping you might suggest some sustainable forestry practices I could use at North Country Woodlands."

"I've made a couple of trips to the Menominee Indian Reservation in Wisconsin. They've been practicing sustainable forestry for one hundred and forty years and have one of the best examples of this type of management in the country. The corner stone of their success is an understanding that the whole resource is needed to protect any individual part."

"I'm not surprised that Native Americans would be practicing sustainable forestry."

"I think you could use some of their methods," said Dr. Holt.

I took a deep breath and let it out slowly. "If I take the job, would you be willing to help with putting together a specific management plan?"

Dr. Holt raised his eyebrows. "You mean come out of retirement and go back to work?"

"Just for a while."

A thoughtful expression appeared on Dr. Holt's face.

"You would be a big help."

"I'll give you a year. After that, you're on your own."

"Thanks Dr. Holt."

A week later, Susan called and asked me if I had made a decision about her job offer.

"I'll take the job providing you hire Dr. Holt as a consultant for a year and providing you send me a letter authorizing sustainable forestry as the sole forestry practice at North Country Woodlands. I also need to have you acknowledge in writing that you understand profits will be lower than what they were when North Country Woodlands was using high yield production methods."

"You don't want much?" Susan said with a hint of sarcasm. "Alright. I'll give you five years to see if you can produce a reasonable profit with your new forestry method."

The next day I walked into Bill Graham's office and began to go through his cutting records. Dr. Holt and his wife arrived a week later. After he was settled in an apartment we began a tour of three thousand acres of clear cuts that had taken place since I left the company.

Aspen, birch, and other pioneer hardwoods had started to grow on many of these harvested sites. The large timber companies used herbicides to kill these hardwoods so they could quickly plant a monoculture of spruce and fir. We planned to leave these hardwoods to foster the spruce-fir forest that would grow naturally in the shade under the hardwood canopy. Some of these harvested sites were treeless, and we would plant them with native spruce and fir.

Our spruce-fir forests would not be harvested in large clear cuts. Instead, we would cut these species in narrow strip cuts to lessen the impact on soil, ecology, wind damage, and esthetics. We also planned to let these small openings seed-in naturally from nearby standing trees.

By the end of March we had a good idea of the number and size of the sustainable harvest cuts we would do when the spring mud season ended.

When the first sunny day arrived in April, I took the day off to hang Sara's photographs and my interpretive messages in the pavilion. When everything was in place I put up the "Sara's Pines" sign I had made during the winter. It felt good to finish the memorial and to keep my promise to Sara.

Dr. Holt and his wife came to see the memorial the following Sunday, and I gave them a tour. When we finished, Mrs. Holt squeezed my hand and said, "Your wife would be pleased."

Cynthia called and said, "I visited Sara's memorial yesterday, and I know she would be happy with it. I plan to bring all my classes out there when the weather turns nice. Kids in northern Maine need to hear both sides of the debate on cutting old growth forests."

Susan came a week later, and she also wanted to visit Sara's memorial. Arriving at the site, we walked along the trail to the pavilion and entered the building. I glanced at the photographs and was shocked to see they had been defaced with a red crayon.

"Who would do this?" asked Susan.

"The only people I can think of are two students that were in the class I spoke to last fall."

"Are you going to press charges?"

"I don't have any proof it was them."

"What would motivate them to do this?" asked Susan.

"I think they feel threatened by this memorial and what I said about it in their class. The people in northern Maine don't have a lot of options for employment. Many of them depend on the cutting of trees and the timber and paper companies for their livelihood."

We drove to the grocery store and purchased cleaning materials. I felt better after we had removed the crayon from the photographs, but I knew Sara's memorial could easily be vandalized again.

When I arrived home, I called the police and told them what had happened. They said they would keep an eye on the pavilion, but I knew it was out of their way, and that they had more pressing things to be concerned about. I would be lucky if they patrolled the site once or twice a week.

Several weeks went by with nothing happening to Sara's photographs. Then in early July I found the photos vandalized again with red crayon. I cleaned them and left the pavilion feeling angry, frustrated, and hurt.

I called Cynthia. She told me Jed and Lisa had broken up after graduation, and Jed had taken off for California. She also said Lisa was spending the summer hanging around town.

"I wouldn't put it past Lisa to do something like this," said Cynthia, "but you'll have to catch her doing it."

I thanked Cynthia and hung up. It was clear I would have to stay overnight at Sara's memorial if I was to catch the person vandalizing Sara's photographs. I decided to sleep in the rafters of the pavilion.

The following day I quit work at supper time, purchased a pizza, and ate it on the way to "Sara's Pines." Using a ladder I had brought with me, I climbed up to the trusses and tied my jungle hammock between two of them.

I also tied a rope to another truss that would enable me to swing to the floor from my hammock. Climbing up to my hammock, I made a practice swing to make sure I would have no problems doing it in the dark.

When everything was set up, I parked my truck in the woods down the road and hiked back to the pavilion. Returning to my hammock, I pulled the ladder up and positioned it on the trusses where I could get it when I needed to climb down.

Lying in my hammock, I wondered what Sara would think of my guard duty. I chuckled to myself when I thought about her sleeping in the rafters with me.

I thought about Susan and how much she had changed. She had made it possible for me to practice sustainable forestry at North Country Woodlands, and I was grateful. I hoped we could produce a reasonable profit for her and protect forest ecology at the same time.

My thoughts turned to Lisa. I hoped she wasn't vandalizing Sara's photographs, but all my hunches pointed in her direction. I wondered what Sara would say to her. No doubt she would try to help her in some way.

When I finally fell asleep I slept soundly. Early sunlight woke me the next morning. No one had visited the pavilion during the night. I went to work and returned in the evening to continue my vigil. Again there were no visitors.

Three weeks passed, and I was getting a back ache from sleeping in my hammock. Lisa was winning the game, and I was going through a lot of effort to catch her. Only Dr. Holt knew I was sleeping in the pavilion, and he kept saying that persistence would pay off.

One night, I was awakened from a deep sleep by a noise below. Carefully, I reached for the rope and swooped down from the ceiling like a super hero. My sudden appearance scared my adversary, and he took off howling, yipping, and barking as he ran down the road.

By early August I was seriously thinking of giving up my nightly watch. Dr. Holt suggested I keep at it for another week, and I told him I would continue to the end of the month.

The next night, I was about to fall asleep when I heard a motorcycle on the road. Footsteps sounded on the wooden floor of the pavilion. A beam of light illuminated one of the photographs, and I saw someone standing below me. Red mist hissed out of a can and fell on one of Sara's photographs.

Quietly, I grabbed the rope and swung through the air. My feet hit the wood floor with a thud. The culprit jumped and screamed. I grabbed her, and she turned on me, kicking and scratching. She tried to pull away, and I wrestled her to the floor. She calmed down when I sat on her. It was Lisa.

"Let me go," she hollered.

"Why are you vandalizing my property?"

"I don't like your wife's photographs."

"Why?"

"Because you are hurting people who are trying to make a living."

"How can these photographs hurt people?"

"You and environmentalists are trying to shut down the woods to logging, and that puts my dad out of work."

"I'm not trying to shut the woods down. It's more complicated than that."

"I've heard your bullshit."

"I'm not going to let you up until you listen."

Lisa didn't respond.

"Preserving the King's Pines was not shutting the woods down."

"There was nothing wrong with cutting them, and there is nothing wrong with clear cutting," said Lisa.

"The timber companies don't want you to consider that the ecological health of a forest is important. So they use the excuse of losing jobs as a scare tactic to protect their excessive clear cutting practices."

"My dad lost his job when environmentalists took him to court."

"Your dad was clear cutting to the edge of a stream without leaving a buffer strip. He knew he was in violation of the law, and he did it anyway. I'm sorry he had to pay a fine and lost his job. I know you're upset. But you have to see beyond the timber companies telling you there will be no work if we regulate the size and spacing of clear cuts and use other harvesting methods."

"I see my dad out of work, that's what I see."

"I'm not moving until you let me finish."

When Lisa realized I was not going to let her up until I had my say she quieted down.

"Alright, talk," she muttered.

"The big clear cuts remove a lot of wood and produce a lot of jobs. But it also means you have to continue to do big clear cuts to keep all those people employed. What's going to happen when the demand for wood decreases, or they can't grow trees fast enough for all those people to keep their jobs?"

"I don't know."

"Suppose we produce a steady flow of timber from a healthy forest, what happens then?"

"I don't know."

"With a steady supply of timber we stabilize the local economy and improve job security. With good management we can also improve timber quality and create jobs in wood products manufacturing. There are other options, but the timber companies don't want to talk about them."

"Yeah, sure. You've got all the answers."

"Why don't you take a look at what we're trying to do at North Country Woodlands?"

"I don't care what you're doing."

"I'll make a deal with you. I'll hire you to help us. You can see firsthand what we're trying to do. But, you have to clean up the photograph you sprayed and promise me you'll stop vandalizing my property. If you do what I say, I won't press charges. The decision is yours."

"I don't know."

"I'm not fooling around. I'll press charges if you don't accept my offer."

"How long do I have to work for you?"

"To the end of October."

"You don't leave me much of a choice."

"You're catching on."

"Okay, okay, I'll work for you."

"Good! Be at the North Country Woodlands office at eight o'clock tomorrow."

"That's early."

"Be on time, and change your attitude before you come. I'm not playing games with you. We work a long day. You are either on the team or you'll be talking to the police."

Lisa looked at me bug eyed. She swallowed and in a softer voice said, "Let me up."

I helped her to her feet. She picked up her flashlight and shined it on the sprayed photograph.

"There're cleaning materials in my truck."

She looked at me and said, "Where's your truck?"

"I'll show you."

We returned with my truck, and Lisa cleaned the paint from the photograph. When she finished she said, "I'll be there at eight tomorrow."

Lisa was waiting at the North Country Woodlands office when I got there the next day. I explained the situation to Dr. Holt and then called Lisa into my office. I offered her a cup of coffee and told her to have a seat.

"Your assignment is to assist us. In the mornings you can gas the truck and help us to get organized and underway. In the field we'll instruct you as we go. In the office you can help with our forest inventory work."

"My dad needs a job, not me."

"Tell him to call me, and I'll find work for him."

Lisa looked surprised and said, "I'll tell him...thanks."

I took a sip of coffee and said, "There's one more thing I want you to do. Have you been to Baxter State Park?"

Lisa raised her eyebrows. "No. Why?"

"I want you to spend a week there as part of your work assignment."

"What for?"

"In a few weeks the autumn leaves will be at their peak of color. It would be a good time for you to spend a few days close to nature. I want you up every morning before sunrise and to be in a beautiful place to observe the dawn of a new day. Sit by a pond, or on a mountain top, or just sit in the woods, and see what's happening around you. When you come back, I want to hear about the places you saw and what you thought of them."

Lisa looked at me like I had lost my mind. "What's that supposed to accomplish?"

"Let's just say it's part of the job. I'm also paying you to do it."

"Okay, okay, whatever you say, you're the boss."

Lisa surprised me during the next few weeks. She was very bright, learned quickly, and never complained about the long days we worked. She also showed a great deal of interest in what we were trying to do. Dr. Holt took a liking to her, and they had long talks about a lot of things.

I had not heard from Song Sparrow in a long time. I decided to write to her and tell her about my new job, and that we were using some of the sustainable forestry practices that we had learned from the Menominee Indians. At the end of the letter I expressed my concern for her safety, even though I knew she would not stop her work on Discovery Day.

A week later, Susan came for an unexpected visit. We went for a walk down a woods road through a forest of sugar maple, yellow birch, and beech. I pointed to the trees and explained that sustainable forestry practices worked well with this forest type, and that we were working to expand our hardwood markets.

We came to a fallen tree and sat down. We didn't speak for a while.

In a whisper Susan said, "I want to talk about us. I still love you."

An awkward silence ensued as I stared at Susan, unable to speak. Finally, in a gentle voice I said, "I was hoping we could just be friends."

"I was hoping we might start to see each other again."

I picked up a fallen maple leaf and played with it nervously. Focusing on the leaf I said, "I don't want to hurt you. You've been a good friend, but I have to be honest with you, and with myself. I don't know if I could ever feel love for another woman after Sara."

"I don't need to hear that you love me," said Susan. "I just want to give us a chance and time to see what can develop. Is that too much to ask?"

"I don't want to give you false hope. I don't believe time will change the way I feel. You've been a wonderful friend. I would like to continue to have you as a friend. If we saw each other in a more serious way, things could get complicated."

I felt ill at ease. Susan looked crushed. She had tears in her eyes. I knew she was hurt and disappointed.

"I'm sorry," I said. "I don't want to hurt you. I know what it's like to lose a person you love. A lost love is always painful, no matter what the circumstances might be. I would not be helping you, or myself, if I tried to pretend that I felt different. Let me be your friend."

There was nothing more I could say. I took a deep breath, slowly exhaled and said, "Perhaps we should go."

"Yes, it's getting late."

I drove Susan to her motel. The silence that passed between us was agonizing for both of us. I had been honest with her. I could only hope she would understand.

Susan flew back to Colorado the next day. A week passed, and I received a card with a fall scene on it from Susan. On the inside she had written, "Friends." I felt a huge sense of relief.

The next day Lisa went to Baxter State Park. The forecast was for warm and sunny weather. I hoped she would have an opportunity to experience nature's beauty.

I went home in the evening, showered, and started to make supper. The phone rang. I picked it up and said, "Hello."

A female voice said, "May I speak to Kirk Weber."

"This is Kirk Weber."

"This is Cloud Watcher. Song Sparrow has disappeared."

CHAPTER 16

"Tell me what happened."

"Song Sparrow was on a TV talk show in Billings yesterday. She was driving back to the reservation in the evening when she disappeared. They found her car parked by the side of the road this morning. The authorities have been searching the surrounding country, but have found no sign of her."

"What was discussed on the talk show?"

"Changing Columbus Day to Discovery Day."

"I'll be there as soon as I can."

I quickly thought about flying to Montana, but decided I needed my truck to get around and camp. It took me an hour to pack. Then I got in my truck and started driving. When I was too tired to drive, I slept in my camper. Three days and one sleepless night later I arrived on the Crow Reservation and called Cloud Watcher. She told me to meet her at the guest trailer I had stayed in after Strong Bear's funeral.

Cloud Watcher greeted me at the door of the trailer and invited me in. Red, puffy eyes told me she had been crying.

"We have to believe Song Sparrow is still alive," I said, "and that we're going to find her. We're not giving up hope until we find out differently."

Cloud Watcher nodded and bit her lower lip. "How can I help?"

"Start from the beginning. Tell me everything you can think of."

Cloud Watcher took a deep breath and said, "A talk show host at the Billings TV station invited her to be on his show, and she accepted his invitation. Normally, one of our reservation police officers goes with her when she has an engagement like this, but his wife started to have labor pains at the last minute, so Song Sparrow went by herself."

"Are there other details that you can think of?"

Cloud Watcher looked thoughtful and said, "The police told us there were some bikers camped about a mile from where they found her car. They told the police they heard a helicopter fly over their camp a couple of hours after dark."

"That's interesting. A Huey Helicopter was used in the Missouri River massacre, and a Huey Helicopter was also used by the grizzly poachers in Yellowstone. I never made a connection between the two incidents until now.

"I think the white supremacy group that killed Strong Bear might be based here in Montana. It might also be the same group that abducted Song Sparrow. Were there any progress reports on Strong Bear's investigation?"

Cloud Watcher shook her head and said, "Nothing. Song Sparrow called the authorities every month, and they kept saying they were working on the case. That's all they would tell us."

"I'm going to start my own investigation," I said. "Can you have your reservation police provide me with a list of white supremacy groups, militia groups, hate groups, and religious cults that are in Montana? I'm especially interested in groups that own land in isolated areas, where they might have a large building to hide one or two helicopters."

"I can get that information for you. One of our officers has good contacts with the outside authorities."

Cloud Watcher went to the bathroom, and I thought about what she had told me. When she came back I said, "Can you also find out if there's a bar somewhere where these people hang out. I might pick up some information by spending a few nights in one of their hangouts."

"I can do that."

"I also want to see the place where they found Song Sparrow's car. Can you take me there tomorrow?"

"Yes."

Cloud Watcher looked at her watch. "It's getting late. I have to pick up some groceries. My daughter is taking care of Stray Wolf, Song Sparrow's adopted son."

"I didn't know Song Sparrow had an adopted son."

"Stray Wolf's parents were killed in an automobile accident, and Song Sparrow and Strong Bear adopted him just before they went to Cahokia."

"How old is he?"

"Four."

"I'd like to meet him."

We went to a reservation grocery store and then to Cloud Watcher's place. Stray Wolf was running around the small house and getting into trouble wherever he could find it. Cloud Watcher and her daughter were very patient with him, and I could tell they loved him very much. I stayed for a while and then drove back to the guest trailer.

The next day Cloud Watcher drove me to the place where Song Sparrow had been kidnapped. We looked around but found nothing that would help us.

Back on the reservation Cloud Watcher's daughter handed us a list the reservation police had dropped off. It had four names on it, but only one group owned land. I decided to check it out.

The place was near Helena, and when I drove past their entrance road I saw a large building that could be used to house a helicopter. Hiding my truck in some cottonwoods a short distance from the complex, I waited for darkness.

At two o'clock I made my way through the trees to the compound. There were no guards or dogs, and I was able to look around without a problem. The large building was a barn, and I found nothing suspicious in it or in any of the other buildings. I left feeling disappointed.

Cloud Watcher called the next day and said, "The Patriot House is a bar in Billings where a lot of white supremacy people hang out."

"I'll go there tonight."

Cloud Watcher gave me instructions on how to get to the bar, and I hung up. I took a shower, ate some food, and got some sleep. At three o'clock my alarm went off, and I headed for Billings.

The Patriot House was on the outskirts of the city. It was the only business establishment in an old two story brick building. The smell of stale beer penetrated my nostrils as I walked into the bar and sat next to a guy with a knife tattooed on top of his hand. A grimy, bald headed bartender took my order for a beer.

Setting my beer in front of me, the bartender belched, looked at the man sitting next to me and said, "I don't know when whites in this country are going to wake up and stop taking all of this shit."

The man next to me took a bite of beef jerky and replied, "Assholes are always telling us what to do. Now the damn Indians want us to get rid of Columbus Day."

The bartender shook his head in disgust and said, "If Indians don't like American history they should move to another country."

Looking at me the bartender said, "What do you think of all this?"

"The history books say the Indians were here before Columbus arrived."

The man next to me snapped, "That may be, but the history books also say we beat the shit out of them, and that proves that whites are the superior race."

The bar was beginning to fill up, and it looked like a rough crowd. I told myself I needed to watch what I said to these people because this would be a bad place to get into a fight. Someone sat down next to the man with the knife tattoo, and they started to talk. I was relieved his attention was diverted away from me.

My next conversation was with a guy who had too much to drink. He tried to persuade me to join the Citizen's Army of Montana. I pumped him for information about the size of their operation and what kind of military equipment they trained with. He said nothing about helicopters or big hardware.

An hour later, a big man with an unlit cigar in his mouth and a shaved head sat next to me. He looked at me as the bartender put a beer in front of him and said, "My name is Bill Custer, no relation to George Custer, but I wish there was. General Custer was a real warrior. Are you a vet?"

"I flew helicopters in Vietnam."

"We should never have lost that war," Bill said. "We should have bombed the piss out of those bastards."

"We tried."

Bill finished his beer and set the glass on the bar. "We didn't hit them hard enough. I was there for three tours of duty. That war

232

was the beginning of the deterioration of America. Now we fight half ass wars and let everyone walk over us."

Bill ordered another beer and a bag of beer nuts. He popped a couple of nuts into his mouth and took a gulp of beer.

I decided to change the subject and asked, "What do you think of the Indians saying we should get rid of Columbus Day?"

"I think its bullshit. Men like Columbus and Custer set things straight, so whites could live and prosper. We need to honor them for what they did for our country. That Indian woman on the talk shows likes to blame Columbus and the Spanish for killing those Indians back then. The truth is those Indians died from disease because they were weak."

Bill looked at me for a reaction. I stayed poker faced and said nothing. He kept talking.

"We're losing everything that Columbus, Custer, and other patriots did for us. Now we give jobs to blacks that have always belonged to whites. Environmentalists tell us that we can't keep the fish we catch, that we can't hunt in national parks, that we can't cut trees down, and that we can't use our God given resources.

"When whites finally wake up in this country, it's going to be too late. I give thanks every day for the brave warriors that are committed to God, guts, and guns to keep us free."

I left the bar at two o'clock and drove to a campground outside of town where I had made a reservation earlier in the day. It had been a long night, and I had heard nothing that would help me find Song Sparrow.

The next day, I hung around Billings and went back to the Patriot House in the evening. I was getting good at listening and asking the right questions to keep people talking. Again I left the bar without any leads.

I decided to spend one more night at the Patriot House before heading back to the reservation. I was recognizing some of the regulars that came to the bar and was hoping none of them would become suspicious of a stranger coming to their place three nights in a row.

It was Friday night and the bar was crowded. I spoke to several people but heard nothing that could help me. I looked at my watch as midnight approached and felt discouraged. Trying not to be obvious, I glanced at the men who were there, hoping to see something that might help me.

My eyes focused on the back of a man with long, stringy, blond hair standing by the pool table. I moved to my right a few steps to get a better look at his face. He turned. It was Hook Nose. With incredible luck I had found Hook Nose.

He was watching the pool game, and I decided to leave before he had a chance to look in my direction. Quietly I slipped behind two men engrossed in conversation and headed for the exit.

Cold air brushed my face in the parking lot. It felt good to be outside. Walking to my truck, I felt exhilaration over my good fortune. I had found Hook Nose. In my gut I knew he was somehow involved with Song Sparrow's abduction.

Sitting in my truck, I watched the two exits from the bar and tried to stay calm. An hour passed and my excitement turned into impatience. Trucks and cars came and went, but I didn't see Hook Nose get into any of them. I thought about going back into the bar to check on him, but decided it was better for me to stay where I was.

Another hour passed before Hook Nose came out of the bar and climbed into a large 4 x 4 truck covered with chrome and lights. I gave him time to pull down the street before I followed him with my headlights off.

He stopped for a traffic light. I waited for him to turn and put my lights on when I was sure he couldn't see my vehicle. He drove to I-90 and turned onto the ramp heading west. Ironically, he got off at a town called Columbus and headed south. I pursued a good distance behind him, hoping he wouldn't become alarmed with the headlights in his rearview mirror.

Several miles down the road he turned onto a gravel road. I slowly drove past the road and saw lights in the distance and a sign, which read, Alliance of the Select. I had the information I needed. Further down the highway, I found a place to pull into a wooded area to bed down for the night.

Sunlight filtering through the window of my camper woke me the next morning. After a quick breakfast, I drove down the highway and clocked two miles to the gravel road by the sign I had seen the night before. Turning around, I studied the tree-covered ridge on my right as I traveled back to where I had spent the night.

Reaching my campsite, I pulled my truck further into the trees, so it would be hidden from the highway. I made several sandwiches and loaded my backpack with my jungle hammock and things I would need to camp for a night. My plan was to hike along the ridge until I came to a place where I could observe the Alliance of the Select.

The ridge was covered with rocks and ponderosa pine, and it was slow picking my way over the rugged terrain. It took a while to find a vantage point that would allow me to view the compound. I tied my jungle hammock to two trees and settled down to wait and scan the buildings with my binoculars.

All of the structures appeared to be cheaply constructed of plywood or cinder block. There was no attempt to make them look attractive. One large building had a cross on it, probably some kind of a church. There were two large barns and cattle in the fields beyond them.

Late in the afternoon, men and a few women started to come out of buildings that looked like dormitories and work places. Most of them headed for a grey building near the church, which I assumed was a cafeteria.

Near sundown the temperature began to drop. Outside lights came on to illuminate the grounds and buildings below. People started to leave the cafeteria and to head for the dormitories. I ate two sandwiches, drank some water, and climbed into my sleeping bag to stay warm. I was too keyed up to fall into a sound sleep, but I dozed for a few hours.

By three o'clock most of the lights were off in the dormitories, but the outside lights were still on. It would be difficult to get near the buildings if the area was patrolled, but I had to see the complex, and I couldn't wait any longer to do it.

A bright moon helped me to find my way off the ridge. It took almost an hour to reach the two barns. I was hoping to find a helicopter in one of them. I found only farm equipment and hay. There was a ditch by one of the barns, and I used it to crawl to the back of the church.

I entered the church through a rear door and walked down the aisle to the front of the building. Looking through the window in the front door, I saw a guard with an assault rifle coming out of another building.

My heart pounded in my chest as I watched him walk to the front of the church where he stopped and lit a cigarette. He was joined by another guard who bummed a cigarette from him. I was hoping there would be no guards. Carefully, I eased the door open a crack so I could hear them talk.

"It looks like another quite night."

"I like quiet nights."

"Where's Slim?"

"I saw him heading toward the barns."

"I don't see why we need three guards patrolling this place every night."

"Orders are orders."

I had heard enough. It would be difficult to look into other buildings with three guards, but I had to check the place out. I closed the door and left by the rear exit.

Hugging the outside wall of the church to avoid the light, I made my way to the front of the building. Falling to my knees, I looked around the corner at ground level and saw the two men walking away with their backs to me. It looked like there was a storage building next to the church, and I ran across the lighted area to get to it.

Staying in the shadows, I went from window to window until I found one that was open. Inside, there were shelves stacked with large cans of food. Sacks of flour, corn, and rice sat on the floor. A walk-in cooler was filled with meat. In another part of the building, I entered a room filled with assault rifles.

Leaving by the window, I moved to the other side of the building. I was still hoping to find a helicopter or something that would lead me to Song Sparrow. Again I took a chance by crossing a lighted area to get to another building. Reaching the shadows, I stopped to catch my breath. Sweat rolled down my face.

"Freeze!"

Fear shot through me. I had seen no one when I started across the lighted area. It didn't matter, they had caught me.

"On the ground! Hands behind your head!"

Rough hands frisked me for a weapon.

"On your feet! Walk to that building in front of you."

Nearing the other two guards, one of them snickered and said, "Well, what do we have here, Slim?"

"A snooper."

"Maybe we should shoot him," one of the guards said with a sick grin.

"We can't do that, you know the new rules on killing," said the second guard.

"Yeah, but they're bullshit," said Slim. "Where should we put him?"

"Stick him in the old storage room for the time being," replied the first guard.

"That's a good place," said the second guard.

"Walk to that building," ordered Slim pointing with his weapon.

When I reached the building one of the guards opened a heavy wooden door, and Slim pushed me through the doorway. I fell to the floor. They shut the door. It was completely dark in the room.

I stumbled around and found a chair to sit on. Hours passed slowly, and then the door opened. A man ordered me outside where two other men stood with assault rifles. I blinked my eyes in the bright sunlight.

One of the men was Hook Nose. The other one was the bald man with a kinky beard that was with Hook Nose at Cahokia. Hook Nose gave me a strange look and said, "You look familiar."

I didn't say anything.

"I never forget a face," said Hook Nose, "especially a face I don't like."

"I remember him," said the man with a kinky beard. "He was with the squaw at Cahokia."

"You're right," replied Hook Nose.

"We've got something special planned for you and your squaw friend," Kinky Beard said, "not quite as awesome as the Missouri River shooting, but it'll accomplish the same thing."

"Shut up Jake," hollered Hook Nose. "You talk too much."

"He's not going to be around long enough to talk to anybody," said Jake.

237

Hook Nose didn't answer; instead he ordered me to put my hands behind my back and roughly placed a set of handcuffs on my wrists. Then he growled, "Move to that truck."

I walked to a black truck with a cap over its bed. Jake opened the tailgate and yelled, "Get in."

With my hands handcuffed behind me, I struggled to get into the truck. They laughed and one of them gave me a push. I fell forward and managed to twist my body so I didn't hit the bed of the truck with my face. They shackled my legs, threw a tarp over me, and closed the tailgate.

The truck barreled down the gravel road, made a right turn, and accelerated on the highway. I have no idea how long we were on the highway, but some time later we turned onto a bumpy dirt road. I had cramps in my arms and legs from the handcuffs and shackles and the position I was forced to lie in. The rough road made me even more uncomfortable. I was relieved when we came to a stop.

The tailgate was opened, and one of the men removed my shackles. They pulled me out of the truck. I couldn't stand with the cramps in my legs, and they laughed when I fell to the ground. One of them kicked me. I felt a swell of anger. I told myself to remain calm. Jake removed my handcuffs, and I rubbed my legs while they stood over me with their assault rifles in their hands.

"Get up and walk to that building," barked Hook Nose.

I staggered to my feet. Jake pushed me toward the building with the barrel of his weapon. We reached the building, and Hook Nose unlocked a metal door. Jake shoved me through the doorway.

Song Sparrow rushed to me as the door slammed shut. She threw her arms around me, hugging me. I hugged her back. A low wattage bulb on the ceiling gave a dingy glow to the room.

A sob went through Song Sparrow while we held each other. Gently, I pulled back to look at her. There was a cut over her right eye, and her face looked swollen and puffy.

"Did they beat you?"

"Only after I tried to fight back. I'm all right. I'm glad to see you, but I wish you weren't here. They're going to kill us. They're sick and evil men. They'll stop at nothing to advance their beliefs and their way of life. They're the ones who killed Strong Bear."

"I know, one of them was bragging about it. We have to escape."

"That will not be easy," said Song Sparrow. "This building is built like a fortress."

I studied the room. They had used heavy timbers for its construction, and there were no windows. Song Sparrow was right; there would be no breaking out of this place. The only way out would be through the door.

"Do they feed you?" I asked.

"Once a day they bring a plate of cold beans, a few pieces of stale bread, and a jug of water."

"Maybe we can try something when they bring us food," I said.

"I don't think so. There are always three of them when they bring food or take me to the bathroom. Two come in, one of them has the food, and the other one has an assault rifle. A third man stands outside with a rifle. They don't take any chances."

"They seem to be well trained," I said. "Did they bring you here in a helicopter?"

"Yes."

"Was it a Huey Helicopter, like the one they used for the massacre on the Missouri River?"

"I think so."

"The grizzly poachers also used a Huey Helicopter," I said. "I think the same group is responsible for both crimes."

There was a mattress on the floor, and Song Sparrow motioned for us to sit on it. She offered me a drink from a jug of water, and I took a swallow.

"How did you find out I was kidnapped?"

"Cloud Watcher called me. I dropped everything and came to Montana."

"You're a loyal friend."

"I'll always come when you're in trouble."

Our eyes met awkwardly. In the depths of her soft gaze I could see fear and for a fraction of a second, perhaps something else. Feelings that had been dormant since Sara's death suddenly stirred in my heart. I couldn't explain what I saw and felt, but my arms ached to hold Song Sparrow and to comfort her. Our eyes had locked for only a moment, but in that instant unexpected emotions were communicated.

Song Sparrow looked away quickly, perhaps a little embarrassed. I looked at the floor and hoped I had not betrayed her trust in our friendship. Strong Bear had been my friend, and I would always respect the love between him and Song Sparrow.

Was I really beginning to feel love for Song Sparrow? I didn't want to answer that question, at least not in the desperate situation we were in. I told myself I needed to suppress whatever I was feeling and concentrate on escaping.

An uncomfortable silence filled the room, which seemed to give credibility to what we may have been feeling. Avoiding my eyes Song Sparrow asked, "How did they capture you?"

"I saw a man in a bar in Billings that I had seen in the crowd at Cahokia. When he left the bar I followed him to a place called the Alliance of the Select. They caught me looking around their compound and brought me here."

Another painful silence followed. I tried to think of something to say, but nothing came to mind.

"I don't understand why they don't shoot us," said Song Sparrow.

We looked at each other and this time we seemed to have control over our emotions. I said, "I don't think they want another incident like the Missouri massacre. Too much publicity. Too many cops. They also don't want to call attention to their hideout in Montana."

"But why did they kidnap me?"

"I don't think they like your idea of changing Columbus Day to Discovery Day. They seem to think your idea will disappear if you disappear. Strong Bear's campaign to do away with Columbus Day may have been one of the reasons they attacked you on the Missouri River.

"I also think they saw your journey to Cahokia as a positive demonstration of Native American power and solidarity that they wanted to put down before it grew into something bigger. Most of these groups do a lot of talking, but this group seems to believe in violence to achieve their goals, and that makes them dangerous."

"But why are they so upset with Strong Bear and me trying to change Columbus Day?"

"They see it as a threat to their way of life. They're a white supremacy group. They think this country should only exist for whites. They also believe Columbus discovered America, and that he was a hero."

"I had no idea that changing Columbus Day would cause so much violence. Strong Bear was a man of principle, and I believe he was right in doing what he did. But I didn't think it would cost him his life, or that I would be kidnapped because of it."

"I've been worried about your safety for a long time."

"I know and I appreciate your concern, but I had to continue with Strong Bear's work even if it put me in danger. Native Americans are the forgotten people in America. Changing Columbus Day may seem insignificant to many Americans, but it'll help my people to feel that their history is also important."

I nodded and took another drink of water. "How did they capture you?"

"I was driving home after a talk show in Billings. It was dark. I came around a bend in the highway and saw a man lying in the road. I stopped to see if he was hurt. When I bent over him to see if he was breathing, he grabbed me! I struggled to get away. Several other men ran into the road, picked me up and carried me to a van. They drove a short distance and loaded me into a helicopter, which brought me here."

"What is this place?"

"It's a ranch, but I think they store a lot of their military equipment here. There's a big barn where they keep two helicopters."

I stood up and walked around the room. "We've got nothing to lose by trying to escape if they're planning to kill us anyway, but we need to wait for the right opportunity to make our move."

We heard someone unlocking the door. Two men came into the room. One of them carried a tray with two plates of cold beans and a few slices of bread. The other man carried an assault rifle and placed a fresh jug of water on the floor.

"I have to go to the bathroom," Song Sparrow said.

A man standing in the doorway holding an assault rifle said, "Come with me."

241

When Song Sparrow returned, I made a request to go to the bathroom. The man gestured for me to come with him. Another man joined him to escort me to an outhouse. I walked slowly, hoping to see a way we might escape. One of the guards shoved me from behind and snarled, "Hurry up...we ain't got all day."

When I finished, they hustled me back to the room and locked the door. I sat on the mattress and said, "They always have plenty of guards, and they don't take chances. It won't be easy getting out of here, but there has to be a way."

After we had eaten, Song Sparrow fell asleep on the mattress. I sat on the floor watching her. Opening her eyes she saw me looking at her. Blushing she said, "I hope you weren't staring at me the whole time I was asleep."

"I'm sorry; I didn't mean to make you feel uncomfortable. I..."

I could feel blood rushing to my face, and I didn't want to appear embarrassed. I quickly added, "I was thinking about your name and wondered if there's a special meaning attached to it?"

Song Sparrow laughed. I think she knew why I was changing the subject. She said, "A lot of people ask me that question. I have a Christian name, but I prefer to use my Native American name. Crow names are usually given by clan fathers or clan mothers. When I was a baby, one of my clan mothers dreamed that I would someday be a person that commands attention by having something important to say in a beautiful way, the way a song sparrow sings."

"I've never heard a song sparrow sing."

"They usually sing sitting on a branch in a prominent place, and when you hear their beautiful song your attention is easily drawn to them."

Our eyes met, and we held eye contact. "I think she picked a good name for you."

Song Sparrow glanced at the floor, and another awkward quiet came between us. I tried to think of another subject to talk about.

"I met Stray Wolf, your adopted son. Cloud Watcher told me his parents were killed in an automobile accident."

"He used to be called Grey Wolf, but when his parents died, one of the clan fathers gave him the name Stray Wolf. We never had a child of our own. Strong Bear was pleased to have an adopted son.

He wanted to take him to Yellowstone and show him the cave when he got older."

Song Sparrow tried to suppress a sob and said, "If I die he'll be an orphan again. That's too much for a small child to endure."

Song Sparrow started to cry. I felt terrible.

"I'm sorry," I said.

Fighting back tears Song Sparrow looked at me with sadness on her face. Trying to sound encouraging I said, "We will get out of this."

Song Sparrow wiped a tear from her cheek and rolled over on the mattress facing the wall. Eventually, her breathing told me she had fallen asleep.

I thought about the routines of the men bringing us food and taking us to the outhouse and tried to think of a way to use one of these opportunities to escape. We didn't have many options. I knew they wouldn't hesitate to shoot us if we tried something. I concluded they planned to take us somewhere to kill us in a way that wouldn't call attention to themselves. I also concluded that this might be the best time for us to make a move.

Two days passed. Then, in the middle of the night, the sound of someone unlocking the door woke us up. Hook Nose, Jake, and another man entered the room holding assault rifles. They ordered us outside where we found two more men with assault rifles. We were lightly dressed and began to shiver in the cold night air.

A man with a red kerchief tied over his head and an unshaven face ordered us to walk to a Huey Helicopter in front of a barn. We obeyed his command without saying anything. Reaching the chopper, Hook Nose told us to climb into the rear compartment, where he handcuffed us to the seat.

Hook Nose and Jake climbed into the front seats. Two other guards got into the rear compartment with us and left the side doors open. We lifted off. The men sitting with us wore heavy coats, and the cold didn't seem to bother them. We were quickly chilled to the bone.

A bright moon made it easy to see the landscape below. Occasionally, I saw lights from an isolated house, but mostly the country showed little sign of human life. I began to see a dusting of snow on the ground. We flew over a range of mountains and saw more snow, and I realized we were in Yellowstone National Park. The chopper circled and came down for a landing in a large meadow.

The pilot turned the engine off and one of the guards yelled, "This is where you get off."

"What do you mean?" I asked.

The guards unlocked our handcuffs and one of them bellowed, "We're leaving you here for the cold to take care of you. Get out of the chopper."

I hesitated. The guard stuck his assault rifle in my face and screamed, "Move asshole, or I'll blow your brains out."

We jumped into ten or twelve inches of snow. Hook Nose and Jake stood in front of us with grins on their faces. Jake snarled, "Start running."

All of them broke into howls of laughter as we ran further into the meadow. Stopping, we turned around and watched the helicopter take off. A shiver went up my spine. The sound of thumping blades faded in the frigid air.

CHAPTER 17

Fear crept into my body and grew into a feeling of panic and helplessness. We were in a terrible predicament with no warm clothes, no matches, and no food. I glanced at Song Sparrow. To my surprise, the moonlight revealed a smile on her face. Before I could say anything she said, "We're not too far from the cave."

"Are you sure?"

"I'm sure. The trail is over there."

Snow crunched under our feet as we ran to the edge of the meadow. It was cold, perhaps near zero. There was less moonlight in the pines, but Song Sparrow knew the way. We didn't talk because we needed all of our energy to run and to fight the penetrating cold. It was even darker in the small canyon with the stream. We picked each step carefully because we didn't want to risk a fall.

Reaching the stream crossing, Song Sparrow jumped to the first rock, and I waited for her to get to the other side before I followed. I made it to the first rock, but when I jumped to the next one my foot slipped, and I tumbled into the swirling flow. Frigid water engulfed my body.

The water was three or four feet deep. I went under and rolled with the current a short distance. I grabbed a rock and pulled myself to a standing position in the churning water. Wet clothes clung to me, accelerating the loss of precious heat from my body.

Shivering uncontrollably, I waded to the bank. Song Sparrow yelled, "We have to get to the cave. Follow me."

Ice was forming on my pants and heat and energy were draining from my body at an alarming rate. I tried to run but numbness in my legs made it difficult to move. Each step required enormous effort, but I dared not stop for fear of my body shutting down completely.

Song Sparrow ran ahead and shouted, "Keep moving."

Her body was like a ghost in front of me as I put every ounce of strength I had into keeping up with her. Darkness, cold, and mental confusion prevented me from knowing where I was. Several times I stumbled and fell to the ground, and Song Sparrow ran back to help me to my feet.

"Not much further, don't give up," she encouraged.

I'm not sure I remember entering the cave or falling to the floor. A veil of confusion seemed to fall upon me, making everything vague and unclear.

In glimpses of clouded consciousness, I sensed Song Sparrow taking my clothes off and wrapping me in two sleeping bags. Brain fog and fatigue blurred my thoughts and tugged on my ability to stay awake.

Then, like a dream, Sara appeared out of nowhere. She was naked and beautiful. She seemed to float through the air, and her body radiated warmth as she surrounded me. I tried to reach out and embrace her, but I couldn't move.

Sara's image started to fade, and Song Sparrow's presence grew stronger. It was now Song Sparrow's warm body that held me, and I thought I heard her whisper, "Please don't die. I love you."

I tried to say something, but was unable to speak. Then I lost consciousness.

When I opened my eyes my vision was blurred. Shutting my eyes, I kept them closed for a short period of time. Opening my eyes again, I was relieved to see the rocky ceiling above me slowly come into focus.

I turned to look for Song Sparrow and saw her sitting by the fireplace. She was wearing her buckskin dress, and she looked the same way she had looked when I first saw her in the cave.

She glanced at me, jumped to her feet, and ran to my side. "Are you alright?"

"I don't know. I feel like I can't move."

"You're exhausted from your ordeal. I wasn't sure you were going to make it. You need hot liquids and more rest."

Song Sparrow made soup from dried beef, vegetables, and rice that were stored in the cave. When it was hot she began to feed me.

"It tastes good," I said. "Your cave has saved me again."

246

"It has saved Strong Bear and me many times."

I felt a powerful urge to hold Song Sparrow, but I told myself I needed to suppress these ideas. I thought about the words I thought I heard her say just before I passed out. I concluded they were part of a dream or caused by the incoherent state I was in.

Song Sparrow would always love Strong Bear. I had to accept that. I also had to stop thinking that she might love me. I finished eating and drifted into a sound sleep.

Two days passed with food and rest helping to strengthen me. Toward evening of the third day it began to snow. We built a fire and watched the flames dancing in front of us. Song Sparrow seemed caught up with her own thoughts. I asked her what she was thinking about.

She smiled and said, "Oh...I was thinking about Strong Bear and how much he loved the cave."

"I wish he was here," I said. "I liked talking to him."

"This is the first time I've been here since he was killed," said Song Sparrow. "It's not the same without him."

"He belongs here with you."

Moisture appeared in Song Sparrow's eyes. "He liked you. I remember we talked about your journey. Tell me how it went."

I laughed. "My journey will never be finished. That much I've learned."

"That's the way of a good journey. Tell me what else you have learned. I will listen for both Strong Bear and myself."

"In Yosemite I photographed an incredible display of light, mist, and landscape. It had a profound effect on me. When I returned to Maine, I realized I had developed the same love for nature that Sara had."

"You have journeyed a great distance."

I paused and thought about what I wanted to say next.

"For most of my life, I didn't think love had anything to do with nature and the way humans treated the environment. I believed nature existed for the sole purpose of supporting humans and that we had the right to take whatever we wanted, regardless of its impact on the earth.

"I was firmly entrenched in this philosophy. I practiced it in forestry and in everything I did. I never gave the exploitation of natural resources for wealth and greed a second thought."

A piece of wood popped in the fire. I thought for a few seconds and added, "I now realize that nature has its own inherent value. I also realize that when we destroy nature, we often harm ourselves."

Song Sparrow poured hot water into a cup, added a tea bag, and set the cup on a rock. Looking thoughtful she said, "Many of the things you experienced were spiritual. Perhaps you need to continue in this direction."

I waited for Song Sparrow to say something more, but she didn't.

Left to my own thoughts, I began to ponder my journey and what Song Sparrow had just said to me. Were my experiences with nature spiritual experiences, or were they just meaningless occurrences that happened?

I thought about the two Bible quotes and the two sentences Sara had written on the piece of paper in her photo file. Could those quotes be plausible? Perhaps, but there had to be a God for them to be true, and if there was, then it made sense that His Creation might enable a person to know something about Him.

I wondered if Sara had thought she had found God in the King's Pines? Could this have been the reason she had fought so hard to save the big trees? I didn't have an answer to this question.

There was a lot I didn't know or understand about Sara even though I had been married to her for twenty-six years. In many ways she would always be a mystery to me.

All of this was confusing and intimidating, and I didn't know what to think or believe. I wish Sara was alive to help with some of these things. Then I realized if I was to continue my journey I would have to travel its path by myself. And I would have to go wherever its path might take me.

The next morning I told Song Sparrow I felt strong enough to hike to the road, and we started to get ready to leave the cave. The sound of a helicopter reached our ears. Song Sparrow looked at me with horror on her face.

"They're coming back."

248

Before I could respond she added, "Why are they coming back?"

"To see if we're dead...or to poach a grizzly."

"We can't let them kill a grizzly bear," replied Song Sparrow.

"Do you have any weapons in the cave?"

"Yes."

Song Sparrow took me to the back of the cave and showed me two bows and two quivers of arrows. There was also a lance.

"Strong Bear always kept weapons in the cave for protection. He used the lance to kill the buffalo. That was the only time he killed anything in Yellowstone. Can you use Strong Bear's bow and arrows?"

"I never used a bow. I might do better with the lance."

"I'll take my bow and arrows," said Song Sparrow.

"These weapons will be no match against their assault rifles," I said. "But if we can surprise them, we might be able to get one of their guns."

Song Sparrow handed me a buckskin shirt and a down vest. "These also belonged to my brother. There is also another pair of his boots, and I have some extra winter clothes I can wear."

We dressed quickly, grabbed our weapons, and ran to the canyon. Approaching the meadow, we stopped in the pine trees to catch our breath and to listen. The noise of the chopper had disappeared.

"Maybe they're not going to land here," said Song Sparrow.

We waited, and then we heard the helicopter returning.

"They're looking for a bear," I said.

A Huey Helicopter came into view, and we watched it crisscross the meadow in a search pattern. It stopped and hovered over a hollow in the terrain. Then it flew in our direction and landed a couple of hundred yards in front of us. Two men jumped to the ground with assault rifles. The helicopter took off, circled the meadow, descended closer to the ground and advanced slowly, sweeping back and forth.

"What are they doing?" asked Song Sparrow.

"Herding a bear in the direction of those two men. We have to get closer."

Staying in the pines, we moved to within thirty or forty yards of the men. Dropping to the snow, we crawled closer, using willow in the meadow to conceal us. Raising my head above the willow, I saw the poachers crouched behind a rock, a stone's throw away.

Lowering myself I gestured to Song Sparrow where the men were located. She took an arrow from her quiver and notched it in the string of her bow. My hand tightened on the lance.

I took another look and saw a grizzly running with a limp toward the poachers.

I bent down and whispered, "They're herding the grizzly that Strong Bear healed toward the poachers on the ground."

Song Sparrow jumped to her feet and pulled the arrow in her bow to a place on her cheek. Releasing her fingers on the string, the arrow flew through the air and landed in the snow where the men could see it. They turned around and saw us before we could drop to the ground. Bullets whizzed over our heads. We started crawling back to the trees as more bullets zinged above us.

The chopper came to a hovering position to the right of us. We jumped up and started running. The men on the ground began chasing us. The side door of the chopper opened and bursts of gunfire peppered the snow around us.

We ran into the trees. Song Sparrow fell. I helped her to her feet. My heart was pounding. We ran further and stopped to listen. Sounds of dead branches breaking on pine trees told us they were pursuing us. Song Sparrow notched another arrow. The chopper was coming down for a landing in the meadow. Song Sparrow gave me a worried look.

"Follow me," I said.

Knowing we needed room to fight with our primitive weapons, I headed back to a small clearing we had previously run through. Reaching the place I said, "Let's get in those pines over there and surprise them when they follow our tracks into this opening."

We hastened into the trees and waited. Song Sparrow readied her bow and arrow. I did the same with my lance.

A voice behind us sent a chill through me. It sounded like Jake shouting, "Where are you?"

"We're following their tracks," a man answered in the trees in front of us. "Keep your eyes open. They're somewhere between us."

Two men entered the clearing. Song Sparrow released her arrow. It flew through the air and sliced into the chest of one of the men. He fell as I hurled my lance at the other man. The lance hit the ground in front of him, and he opened fire. We dropped to the ground. Bullets hissed over us.

The shooting stopped. A horrible scream pierced the air. Cautiously I lifted my head to see what had happened. The second man was staggering, trying to stay upright. Half of his face was missing, replaced by a bloody gash.

Behind him stood the great bear, and he was not finished with his attack. With a ferocious growl of rage he charged the man. Huge claws ripped and tore at the man's body until there was no life remaining in what had become a bloody corpse. When the bear was satisfied the man was dead, he turned around and walked into the trees behind him.

Jake was standing to the right of us, wide-eyed with fright. The bear attack had diverted his attention, and he had not seen us. When he glanced in our direction, Song Sparrow had her bow drawn with another arrow. Jake quickly disappeared into the trees before she could release her fingers on the bow's string.

I ran to the two men on the ground, grabbed one of their assault rifles and dashed after Jake. Song Sparrow grabbed the other rifle and followed me. Approaching the meadow, I saw Jake running toward Hook Nose, who was standing next to a helicopter.

"Let's get out of here," yelled Jake.

Both men got into the helicopter. The engine started. I slipped out of the trees and started shooting at the chopper. The side door opened as the blades picked up speed. Jake pointed his assault rifle at me and fired. I retreated back into the forest and watched the chopper lift off and disappear over a distant ridge.

My adrenalin subsided, and I felt pain in my upper arm. Blood oozed out of a bullet hole near my shoulder.

I looked for Song Sparrow and saw her in front of me staring at a shaft of sunlight in the meadow. I was about to say something when I saw the bear standing in the sunbeam. Song Sparrow walked closer to the bear and stopped about eighty yards from him. They seemed to be connecting in some strange way.

The bear stepped out of the light, and Song Sparrow watched him amble toward the timber. When he had vanished in the trees, she came back to where I was waiting for her.

Looking at me, she saw the blood on my shirt. "You're hurt."

"I'm okay. It's more important we get to the road and notify the authorities before these guys pack up and leave. We don't want them to escape."

Song Sparrow's brow furrowed with concern. "I think we should go back to the cave and take care of your wound."

"It's not serious."

"It needs to be taken care of," replied Song Sparrow in a firm voice. "I don't want you having problems on the way to the road."

I shrugged, thought about disagreeing, and then accepted the fact that Song Sparrow wasn't going to change her mind.

Back in the cave Song Sparrow put a pot of water on her stove and got her first aid kit. She said, "Take your shirt off and let me have a look."

Pulling the shirt over my head caused me to grimace with pain. Blood had crusted over what appeared to be a surface wound. It looked worse than it really was.

Squeezing warm water out of a cloth Song Sparrow gently washed the blood away. "You're lucky; the bullet only nicked you."

She applied antiseptic salve, and while she was securing a bandage I thought about pulling her closer and holding her in my…

"How does that feel?" she asked.

"Oh…it feels better. Thank you. I think we should leave tonight. Those guys know we're alive and that we know they were responsible for the Missouri massacre. We have to alert the authorities before they get away."

Song Sparrow gave me an anxious glance. "We'll see how you are in the morning."

"I'm fine."

"It's a long hike to the road and you'll…"

Her eyes softened as her gaze locked with mine, and then she abruptly turned away. I swallowed. Without looking at me she said, "You need to rest. We'll see how you are in the morning."

She went to the back of the cave to put the first aid kit away and was there for what seemed like a long time. Was she feeling what I was feeling? Was it love that I thought I saw in her eyes?

Eventually she returned and asked, "Are you hungry?"

"I could eat something."

Song Sparrow prepared a meal. While we were eating she asked, "Can I ask you something personal?"

"Sure."

"Where did you meet your wife?"

"In college."

"Was it love at first sight?"

I shrugged. "I don't know. It may have been. I'm not sure I recognized those early feelings of love, but when I realized I was truly in love with Sara, it was quite a shock."

"What do you mean?"

"I didn't feel like eating. I couldn't sleep. I kept thinking about Sara all of the time."

"It was also like that for me when I fell in love with Strong Bear. Only I felt that way the first time I saw him."

"How did you meet?"

"There was a dance contest on the reservation. He was a competitor. He came out of a door dressed in beautiful traditional clothing. When he finished dancing, he explained the meaning of his dance to the audience. I couldn't keep my eyes off of him. He was an excellent dancer, and he won the contest. Later in the day one of my friends introduced us. I loved him from that day on."

Song Sparrow smiled and added, "My mother said I was in a fog for weeks after that dance contest. What was your wife like when you first met?"

I took a deep breath and thought about Sara. "She was beautiful and full of life. She was very idealistic and passionate, especially about the environment."

I paused and added, "I wish she had lived long enough to see how I feel about nature now."

"I think she knows."

Afternoon light faded to twilight. Song Sparrow lit a few candles, and we continued to talk about our spouses and how much we missed them.

"Would you consider marrying again?" asked Song Sparrow.

"I never thought about it."

Song Sparrow looked embarrassed. "I'm sorry; I shouldn't have asked such a personal question."

"That's okay. Would you consider it again?"

"I might. At times I'm lonely. I also want Stray Wolf to have a father."

We ate and went to bed early. I didn't fall asleep right away, but kept thinking about Song Sparrow. When I opened my eyes the next morning she was staring at me from her sleeping bag. I laughed.

"What are you laughing at?" she asked shyly.

"I'm not used to people staring at me."

Song Sparrow moved closer to me.

"Only people who like you stare."

"What do you mean?"

Her eyes looked into mine and it seemed she was trying to evaluate what I was feeling. She started to speak, hesitated, and said, "When I was near the bear yesterday I felt close to Strong Bear. I felt his presence telling me to move on."

She paused, swallowed, and added, "I believe he would be happy with my decision to give you my heart."

Without thinking I said, "I love you."

Song Sparrow caressed my cheek with her hand. Her touch was soft, like a summer breeze, but it sent an electric shock through me. I leaned toward her until my lips touched hers. She sighed as her lips parted under our deepening kiss.

Her hand cupped my face and then slid gently around my neck. I kissed her lips again and then her throat. She stood up and removed her dress. I looked at her and said, "You're a beautiful woman."

I removed my clothes and she arched her hips against mine. My hand stroked the supple warm skin of her back. She gasped in anticipation. It had been so long since either of us had received or given ourselves in love.

Our passion increased in intensity. She closed her eyes as our love making reached its peak.

I held her still trembling body against mine and said, "I never expected to feel love again."

We continued to hold each other as our breathing slowed. I gently pulled away from her and studied her face, looking at her nose, mouth, and eyes. Again I told her how beautiful she was.

She smiled in acceptance of my compliment and rested her head on my chest. I put my arm around her and held her close.

"I was uncomfortable with my growing love for you," I said, "because I respected you and Strong Bear as friends."

"Strong Bear liked you. He would be happy for us."

"I don't want to dishonor his memory."

"He would be pleased that we found love and joy in each other after such a long time without love."

"I hope so."

"What would your wife say about me?"

"She would like you and be happy I've found someone I can love again. Loving you doesn't mean I've stopped loving Sara, if you know what I mean?"

Song Sparrow nodded and said, "If I had died in the massacre I would have wanted Strong Bear to find a woman he could love. Being in love is wanting what's best for your loved one. I'll always love Strong Bear in the same way you'll always love Sara. But now there is room in our hearts for new love.

"You became a special friend when you came to our camp on the Missouri River. That was a horrible time for me. I needed a friend, and you were there. I fell in love with you when we were prisoners on the ranch. Again you came when I needed someone."

Making eye contact I said, "I'll always be here for you. I'll…"

I stopped talking because I suddenly saw terror in Song Sparrow's face. "Do you hear helicopters?"

The muscles in my body tightened. "They're coming back. We have to leave right away. Is the trail in the canyon the only way out of here?"

"Yes. We could try climbing the canyon walls, but they're steep and snow will make them slippery."

"We don't have a moment to lose. We have to get out of the canyon before they find our tracks in the snow. If we can make it to the meadow we'll have a better chance to defend ourselves."

We quickly got dressed, grabbed our assault rifles, and started running down the trail. In the canyon I stopped to listen.

"They're landing," I said.

We came to the stream crossing and hastened across the rocks to the opposite bank. Stopping to catch our breath Song Sparrow whispered, "I hear voices coming down the trail."

I looked around. "Where can we hide?"

Song Sparrow pointed to a place behind a few large rocks next to the trail. Three men came into view just as we concealed ourselves. Song Sparrow grabbed my hand and squeezed it tightly as they passed within touching distance of us. They would find the cave, if we didn't stop them.

One of the men crossed the stream and yelled, "There are fresh tracks over here, probably made this morning by two people."

The other two men started to cross the stream. I couldn't wait any longer to do something. Jumping up I shouted, "Are you looking for us?"

My voice startled them. One of the men standing on a rock lost his balance and fell into the stream. The other two started to raise their rifles.

I opened fire on them. All three men were dead when I stopped shooting.

Primitive instincts of survival swirled up from the depths of my body as adrenalin rushed through me. The shooting was over in seconds, but in those few seconds I had returned to the horrors of combat in Vietnam.

"There are more men in the meadow," I yelled. "The shots will bring them running."

Song Sparrow stared at the three dead men with shock on her face. I nudged her and said, "We have to get to the meadow before they come down the trail."

I grabbed Song Sparrow's hand. "Come on."

We hurried up the trail. As soon as we were out of the canyon we darted into the trees and continued running until we reached the meadow.

A few hundred feet in front of us was a Huey Helicopter with its pilot standing in front of it. He was watching two men on the far side of the meadow running towards his chopper. I knew the pilot had heard the shooting in the canyon, but it appeared he had orders to stay with his helicopter.

"Follow me," I whispered to Song Sparrow with urgency.

We bolted for the helicopter and used it as cover to keep the pilot and other men from seeing us. I ran to the front of the helicopter and hit the pilot with my rifle butt in the back of his head. He fell to the ground.

"Get into the rear compartment of the chopper," I yelled to Song Sparrow as I picked up the pilot's assault rifle.

I climbed into the pilot's seat and started the engine. The rotor blades began to turn slowly. A minute or two crept by. The men in the meadow were getting closer. They would soon be in firing range.

"Shoot at those men in the meadow if they fire at us," I shouted to Song Sparrow.

Blades kept speeding up. Bullets slammed into our chopper.

Song Sparrow fired back. One of the men went down. Blades were accelerating. The other man began to drag the wounded man behind a rock. We lifted and rose in a steep climb that quickly took us away from the two men on the ground.

Climbing higher I saw another Huey Helicopter ascending. My course took us over the rising chopper. Hook Nose was in the pilot's seat, and Jake was sitting next to him.

Gunfire erupted from the other chopper's side door. I veered sharply to the left to avoid their bullets. The other Huey was on my tail, and we began a cat and mouse chase.

"Use your rifle when I get you into a position for a shot at the other helicopter," I yelled to Song Sparrow.

I turned sharply, climbed and dived abruptly, and used every combination of changing direction that was possible with a Huey Helicopter to keep them from getting a shot at us. At the same time, I tried to position our chopper to give Song Sparrow a shot at their helicopter. I heard Song Sparrow firing her rifle, and I heard bullets popping holes in our aircraft.

The canyon of the Yellowstone River came into view. I descended to the river's surface and challenged Hook Nose to follow me through the twists and turns of the chasm. At times I flew dangerously close to the canyon walls, hoping to encourage Hook Nose to make a mistake and crash. He dropped back, and I gained a small lead on him.

257

My plan was to follow the river to park headquarters at Gardiner and to land there; knowing Hook Nose would abandon the chase when he saw where I was going.

We left the Yellowstone canyon, and Hook Nose closed in on me. I went into another series of maneuvers to avoid his bullets. He was getting use to my dodging tactics and was beginning to stay longer on my rear.

"I'm out of bullets," yelled Song Sparrow.

More shots riddled our chopper. I quickly banked to the right to get away from Hook Nose. Without ammunition Hook Nose had the advantage. The time had come to execute a desperate move that a pilot in Vietnam had told me about.

I reduced my speed to encourage Hook Nose to close in on me. When he began to hug my tail, I advanced the throttle and brought the nose of my chopper up sharply, approaching an angle of ninety degrees. Not realizing what I was doing, Hook Nose flew under me.

Just as quickly, I brought my nose down into an angle of forty-five degrees behind him. In this position, I was able to keep our main rotor blades away from each other. With a steady hand, I eased my chopper forward and down, bringing my metal landing skids into his tail rotor. The whirling blades were instantly sheared off, and I rapidly pulled away from him.

Without a tail rotor, Hook Nose lost control of his helicopter, and it spiraled toward the vertical side of a nearby mountain. The blades of his main rotor hit the rock wall and shattered. Stripped of its ability to fly, the chopper plummeted to the earth, slammed into the ground, and exploded in a ball of fire.

My attention turned to my helicopter. Glancing at my gas gauge I saw we were losing fuel. I looked back at Song Sparrow. She had collapsed in her seat.

CHAPTER 18

I shouted Song Sparrow's name. She slowly lifted her head. Her face was contorted in pain. She put her hand over the right side of her chest, and I concluded that was where she had been shot.

Nervously I glanced at the fuel gauge again. It was going down quickly. I had to keep the chopper in the air and get Song Sparrow to Gardiner. The next time I looked at the gauge it was frozen on empty.

Structures loomed in the distance. I headed for a cluster of buildings with red roofs that looked official. People came out of a building as I landed in a vacant parking lot. I turned off the engine, jumped out of the helicopter, and ran to the closest person in a National Park Service uniform.

"I have an injured woman in the chopper," I shouted.

"What happened?" asked the ranger.

"She's been shot in the chest. We need a stretcher."

The ranger gave instructions to two other uniformed men, and they ran into a nearby building. We went to the chopper, and the ranger did a quick assessment of Song Sparrow's injuries.

"I think she has a broken rib," said the ranger. "It might have punctured her right lung. We need to be careful moving her."

The other two rangers returned with a gurney. We carefully lifted Song Sparrow onto it and wheeled her into the building where it was warm.

"I'll see if Dr. Harrison is home," said one of the men.

"Will your chopper make it to the hospital in Bozeman?" asked the ranger.

"No, the gas tank has been shot up."

A woman arrived with a first aid kit, and she cut away part of Song Sparrow's dress so we could see her injury.

"I'll put a dressing on her wound until the doctor gets here," she said.

A man came out of an office and said, "We have a chopper on a wildlife project not too far from here that we called in. It will fly her to Bozeman."

A grey-haired man with a medical bag arrived and began to examine Song Sparrow. One of the rangers took me aside and said, "We got a call about two choppers shooting at each other. Was that you?"

"Yes."

"What in God's name were you doing?"

"We were trying to escape from a white supremacy group that had kidnapped us and left us to die in the back country. They're the people responsible for the Missouri River massacre and the grizzly poaching in Yellowstone. They call themselves the Alliance of the Select."

"I'll call the authorities," replied the ranger. "Can you come with me and give me a few more details?"

I followed the ranger into his office and showed him on a map where the Alliance of the Select was located and where I thought their ranch could be found. I also told him about the Huey Helicopter that had crashed near the Yellowstone River. He said he would take care of it.

Returning to Song Sparrow, the doctor told me he had inserted a tube into her chest to help her breath. He wanted to get her to a hospital as fast as possible. While he talked, a helicopter landed in the parking lot.

We lost no time getting into the chopper and taking off for Bozeman. The doctor came with us and asked the pilot to radio ahead to have a doctor waiting at the hospital. The flight took about thirty minutes, but it seemed longer to me. When we arrived at the hospital they took Song Sparrow into the emergency room. I waited in a nearby lounge.

I was worried about Song Sparrow and realized my journey had also been about finding a new love. I didn't think Song Sparrow would die, but the thought of losing a love for a second time scared me.

A half hour passed, and a doctor came to the lounge to talk to me. "We took an X-ray. A bullet grazed the side of her chest and fractured a rib that punctured her lung. We want to keep her overnight."

I thanked the doctor, and he left. A nurse came to tell me I could see Song Sparrow. As we walked to her room the nurse said, "She has been given pain medication and is probably groggy."

Song Sparrow recognized me, but didn't want to talk very much. When I gave the nurse a worried look she gave me a reassuring smile and said, "It's the pain medication."

"I want to stay with her," I said.

Song Sparrow smiled.

The nurse nodded and said, "I'll be back later to check on her."

I bent over Song Sparrow and kissed her on the forehead. She smiled, closed her eyes, and went to sleep. I sat in a chair next to her bed and eventually fell asleep. I woke up several times during the night and looked at Song Sparrow. She seemed to be resting peacefully. When I woke up again it was morning, and Song Sparrow was awake.

"I still want to be your wife," she whispered.

"You will be, as soon as you get better."

"I have one condition that is very important to me. Will you agree to raise Stray Wolf in Native American traditions?"

"Yes."

"Stray Wolf will also need to know about your world, and that is where I'll need your help."

"I'll help in any way I can."

"What happened to the other helicopter?"

"It crashed into a mountain."

"I'm glad they didn't get away."

"They got what they deserved."

"When will I get out of here?"

"We have to see what the doctor says."

I leaned forward, kissed her, and said, "I love you."

"I love you, too," she whispered.

The doctor came into the room and examined Song Sparrow. He told us he wanted another X-ray and left. I told Song Sparrow I was going to the cafeteria to eat breakfast. When I returned the doctor was talking to Song Sparrow.

He looked at me and said, "The lung looks good and the rib is in place. She can go home, but I want to see her in a couple of days. Her rib is going to be painful. She needs to take it easy until it heals."

I rented a car and drove Song Sparrow to the reservation. At the end of the two months it took for her to heal, I felt I needed to get back to Maine and check on things. Song Sparrow wanted us to get married before I left.

We decided to have a small, traditional wedding on the reservation. Only immediate family and friends were invited. Annie flew out, and I was glad she was there. The ceremony was a personal expression of our love for each other, and we were happy with it.

The following day we snowshoed to the cave in falling snow. I pulled a small sled with food and supplies, and Song Sparrow carried a small day pack. She was worried that some of the men from the hate group might have followed our tracks to the cave. Arriving at the cave, we inspected it, and concluded that no one had been there.

In the evening, we built a fire, and made love. We fell asleep in each other's arms.

We stayed a week in the cave enjoying each other's love. The night before we were planning to leave I said, "Being here with you gives me a feeling of peace that I have not experienced very much in my life. I wish we didn't have to go back."

"I know," said Song Sparrow. "I've had that feeling many times when I'm here. It has always been a special place. I worry that a hiker or the Park Service will someday find the cave."

"What will you do if that happens?"

"Stay away."

"Why?"

"Because it will not be the same."

Before I left for Maine, Song Sparrow received a phone call from the FBI. They said they had apprehended all the members of the white supremacy group that were involved with the Missouri River massacre and the grizzly bear poaching in Yellowstone National Park. Apparently Hook Nose had been one of the leaders of the group. They also said that the Huey Helicopter used in the massacre was hidden in Missouri for several days and then flown back to Montana at night.

Song Sparrow and I also talked about practical aspects of our marriage. We knew our relationship was unique and that it would

262

require adjustments and compromises. We were both very independent people, and we were aware of the cultural differences that could impact our marriage. But we were also mature people and knew about life and the need to get along. We also loved each other very much.

I wanted to work four or five years to set up a workable, sustainable forestry operation at North Country Woodlands. Song Sparrow wanted to spend time in Montana working on changing Columbus Day to Discovery Day.

We would have to accept the fact that we would be separated for long periods of time, and that we would be doing a lot of traveling. When I finished my work at North Country Woodlands I would move to Montana, and we would no longer be separated.

Back in Maine, I found that Dr. Holt and Lisa had accomplished a great deal. On the first day in the field with Lisa she said, "I've learned a lot about forests and forestry from Dr. Holt. Please accept my apology for all the trouble I caused you. Managing a forest is more complex than I thought it would be."

"Apology accepted. Dr. Holt told me you would like to study sustainable forestry in college."

"I would, but I can't afford to go to college."

"I know the owner of North Country Woodlands. She might be able to help you with college if you promised to work here a few years after you graduate."

"I would be happy to come back. I want to stay in Maine."

"By the way, how was your visit to Baxter State Park?"

"I thought you were really nuts making me go to Baxter, but I'm glad I went."

"Why?"

"I met this really cool guy who's studying ecology at the university. He took me to a pond one morning to see the sunrise and...and..."

Lisa paused like she wasn't sure she wanted to tell me something.

"What did you see?" I asked.

"Mist was rising, and Mount Katahdin was reflected in the water. The leaves were brightly colored and covered with frost and...and we saw a moose walk into the pond...it was awesome."

"It sounds like it would have made a great photograph."

"It would have made a terrific photograph. I've never seen a morning like that. This may sound weird, but I never thought about the woods as being beautiful. I always thought of them as a place to work."

"Did your dad take you to the woods?"

"No. He doesn't like working in the woods. I never heard him say they were beautiful. When he came home from work he was usually tired and grumpy. He would take a shower, drink a beer, and watch TV. He always worried about putting food on the table."

"Sometimes you have to see something for yourself and form your own opinion about it," I said.

"I wish my dad could have been at that pond with me and seen what I had seen. He never went hunting, fishing, or camping. He never went to the woods on his day off. The only time we went on a picnic was on the fourth of July in City Park."

"I'm sorry."

"Don't be. I love my dad, that's just the way he is."

"Did your friends go to the woods?"

"Some of them hunted and fished, but they never invited me to go."

"What did you do?"

"Not much. I hung out with my friends and drank and smoked pot and had a good time. But now I want to go to college. Now I see things differently, thanks to you and Dr. Holt."

"Dr. Holt likes you."

"He has taught me a lot of stuff. He also likes David, my boyfriend."

"I'd like to meet David."

"You will. He wants to meet you. He also wants to work with the forests in Maine. I may even marry him."

"Sounds like you've got it all planned."

"I hope so."

A few weeks after Christmas, Song Sparrow and Stray Wolf came to Maine. The day after they arrived we visited Sara's memorial and went to dinner at the Lake View Inn. A lot of people were surprised when I introduced her as my wife. People stared at us through dinner. I knew they were talking about us, but I didn't care.

I was already a subject of gossip in Spruce Mills for the changes I was initiating at North Country Woodlands. Marrying a Native American just added to the chatter. I was never a member of the so-called socially elite of Spruce Mills, so their opinions were of little concern to me. I had found happiness with Song Sparrow, my new son, my work, photography, and with nature. That was enough for me.

Song Sparrow and I adjusted quickly to living in my house. In the evenings she sat at Sara's desk and worked on changing Columbus Day. I worked on forest management plans or played with Stray Wolf. At first it was strange to see Song Sparrow sitting at Sara's desk, but after a few nights it seemed normal.

Stray Wolf was sleeping in Annie's room, and I was adjusting to my new role of being a step dad. I took Stray Wolf sledding and played with him in the snow. I tried to budget special time for him whenever I could. I planned to take him camping and to teach him photography when he got older. I enjoyed having a son more than I realized.

I continued to work on management plans, and by March we were mailing letters to loggers soliciting their bids on five sustainable harvest cuts. By early May I had signed contracts for all of the work.

Song Sparrow was anxious to get back to Montana, and I planned to go with her. The night before we left we made love and were resting in bed. The window was open and moonlight filled the room. A coyote called in the clear-cut behind the house. I pulled Song Sparrow closer and fell asleep.

Susan called the third week we were in Montana and invited us to Henry's place. She said she needed help with the interpretive program she was setting up as part of her project to make the Autumn River area into a park.

Nearing Henry's shop we saw a large travel trailer parked by the side of the road. Susan stepped out of the trailer as we got out of my truck. She smiled and said, "I have a surprise for you. Matt, would you please come out here for a minute."

Matt came to the doorway and said, "Hi Kirk. I see you have met my new-old wife."

Susan and Matt laughed.

"You two are married?"

"We were remarried a few weeks ago," replied Susan, "and we're on our honeymoon."

Matt put his arm around Susan and kissed her. I watched with my mouth open.

"I'm happy to see you two are back together."

"Thank you, Kirk," said Susan. "It has been a long journey for some of us, but I've never been happier."

I laughed. "I know a few things about journeys. I'm happy for both of you."

"Enough talk," said Matt. "We have supper on the grill, and we have enough for both of you, so come in."

Over cold drinks and hamburgers we talked about Susan's plans for The Autumn River Park. When we finished eating Susan said, "I want to establish an environmental review board at WestSun Resorts, and I want you to be on it. Is that okay with you?"

"I would be happy to do it."

"Good. One more thing. Matt and I have not been able to determine which pool is Looking Glass Pool. Can you show us?"

"Yes. The light should be just right in a few more minutes to see into its depths."

We walked along the river and saw numerous small trout rising to flies. It would take a few years for them to grow into larger trout and then the Autumn River would be completely restored to its previous glory.

We climbed up on the big rock that overlooked Looking Glass Pool and gazed into the crystal clear liquid. Susan asked me to tell the story of how Henry and I saved the big brown trout. I chuckled at the thought of her wanting to hear the story.

When I finished Susan said, "I want to tell that story in the visitor center, maybe with a video. I'll work something out. It will be our version of the old man and the river."

"Is there any chance the big brown trout might still be alive?" asked Matt.

"He was an old fish three years ago. He's probably dead by now."

A golden brilliance illuminated the landscape and the watery interior of Looking Glass Pool. I pointed to the submerged rock in the middle of the pool and said, "That rock was the hiding place for the big brown trout."

A huge tan shadow emerged out of the depths of the pool. As it neared the surface, we saw red and black spots on its yellowish brown body. With grace and dignity the fish took a fly from the glassy sheet of water.

The big brown trout had returned to Looking Glass Pool. We all saw him. Song Sparrow's hand touched mine and our hands closed together. Susan and Matt were also holding hands.

Each of us was lost in our own thoughts. I saw Henry in my mind's eye, casting a fly over the slick currents of Looking Glass Pool. Then I saw Strong Bear standing with the great bear on top of a hill. Sara came to mind next. She was taking a photograph of the King's Pines. Looking up from her camera she smiled at me. I smiled back.

The big brown trout rose to another fly. Ripples spread over the placid surface from the rise and traveled downstream on the smooth flow. The sun eased below the ridge behind us, and we could no longer see into Looking Glass Pool.

Third party sustainable forestry certification of timber companies began in the mid-1990s and continues to the present.

The path to appreciating nature that Kirk travels in THE FORESTER has always existed. Its presence has long been recognized and verified by countless poets, writers, painters, photographers, native people, and many others. Everyone can travel this path of bonding in their outdoor activities and experiences if they go with a heart and mind that is open and receptive.

James Kraus
January 22, 2013

Bibliography

Adams, Ansel. *Yosemite and the Range of Light.* Little Brown & Company, Boston, Mass., 1988. Cover Photograph: "Clearing Winter Storm" Internet Search Engine: Ansel Adams Photo: "Clearing Winter Storm."

Adirondack Park Agency - Website: apa.ny.gov/
N.Y. State Agency That Regulates Zoning & Development On The 3 Million Acres Of Private Land & Manages The 3 Million Acres of Public Land Which Makes Up The 6 Million Acre Adirondack Park.

Baskahegan Timber Company - Website: www.baskahegan.org
Timber Practices Are Certified by the Forest Stewardship Council

Cahokia Mounds State Historic Site – Illinois
Website: www.cahokiamounds.org
Watch: "City of the Sun Video"

Carson, Rachel. *The Sense of Wonder.* New York: Harper & Row, 1956.
Website: http://rachelcarson.org/BooksBy.aspx
On the Human Relationship with Nature she writes, "…it is not half so important to know as to feel…etc."
(Rachel Carson also wrote, *Silent Spring,* her most famous book.)

Crow Tribe – Apsaalooke Nation - Website: www.crowtribe.com
Read History Section – Quote: "While we were People of the Earth, when the birds and animals could talk…"

Diamond, Jared. *Collapse.* Penquin Books, 2006.
Chapter 1 Presents A Spotlight On Montana's Development & Mining Situation Which Is Similar To The Situation In Colorado.

Forest Stewardship Council – FSC - Website: www.fscus.org
Third Party Sustainable Forestry Certification for Timber Companies

Franklin, Jerry F. & Kohm, Kathryn A. (Editors). *Creating A Forestry for the 21st Century – The Science of Ecosystem Management.* Island Press, Washington, D.C. – Covelo, California, 1997.
Read: Page 125 – "Menominee Sustainable Forestry"

Josephy, Jr., Alvin M. *500 Nations, An Illustrated History Of North American Indians.* Alfred A. Knope, New York, 1994.
Read: History of Columbus – Pages: 120 to 127.
"Five Hundred Nations" is also an Eight Hour Video Produced by Kevin Costner. Watch: "500 Nations & Columbus" on YouTube.

Leopold, Aldo. *A Sand County Almanac.* A Sierra Club/Ballantine Book, Oxford University Press, Inc, 1966.
Website: http://home.btconnect.com/tipiglen/landethic.html

Louv, Richard. *Last Child In The Woods.* Algonquin Books of Chapel Hill, 2005. - Website: richardlouv.com
Book Deals With Younger Generations Not Bonding With Nature

Menominee Tribal Enterprises - Website: www.mtemillwork.com
Read: "Our Forest – Stewards of the Earth"

Muir, John. *The American Wilderness – In the Words of John Muir.* By the Editors of Country Beautiful, Waukesha, Wisconsin (no copyright date).

Navajo Legends
Website: navajopeople.org/Navajo-legends.htm

New American Catholic Edition. *The Holy Bible.* Benziger Brothers, Inc., New York, 1950. (Book of Wisdom is found in the Catholic Bible. Romans is found in most Bibles.)

Olson, Sigurd F. *The Singing Wilderness.* Alfred A. Knope, New York, 1990. (Olson Compares the Beauty of Nature to Music.)
Website: The Sigurd Olson Website
Book Provided Inspiration for the Writing of the Nature Scenes

Seven Islands Land Company - Website: www.sevenislands.com
Timber Practices Are Certified by the Forest Stewardship Council

Society of American Foresters - Website: www.safnet.org
Read Papers: "Old Growth Forests," "Sustainable Forestry," &
"Biodiversity."

Trout Unlimited - Website: www.tu.org

Zinn, Howard. *A People's History of the United States, 1492 to Present.*
Perennial Classics, 1999.
Read: History of Columbus, Pages 1 to 8.
YouTube - Watch: "Howard Zinn & Columbus" & "True Columbus."

About The Author

James Kraus published a photo book entitled, *Adirondack Moments* in 2009. He has also written and produced numerous articles, short stories, filmstrips, videos, and formal slide shows on a variety of outdoor subjects. He is a graduate of Colorado State University with an MS Degree in Outdoor Recreation and has taught forestry at Paul Smith's College for thirty years. *The Forester* is his first novel.

CPSIA information can be obtained
at www.ICGtesting.com
Printed in the USA
LVOW01s0112101115

461818LV00014B/73/P